PRAISE FOR
Exiles in America

"Christopher Bram's brave new novel, *Exiles in America*, is a tender tale of two couples (one gay, one straight; one 'American,' both displaced) and of the art, love, religion, and family that weave us in their tangled and oh-so-human web. A timely, gripping work of sure imagination, moral courage, quiet astonishment—and a parable for our times."
—Brenda Wineapple, author of *Hawthorne: A Life* and *Sister Brother: Gertrude and Leo Stein*

"Bram's novel . . . [with] its well-made plot . . . grapples with big issues—passion versus reason, the nature of marriage, the intersection of private and public lives." —*New York Times Book Review* (Editor's Choice)

"What is love? . . . [Bram's] enthralling . . . story challenges us to broaden our search for answers." —*USA Today*

"Bram creates a labyrinthine web of relationships, emotions, sexual hi-jinks, denial, betrayal, love, and lust that builds, exasperates, explodes, and deepens. He also explores cultural, religious, and social dimensions that expose American provincialism and widen his tale to question every conventional value and perspective that many of us cling to through our own dark nights of the soul. . . . This intricate, emotionally layered novel is one of the best I've read in years. We come to love these very human, extremely articulate creatures. . . . Who finally are the exiles in America? This brilliant, soul-wrenching, heart-penetrating novel suggests that we all may be." —*Providence Sunday Journal*

"The predicaments Bram has set up for his characters are interesting . . . compelling." —*Washington Post Book World*

"Bram displays a relaxed mastery of dialogue and captures the rich emotional state of a character in a few deft sentences. He nicely melds contemporary issues of gay rights, Christian fundamentalism, national security, and the difficulties of marriage. . . . This love story set against a political/academic landscape . . . keeps you turning pages." —*Denver Rocky Mountain News*

"Strong, interesting, and complex." —*Baltimore Sun*

©Draper Shreeve

About the Author

CHRISTOPHER BRAM is the author of eight novels, including *Father of Frankenstein,* which became the Academy Award–winning movie *Gods and Monsters; Lives of the Circus Animals;* and *The Notorious Dr. August: His Real Life and Crimes.* He also writes book reviews, movie reviews, and screenplays. He was a 2001 Guggenheim Fellow and received the 2003 Bill Whitehead Award for Lifetime Achievement. He lives in New York City.

Exiles in America

Christopher Bram

NEW YORK • LONDON • TORONTO • SYDNEY

HARPER ● PERENNIAL

A hardcover edition of this book was published in 2006 by William Morrow, an imprint of HarperCollins Publishers.

HarperCollins books may be purchased for educational, business, or sales promotional use. For information please write: Special Markets Department, HarperCollins Publishers, 10 East 53rd Street, New York, NY 10022.

FIRST HARPER PERENNIAL EDITION PUBLISHED 2007.

Designed by Susan Yang

The Library of Congress has catalogued the hardcover edition as follows:

Bram, Christopher
    Exiles in America: a novel / Christopher Bram.—1st ed.
        p.   cm.
    ISBN-13: 978-0-06-113834-8
    ISBN-10: 0-06-113834-7
1. Painters—Fiction.   2. Psychiatrists—Fiction.   3. Gay couples—Fiction.
4. Iranians—United States—Fiction.   5. Triangles (Interpersonal relations)—Fiction.
6. Psychological fiction.   I. Title.

PS3552.R2817E95 2006
813'.54—dc22   2006041227

    ISBN: 978-0-06-113835-5 (pbk.)
    ISBN-10: 0-06-113835-5 (pbk.)

07 08 09 10 11 NMSG/QWF 10 9 8 7 6 5 4 3 2 1

For David, Michael, and Geoffrey

A SORT OF FRIENDSHIP RECOGNIZED BY THE POLICE.
—*Robert Louis Stevenson on marriage*

I

Zachary Knowles and Daniel Wexler had been together for twenty-one years. They did not describe themselves as "married." Their generation distrusted the word.

Zack was forty-eight, Daniel forty-seven. They lived in Williamsburg, Virginia, in a 1930s colonial brick house on Indian Springs Road, a quiet residential street near the College of William and Mary. Daniel taught studio classes in painting at the school. Zack was a psychiatrist, Dr. Zachary Knowles, with a small practice in town and an office at home, just off their living room.

Nothing much ever happened in Williamsburg, and people at the college tended to become set in their routines. When an Iranian painter, Abbas Rohani, came to town to be artist in residence in September 2002, nobody thought to invite him and his wife to dinner. Daniel persuaded Zack that they should have them over.

"What if they don't like homosexuals?" said Zack.

"Hey, they're Muslims," said Daniel. "What if they hate Jews?"

Only Daniel was Jewish, born in Brooklyn and raised on Long Island. Zack was a native Virginian, a lapsed Methodist who had escaped to New York after med school to finish his training in the city of psychoanalysis. He had met Daniel in New York. They had moved south to Zack's home turf ten years ago, when Daniel took a teaching job at this small state college.

Daniel left a message in Rohani's voice mail inviting him and his wife to dinner. It was the wife who called back.

"This is Elena Rohani. We shall be delighted to come. Do we need to bring anything? Is it—how do you say?—potluck?"

Daniel assured her that all they needed was their appetite.

And so, late one afternoon early in September, the Friday before classes started, Daniel stood in the kitchen, slicing fresh tomatoes and squash from Zack's garden to grill on the hibachi while he talked to their good friend Ross Hubbard, who stood by the back door with a glass of red wine. The door was wide open—the weather remained warm and humid—and looked out on a narrow concrete terrace with an iron railing. A small wooded ravine sloped behind the house, its curtain of trees level with the railing. The last cicadas of the summer chirred in the leafy branches. Zack was at the other end of the house, seeing his last patient of the day.

"An artist who paints paintings?" asked Ross in his deep, leisurely drawl. "Isn't that kind of old-fashioned? I thought you said painting was what the dinosaurs did."

"He's Iranian. Maybe he doesn't know any better," said Daniel.

"You joke, but you may have hit on something. He could be in a time warp. Fundamentalist Islam forbids graven images. Figurative painting could be very avant-garde."

Ross was a courtly Southerner of the old school, handsome and hetero, almost sixty, much married and much divorced. He owned and managed the movie theater on Merchants Square, an art house that showed foreign and independent films and occasional classics. Zack and Daniel were among his handful of regulars. Ross was a rare kind of straight man. He loved books, art, music, and old movies. He had served in Vietnam but broke the stereotypes there, too. He loved to travel—he'd visited the Middle East twice. He might have been happy if he didn't fall in love with a new woman every five or six years. Currently between marriages, he seemed like the perfect extra guest for tonight.

"What're the paintings like?" he asked. "Have you seen any?"

"I've seen slides and a catalog from a show in Paris. They're figurative, but in an abstract way. Like Picasso or Klee. But not pastiche. Kind of neo-Expressionist, like Francesco Clemente from a few years back. But I like his stuff." Daniel liked it very much, in fact.

"So it's not ethnic or primitive?"

"Hardly. He studied in Paris and Berlin. He's probably better trained than I am."

They could hear Zack out front, bidding goodbye to his patient, an elderly woman who responded with a deliberate, end-of-the-session cheerfulness. Daniel knew that chirpy tone all too well.

"It must make you glad," said Ross. "To have a real painter in town, someone you can talk shop with."

Daniel frowned. "Not really. I don't especially like other artists. I just want to be friendly. I remember what it was like when *we* first came here and nobody gave us the time of day." Daniel wasn't entirely sure why he wanted to know the man. "It's not like I'm an artist myself anymore. I'm a teacher now. Full-time. I don't miss all that my-paintbrush-is-bigger-than-your-paintbrush macho bullshit."

There was a tread of shoes coming toward the kitchen, and a clack of toenails against the hardwood floor. A large black poodle with a pink tongue trotted into the room, Jocko, followed by Zack, a solemn man with a pale beard and a starched blue shirt.

"Hey there, Jock," Ross sang out, crouching down to scratch the happy dog behind its ears. The poodle wasn't trimmed like topiary but left woolly all over. "Hey there, Zack. How you doing?"

Zack only nodded, looking preoccupied, distant, sad.

"Bad session?" said Ross.

"Who-what?" Zack snapped his eyes open and saw Ross. "Oh, Ross. Sorry. No. Good session. Actually. Very good. Hi."

Zack was often like this after seeing a patient, spacey and distracted, still listening to the conversation in his head.

He went over to Daniel and kissed him on the temple. "That's right. We got company. Need any help?"

"No, dollface. We're fine," said Daniel. "Why don't you pour yourself some wine?"

Gay male couples are said to grow more alike over the years, like people and their dogs, but it isn't true. More often, each man looks more different over time, half-consciously marking out a territory of his own. Zack and Daniel were roughly the same medium height, but Daniel was trimmer, clean-shaven, and bald—not entirely bald but with two cropped wings of short brown hair left over his ears. He joked that without the hair he'd look like Henry in the old comic strip. Yet his profile was strong, and he had the handsome, masculine baldness of a Roman statue, not a debauched emperor but a young senator or maybe a general. He looked butch enough that he wasn't afraid of acting nelly now and then.

Zack was stocky and bearded with a full head of hair—hair and beard were the color of flat ginger ale. If Daniel didn't remind him to visit the barber, he began to look like an old hippie or Civil War reenactor. Zack dressed much as he'd dressed for the past twenty years, in oxford cloth and khaki, while Daniel wore the clothes of his students: this year it was baggy jeans or cargo pants and long-sleeve T-shirts. Daniel visited the college gym regularly and swam laps in the pool there. The only exercise Zack ever got was on the days he bicycled out to Eastern State Psychiatric Center, where he was a visiting psychiatrist.

"What's for dinner?" Zack asked.

"Grilled veggies and burgers. Muslims eat cow, don't they?"

"Or they'd starve," said Ross. "If they're good Muslims, they might not drink."

"Not drink?" said Daniel. "An artist doesn't drink? I can't believe that."

"If they've come to the land of the Great Satan," said Ross, "*and* he paints figures, they can't be very good Muslims."

"Is that true about artists and alcohol?" asked Zack. "They don't *all* drink, do they?" He was still locked in earnest therapist mode.

Jocko let out a soft woof, more like a burp than a bark, just before the doorbell rang.

"Speak of the devil." Daniel hurriedly wiped his hands on a dish towel. "I'll get it." He readjusted his cargo pants over his ass and calmly walked out to the hallway.

2

THEY STOOD SIDE BY SIDE on the brick porch, lit from behind in the dusty copper sunlight: a tall, elegant woman and an even taller, elegant man. They both wore glasses; they both had dark hair. The woman's skin was paler than the man's.

"I am Elena Rohani," she declared in her lovely musical accent. "You must be Daniel." She laughed and shook his hand. Her fingers felt cool and delicate.

"A pleasure to meet you," said Daniel. "Good to see you again, Abbas." He shook his hand, too. The Iranian's grip was firm.

Daniel had met him only briefly, introduced by Jane Morrison, the department chair, when she gave the man a tour of the art building. Abbas looked more distinct in daylight than he had indoors. He had an umber-olive complexion, heavy eyebrows, and a very high forehead. He was younger than Daniel—in his mid-thirties—yet apparently losing his hair as quickly as Daniel had lost his.

"What a pretty house," said Elena as they passed through the living room full of comfortable old furniture, including pieces inherited from Daniel's mother. "Very homey, very open."

Abbas said nothing but gazed intently at the drawings, watercolors, and photographs on the walls. None of this work was Daniel's, however; it was all by friends in New York.

"What a pretty dog," said Elena when Jocko danced forward to say hello. She gingerly stretched out her fingers to tap the top of his head. "Like a big black sheep."

"There's a cat around somewhere," said Daniel. "I hope you're not allergic." Balthus usually made herself scarce when strangers were present.

Ross and Zack came out of the kitchen and introduced themselves. Abbas only nodded after each name: Daniel wondered if he was arrogant and haughty or just unsure about his English.

"What a pretty view," declared Elena a few minutes later when she stood outside on the terrace, a glass of wine in one hand, a cigarette in the other. "Don't you think, Abbas?"

Again Abbas only nodded before he took a long suck off his own cigarette. Not only did the Rohanis drink but they smoked—like chimneys. Zack dug out an ashtray from the back of a kitchen drawer. Even without cigarettes, they looked more French than Muslim. They certainly dressed French, elegant in casual clothes, especially Elena. She wore a silky saffron blouse with her jeans. Her long face initially struck Daniel as horsey, but her strong features—her blade of nose and broad cheekbones and cool gray eyes—grew on him, and she became oddly beautiful. She was clearly older than her husband, although Abbas looked simultaneously young *and* old. His short black hair formed a widow's peak halfway up his skull, yet his umber skin was boyishly smooth. His dark brown eyes were caged in narrow, black-framed designer glasses like a raccoon mask.

Ross promptly struck up a conversation with Elena. He seemed quite taken with her: his Southern accent grew just a little thicker.

"Tehran?" she replied. "Oh no. I have never lived there. I have only visited. You see, I am not Persian. Only Abbas is Persian. I am Russian. Or was until the Soviet Union went kaput. I am from Uzbekistan. Which means I am Turkic. Not Turkish but Turkic. Of Central Asia. With *some* Russian blood. I have not been back in years. I hear it is unlivable."

Abbas stood off to the side, warily watching Ross. "*You* have been to Tehran?" he asked.

"Ages ago," said Ross. "Back at the time of the Shah. So it was—what year?"

"Before 1979," said Abbas. "That was when my family left. When I was fourteen." He spoke very carefully, in a soft, low, husky tenor, like a muted clarinet.

"Your family, uh, emigrated?" asked Zack.

"We fled. To Paris. I grew up in Paris. I have been back to Tehran only to visit my brother. Who returned after the death of Khomeini. But it is still an impossible country for artists."

"And for women," said Elena.

Ross said something in French, and Abbas answered in what sounded like fluent French. Daniel didn't know the language.

"We met," Elena announced, "in Berlin. And we lived in Paris for a time. And now we are here. We are going to be Canadian next. We await our papers. When we finish here, we will go to Toronto and become *Canucks.*" She happily puckered her lips around the strange, new syllables, almost kissing them. "That is the word?"

Ross assured her that that was the word.

The sun was down now, the leafy green trees full of inky blue shadow. Husband and wife blew their silky streams of smoke into the gloaming. Daniel noticed Zack twitching his nostrils, not in distaste but in nostalgia. Zack used to smoke himself.

"So how do you like Virginia so far?" Zack asked.

"We like it enough," said Elena. "We find it hot and damp, but we hear it will change."

"Have you visited Colonial Williamsburg yet?" asked Ross. "That can be a hoot. Our cartoon America."

"We walked in it yesterday. We found it very cute."

She used *we* a lot, a word that Daniel tried to use carefully, saving it only for special occasions.

"Zack, darling? Why don't you start the grill?" He wanted to remind the Rohanis that he and Zack were a couple, too. "We're going to keep it simple. A plain old American cookout."

Zack stepped to the end of the terrace and began to arrange a neat black pyramid of charcoal in the hibachi.

"Such a quiet town," said Elena. "Is it safe to walk at night? They give us a house one street over." She waved her hand at the trees. "I go out at night or take Osh and Mina to the library, and the place is like a tomb. That will change when school starts?"

"Yes and no," said Daniel. "The students usually stay in at night, studying or visiting cyberspace."

"They can't talk to each other face-to-face anymore, only on computer," grumbled Ross. "They don't go to bars. Or to the movies." He blamed computers for the fact his theater was always hanging by its financial thumbs.

"The whole town shuts down at six," Daniel explained. "When we first moved here from New York and I went out walking at night, it felt so quiet. You could hear nothing on the street but the whisper of televisions. I was afraid to fart."

Elena stared at Daniel, narrowing her eyes. Then she burst out laughing. She covered her mouth and tried to stop but only laughed harder. She saw Abbas frowning and quickly regained control. She translated for him, not into French but another language.

"Ah," said Abbas and nodded. "Very amusing."

The charcoal was ablaze now. Zack returned from the fire just as Ross worriedly asked, "You mentioned Mina and—another name?"

"Osh. For Arash. Our son," said Elena. "A son and a daughter. Mina is ten, Osh six."

"Our beautiful children," Abbas proclaimed.

"We had a difficult time finding a child sitter," said Elena. "But one of Abbas's future students said she would sit."

Ross tilted his head to study Elena at a new angle, distressed to hear she was a mother.

"I'm sorry we didn't know," said Zack. "You could've brought them. It's always fun to have kids around."

Daniel exchanged a concerned look with Ross. Neither he nor Ross wanted kids here. Daniel must have known that there were children, but it had slipped his mind.

"Maybe next time," Zack said cheerfully.

3

WHEN THE FOOD WAS READY, they all went inside and sat at the dining room table. The house was very bright after the darkness of the terrace. Daniel served while Zack opened another bottle of wine.

"This is a real American cookout?" said Elena, taking a burger and a swatch of grilled vegetables from the serving platter.

"With a few modifications," said Daniel.

The two couples sat facing each other: Abbas and Elena on the window side of the table, Daniel and Zack opposite. Ross sat at the end between Zack and Elena.

"The art students here?" asked Abbas. "Are they any good?"

"Oh, they're a nice bunch of kids," said Daniel. "We're chiefly a liberal arts school. Now and then we get someone truly talented, but not often. Mostly we just teach teachers how to teach."

"Then I should have time to do my own work?"

"I would think so. You have only one workshop class, right?" Whereas Daniel had three studio classes, a history of art technique class, and endless departmental business. He barely had time to shit once the semester started.

Zack addressed Abbas. "I haven't seen your work yet, but Daniel speaks very highly of it. And he's not an easy critic."

Daniel was both pleased and embarrassed that Zack spilled the beans about his admiration. He was ready to make a joke about it, but Elena jumped in.

"He is a great painter!" she declared. "A brilliant painter. Which the world does not yet appreciate. But they will."

The "great painter" made a face and patted the air with his hand to signal her to be quiet.

"But it is true! Do not hide your light. You may not be able to say so, but I can." She addressed the table. "He *is* great. He paints beautifully. Things I have never seen. Things nobody has ever seen. A modern hieroglyph like a new alphabet. With the most wonderful colors and textures. Critics compare him to Picasso and Chagall and—" She snapped her fingers. "Who is the clumsy Italian?"

"Clemente," grumbled Abbas, now bent over his food.

"None of whom hold a candle to him! Or if they are great—and Picasso *can be* great," she admitted, "they are great in different ways. Abbas is original. Abbas is new." She noticed how the men were looking at her, all except Abbas, who continued to eat. "You think I am not objective because I am the wife?"

"Not at all," said Zack in his kindest doctor voice. "But your love for him *might* help you see things that are harder for the rest of the world to recognize."

She shook her head. "No. I love his paintings more than I love him. I put up with his faults as a husband because I love him so much as an artist."

Abbas glanced sideways at his wife. "You must forgive our way of speaking," he said. "English is not our first or even our second language. So we say things more bluntly than is proper. And not always accurate."

"Nonsense!" said Elena. "I am as blunt in Russian or French as in English." And she laughed, tossing an imaginary handful of bluntness over her shoulder. She pointed down at her food. "Your grilled squashes are delicious."

All was not right in this household. It was confusing to stumble so soon into another couple's private trouble. Nevertheless, Daniel couldn't help thinking: Zack never praised my work like that.

Zack was watching Elena. "Are you an artist yourself?" He often picked up on such things more quickly than Daniel.

"No, I am not a painter. But I am a poet."

"A wonderful poet," said Abbas.

"But you don't know," she told him. "I am wonderful only in Russian and you do not know Russian."

He took a deep breath, then shrugged. "No," he admitted.

"But I am a good translator," she told the others. "From other languages into Russian. I comprehend English better than I speak it. There you must trust me. I am a wild speaker, I know."

"You'll teach classes while you're here?" asked Ross.

"It is not necessary. Our house is paid for. We do not need the money. So I can take care of the children. Work on my English. And do all I can for my artist. Because he is my true job. I write to the dealers and send out the slides and inspect the contracts and prepare the press statements. He gives my life purpose."

Her English was too shaky for Daniel to tell if this last statement was sarcastic or not. It *sounded* sincere.

Abbas turned to Daniel. "You paint, yes?"

Perhaps he only wanted to change the subject, but his attention pleased Daniel. His squinty black glasses might look mean, but his eyes seemed friendly enough.

"When I have time for it. I'm more teacher than painter now."

"He's a terrific painter," said Ross. "And a great cartoonist. He's done some clever things for the ads and posters for my theater."

Zack nodded in agreement but said nothing. He watched Daniel, as if waiting for permission to praise him. Because praise, in fact, often annoyed Daniel. He feared he didn't deserve it. But tonight he wanted Abbas Rohani to hear other people celebrate his work.

"These are not your things on the wall?" said Abbas, pointing into the living room.

"Oh no, they're all by friends. I keep my stuff downstairs. I have a studio in the basement."

"Oh?" said Abbas. "When we finish dinner, can I see?"

"Uh, if you like." Daniel was suddenly very nervous, very excited. Which was stupid. Why should he care what this Euro-trash Muslim thought of his work?

"And you are a shrink?" Elena asked Zack. If Abbas got Daniel, she got Zack—or so it seemed. "We can say *shrink*? Or is it an insult?"

"Oh no. *Shrink* is perfectly acceptable," said Zack.

"Are you the kind who gives drugs or do you only talk?"

"I do both. But I prefer talk to medication. Which I couldn't always do in New York. My caseload was too heavy. But here I see fewer patients and I can talk more."

"There are fewer crazy people here?" she asked.

Zack smiled. "No. Just fewer who know that they're crazy."

"Correct me if I am wrong," interrupted Abbas, "but this is an American thing, yes? In other countries we are happy when we are happy, and sad when we are sad, and there is nothing more to say. But in America people want to be happy all the time. And so they go to psychiatrists."

Zack did not take offense—Daniel knew he got this kind of criticism all the time. "But it's only human to want to be happy," he said gently. "There's nothing frivolous about it. Although many of the people I see are too wounded or paralyzed by other issues to even *begin* to think about happiness."

Elena abruptly turned to Ross—it was as if Abbas had spoiled Zack for her just by talking to him. "How is it for the homosexuals here? Are you persecuted or do they leave you alone?"

Ross let out a friendly laugh. "You'll have to ask them, not me. I'm straight, sorry to say."

"Oh?" Elena looked more closely at Ross, as if seeing him for the first time. "And you are sorry? Why sorry?"

Before Ross could explain that he was joking, Abbas jumped in and snatched this subject, too. "Yes, yes, yes," he said. "We hear there are many super-Christians in this part of the country and life is hard for gay persons."

"They leave us alone," said Zack. "For the most part."

Ross remained focused on Elena. "I gather neither you nor your husband are religious?"

"Not a bit," she replied. "Religion is for cowards."

"My wife was brought up a godless Communist," said Abbas. "I was brought up by a liberal father who thought the Koran and Khomeini would save his country from the Shah. But they wanted to save the country from men like my father, too, and they drove him away. So no, we have no great love of religion."

"Islam is for idiots," declared Elena. "For people who do not like to think. Who do not want complication."

Abbas frowned. "I do not go so far. They are not all idiots. There are good Muslims. But it does attract many fools."

"And how do they treat the Muslims here?" asked Elena. "After Osama bin Laden and the terrorists and the war?"

"But we are not Muslims," said Abbas. "It does not concern us."

"But strangers will not know," Elena argued. "They will see your skin and hear your voice and think what they think, true or not. And this is Virginia. It is not Canada or New York."

"The college community is fairly liberal," said Zack when the Rohanis paused long enough for someone else to speak. "Many students come from D.C., which is an international city. The town itself is more Southern—"

"He means redneck," said Ross.

"But it's old South," Zack continued. "There's lots of born-again Christians. But people want to be nice. Virginia good manners tend to keep the righteousness in check."

"Zack grew up down here," Daniel told the Rohanis.

"But I work with all kinds of people as patients and see their softer sides," Zack explained. "I'm not defending them. I'm just pointing out that people will probably be very civil and even friendly in person. No matter what gets said in the newspapers."

4

THEY FINISHED EATING and Daniel led everyone downstairs to his studio. His nervousness returned, a confusing, annoying giddiness, as if he were a student and Abbas a teacher. It was ridiculous. Daniel liked the man's paintings and wanted the man to like his. That's all.

Their house was burrowed in the hillside that sloped away from the street; the basement level opened on the carport and yard out back. Everyone trooped down into the rec room, with its knotty pine walls and fieldstone fireplace, then turned a corner to a short hall that led past the laundry room into Daniel's work space.

"You have a washing machine!" exclaimed Elena, stopping to look. "You lucky dogs."

"There's no washer and dryer at your place?" asked Zack.

"Oh no. The college says there is a laundrette in town and I can go there. But with two children I will be going often."

"If we're home and you give us enough warning," offered Daniel, "you can always use our machines."

Elena looked surprised. "I do not wish to impose."

"Not at all," said Zack. "You got two kids. They make tons of dirty clothes."

He must have been thinking the same thing but had been waiting for Daniel to suggest it first. "Use us. Please."

"Thank you. Yes. Maybe I will. That is very kind."

Daniel entered the studio and turned on the light; the fluorescent tubes fluttered and caught.

The whitewashed brick room glowed like a jail cell. The space had been cleaned, but the workbench was still speckled like a palette, the concrete floor stained with colored shadows. There was almost no smell—Daniel worked in acrylic. A large wooden rack filled one corner, where Daniel stowed his more recent, stretched canvases. His older, dead canvases were rolled up and stacked in the storeroom behind the water heater.

"You are very tidy," said Elena.

"Not really. I just finished putting everything away for the winter. You should see this place when I'm working. I can't paint while I teach. It only makes me unhappy when I try, so I don't try anymore. Besides, I paint primarily for myself now, for my mental health." Which was what he always said; it was sometimes true.

Abbas wasn't listening but peering sideways into the rack, frowning vertically.

Daniel went over and pulled out a small landscape. One of his river paintings: precise patches and beads of bright color on a long rectangle of canvas, a view of flat, curving water flanked by marsh grass—like Corot in quotes, Corot in the age of Kodachrome. He couldn't say that aloud, however. He had to let the pictures speak for themselves.

Abbas sniffed, as if smelling the image. "You are photographic?"

"I work from photos, yes."

"You are a photo-realist?"

"Which is so seventies, I know," said Daniel with a guilty laugh. "What can I say, honey? I'm a child of the seventies." He tried to protect himself with a touch of camp.

Abbas didn't even smile. He waved his open fingers at the canvas as if to say, "Next."

Zack stood to one side, looking worried. He claimed not to understand how painters could examine each other's work and say so little. Or hear so much in each other's silences. But then words were Zack's medium.

Daniel brought out another landscape, this one larger, a wide stretch of the Chickahominy River near Ross's house, the water as smooth as glass, the eye nearly level with the watery mirror.

"My river!" Ross said proudly. "The view from my dock. I love this one." He'd seen all these paintings before; Daniel had done them over the past two summers. "Look at the way the river opens and closes," he enthused. "In chambers, like a cow's stomach. A green stomach full of blue sky."

"Very green," said Elena uncertainly. "Very—luscious?"

It was always the non-painters who did the talking, as if silent images made them uncomfortable.

Daniel carefully turned the canvas against the wall. He hauled out another: a view of woods. The ferny floor was roofed by oak trees, a green twilight caged with tree trunks.

"This is my favorite," said Ross, bending forward, supporting himself with his hands on his knees. "I could fall into it. It has an unearthly hush, like 'Stopping by Woods on a Snowy Evening.' Only it's summer, not winter."

Ross loved Daniel's work, but Ross didn't count. He and Zack were amateurs; they saw the pictures only from the outside. Daniel saw them from the inside and recognized everything that was wrong with them. He wondered what Abbas saw.

Abbas said nothing. He pursed his lips and lifted his chin; he seemed to look down his nose at the painting. Or maybe his glasses were bifocals and he was looking through the reading lenses.

"There is much control," he declared. "Much craft."

And no imagination? Is that what he meant?

He turned to Daniel. "These are exercises for your students?" he asked. "To show them how to paint?"

"No. They're for me. To show *me* how to paint."

"And now you know." Abbas smiled—a mild twitch of mouth. "Still. They are nice. For what they are."

Fuck you, thought Daniel. But he was right. The pictures were nothing but exercises, busywork, anxious displays of craft. Daniel was furious with himself for showing them to the younger painter.

"But they're beautiful," said Zack. "They're not just exercises."

"I love them," said Ross. "I love the landscape around here anyway. But these paintings have a real peace. A real serenity."

They could see that Daniel was upset, but their sympathy did not make him feel better.

"And so on and so forth," he declared, waving at the other frames in the rack. "More exercises in peace and serenity. All very good for my mental health."

"And you always work in photo-realism?" Abbas was looking back at the storage rack. He did not hear Daniel's bitterness, did not seem to know he had offended him.

"Oh no. I do other things. Some abstraction. Photo collage. I keep coming back to landscape, however." He surveyed the rack until he spotted an edge of orange-pink canvas. "But sometimes I feel transgressive. Here's a different kind of landscape." He angrily tugged at the heavy five-foot-by-six-foot frame.

Zack recognized the first inches of flesh color. "Daniel? You sure you want to show that? Before they know us better?"

"Hey, we're all grown-ups." Daniel hauled the frame out and turned it around and slammed the bottom end against the concrete floor. The taut canvas trembled like the skin of a bass drum.

He stood beside it, staring at the faces staring at his painting.

Ross clapped his hands and laughed. "God, I love this picture!"

It was a self-portrait, rougher than the landscapes, the brushstrokes looser, the colors gaudier. Daniel's bald head and bare shoulders filled the bottom half of the picture, with a stomach in the upper half, not his own naked belly but another man's alluvial plain of muscular abdomen. Daniel's pink face sheepishly looked up from between the man's nude legs, his eyes cartoonishly big, his full mouth rounded in a happy "Oh!"

"Oh," went Elena and jerked her head away.

Abbas didn't even blink. He studied the picture, pursing his mouth again, solemnly nodding. "This too is from a photo? Did you take it?" he asked Zack.

Zack frowned at Daniel, letting him know that he would say nothing and Daniel could answer however he pleased.

Daniel could have lied—Abbas wouldn't know that Zack's stomach could never look like that, not after a thousand sit-ups. But Daniel said, "No, a friend took the picture. A young friend." He smiled. "The sacrifices we make in the name of art."

Elena stole another look over her shoulder, then glared at her husband. "Smut," she said. "Schoolboy smut." She turned to Daniel and laughed. "Ha ha ha." She actually spoke the syllables. "You are a silly man and this is silly smut." She lowered her head and charged from the room. They heard her shoes clatter up the stairs.

Daniel had been so determined to shock the husband that he'd forgotten he might shock the wife as well. Her reaction threw him.

Abbas frowned at Daniel, disapproving of the painting or his wife or Daniel, it was hard to tell. He shook his head. "Excuse me," he murmured and followed Elena upstairs.

"Anyone want coffee?" Zack called after them. "I'll be right up and make coffee." He gave Daniel a hurt, weary, chiding look.

Daniel smiled and shrugged and prettily batted his eyes, an ironic pose of innocence that he'd learned from Charlie Chaplin.

"You guys," said Ross, still studying the painting and grinning. "There are no secrets in this household."

5

They found Elena and Abbas upstairs, out on the terrace, whispering in French while Elena finished a cigarette.

"Coffee? No thank you," she said. "This is lovely but we must go. We must relieve the sitter." She was smiling sweetly, pretending nothing was wrong. "Oh, Abbas?" She opened her purse and began to rummage inside. "You should show them our children."

She gave him a handful of pictures, and he proudly passed them around, color photos of a pretty girl and boy whose eyelashes were so dark that both seemed to be wearing mascara.

When they said good night, Elena gave each of the men double air kisses—Daniel wetly kissed one cheek before he understood—and Abbas shook their hands. The Rohanis strode off into the darkness, the wife's shoes clopping down the street like petulant hooves.

Ross stayed behind for a last glass of wine while Daniel and Zack cleaned up. "So she's Russian," he said. "Not Iranian but Russian. From Uzbekistan?" He shook his head in wonder. "So beautiful. Like an Uzbek Anouk Aimée. If you guys get the husband, I get the wife."

"The husband?" said Daniel. "What makes you think we want the husband?"

"I assumed you found him attractive."

"He has a certain sultry quality," Zack admitted.

"He has a certain asshole quality," said Daniel. "Just another holier-than-thou straight male genius."

"And that's why you showed him your *Portrait of the Artist Giving a Blow Job*?" said Zack. "To slap him in his holiness?"

"I love that picture," Ross repeated. "It's like dirty Escher. Male or female, the viewer gets their dick sucked by you, Daniel. Too bad you can't show it at school. What happened to John Wilson anyway?" Who was the blowee, a bleached-blond assistant gardener for Colonial Williamsburg with whom Daniel had had a fling three years ago.

"He went off to L.A. to seek fame and fortune," said Daniel.

"He still sends us Christmas cards," said Zack.

Ross knew all about their open marriage. He was intrigued, even envious—"Silly me, I think I have to marry them"—although he had also learned that it was not without complications.

"The painting disturbed her more than it did him," said Zack.

"You think?" said Ross. "See, I found his reaction fishy. I can't believe the guy was as blasé as he pretended."

Zack shrugged. "He's an artist. He's lived in Paris and Berlin. He's probably seen it all."

"So have I," said Ross. "But first time I saw that picture, I freaked. I mean, I'm not totally comfortable seeing a guy go down on me, especially a good friend."

"Just drop it," said Daniel. "Please? I don't care what either of them thinks. Of me or my work or cocksucking or any of that. I don't know why the hell I showed them that damn painting."

He could feel Zack looking at him, wondering what this was really about. Well, they could talk about it later, maybe.

Then Ross asked Zack, "I know I have no business asking for a professional opinion. But didn't they both seem just a little nuts?"

"They're wound a bit tight," Zack admitted. "But considering the lives they've led, it's a wonder they aren't wound *tighter*. They have their own gestalt, that's for sure. But they seem to make it work."

After Ross left, Daniel took Jocko for his walk, a quick trip around the block. Williamsburg really was a ghost town after dark, the peace more unnerving than soothing. The cicadas continued to buzz and chitter like a short circuit in the night's wiring.

When he returned, their tiger-striped tabby, Balthus, had come out of hiding to waddle around the living room, fat and possessive, making sure nothing had been stolen. Jocko sniffed the cat hello, then followed Daniel down the hall to the bedrooms.

They found Zack in his room, already in bed, sitting against the headboard in his yellow nightshirt, with a Penguin paperback in his lap, something else Victorian.

"Hello, buddy," said Zack when Jocko jumped up beside him. The dog turned a few times, making a mental nest at the foot of the bed, and lay down.

Daniel remained in the door. "So. Have a good time tonight?"

"I did. I always enjoy seeing Ross. And I like meeting new people. Even if they're strange." Zack was watching Daniel.

"They are strange, aren't they?"

"But interesting. Different." Zack closed his book, signaling that they should talk. "I hope they're not too unhappy being stuck in Williamsburg for a year."

"We don't have to worry about him," said Daniel. "He's the kind of cocky young artist who doesn't need anybody or anything."

"So what did you want from him?"

"Nothing. What's to want?"

"Did you ask them over tonight because you're interested in him as a painter?" said Zack. "Or in him as something else?"

Daniel frowned. "What do you mean?"

Zack broke into a smile. "What do you mean, what do I mean?"

And Daniel laughed. It was a nuisance to have a boyfriend who could read you so quickly, who knew there was no such thing as a meaningless impulse. There is much in life one prefers to leave unexamined, but Zack saved them countless hours that would otherwise have been lost in silences or secrets.

Daniel came into the room and sat on the bed. "Handsome, exotic, thirty-something guy? Yeah, I found him attractive. Despite his being married. And the two kids. Although I forgot about the kids." He scratched Jocko behind the ears: the dog opened his mouth and grinned. "But you can be attracted to someone without wanting to go to bed with them. He's interesting. He's a new face. I like his paintings. Or I did. But he's just another snotty frog."

"A snotty *Muslim* frog," said Zack. "A *sexy* snotty Muslim frog."

"You think he's sexy?"

"Sure."

"Then why don't *you* pursue him?"

"Because I'm lazy. And he's straight. And I don't care about that stuff any-more." He lightly touched Daniel's hand.

Daniel touched back, brushing a thumb with a finger. "I don't know what I wanted. If it were just sex, it'd be simple. 'Wanna mess around? No? Okay. Bye.' But I wanted a friend. A peer. Maybe I just wanted him to like my work as much as I like his. Which is stupid."

"Not stupid," said Zack. "It's what we all want. Respect from people we respect."

"But most artists can't love anyone else's work without doubting their own. They're too competitive."

"You admire other people's work."

"Because I already hate my own stuff."

Zack hesitated. "No, you don't. You're just frustrated right now."

"We're not gonna go there tonight."

"Okay. We won't."

But if they couldn't talk about that, they didn't know what to say next. They said nothing for a moment.

"I'll let you get back to your reading." Daniel tapped the book by the pil-low: *Wives and Daughters* by Elizabeth Gaskell. Zack had read all the giants and was growing more and more obscure.

Zack opened the book. "Well, we have the whole school year to figure out the Rohanis," he said, pretending that was all they'd been talking about.

"Or never see them again," said Daniel.

"Except we did offer her the use of our washer and dryer."

Daniel groaned and rolled his eyes. "I think I scared her off." He kissed Zack on the forehead. "Good night, love," he said. "Good night, Jocko." And he went next door to his bedroom.

They slept in separate rooms but kept their doors wide open. Zack snored, but not so badly that it carried down the hall. They had slept apart for so long now that they did not miss each other's body. In fact, each man remained intensely conscious of the other's presence in the next room, almost as if he were sleeping beside him. Jocko would shift from bed to bed in the night, depending on his mood.

Life in couples usually writes white upon the page, except in times of crisis. Zack and Daniel believed their private crises were all behind them. Over the past twenty-one years they had fallen in and out of love with each other more than once, and not always at the same time. They had come to believe that they would always have each other, no matter what might happen to them separately or together.

6

THEY MET IN NEW YORK CITY IN 1981, at the monthly gay and lesbian dance at Columbia. They were two young men in their late twenties—they did not know how young they really were—with the spotless preppy clothes and skinny El Greco bodies of the period. Neither was looking for a boyfriend that night. Both just wanted to get laid. Daniel was getting over being dumped by a middle-aged art dealer. Zack was in the middle of his residency and had no emotional space for anything like love. He was just beginning to enjoy sex for the sake of sex. Back in Virginia he used to fall in love with any man who was kind enough to go to bed with him.

It was after midnight, and all the pretty undergraduates had paired off. They noticed each other across the room. Daniel strolled over. "Hey, handsome. Wanna dance?" Zack disliked this New York smart-ass manner, but he nodded and stepped out on the floor. Years later, he remembered a song by the Beach Boys, Daniel insisted it was the Supremes. "My name's Daniel. What's yours?" "Zachary Knowles." "Oh. You're from the South." "How did you guess?" "You got an accent, sweetheart." "Damn. I'm trying to lose it."

They danced a second dance and Zack decided the guy was cute enough. Zack disliked dancing—he knew he moved like a wooden Indian—so he cut to the chase. "You wanna go back to my place?" Daniel laughed. "Not too impatient, are we, sweetheart?" "Sorry. I'm on a tight schedule." "What am I, a train?" "It's just that I can't afford to waste time." "You sure know how to romance a girl." Zack disliked this kind of faggy talk, but he hated himself for disliking it. "Sorry. That was a stupid thing to say. I apologize." "No apology necessary," said Daniel. "Besides, it is getting late. Where do you live?" He lived downtown, only a few blocks from Daniel's place. It'd be easy enough to get home afterward. "Oh, why not?"

They caught a cab, and Zack became nervously quiet on the ride down, Daniel nervously chatty. He talked about politics, first Jimmy Carter, then Ronald Reagan, wanting to prove he had a serious side. They arrived at Zack's building, rode in the elevator up to his apartment, walked through the door—and mutually pounced. They became two frantic, groping, greedy, generic bodies—for twenty minutes or so. Their first sex was friendly, efficient, and forgettable. Then, while Zack considered going to sleep and Daniel considered getting dressed and going home, they began to talk again.

"A shrink?" said Daniel. "A shrink who's not a Jew?" He'd been in therapy for most of high school, and there was a kinky thrill in being naked with a psychiatrist, even one from Virginia. "So you're a bagel queen. You love psychiatry, New York, and Jewish boys."

"Nooo," said Zack. "I just like smart guys. They don't have to be Jewish." He ran his fingers through Daniel's hair—Daniel still had a full head of soft brown hair; Zack was still clean shaven. When Zack thought back years later to this time, he could not help picturing their faces as they were now, only smoother, vaguer, not yet in focus. "So you're an artist," he said. "All I know are nerd doctors."

"We're pretty wild, you know. Flaky and unpredictable."

"I'm a grind," said Zack. "I work all the time. I'm not much fun."

Each tried to tell the other that they were a bad match and shouldn't see each other again. Nevertheless, Daniel spent the night.

They went out for breakfast the next day, the civilized way of saying goodbye to the total stranger who had gotten his pubic hair in your mouth the night before. In diners all over town, one-night stands were saying farewell over bacon and eggs. But when Zack and Daniel got up to go back to their real lives, they went for a walk instead.

They spent the whole afternoon walking, ambling around the West Village, strolling up into the overcast sky by the Hudson River piers—the abandoned elevated highway still stood on stilts over West Street—telling stories about work and family and school. The tops of the skyscrapers downtown dissolved in the low ceiling of gauzy gray clouds. They wasted the entire day together and decided they might as well have dinner. Afterward they went back to Zack's place and ended up in bed again. They lay there after sex, sharing Zack's cigarettes and opening up the rest of their lives, telling about the first men they loved, the first men they slept with, the first time they told friends. Neither man had told his parents yet.

They met on a Friday night and did not say goodbye until Sunday afternoon, when Zack had to report back at the hospital. He was on twenty-four-hour duty until Wednesday. Then he spent Wednesday night with Daniel, and Thursday night, and Friday night.

It was so easy, so painless. It felt too good to be true. Zack was twenty-seven but had never experienced requited love before. Daniel was twenty-six and had been through several messy, manic affairs with hot men who loved sex but hated love. Zack seemed so sane and sweet by comparison.

They did most of their talking in bed during their first month.

"Sex is such a nice way of getting to know somebody," Zack purred into Daniel's ear.

"And *after* you know them?"

"Oh, you can never know anyone *completely*," he claimed.

More important for Zack than the pillow talk was the first time Daniel took him to his studio. Daniel taught part-time at Parsons, but he rented space in an old building on lower Broadway. His fiberboard cubicle was full of paintings in a variety of styles, but all very precise, measured, and beautiful. Zack knew nothing about art, but he could tell when someone cared about his work. He did not want to fall in love with a man who was faking it. Daniel clearly loved his vocation as much as Zack loved his.

Daniel didn't need a turning point. Somehow he knew after their first day-long walk together that they were right for each other. He should have worried about binding himself to a therapist, a highly trained conscience, like Jiminy Cricket with a medical degree. Yet that never bothered Daniel. He liked the idea of sharing his life with someone who was smarter than he was about certain things, not everything but some things, like psychiatric theories and mental illness, which were only a small part of existence anyway. He joked to his pals that his new boyfriend had access to great drugs. It was months before he could share the joke with Zack, who found it very funny, since it wasn't true.

They moved in together, into Zack's apartment, which was bigger, with a real lease. They both had siblings and knew how to live with other people. They understood difference; they did not expect oneness. Zack loved classical music and social history, both of which left Daniel cold. Daniel enjoyed ballet and cooking and bad pop songs—the trashier the better—all foreign to Zack. But they both liked women and they both hated Reagan, and they both adored silent movies.

Actually, silent film was Daniel's bug; Zack caught it like the flu. Despite what many people think, silent movies aren't failed talking pictures but a whole different art form. They need music to work, and Zack already loved music. Daniel took him into a new world of old images and live music. New York in the 1980s was filled with it: Lee Erwin played a mammoth church organ for summer screenings at St. John the Divine; various piano players performed at the Thalia; entire symphony orchestras accompanied rediscovered epics at Radio City Music Hall.

They adored the comedies, of course: Chaplin *and* Keaton. Zack preferred Chaplin and Daniel preferred Keaton, but they admired both—only dilettantes claim Keaton is greater—and in later years they would switch favorites. But they also loved the melodramas, which are like pantomime operas full of high, absurd emotion. It's the convention of talk that makes such excess feel ludicrous. They would sit side by side, staring ahead, transfixed by the sorrows of a disfigured clown in *The Man Who Laughs* or the pathos of a beaten child in *Broken Blossoms* or the reconciliation of an unhappy husband and wife in *Sunrise*. Without the distraction of words, such stories can pierce the heart like a knife. When the lights came up, Zack and Daniel would slowly rise to their feet, shake themselves out of their different dreams, and turn to each other, grinning.

7

Something terrible is going to happen. That's what I feel during these attacks. I feel it first in my tummy, then it rushes up to my head and out to my hands. A cold, icy panic."

"Something terrible will happen to you?"

"Or to my family. Or a neighbor. Or maybe just in the world. I don't know. Which makes the fear even worse. It'd be easier to handle if I thought it was going to happen to me."

The office was dark, the curtains drawn, the air conditioner running. September remained warm and humid. Two bookcases flanked the curtained window, one full of psychiatric texts, the other full of Victorian novels, biographies, and history. A soft, black leather chair squatted against the opposite wall. Fay Dawson sat very ladylike in the chair, staring down at the hands she kept neatly tucked in the folds of skirt between her knees.

"Prefers worrying about others to worrying about self," Zack scratched in pencil in his spiral notebook.

His work was about stories. Everyone had stories. Many stories. And Zack knew how to listen. In recent years he sometimes feared that he'd forgotten how to speak, but he did know how to listen.

"I imagine these episodes are not only frightening for you but disruptive?" he offered. "Sometimes inconvenient?"

"You better believe it," said Fay. "Twice I had attacks while I was driving. I had to pull over and call home. Which is why I don't drive anymore. I have to get my son or husband to take me places."

"That must be limiting."

"Yes." She lowered her eyes. "Embarrassing, too."

Fay was a petite, pretty woman a few years younger than Zack, an ageless Southern good girl with short hair and no makeup; her smart clothes gave her a feminine tomboy look, like a motel manager or real estate agent. She'd been referred to Zack by her family doctor, Jack Sturgeon, for panic attacks. She wanted something for her nerves, that's all. Zack said he'd be happy to write her a prescription, but he wanted to talk with her first, then meet with her while she was on the medication to monitor its effect. Since they'd be meeting anyway, they might as well explore possible causes for her anxiety.

"Have you discussed these attacks with anyone?"

"I tried talking with Donald Kane, our minister. We belong to the Rock Church, you know. Pentecostal. But all Donald can say is that I must trust in Jesus. And he quotes scripture at me. And scripture is not what I need right now."

"No. Sometimes we just need someone to listen," said Zack. "And your husband? Can you talk about it with him?"

"Oh, Yancy means well, but you know how men are. Well, maybe you don't." She caught herself; her cheeks and neck turned bright red. "Sorry. I didn't mean you're *not*. A man, I mean."

"No offense taken." Zack smiled. "And gay men can be just as oblivious as straight men."

"They can? Truly? I didn't know." She tried looking him in the eye but couldn't.

Despite what he'd been taught, Zack had learned to establish as soon as possible that he was a gay man with a boyfriend. This was a small town, and people were going to know anyway. He hoped to reduce the elaborate tap dance around I know/you know/I know. Most of his patients were women. He saw a few men, chiefly students from the college, but mostly it was women. Daniel joked that Zack was like a hairdresser for distressed psyches.

"You have children?" he asked.

"Yes, two. A boy, Malvern, who's a teenager. He's seventeen. And Melissa. Who's twelve."

Zack wrote everything in his notebook. "How long have you and Yancy been married?"

"Nineteen years. Is that right? Yes. Nineteen years in October." She paused. "You're going to ask me about our sex life, aren't you?"

All patients fretted about this during their first visit; Zack admired Fay for having the courage to come right out and ask. "Probably. But not today," he assured her. "Eventually."

She smiled and took a deep breath. "I know it sounds awful, but I'm not much interested in sex anymore."

"It often happens when people get to be our age." He hadn't meant "our" to slip out, but it did.

"It's terribly private. Marriage. So hard to talk about. You sound mean-spirited if you complain, or like you're fooling yourself if you praise it. You and your, uh, friend. How do you talk about it?"

"Fay, we're here to discuss you today, not me."

"Of course. I'm sorry. It's my old-fashioned Virginia manners." Fay let out a nervous laugh. "It's how I was brought up, Dr. Knowles. I feel funny doing *all* the talking."

Zack smiled kindly. "You can forget your good manners here," he told her. "How would you describe your marriage?"

She took another deep breath. "We're happy. Well, as happy as anyone can be. There are times when we don't like each other very much. But we love each other. We do."

He respected her for offering such a realistic appraisal right off the bat. She was a very intelligent, self-aware woman. She reminded him of someone. He could not let himself be distracted by memories, yet he felt this was someone he liked.

"And the Rock Church helps," she said. "It gives me and Yancy something to share, something to lean on. I didn't mean to bad-mouth it earlier. Truly. Do you believe in God?"

Zack was not totally surprised by the question. He saw a fair share of extreme Christians out at the state hospital, but rarely in his private practice. For an evangelical or fundamentalist believer, seeing a therapist was like admitting Jesus couldn't help. But Fay was bolder and more curious than most born-again Christians.

"Why do you ask, Fay? Do you feel we have to think about God in the same way for us to work together?" She didn't need to know that she was dealing with an atheist.

"Oh no! Not that. I was just asking. Curious. That's all."

Zack had a new idea. "Do your panic attacks affect your faith?"

"What do you mean?" She looked worried.

But she had brought up God and Zack thought he should explore. "They don't make you feel God has abandoned you? Or are they about something else entirely?"

She stared at him as if he had insulted her. "God has nothing to do with my attacks. They don't put the fear of God in me, if that's what you mean. Because I always have the fear of God. And the *love*!" She looked down at the hands in her lap. "I'm not upset about *God*!" she argued. "I'm not upset about the Rock Church! I'm not even upset about Reverend Donald! I don't know why I'm so upset. Except—" Her face snapped back up with a fierce look of hurt. "My daughter almost died, you know!"

Zack was stunned. "I didn't know. I'm sorry." It took him a moment to recover. "I can know only what you tell me, Fay. I can't read your mind."

"Sorry, sorry," she whispered, lowering her head again, frightened by her anger. "I didn't mean to take that tone with you."

"Don't worry about *my* feelings. I have a very thick skin." He had crossed a line, but it gave them something valuable. "So what happened to your daughter? This is Melissa?"

"Yes. Melissa. This was last spring. This year."

Fay told the story in a soft, muttering tone, with many pauses and grimaces. Her daughter went to school one day and was fine. The kids were playing dodgeball on the playground. And Melissa suddenly collapsed. The ball hadn't hit her; she just fell, unconscious. And she stayed unconscious and was rushed to the hospital. The doctors thought it was a cranial blood clot and were certain she'd die.

Zack set down his pencil, listened, and said nothing.

"And I was ready to accept it. I was ready to say goodbye and let her go," said Fay. "With an ease that amazed me."

He thought he knew where this was going: She was angry with God— that's why she had lost her temper. She was angry with God and her church, and her anger frightened her.

But then Fay said, "And I realized I could let go of *all* of them. Every last one. My daughter, my son, my husband. They could all die tomorrow and it wouldn't mean a thing." She stared at Zack. "Isn't that awful? They could all drop dead and it wouldn't hurt me a bit. They'd be out of my hair and I'd be sad, but I could go on with my life. Because I don't love them. Not really."

"You mean to say that you felt—"

Fay rushed back into her story. "She was unconscious for thirty-six hours. That's all. A day and a half. I came back to her room from the cafeteria and— there she was! Wide awake! Sitting up in bed! My darling little angelcake. And I was so glad. I was!" she insisted, as if anyone could doubt her. "She was fine, like it was nothing but a long nap. I was so happy to have her back." She paused again and bit her lower lip. "Not until weeks later did I remember my *real* feelings. When the doctors told me she might die." She drew her mouth down in a rubbery frown. "That's the kind of mother I really am. A cold mother. A selfish mother." Her face folded up between her frown and her eyes, and she broke into loud sobs.

Daniel called this "the room where women come to cry," but men cried here, too. Zack could feel his own eyes prickling. He stood up and crossed to the box of Kleenexes on the table beside her. He knelt down on one knee and held out the tissues. "Fay, you don't *sound* like a selfish woman. You don't talk like a cold mother."

She took a tissue and covered her eyes.

"You sound like someone who was only protecting herself from a possible loss."

"But I don't care about any of them!" she cried behind the crumpled mask of paper. "I don't love them."

"But you must," said Zack. "Or you wouldn't be so afraid that something else might happen to them."

She clutched her nose in Kleenex. "What do you mean?"

Zack knew he'd jumped the gun. This was a premature interpretation and he was saying too much too soon, but she was upset and he wanted to offer some kind of solace. "You do care or you wouldn't be afraid other terrible things could happen to them."

"You mean my panic attacks are about them and not me?"

"Maybe, maybe not," said Zack, backtracking. "We'll have to talk about it later. In our next session." He smiled apologetically as he got up off the floor. "We're almost out of time today."

This was a cruel place to leave things but a useful place, a productive place. Zack hoped to make up for having said too much.

He wrote out two prescriptions, explaining how the Paxil would re-up her serotonin and the Xanax would stop the panic attacks until the Paxil became effective. "Once the Paxil kicks in, we'll take you off the Xanax, but save it for emergencies."

Zack escorted her out to the bathroom in the front hall so she could wash her face.

A man sat in the living room, an eighteenth-century figure dressed in green knee britches and a brown waistcoat, like a hallucination from the Age of Reason.

"Hello, Carter. Go on in. I'll be with you shortly."

Carter Mosby worked for Colonial Williamsburg, a silversmith in one of the craft shops. He came to sessions straight from work.

Fay stepped out of the bathroom, fully reassembled, her face almost sunny. "Thank you," she said. "This has been very interesting. Could you walk with me to the car? I'd like my son to meet you. So he'll know you're not the boogeyman."

Zack escorted Fay outside to a Jeep Cherokee parked at the curb. Her son sat at the wheel, one of those teenage boys who already worked out at the gym, a baby-faced child with a boxy build, like an SUV. Sullen and mumbly, he did not look terribly lovable; Zack wondered if he were part of Fay's problem. The boy kept his eyes averted when she introduced Dr. Knowles, but no teenager is going to be happy his mother is seeing a psychiatrist. Fay had brought them together in order to declare, "See, I am not ashamed."

"You have my number if you need anything," Zack told her. "But you're in good shape. I'll see you next week. Nice to meet you, Malvern. Goodbye."

Zack went back inside and found Carter in his office, sitting smugly in the black leather chair.

"Hello, Dr. Knowles. You have a good week? I know I did," he said in his usual robotic tones. "I made out like a bandit."

Carter was twenty-nine years old, a cold, affectless, unhappy man who loved crafting silver and pewter but could connect with people only through sex. He connected constantly, nearly every night in fact, usually with men but sometimes with women. He met them on the computer or through phone sex lines—there were phone sex lines even in Virginia.

"Did you meet anyone you *liked*?" asked Zack.

"No, they were all jerks."

Carter claimed to prefer women, insisting he was straight. Zack thought this was possible. The man was schizoidal and unable to form any kind of relationship. A previous therapist had convinced Carter that he'd been sexually abused as a child. Zack didn't think this was the case, but Carter had constructed a shell identity around the idea and Zack was afraid to crack it. The man had a terrible temper. His remoteness could be broken only in orgasm or anger.

"All right then," said Zack. "Let's talk about the people you met. Maybe they weren't all total jerks. And concentrate on what you felt. We don't need to talk about the sex."

Zack heard too many sad, dreary tales about bad, dreary sex. There was a time when therapists had to work at getting patients to talk about their sex lives. No more. Zack had to work through the sex, at least with patients like Carter, to get at the rest of life. No wonder he enjoyed meeting someone like Fay Dawson.

Listening to Carter describe his week of tricks, Zack found himself missing Fay. And he suddenly realized who she reminded him of: his mother. She had Doris Knowles's confusing mix of timidity and boldness, convention and rebellion, Southern other-directedness and deeply private dreaming. Was that why he'd been so quick to assure Fay that she didn't hate her family? Zack couldn't guess if Mom ever imagined their family dead, but he couldn't ask her. She had died seven years ago.

This was a special variety of countertransference, of course. There are more dangerous forms; but it couldn't be healthy for a psychiatrist to confuse a patient with his mother. Besides, Zack knew he usually reminded patients of *their* mothers.

8

The semester began, and Daniel was actually happy. He always found the first weeks of school oddly invigorating. There was the challenge of classes, the thrill of performing. His days were suddenly full again, and he had no time to worry about his own life and work.

"Welcome to Fine Arts 101, Fundamentals of Form. My name is Daniel Wexler. You can call me Daniel or Mr. Wexler or even Wexler. But don't call me doctor or professor, because I'm neither."

He looked out on the usual assortment of bland, blank faces, like clock faces without hands. The students continued to appear younger and younger, despite recent efforts to age themselves with piercings and tattoos. The guys were never very interesting as people or artists. Oh, some were cute, but Daniel had learned long ago that chicken was more trouble than it was worth. Occasionally there was a talented female—Daniel liked the girls and they liked him—but the talented boys went to other schools.

"Don't be afraid of making mistakes. Don't be afraid of feeling frustrated. Let yourself get angry. Henri Matisse, the creator of so much perfect beauty, once said, 'I work like a drunken brute trying to kick the door down.' We're all trying kick a door down."

But these kids did not believe in struggle. They wanted instant product, immediate results: conceptual art, collage, found-object sculpture, digital photography, video. Painting required too much work. "We're here to put the pain into painting," Daniel told his First Year Painting class and assigned their opening project, the White Box, where they put objects in a box, painted the whole thing white, then painted paintings of that. It was a great exercise for studying light and shadow, but students complained that Daniel was stifling their expressiveness. They didn't realize they had nothing to express yet.

His favorite student last year had been Maureen Clark, a tough little redhead from Goochland County with a good eye and a nice, dry sense of humor. Maureen was not in any of his classes this semester, but he ran into her one afternoon smoking a cigarette on the wide steps of Andrews Hall, the home of the Fine Arts Department. Girls were the only ones who smoked anymore, their way of keeping thin.

"How's the semester look?" he asked. "Aren't you doing the workshop with the artist in residence?" Daniel hadn't seen Rohani since the dinner. He lowered his voice. "What's he like?"

Maureen shrugged. "Good looking. And weird. He stood in front of us the first day and went, 'You must forgive my bluntness' "—she took on a gruff, foreign voice—" 'but English is not my first or second language. Paint is my first language, Farsi my second, French my third. So if I am rude in English, you must cut me the slack.' "

Her impersonation was good. It was interesting to learn that "English is not my first or second language" was part of his schtick. And why not? It was a good line.

"I've met his wife, and she's weird, too," Maureen continued. "And they got two kids, and the kids are weird. But sweet. I've babysat for them twice."

"*You're* the student they roped into babysitting? I should've known." Unlike most undergraduates, who stuck to their peers, Maureen spent as much time as she could with teachers. She enjoyed being around grown-ups.

"Hey, we never got any Persian painters or Russian poets back in Goochland," she said. "I'm making up for lost time."

Departmental silliness resumed with the school year. Rohani did not attend the first faculty meeting, but everyone else was there.

"My students attack me because I'm not part of this *net* thing," grumbled Samuel Clay Brooke, a tall, elderly bachelor with the dotty grandeur and rolling baritone of an Anglican minister. He taught British art history and wrote about Hogarth, Fuseli, and Rowlandson; he could have modeled for all three. "I refuse to be treated as a woolly mammoth."

"Nobody's attacking you, Samuel," said Jane Morrison. "The students are just used to doing things a certain way."

"I can show you how to get online," Daniel offered again.

"You'll love it," said Warren Bates, who taught American twentieth-century art; he'd been working on a biography of Thomas Hart Benton for the past thirty years. "My wife uses it for shopping, and I use it to download music. It's better than TV."

"I don't own a TV," Samuel said proudly.

This was a small department, divided equally between teachers of art history and teachers of studio art. The art history people tended to be older, but nobody new had been added since Daniel arrived ten years ago. He had heard about the job from Jane, who had known him since grad school at Penn. Jane was a graphic artist and printmaker, a stocky, down-to-earth woman with enormous forearms. She was assumed to be lesbian until people met her stocky, down-to-earth cabinetmaker husband, John, whose forearms were even bigger. The joke among students was that they'd met at a national arm-wrestling championship.

"Samuel, it'll save *you* time," said Jane. "Think of all the hours you waste sitting in your office on the chance that a student might drop by. This way they can make appointments."

"No!" said Brooke. "In our inhuman age of cold technology, I will continue to offer my students a warm island of humanity."

What sometimes sounded like dry wit from Brooke was almost always sincere. The man had a mad, sweet, exasperating innocence.

The meeting ended without any mention of Rohani, but an artist in residence was not part of their routine. The residency program cycled through the school from department to department—English, music, theater, and fine arts—so all could benefit from the presence of a living genius every four or five years. The last resident in fine arts had been Lucinda Johnson, a sculptor whose hammered copper abstraction *Somalia* still lurked in the garden between Andrews and Swem Library like a tall, sinister bird.

The following week Daniel and Zack walked down to Merchants Square to see *Double Indemnity*. Ross was running a Monday night film noir series for the English Department. The college paid for the screenings, but the theater remained open to the ticket-buying public. Ross did whatever he could to keep his business going.

They found him working the popcorn stand in the mock-colonial lobby. "Guys! Was hoping you'd come tonight. Nothing but students in there. People don't appreciate the classics."

" 'Don't nobody come to the picture show no more,' " said Daniel in his best Texas accent.

"Ain't it the truth. Not even our Iranian friends. I was hoping I'd see her here sometime. Maybe she doesn't like movies."

"You mean Elena?" said Zack.

Ross heard a soft accusation, which people often did with Zack, simply because of his profession. "I know, I know," he said with a guilty smirk. "She's a married lady. I'd just like to see her again. That's all. She's interesting. They both are. I'd like to see them both."

"They keep to themselves," said Daniel. "I don't even see the husband at school. He has a studio there, but he's never in it when I'm around." He shrugged. "I've forgotten all about them."

Daniel went for a morning swim at the college gym every Monday, Wednesday, and Saturday. Saturday was his favorite day, simply because students slept late and he usually had the pool to himself. The Saturday after *Double Indemnity* he drove over in the car—the gym was only a mile away, behind the fraternity houses, but walking took too long. The weather was now cool and schoolish in the mornings.

Daniel was in the locker room, pulling on his Speedo, when he heard a high-pitched squeal out in the echoey pool. It sounded like a child. He hung his goggles around his neck, walked through the men's showers, and came around the corner.

The enormous sky blue room appeared empty at first, its liquid blue floor full of wiggling black lines, nothing else. Then Daniel saw the figure standing on the curb at the shallow end, a dark body in tight red trunks: Abbas Rohani.

There were two children in the water at his feet, a laughing little boy and a solemn little girl. Abbas clapped his hands at them and said something in French. He turned when he noticed his daughter staring at someone.

Daniel felt embarrassed, as if he'd walked in on a very private act. But the man was only playing with his kids. "Good morning," he called out. "These yours?"

Abbas glared at him, squinted and frowned. Startled, Daniel was ready to turn and walk away when Abbas broke into a grin—a warm grin displaying a mouthful of small, neat teeth. "Good morning, Daniel. It is good to see you again. Yes. These are my children."

He wasn't wearing his glasses—that's all his frown meant. He was actually pleased to see Daniel.

"Hel-lo. What-is-your-name?" chanted the little boy hanging on the side. "My name is Osh. Hel-lo. What-is-your-name?" he repeated. They were memorized sounds, not words. "My name is Osh."

"Poppi!" cried the girl. "I'm cold!" She held up a hand signaling that she wanted to be pulled out.

He bent over and lifted her up. The red trunks hugged his narrow ass like paint. The backs of his thighs were black with hair.

The girl stood beside her daddy, holding herself in her skinny arms and stamping her little feet. Her eyes were so dark that they looked rimmed with kohl, a baby Theda Bara.

"This is Mina," said Abbas, setting both hands on his daughter's shoulders. "And that is Osh." He nodded at the boy. "And this is Daniel, who is a painter like your poppi."

The girl knotted up her mouth in a frown.

"You come here every day?" Abbas asked.

"Every other day," said Daniel. "To swim laps."

"A lovely pool. I am surprised no one else is here. Elena and I have an arrangement. I take the kids on Saturday and she can have time alone. Is only fair, yes? So I come here. It is our first visit."

The little girl continued to frown at Daniel. He suddenly felt very naked standing before this family in his dinky black Speedo—and very gay. He shyly stepped back. "Have a good time," he told them. "Enjoy yourselves. See you later, Abbas."

"Yes, yes, Daniel. Enjoy your laps."

Daniel hurried away, fearing he looked awfully nelly tiptoeing over the tiles. He quickly snapped his goggles over his eyes and dove into the pool. He clothed himself in water.

He began to swim, solidly and briskly. This was his element, his habitat, his home. He climbed through the mild, peppery burn of chlorine, reached the end of the pool, and spun around. He wondered why he had felt so self-conscious around the Rohanis, so nervous. He soon calmed himself in the meditative rhythm of counting off laps.

Abbas wasn't such a bad guy, Daniel decided. He wasn't at all snotty or arrogant the way he'd been two weeks ago, when he was new in town and still on guard. "English is not my first or second language." And Daniel had been in a testy mood that night. He felt a teensy bit guilty now for checking out the younger man's body when the man was with his kids. But the man had a nice body, and the kids wouldn't know. Abbas might not know either.

Rotating his head to breathe on every other stroke, Daniel caught sight of the family now and then, three toy figures at the shallow end, one of them dabbed with a harsh dot of crimson red trunks. Two-thirds of the way through his laps, the toy figures disappeared.

Daniel swam half a mile on Saturdays, which took twenty to thirty minutes. When he was done, he climbed out feeling purged and solid and whole. There was a pleasant burn in his lungs, a sweet buzz in his muscles. He assumed the Rohanis were long gone.

His ears were stopped up and he heard nothing as he stepped into the men's showers. He was surprised to see a small boy standing in the corner, under a cone of spray. Abbas squatted in front the boy, trying to untie Osh's bathing suit.

"*Merde,*" he said, smiling at Daniel, amused to be caught in his helpless pose. He'd taken off his own suit and was as naked as a cat.

Daniel hurried over to a showerhead in the opposite corner, turned on the water, and looked away.

"Owww!" cried Osh as his father skinned the little trunks off.

Abbas stood up, shaking the tiny garment and inspecting the knot, which was still tied. "He makes a knot I can never undo."

"Granny knots are the worst," said Daniel.

Now he was looking, of course. He saw a trim, dark, hairy-assed nudity. Hairs twitched in the spray like iron filings teased by a magnet. The dick was short, plump, and circumcised, which surprised Daniel until he remembered that the phrase "uncircumcised dog" originally meant Christians: Jews and Muslims shared that heritage.

Daniel kept his own suit on. "Where's your daughter?"

"She is in the ladies' locker room. She is a big girl. She can take care of herself. Come here, *mon bébé.*" Abbas squirted shampoo into his hand. The little boy squeezed his eyes shut and made a face while his father soaped his head.

The bare child like an elongated Baroque infant made Abbas look even hairier and darker. Daniel remembered when he was the boy's age and took showers with his own father. He was never aware of his father's genitals, only of his dark, tree trunk body.

He waited until father and son had finished and padded into the locker room—"Later," said Abbas—before he peeled off his Speedo.

There is something wonderfully primal about fathers and sons—fathers and straight sons anyway. With gay sons, fathers often draw away. At least Daniel's father had. Daniel and Zack used to argue about this, whether it was universal that straight men fear their gay sons. Zack wasn't so sure. He and his straight brother had the same cool yet polite relationship with their father. Whatever the case, Abbas and his son were still in their honeymoon phase.

When Daniel came out, a towel tied securely at his hip, he found the father and son still in the locker room. The boy was fully dressed and stood in front of Abbas, who sat on a bench still wearing his towel, tenderly combing his son's hair.

"Now you are perfect," he told the boy and kissed him on the forehead. "I see they have a sauna," he told Daniel. "I have turned it on. Will you join me for a quick sweat?"

What was this? Had he noticed Daniel giving him the once-over? Was he testing him? Was he flirting? Or was this just Middle Eastern male bonding?

"Thanks, no. I need to get home."

"Oh, please. Just a few minutes. It is no fun to sit alone. And it is too hot for Osh. Osh, darling. Go meet your sister outside. Tell her I will be out in five minutes. You can play your Pokémon game."

Osh trotted off, and Abbas stood up, readjusting his towel.

"Oh, why not?" said Daniel.

He followed Abbas to the windowless redwood box between the lockers and the showers. They stepped into the oven air.

Abbas promptly whipped off his towel, spread it on the wooden bench, and sat there, as plain as could be. Daniel dropped his own towel and sat facing him. Their knees were less than ten inches apart. Daniel carefully set his bare feet on either side of the Iranian's toes.

Already he could feel prickles of sweat in his crotch and armpits and the bald zone of his scalp.

Abbas smiled at Daniel.

Daniel smiled back. "You have beautiful children," he said.

"Oh yes. They are my pride and joy." Abbas jiggled his genitals, separating his cock from his balls in their nest of jet-black hair.

Daniel leaned back, lifting one knee to display himself and prove he wasn't intimidated.

Abbas closed his eyes and took in a deep breath of baked air, salty perspiration, and masculine musk.

It was incredibly sexual. Daniel knew not to confuse imaginary sex with real sex, and this sex was all in his head. Maybe it was their cultural differences. Something was lost in translation—or gained. Thoughts were distorted as they passed from one language to another, like light passing through a glass of water.

One dim incandescent bulb glowed in the ceiling. Abbas's body began to glisten. He kept his eyes closed when he spoke.

"I enjoyed the other night very much. The dinner and conversation. And your painting. Not all your paintings but one. You know the one. Very— witty." He opened his eyes and smiled again. "You and your partner are like me and Elena."

"Oh?"

"We see other people."

"*Oh.*" So that's why he wanted Daniel here. He was using the sauna as a confessional. "You see other women?"

Abbas shrugged. "*And* men," he said, as if this were of no importance. "Men are more available. And understanding."

Daniel crossed his legs. Then he uncrossed them. His legs were slippery with sweat. His heart was racing like a stopwatch.

So it was not a mistranslation, not just imaginary. The sexual feeling in the sauna was real. Daniel had sensed something about Abbas ever since he first met the man, another side to the painter that could bring the two men together in friendship. He had thought it was art they shared, but it must be their sexuality. Or was Abbas offering more than friendship?

"You mean you're bisexual?" he said.

Again Abbas shrugged. "I prefer women for love and men for sex. And I love Elena. But I have my needs and she prefers I satisfy them with men."

He chuckled and stretched, arching his back and spreading his arms and legs, opening himself out. His sweat glands threw off a faint spray, like the mist you get when you bend an orange peel.

"This is lovely. Reminds me of Berlin. Have you been to Berlin? I used to go there to the Apollo Sauna. Very nice. Very relaxing."

Was he hoping to relax this morning? Was that what he wanted? Did he expect a hand job here and now? Daniel wasn't *that* cheap. Plus they were faculty, in the same department. And the man's kids were just outside! Yet he did look awfully appealing sprawled in front of Daniel like a starfish.

"No. We're not monogamous," said Daniel. "You saw my self-portrait. We see other people. Now and then." All right, he thought. Your move.

"And where do you meet these other people?" asked Abbas.

"Oh, on the Internet. And at bars. There's a couple of bars down in Norfolk. Which is a big navy town."

"But nothing here?"

The sauna door burst open in an explosion of light.

Three frat boys stood outside. They came to a dead stop when they saw two grown men inside—two *naked* grown men. The boys wore baggy bathing suits and large, droopy T-shirts.

Their timing could not have been better if this were a porn movie. But it wasn't a porn movie.

"Come in, come in!" called out Abbas. "There is plenty room."

"Sorry, man. Hey. We're cool. But we're gonna go swim first. Bye." And they quickly shut the door.

"You should know," said Daniel, "that the students here are big prudes. And legally out of bounds. So you can forget about them."

"Pity," said Abbas. "When I was their age, I was a big prude, too. Which might be why I prefer younger men. To make up for my lost years. So American students are as uptight as Muslim students?"

"The majority. Yes." Of course Abbas wanted younger men, thought Daniel. Who didn't?

"But there are sailors nearby? Sailors are good."

"Oh yeah. Norfolk is full of sailors. And marines, too."

So Abbas didn't want Daniel. He wanted only his data, his know-how, his local knowledge. Which was a relief. It *was* a relief, wasn't it? It was so much safer and saner this way.

They sat together for another five minutes, companionably naked, making plans while the perspiration poured off their bodies like tears.

~ ~

"So I offered to take him down to Norfolk tomorrow and show him the bars and go to a few tea dances. He and Elena have a deal where he takes care of the kids on Saturday and can spend Sunday however he pleases. He usually spends it painting. But man cannot live by bread alone."

They were out in the garden behind the house, where Daniel had found Zack when he got home. Zack was on his knees, his sleeves rolled up, his hair and beard speckled with tiny brown leaves. He was clearing away the dead vegetation, pulling up what was left of the tomato, squash, and cucumber plants. Jocko lay in the grass a few feet away, dozing in the honey-colored sunlight.

Zack said nothing for a moment. "Just your typical trilingual, bisexual Iranian painter, huh? And his wife knows?"

"I don't know if he gives her full reports. But he was all too happy to tell me about their open marriage since he knew about ours. Here. Let me help you." Daniel crouched down and began to stack the extracted wooden stakes.

"What're the kids like?"

"Cute. Adorable. He clearly adores them."

"How old?"

"A little boy of six and his grumpy big sister, who must be ten." The grumpy sister had given Daniel the dirtiest look imaginable when he came out of the gym with her father.

"And he wants you only for information?"

"That's right. Silly man. He doesn't know what he's missing."

Zack didn't laugh. "Just be careful," he said.

"I always am, sweetheart. More careful than you are."

Zack opened his mouth as if to argue, then shut it and reached over to jiggle loose another stake.

"Anyway," Daniel quickly added, "nothing's going to happen. I'm not his type and he's not mine. We're too much alike. We're both painters. We're both married. And we're both losing our hair."

9

SUNDAY WAS USUALLY A QUIET DAY for both men. Daniel cooked breakfast while Zack walked down to Merchants Square with Jocko to pick up
a Sunday *New York Times*. They spent the morning in the sunlit kitchen, reading the paper and drinking coffee, occasionally discussing a play or museum
exhibition they might want to see *if* they were still living in New York. Their
if had grown softer over the past ten years, but it was still present.

After lunch, Daniel showered and shaved and tried on shirts before set-
tling on a nifty blue bowling shirt from the sixties. This was hardly a date, but
he wanted to look good. He didn't expect to pick anyone up, but it'd be too
humiliating to get completely rejected in front of Abbas. All he hoped to do
was dance with a cute stranger.

"See you later, dear," he told Zack. "I won't be late."

"Be safe," said Zack—their old slogan from the eighties.

Daniel drove over to the campus, parked in front of PBK Hall, and walked
around back to Andrews. It was three o'clock. Abbas had suggested they
meet at his studio, not because Elena didn't know, he said, but because he
preferred not to rub her nose in his other life. Well, maybe. Or maybe Abbas
and Elena had a don't ask, don't tell policy. Or maybe Abbas didn't tell her a
thing. Whatever their story, it was none of Daniel's business.

The artist in residence had been given the big studio on the second floor for his private work space. Daniel went up the stairs and down the hall. He could hear music ahead. The door was half open. A boom box played loudly inside, some kind of buzzing, rhythmic, Middle Eastern chanting. Daniel knocked on the door as he pushed it open. There was a rich, savory smell of oil paint.

Abbas stood with his back to the door, bent forward in a pair of white bib overalls, hunched over a narrow canvas on stretchers that lay flat on the floor. He was barefoot and shirtless.

Daniel knocked again.

The man's angular butt slowly swung around as he laid a long, slow brush-stroke across the canvas.

"Hey!" Daniel called out.

Abbas stopped and looked over his bare shoulder. He stared at Daniel through his raccoon glasses. He looked down at the painting, then back at Daniel, then at the painting again. He hit his head with the heel of his hand. "Damn, damn, bloody damn!"

"We had a date!" said Daniel. "Did you forget?" He was angry or he wouldn't have said "date."

"No. I do not forget. I come over here dressed for the clubs"—he pointed at a small stack of folded clothes on the sofa—"and then I think, I have an hour. I can fix this. And so I put on my work clothes and go to work and I lose track of time. Now I am in the middle and cannot quit." He nodded at the door. "Go on without me."

Daniel knew how easily one can be swallowed by a picture, but he still felt insulted that Abbas could choose work over an afternoon with him. "No way," he said. "It's no fun doing Norfolk alone." He immediately stepped toward the canvas for a look.

There was a parade of figures on a burnt sienna background. The figures suggested calligraphy, elegant squiggles of Arabic struggling to become bod-ies. And it was oil paint, not acrylic, so the colors had a solid, luminous qual-ity, even under fluorescent light. Plump snails of pure color sat on Abbas's palette on the floor, a raw square of plywood, not mixed or blended together but applied straight to the canvas. A bouquet of brushes stood in a glass of turpentine by his foot. His toes were spattered with paint.

"How long will you be?" asked Daniel. "I don't mind hanging."

"An hour? I can promise I will finish in an hour."

If he were anything like Daniel, an hour could stretch into two. But Daniel didn't want to leave.

"Or you can come back later," Abbas suggested.

"No. Let me hang here. Then I can make sure you finish." And he could watch Abbas work.

"Do you mind? Because I want to finish this. But I also want to go to Norfolk and meet sailors. Life is full of trade-offs."

"I'll say. Go ahead. I'll be fine." Daniel was already walking toward the wall to study the handful of sketches tacked there.

If Abbas had been looking at Daniel's work, Daniel would've been paralyzed with self-consciousness. But Abbas automatically went back to work.

So few people used oil paint anymore that it was a memory aroma now, like a forgotten soup or stew made by a favorite grandmother. Under that smell was another forgotten scent, the pleasant stink of cigarettes. Daniel saw the empty coffee can full of butts and ashes. The smoke detector hung open on the ceiling, gutted of its batteries.

The sketches on the wall looked like pen and ink, but no, they were also paint. Crucified on white paper, the simple brushstroke figures really did look like letters, not Arabic but an alien, extraterrestrial alphabet.

"Pay no attention to those," said Abbas. "They are only thoughts."

A finished canvas on stretchers leaned against the rear wall. The top half of the canvas was greenish blue, the bottom half saffron yellow: sky and beach. An abstract family of four figures battled a large, angry, abstract fish. The colors were delicious, clear and direct. Nothing was muddy or overworked.

If he wanted to be mean, Daniel could've said, "Oh, it's like Klee turning into Picasso" or "Giacometti meets Clemente." Because you can always use famous names to dilute another artist's identity. But the truth of the matter was, despite the echoes, the work was fresh and alive—both the finished and the new piece. Daniel had seen only slides and reproductions, which did not fully capture the man's gift for color and texture. The things themselves were richer, more beautiful and mysterious. There was a Middle Eastern quality, too, although that may have been an effect of the music on the boom box.

Just then the CD jumped into a new track, a bongo-driven thing that sounded more Indian than Middle Eastern.

"This isn't Iranian music," said Daniel.

"Oh no. Iranian music is all funeral and military marches. Very grim. This is Bollywood. The soundtrack of *Lagaan.*"

"Nice," said Daniel, and it was, a jumpy weave of rhythms and counter-rhythms, so catchy that Daniel half expected the figures in the fish painting to start dancing.

"Iran used to be a beautiful land," said Abbas. "Lush and fun and foolish. But no more. Religion has ruined it."

"You were a teenager when you left?"

"I was fourteen. Before the revolution. But I have been back to visit my brother. A sad, sad country."

He duckwalked around his canvas, as agile as a gymnast. No wonder his body was so lean and taut. An empty easel stood in the corner; he preferred to work on the floor.

Daniel sat down on the sofa, next to the stack of club clothes: it was everything, even his socks and underpants—black boxer briefs. Abbas must really get into his paint when he worked. But he'd told the truth when he said he *intended* to go to Norfolk today.

"How's it coming?" asked Daniel. "Are we there yet?"

Abbas didn't laugh. He didn't respond at all. He was lost in his brushstrokes.

Daniel sighed, sank back, and listened to the music.

Art books from the school library stood in stacks beside the sofa, a hundred or more. Abbas must have checked out half of the modern art section. Several volumes were open, one parked on top of another. Francis Bacon lay on Lucien Freud, who lay on David Hockney. Daniel wondered why Abbas was exploring Brits, but no, the pictures were about all bodies. *Hockney by Hockney*—with green fingerprints in the margins—was open on the Cavafy drawings, scratchy pen-and-ink sketches of boys in bed. There was a book of Muybridge photographs, opened to a multiplied naked runner. Abbas seemed to have a thing about naked men, yet there were no literal naked men in his paintings, only Klee-like ideas of men, boxed or paisley symbols of bodies.

Abbas squatted at his canvas like a rubbery logo, his brown shoulder blotched with green, the white seat of his overalls rubbed with yellow. And here was his black underwear in the stack of folded clothes beside Daniel.

All right, sitting in the man's studio was like getting into the man's head, and Daniel couldn't help wondering what it would be like to get into his pants.

That was why Daniel was here, of course. Sexual curiosity. He had already seen Abbas naked—there was no mystery there—and Abbas looked naked now, his backbone and ass shifting inside his overalls. Daniel had hoped a trip to Norfolk would teach him enough about Abbas to kill off the rest of his curiosity. There'd be no mystery at all, and Daniel could treat him as simply a pal, a peer, a friend. But he liked Abbas's art, which made Abbas sexier. Daniel was jealous of his talent—he admitted it—which made him want to hump Abbas just to get on the other side of that talent. But Daniel wasn't Abbas's type—Abbas had made that clear. Or had he?

This is too silly, thought Daniel. He should just go ahead and get the question out of the way. Unasked questions are the worst. He'd be making a fool of himself, but he had nothing to lose. He decided to treat the idea as a joke.

"Here's a thought," he said. "We don't need to go to Norfolk to get laid, you know. We *could* just do it ourselves."

Abbas stopped. He looked at Daniel. He frowned. "You have sex with your friends?"

"Now and then." Daniel was pleased he didn't have to explain.

"Then you know. Friends misunderstand and want more. Which is why I prefer strangers. But we talked about this already. We are in the same boat. We are not single."

"We're certainly not."

Abbas studied the brush in his hand. It was tipped with white. He turned away. "Let me think about it. See how I feel when I am done. Do you mind?"

"Not at all." He had muffed it. He should have waited until Abbas was finished and they could jump on each other without time to think. "Just an option," he said. "No big deal."

"Hmmm. My colors keep changing their tune." Or did Abbas say "tone"? He was bent over the canvas again, back at work, which was humbling, If Daniel were in his shoes, he'd be too distracted. But Abbas continued to paint, as if he didn't care whether he had sex or not.

What the hell am I doing? thought Daniel. Sex wasn't going to happen. Or if it did, it'd be ugly and humiliating. What did he want from Abbas anyway? His respect as a fellow artist? Or the arrogant sneer that one man gives another when he gets a blow job from him? That was all Daniel could picture happening: himself on his knees, giving head to a visiting faculty member, a Muslim with a wife and two kids. Could life get any tackier?

Abbas's silence was too annoying. "Do you ever show or sell your work in Iran?" asked Daniel, just to say something.

"Oh no. I am too Western and decadent. You should see the art they admire. Hideous murals. Like Soviet propaganda. Elena says it is like the art of her childhood, only it is of Khomeini and the mullahs, not Brezhnev and Kosygin."

It was such a relief to talk that Daniel seized the subject. "But it's not like your work is dangerous. It's beautiful but not political or religious. Not that I can see. You're hardly Salman Rushdie."

Abbas frowned again. "No. I hate politics and fear religion. Not fear. That is the wrong word. I respect religion. But decadence is not in the meaning. It is in the vocabulary. The Shah loved modern art, so now the people of Iran must hate it. The Shah loved all things American, and now the people must hate such things."

"You don't hate America?"

"Oh no. I love American things. Even the kitsch. Because they are things from my childhood. You cannot imagine how soaked we were in American things. Mickey Mouse and Coca-Cola. *American Bandstand.* American English. The English was a status symbol. Everyone wanted to speak it, even those who couldn't. All brochures and advertisements were written in bad, freaky English." He looked up from his canvas, grinning. "There was a brand of rubbers, Iranian condoms, and on the package it said, 'For sanity of penis.' "

Daniel laughed, overdoing it, but the line was funny.

"So when they throw out the Shah, they throw out everything American, good and bad: the condoms and art and secret police. It is too hard to separate the good from the bad so they just throw out everything. They see things in black and white. But life is not black and white."

"Not at all," said Daniel. "It's in color. Like your paintings."

Abbas lifted his eyebrows, as if Daniel had said something important—but Daniel had only been playing with words.

"I hate black and white," said Abbas. "And I hate gray. And all murky things. I love strong color."

He slowly stood up and looked down at his painting. He went to his boom box and turned off the music. He returned to the painting and studied it for a long time. He gritted his teeth.

"It is off. It is no good to continue. Maybe tomorrow." He walked sadly to the sink, his face looking very grim.

Daniel got up to look at the canvas. It was still a beautiful carpet of color, with a parade of cryptic figures, unfinished but promising. What had gone wrong? Was it something he'd said?

"You must know the feeling," said Abbas, pouring turpentine on his hands and forearms. "Everything is going fine, and suddenly, click, it looks flat, dead, wrong. You must walk away or you will tear the canvas up or start hitting walls."

"Oh yeah, I've been there," said Daniel. Was Abbas in such a bad mood now that they could forget about sex? He looked so glum that Daniel wondered if they'd even get to Norfolk.

Abbas finished with the turpentine, then undid the straps of his overalls and squirted liquid soap into his hands. "You are still wanting us to do this?"

"Uh, only if you want to," Daniel said worriedly.

Abbas soaped his arms and chest, looking even more solemn. "Oh, all right. It will get me out of my head and into my body."

"Good then," said Daniel. "Sure." You might think they were agreeing to pull each other's teeth out.

Abbas washed more quickly, splashing water into his chest hair. "I stink like a forest. Or how you call it? A Christmas tree?"

"One of my favorite smells," said Daniel. "Bad Jew that I am."

But Abbas didn't smile. "This is probably a stupid thing to do with a friend," he said as he rubbed his chest with a towel. "But I am in a bad mood now and this is better than hitting walls."

Daniel hesitated. "So long as you don't start hitting me."

Abbas tossed the towel and went to the door. He locked it. "On or off?" He was pointing at the fluorescent lights overhead.

"Off." Daniel usually wanted light, but darkness would be safer.

Abbas clicked the switch, and the studio wasn't totally dark but full of gray, dusky light from the clerestory windows.

Daniel watched Abbas approach. The bib of the overalls was still lowered; he was ghost white from the waist down. He smelled of flowery soap and pine resin. He stood in front Daniel, frowning.

Daniel slipped both arms around him.

Abbas was lean and solid and taller than Daniel.

Daniel went up on his toes to kiss him.

He feared the worst: locked teeth or an averted face, followed by the classic forceful hand on the head, like a policeman pushing you down into a patrol car. But Abbas opened his mouth into Daniel's mouth and their tongues met, like two warm, wet, muscular souls.

Daniel remained on his toes. There was so much of Abbas to rub against. He ran his hands over Abbas's spine and shoulders and down into his overalls to clutch a small, fuzzy bottom.

Abbas moaned into his mouth and Daniel moaned back.

When they released each other to catch their breaths, Abbas was smiling, his teeth showing, his eyes shining. "This is good. Yes?" He reached down to grip Daniel's erection through his trousers. "For sanity of penis."

10

THE BRAHMS PIANO CONCERTO NO. 1 IN D MINOR BEGAN: loud, tragic, glorious bombast. The entire Berlin Philharmonic poured down a mountainside, in cataracts and torrents, sweeping everything in its path. The pianist, Alfred Brendel, threw himself into the flood and tried to swim against the current, frantically, heroically, as if for his life. Then he stopped fighting and let the torrent carry him on a long, lyrical ride down through the mountains.

Zack couldn't play this stuff when Daniel was home. Daniel enjoyed Brahms chamber music but not the big orchestral works. "Nerd music," he called it. Daniel, however, was out tonight and Zack could crank up the concerto. He sat in the kitchen and did his end-of-the-month paperwork, billing patients and insurance companies, while Brahms roared on the stereo in the dining room. Jocko snoozed on the kitchen floor, in his usual warm spot at the base of the refrigerator. Classical music was only white noise to him.

But something outside snapped Jocko awake. He jumped to his feet and trotted into the front hall. A moment later, he returned, herding Daniel through the dining room, happily nudging Daniel's crotch with his snout.

"You can turn the music down!" shouted Zack. "Or off!"

Daniel only laughed, shooed Jocko away, and paused at the stereo to lower the volume. He continued into the kitchen. He looked quite cheerful, even sunny.

"Hello, dear," he said and kissed Zack on the top of his head. He smelled like cigarette smoke, which you'd expect for a man who'd been to the bars, but under the tobacco was a surprising whiff of pine needles.

"Sorry about the Brahms," said Zack. "I didn't think you'd be back until later."

"Oh no, your nerd music sounds good tonight. Just a little loud." He went to the refrigerator to get a beer—a surprising action for someone coming home from an afternoon of bar-hopping.

And Zack began to understand. "You're back awfully early. Norfolk didn't live up to its reputation?"

Daniel sat at the table, suppressing a smile. Or rather, suppressing a variety of smiles. Zack knew, after twenty-one years, that Daniel still had to decide what attitude to take with him, what tone of voice. He could do guilty or bored or boastful or humorous.

"We never got to Norfolk," he finally said, humorously. "We decided to cut out the middleman and make do with each other."

"Ah," said Zack. He almost said "ah" again but decided it might sound too dramatic. "I can't say I'm surprised."

"Well, I was. Some."

"You were?"

"Oh, I knew I could be interested in him, but never thought he could be interested in me. So I didn't consider it. Not consciously anyway. What I didn't realize is how important his work is to him. A trip to Norfolk would have taken three hours out of his life. But there I was, a bird in the hand, so to speak. And we made do with each other."

Zack slowly nodded. "Did you have fun?"

"Yes. It was nice." Daniel took a swig of beer. "Friendly but impersonal. With no embarrassment afterwards." He laughed. "You might've thought we'd just shared a game of racquetball."

Zack raised an eyebrow—he'd heard this line before.

"I'm serious. We talked a bit, then he jumped up and went back to work on a painting. It was the easiest, most matter-of-fact sex I've ever had."

"Is that good or bad?"

Daniel laughed again, a deliberate chuckle this time. "Good, I think. Good for us. You and me, I mean."

Zack made a get-out-of-here face—this didn't worry him.

"Good for everyone," Daniel added. "No complications."

He usually didn't say so much about an encounter. Bad sex produced only a bitter joke or two. Great sex confused him and he didn't talk about it at all. Tonight, however, he was amused and content, so the sex must've been good.

"Are you going to get together again?" asked Zack—the million-dollar question.

Daniel wagged his head back and forth, took a deep breath, and sighed. "I don't know. I enjoyed this afternoon. But I don't *need* to do it again. I was curious, that's all. I've satisfied my curiosity. But we talked about *maybe* getting together next Sunday. Don't look at me like that."

"Like what?"

"Like I don't know myself as well as you know me."

"No, I was thinking you really do seem content and relaxed."

"I am," said Daniel. "Because it was fun. It's fun to have a fuck buddy. That's all this is. Or was. I'm not sure I like him. We talked, but it was all about his work, not mine. He's utterly self-absorbed. Which is fine for a fuck buddy, but not for a friend or lover."

Zack suddenly understood the smell of smoke on Daniel's skin: it was Abbas's postcoital cigarette. Zack didn't picture them having sex—he neither wanted nor needed to visualize it—but he could picture Abbas enjoying a cigarette afterward.

"So is he gay? Or just horny?"

"Oh, he's gay. Or bisexual. Or maybe he just likes sex. But he loves Elena and his kids. He made that clear."

"Will she know?"

Daniel arched his eyebrows. "Beats me. He said she knows he's bi, but I didn't come right out and ask what their rules are."

"Does he know that I'll know?"

"Yes. I told him I'd tell you. He didn't seem to care. Maybe because we're both gay men and he thinks anything goes with us. Or because we don't count. I'm not sure."

Zack was nodding, then he stopped nodding, afraid it looked like he was giving Daniel permission. Daniel didn't need permission. "Well, I can't speak for the Rohanis. They're both grown-ups. My chief concern, as always, is how you might feel when this falls apart."

"But there's nothing to fall apart. We're just messing around."

"Okay. But be careful."

Daniel smiled, a sheepish, guilty, pleased smile. "You know what'll happen? Next Sunday, I'll want to see him again, but he'll be busy or have changed his mind or have found someone else. And I'll be pissed for a week or two. But that'll be the end of it and I can go back to my normal, happy, lazy life."

Zack found himself nodding again and stopped. "But you had fun today?"

"Oh yes. I had fun today."

"Good. I'm glad."

"I'm glad you're glad." And Daniel got up, thanked Zack with a squeeze of his shoulder, and went down the hall to his room.

We are such a pair, Zack told himself. I am such a case. He was pleased that he felt no pain, but guilty he felt no pain. He did not feel jealous. He did not even feel envious. Those emotions were merely childish expressions of private dissatisfaction; he was glad to have outgrown them. But could one be fully human without feeling jealous now and then?

Brahms continued to whisper in the dining room, finished with the frantic first movement and humming the middle section: mature, sweet, and melancholy.

11

During their first years together, Zack and Daniel had each other and they had their work, and that was plenty. Work was important to both men, and more difficult and challenging than love.

Zack did not have an easy time starting out as a psychiatrist. Homosexuality was no longer labeled a disease in 1981, but the psychoanalytic community still treated it as a moral failing, even in New York City. Zack's own supervisor, who was gay, advised him to stay in the closet until he got his certification. Zack refused, and the New York Psychoanalytic Institute rejected his application. He turned instead to the less prestigious National Psychological Association for Psychoanalysis, with its motley offices in an old row house on West Thirteenth Street, and its motley people, more social workers than doctors, flakier than Zack's other peers but also looser and more human. Zack grew fond of the NPAP. Their reputation may have slowed his career, but he was later glad of that. He avoided the faster track, the traps and pressure of expensive success.

When AIDS came along, sexual honesty became not just a political good but a moral necessity. Zack did an enormous amount of volunteer work through Gay Men's Health Crisis. He saw many sick men, and even more men who were healthy but scared. It was a crash course in the dangers of self-pity

and self-hatred. For a time Zack wondered if gay men were the most dysfunc-
tional people on the planet. Then he began to see more straight people—
GMHC reached out to all communities—and learned how confused and
frightened everyone was.

Meanwhile Daniel continued to paint and teach. His MFA from Penn led
to an instructorship at Parsons, then one at Pratt. He enjoyed teaching. He
liked the give-and-take, the public performance, the occasional sense of accomplishment. He slowly understood that he liked teaching more than he
liked painting. He felt so smart when he taught, and so stupid when he
painted. Painting offered a strenuous, masochistic kind of pleasure, but it felt
private and trivial, especially when no major galleries showed interest in his
work. He changed his style again, and again, and yet again, and still nobody
bit. He began to lose faith in the future. Around the time he turned thirty-six,
Daniel decided he was never going to be a successful painter. He would be
only a teacher, a good teacher maybe, but only a teacher. He became very unhappy. This was when he went into his tomcat phase.

Right from the start, during their first year together, Zack and Daniel had
agreed that monogamy was neither important nor realistic. AIDS didn't scare
them off sex, but it made them more careful. Not that they did very much—
they were usually too busy. They tried a couple of threeways early on, as the
high of requited love wore off and they wanted new thrills. But affection and
voyeurism didn't mix. Each felt silly watching the other take his turn with a
happy, horny florist from New Jersey; they both became terribly self-
conscious over what they could and couldn't do with the cute young translator from Finland. So they dropped the threeways but allowed each other to
mess around when one of them was out of town, so long as he was safe and
told the other. Zack enjoyed hearing the stories; Daniel didn't. Daniel didn't
enjoy telling stories either, so their reports became short and simple: twenty-
five words or less.

When his crisis struck, Daniel no longer waited for one of them to be away.
He told Zack what he was doing and began to go out regularly to bars and sex
clubs and back rooms. This was 1991, when gay men rebelled against the epi-
demic and openly played around again. There was a renaissance of raunch, an
era of safe sex sleaze. Zack stayed home and enjoyed the peace and quiet. He

understood what was driving Daniel, but his show of sympathy only made Daniel feel worse, feeding his frustration and guilt. Daniel tried having an affair with a student but found there is nobody more calculating and heartless than a young artist who has just moved to New York. He told Zack it was only sex, and maybe it was, although unrequited lust can often feel like unrequited love. No, it was better to stick to strangers and the occasional fuck buddy.

It was during this tomcat phase that the job at William and Mary opened up. Jane Morrison, his good friend from Penn, was teaching down there and reported that they needed someone for next year. It was a short gig, although the job could lead to a tenure track position. Daniel applied. It'd be good to escape the ugly art world and easy sex of New York, he said, if only for a year. But he did not want to live away from Zack, not for an entire year. He had a couple of months to mull it over before he heard if they wanted him or not. While he waited, Zack met Eugene Thomas.

This was E. G. Thomas, the social historian and critic. A fifty-three-year-old professor at Boston University who wore old-fashioned horn-rims and big bow ties, he spoke at a mental health conference that Zack attended in Atlanta. A friendly argument about Foucault led to an invitation up to Thomas's room to find an old article about Quaker asylums. There Thomas confessed that, since his wife died a year ago, he'd been "reconstructing" his sexuality. "I find you very butch and humpy. Please don't take this the wrong way, but I'd very much like to go to bed with you."

Zack flew back to New York the next day feeling foolish and guilty and oddly fond of Thomas. It wasn't the sex, which had been nothing much, just a friendly wrestle with a bulky, middle-aged man. But Thomas had made Zack feel young and lively; Zack usually felt only old and dull.

"So did you behave yourself in Atlanta?" asked Daniel.

"Oh. I went to bed with one of the guest speakers."

"Cute? Young?"

"In his fifties."

"Ugh. I don't want to hear about it."

So Zack told him nothing more.

A week later, at his office, Zack got a call from Thomas. "I just wanted to say hi and see how you were doing. And tell you how much I enjoyed meeting you. And let you know I'd love to see you again. Dammit to hell—I *need* to see you again! If I fly down this afternoon, will you be available?"

It was awful being wanted like that. And embarrassing. And exciting.

Three hours later, Zack was rolling around naked with the man in a hotel room in midtown, understanding as if for the first time why so many of his patients could forget self-interest for the sake of a meaningless lay. And it was meaningless. They spurted, showered, and parted, happy to say goodbye, relieved that they'd gotten each other out of their systems.

"It might surprise you," Zack told Daniel over dinner that night, "but I canceled my afternoon appointments for a quickie."

"It does surprise me," said Daniel. "Who was he?"

"Eugene Thomas. The guest speaker in Atlanta."

"He followed you here?"

Zack could have lied and said he just happened to be in town, but it felt better to tell the truth. "He came here to see me. Yes."

Daniel's face went blank. "Is he still here?"

"No. He took the shuttle back to Boston."

"He's in love with you?"

"No. He was here for sex. That's all."

"So who is he? What's he like? Should I be worried?"

Zack assured him he had no cause for worry. The man was old and overweight and not remotely sexy. And it was over, just a couple of curiosity fucks with a guy he'd never see again.

Daniel's worried look was turning into a glower. "This is your way of getting back at me for messing around," he charged.

"No!" said Zack. He quietly added, "I don't think so. And your messing around doesn't bother me." He paused. "It doesn't."

Zack thought about it during the next few days, sorting through his emotions. He found no trace of anger over Daniel's tomcatting, only guilt that he actually enjoyed having time alone on those nights. Yet Daniel had read anger, and so quickly, as if he were angry with Zack. Why? Zack was shy about turning his therapeutic gaze on his partner, and not just because Daniel hated it. They had agreed long ago that they could never be doctor and patient.

The following week the phone calls from Thomas began, not just at the office but at home.

"Please don't call me here, Eugene. It's a small apartment. I can't talk. We're watching a movie. I'll talk to you tomorrow. Bye."

"Why the hell are you so nice to him?" snarled Daniel. "Just tell him to get lost."

"Because he's not just a trick but a friend," said Zack. "And I enjoy talking to him."

"You just feel sorry for him," said Daniel bitterly.

"I do not," said Zack. But he did.

That weekend Thomas made another visit to New York. He wanted to see Zack again. Zack guiltily said yes. He offered to introduce Thomas to Daniel, but Daniel said no. "I'm going out and getting laid myself tonight. Do what you want. I'll see you tomorrow."

Zack met Thomas at his hotel, went off to dinner, returned to the hotel, and spent the night. He could forget about Daniel—Daniel was off having his own fun—and sprawl in bed with Thomas after sex, talking about nineteenth-century medicine. When Zack woke up the next morning, he felt so content that he wondered if he was falling in love. It was not an all-consuming, exclusive love, but more like a supplemental love, an extra love—like having an extra room in their apartment. Zack badly needed an extra room.

When he got home, Daniel was already back, waiting for him. "I saw you at Café des Artistes."

"You were uptown?"

"I followed you. I hung out outside the hotel, then followed you to the restaurant."

Zack was stunned, frightened, worried.

"A fat academic with a bow tie," snarled Daniel. "Like Senator Daniel fucking Moynihan. What do you see in him? Why do you want to be with him? Do you realize what an insult he is to me?"

"*You?* What're you talking about? He has nothing to do with you."

"You can go to bed with a pig like that, then come home and go to bed with me, and you probably don't even know the difference."

"Daniel? What is this really about? Why are you so angry?"

"Don't use your fucking shrink voice on me."

Zack didn't know how else to continue. "Daniel, don't do this. Do I use your tricks against you? Do I say they insult me?"

"No, but my tricks are only tricks, and I know better than to get too personal with them. I have more experience here than you. I know the difference between love and dick. I don't trust this guy."

"What's going on here?" said Zack. "Why should you be upset about him when you weren't upset about other guys I've seen? Like Ben Brandt, who you found hot and sexy. Or what's-his-name, the piano player at High School of Performing Arts."

"You can't even remember their names!"

"Not all of them, no. Can you remember yours?"

"No!" cried Daniel. "Because mine aren't as important to me as yours are to you. But this Thomas is different. You feel sorry for him, which is like one step from being in love with him."

"What are you talking about? I'm in love with you and I've never felt sorry for you."

"No? Haven't you? Not a little?"

Zack was silenced again, confused by the accusation. It was true that he felt sorry for Daniel. But he felt sorry for almost everyone.

He slept on the sofa that night. In times of insomnia, one of them would often move to the sofa, but they had never begun a night apart. They had never gone to bed so angry that they couldn't sleep together.

Zack hoped they'd find a way to address the subject over the next few days, but Daniel refused to discuss it. Zack feared the crisis would affect his work, preventing him from giving his patients his full attention—he had joined a new clinic in the East Village and was often overworked. But he found that he could actually lose himself in his patients, forgetting his troubles in theirs. He remained clear about other people even when he felt confused about himself.

A week passed and Daniel asked, "So when's he coming back? You seeing him this weekend?"

"No." Zack hesitated, then decided to tell the truth, even though he suspected he was being truthful only because he was angry. "But he's invited me to fly up and visit him in Boston sometime."

"You want to spend good money to fuck an old man?"

"It's my money. He's not an old man. And I don't fuck him, if you have to know."

"I don't want to hear about it. It's too gross to think about." Daniel shook his head. "You are such a sucker. Such a pushover. You'll love anybody who loves you. Anybody."

"Would it make you feel better if I never saw him again?"

"No. Do what you want. You always do."

"And you don't?"

"Not always." Daniel paused. "Maybe I should take this job at William and Mary."

"I told you. You can try it. But I think you'll be miserable down there."

"Why? Because I'm a New York Jew?"

"No. Because you're you. And I know Virginia. It's a nice, safe, boring place. You'll be bored to tears."

"You don't think I'm bored now? I don't hate my life now?"

Zack reached out to hold him. "Oh, Daniel, don't talk like—"

Daniel jerked away. "Don't give me your fucking pity. Save it for your fucking patients." He stormed out of the room.

"Don't be an ass!" Zack shouted after him. "Come back and argue with me! Finish what you're trying to say, dammit!"

Zack flew up to Boston that weekend. He needed to get away from Daniel, and there was no other place to go. He spent the next forty-eight hours in Eugene's town house. Love was not just an extra room but a whole building, its rooms and hallways lined with books. It was May, warm and sunny, and Zack stayed naked for most of his visit, refusing to wear even a bathrobe as he padded about, smoking cigarettes and drinking coffee, wanting to feel cheap and slutty. Eugene got dressed and followed his nude guest, talking about the book he was working on or books he had written or books he hoped to write one day. He asked nothing about Zack, not a word. Zack wanted to talk about his fight with Daniel, although complaining about his partner felt like a worse betrayal of him than sex. But Eugene didn't care that Zack had a partner.

What Zack had read as love was little more than a widower's gratitude that a younger man could share his bed. Zack could not remember his own orgasms ever feeling so deep or leaving him so sad. He passed the weekend in an erotic, melancholy stupor.

When he got back to New York, Daniel was overjoyed to see him again. "William and Mary called," he said. "They offered me the job. I'm taking it. Just for a year. Just to try something new. It has nothing to do with us. It's not because I'm jealous of you and your history professor. I just need to try something new."

Zack could have said: It has everything to do with us. Why can't we talk about us?

Or: There's nothing between me and the history professor so you don't have to pretend not to be jealous.

He could even have said: If you hate your life and need to try something new, that means you hate me, because I am your life.

But there was too much to say, such a backlog of silence. The psychiatrist said only, "You're right. It is practical. It's just a year. You *should* take the job."

And it was practical, a badly needed change, which was how they treated the move over the summer as Daniel prepared by sorting through his clothes and music and art supplies, and buying a secondhand car from friends in Brooklyn.

Zack took the week off and rode down with Daniel to Virginia. It was a six-hour ride to Williamsburg. They enjoyed the trip, the escape from the city, the open road, the chance to play each other's favorite tapes on the car's excellent stereo system.

They arrived and unloaded everything at Daniel's new apartment, the converted garage of a white clapboard house at the far end of Indian Springs Road. The owner, Miss Tolley, was an old-fashioned spinster who lived with seven cats, all named after Greek gods and goddesses. Zack had forgotten how oppressively humid Virginia got in August, how loud the cicadas became after dark, their chatter rising and falling in waves. He and Daniel tried to make love that first night, but it was too hot and their moves were out of sync, their bodies hopelessly out of step. It felt like months since they'd last had sex with each other. Zack couldn't help feeling that they were over, that they were saying goodbye for good.

Daniel drove Zack down to Norfolk the next day for lunch with Zack's mom and dad before Zack flew back to New York.

"How you boys doing?"

"We're doing fine, Mr. Knowles," said Daniel.

"Yes, sir, Dad. We're fine," said Zack.

Even after ten years, Edgar Knowles and Daniel were still on very formal terms with each other. Daniel blamed Zack's father for the formality, insisting Mr. Knowles couldn't get over the fact that Daniel was not only gay but Jewish. Zack said the formality was a Southern thing—he still called his father "sir"—but Daniel was not convinced. There was so much about Zack's life that Daniel didn't get. No wonder they were breaking up. Were they really breaking up?

Zack's mother served a big lunch of ham salad, sliced tomatoes, and cole slaw—"I forget, but you do eat ham, don't you?"

After lunch, Daniel drove Zack to the Norfolk airport. They kissed goodbye in the car: a series of quick, mutual pecks that ended with Zack kissing the bald spot starting to bloom in the crown of Daniel's head, a tender patch of pink.

"Stop fussing," said Daniel. "We need a break from each other. That's all. We'll be fine." He gingerly patted Zack on the shoulder and pushed him out the door.

When Zack got back to New York, the apartment that had seemed so small was suddenly enormous. Nights that had been too short were now endless. Zack thought he'd be able to accomplish a hundred things he'd been putting off: books read, friendships resumed; he might even write a few articles. Instead, he fell into a deep funk. He slept more and watched too much television, not just PBS but sitcoms and game shows. He came to life only when he was seeing patients. He began to grow a beard, partly out of laziness, but chiefly because he now hated the bland, round pan of his face, the timid, chinless thing that returned his unhappy stare every morning. He needed a new look.

"Seeing anyone?" Daniel asked when they talked on the phone.

"My patients."

"I mean people. Friends. Or, you know—guys." He meant Eugene, of course.

"No, I stay in nights. When are you coming home for a visit?"

"Not until Thanksgiving. You should come down here."

"I'd like to, but my schedule is very full for October."

Zack didn't tell Daniel that he was no longer seeing Eugene. They had spent one more night together—here in Zack and Daniel's apartment, in Zack and Daniel's bed—and Zack found himself hating the guy, a smug, fat, naked old man. Which wasn't fair to Eugene—he was what he'd always been, a frisky, oblivious sex buddy—but the next morning Zack apologetically told him that he didn't want to see him again. And Eugene looked relieved. He confessed that he was getting bored and wanted to play the field but was afraid of hurting Zack's feelings. Besides, hadn't Zack said he had a boyfriend?

"If you're not coming down," said Daniel, "could you send me my navy blue overcoat?"

"Sure," said Zack. "Where is it?"

"The drawer of the platform bed."

"All right. There's nothing else you need?"

"Not for now. No. Love you. Bye."

Daniel didn't miss Zack nearly as much as Zack missed Daniel. Which hurt Zack more than he thought possible. As the weeks passed, it began to make Zack angry. He decided to test Daniel. If the next time Daniel called and it was just to chat, then he still loved Zack and they were still a couple. But if he called only because he needed something, a book or a cassette or an article of clothing, then they weren't a couple and it was over.

Zack was a smart man, conscientious and aware. He was a trained therapist. He recognized exactly what he was doing: he had locked himself in a cycle of guilt and punishment, a trap of blame. He was determined to punish himself further. If a patient came to him and told him this story, Zack would help the man find his way out of his narrative trap. But Zack wasn't one of his patients.

One night after ten o'clock, the phone rang and Zack picked up.

"Hello, love. How you doing?"

Zack's heart lifted a little, as it almost always did when he heard Daniel's voice. "Fine. And you? Is it cold down there yet?"

They exchanged pleasantries for a few minutes, and Zack was happy. Then Daniel said, "Oh, the real reason I'm calling— You know the Met catalogs in the bookcase in the front room? There's four or five. From the Bacon and Caravaggio shows and others. Could you pack them up and ship them down?"

Zack sat with the receiver pressed to his newly bearded face. "I have a better idea," he said. "Why don't I just go through the apartment and pack up all your stuff and ship it down?"

Daniel didn't get it. "That's okay, I just need the catalogs."

Zack took a deep breath. "Do you realize you never call except when you need something? This isn't your home anymore. It's just a post office. I'm nobody to you now but your fucking mailman."

Daniel was silent for a moment. "That's not true. I miss you. I just don't want to waste money on long distance. So I wait until I have a practical reason for calling."

"But I want to waste money on *you*!" Zack cried. "Because I miss you. But you don't miss me. Not at all. Jesus Christ. To think I spent all summer feeling guilty for what I did, when you don't give a damn one way or another."

"I give a damn! I miss you. Look, I'm sorry I don't call more, but this is a new life for me. I'm busy adjusting to it. But I do miss you, Zack. Please. Believe me," he pleaded. "I'm sorry."

His apology instantly made Zack feel guilty for his anger. He spoke more softly. "No, *I'm* sorry. I have no business flying off the handle like that. But I'm not myself these days."

"You're telling me. You haven't been yourself for a long time. Not since you started seeing that pig professor." Daniel paused. "I don't believe this. You spent the past six months fucking that pig, and now you're angry with *me*?"

He abruptly turned combative, which was always Daniel's curve in an argument. When the other person was angry, he backed down. But as soon as the other person turned apologetic, Daniel became the aggressor.

"I'm angry with you because you don't miss me like I miss you," Zack argued.

"And whose fault is that?" said Daniel. "I miss you," he conceded. "But I don't miss your smugness. Your calm. Your I'm-so-on-top-of-the-world confidence. I don't miss how you and everyone else in New York make me feel like a failure."

"When did I ever treat you like a failure?"

"Every time you look at me with your poor-little-you eyes. You feel so sorry for me. Poor little Danny. Poor loser Danny. I hate it."

Only when they were four hundred miles apart could they say all the dangerous things that needed to be said.

"I don't think that," said Zack. "I never thought that. I love you. It's not pity. It's love. What else do you want from me? Do you want me to hate you? Fear you?"

"I want you to respect me."

"I respect you. More than you respect yourself." Zack's anger was back, taking control. "You are so spoiled. You're a good teacher, students love you, but it's not enough. You got to be a famous painter. And you're not, so you're pissed at the world. You got to have a grievance. If you don't have a grievance, you feel cheated."

"What do you know about it? Not a damn thing. You are so fucking repressed. I can't say boo to you for fear you'll go to pieces. You white-bread Southern Wasps. You don't know how to argue."

"And you do? Don't give me your Jewish soul crap, because I see enough of all types to know we're all screwed up, and Jews handle anger as badly as everybody else."

Arguing on the phone alters a fight, disembodies it. Your body is no longer afraid of anger because you can't hit the other person. And so you feel free to say anything, even the worst thing.

"Yeah, you know so much about soul," sneered Daniel. "So much about love and sex. Which is why the great love of your life is a dumpy history professor."

Daniel was jealous? That's what this was about, jealousy?

"Not that it matters," said Zack, "but I broke off with my history professor. Last month. I'm not seeing him anymore."

"You're right, it doesn't matter," said Daniel without a pause, not surprised in the least. "Because my anger with him wasn't about him but what he represented."

"Yes? And what did he represent?"

"The fact that you don't love the body the way that I love the body. That you could love him proved how much you hate the body. We were never right for each other."

Zack was stunned by the last sentence. They were *never* right? He didn't know what to say. And while he was silent, his anger built up. Then it broke out.

"Don't give me that mind-body dichotomy bullshit! It's not like you're Mr. Happy Animal Body. Or like I'm Mr. All Brain and No Body. You might want to be all body and no brain, which is why you want to get away from me. But it won't work, Daniel. You'll be just as miserable without me."

"No, Zack. Sorry. I've been down here three months, and I've never been happier. I hate to say it, but life without you is so much easier. It's less complicated. I like being the new kid in town. I like being single. I feel lighter and freer than I've felt in years."

Zack was speechless again. Then he said, "You know what I say? I say fuck you. You were always more trouble than you were worth. I can't believe that I wasted ten years of my life with such a lightweight."

"And you're a ball and chain, Zack. A fucking ton of bricks. And I say fuck you and good riddance. And fuck you and good night!"

And Daniel hung up, not slamming the phone but coldly clicking it off. He disappeared into the sad, outer space roar of a dial tone.

Zack lowered the receiver. What just happened? How had they gone from anger to apology to more anger to the complete burning of bridges? The psychiatrist could reconstruct the argument, but it was a common fool who had said those things. Daniel struck a nerve when he accused Zack of hating the body. It was like calling him bad sex. But Zack never thought that he was great sex, and their love had never been about sex.

With Daniel no longer on the line, Zack could not blame Daniel, he could blame only himself. He felt like he'd just committed murder. He feared he wouldn't sleep a wink that night. Nevertheless, when he fell into bed, he dropped like a rock, exhausted, into a black ocean of sleep.

When he woke up the next morning, he knew what he should do. He canceled his appointments and called National car rental. By ten o'clock, he was on the New Jersey Turnpike, headed south. He hated driving, he drove so rarely, but it seemed the right penance, a four-hundred-mile meditation exercise that would put him in the right frame of mind for saying goodbye to Daniel. That's what he intended to do. You don't terminate a decade of your life over the phone. It was too easy. He had said goodbye only to the sound of Daniel, the idea of Daniel. If he were truly saying goodbye, he must do it face-to-face. Near Philadelphia, he remembered Daniel's stuff at the apartment and wondered if he should go back and bring some of it with him. But no, there'd be other occasions for that, and this way the trip was more irrational, crazy, and pure.

He made excellent time. It was four o'clock when he pulled into Williamsburg. He drove around campus until he recognized PBK Hall and parked out front. He walked around back to the fine arts building and went upstairs to Daniel's office. The door was closed and the whiteboard scrawled in grease pencil: "Wexler Wednesday classes canceled due to family emergency." Which startled Zack. Daniel's mother had been in the hospital back in June, but she was fine now. An office door across the hall was wide open. Inside sat Jane Morrison, talking to a female student.

Zack knocked. "Excuse me. Jane? Hi. I'm Zack Knowles, Daniel's friend. We met back in September."

A square-faced woman with big forearms, Jane stared at him in disbelief. "I remember. Oh my God. Didn't you get Daniel's message? He drove back to New York today."

"New York?" Daniel's mom was in Florida.

Jane stole a peek at her student, then decided to continue. "He said you had a terrible fight over the phone. He couldn't leave things as they were but had to make peace with you face-to-face." She was smiling. "I guess you felt the same." She laughed. "That's very funny. Romantic, but funny, too."

"Very," said Zack. "Can I use your phone?"

He was tempted to correct Jane, but only for a split second. Because he realized that he wasn't here to say goodbye. No. He had changed his mind somewhere on the road. Long before he heard that Daniel was headed back to New York to fix things, he had decided that he didn't want them to end.

Watched by Jane and her student, a pretty girl in a green sweatshirt, Zack called their machine in New York.

"Daniel? Love? It's me. Great minds think alike, huh? I drove down to Williamsburg so I could talk to *you*. And we need to talk. Really talk. I'll go over to your place and spend the night and expect you back tomorrow. Or whenever you come home. But drive carefully. Don't rush. I'll be here. I promise. Bye."

Zack thanked Jane for the use of the phone and left.

"Good luck," said Jane.

"Happy landings," said the student.

Zack went back to his car and drove across the street to Indian Springs Road. He assumed that Miss Tolley had the key and could let him into Daniel's apartment. But the old lady wasn't home. And Daniel, a true New Yorker, had locked his door.

It was the first week of November and chilly outside but warm in the sun. Zack sat in a white cast-iron chair to wait for Miss Tolley. Red and yellow leaves blew down from the trees and rolled over the grass. Cats squeezed out of the boxwood hedge and circled Zack, big black, white, and spotted beasts with names like Zeus, Athena, and Aphrodite, although Zack didn't know which cat was which.

Such a pretty place, he thought. Such a pretty turn of events. He went south and Daniel went north. They really were a couple, weren't they? But they were like a couple in a toy weather house, where one comes out for shine and the other for rain and the two never appear at the same time. Zack had driven down to say goodbye but had changed his mind. Daniel seemed to have known all along that they belonged together, but Daniel often knew these things more quickly. Maybe he was more body than mind.

All right, if Daniel wanted a new life, Zack could give it to him—so long as Zack could be part of it. Zack too was tired of New York. He could start all over. He could build a practice here; there must be a few unhappy people. He loved the smell of the trees in this yard, a rich, sweet ferment like old apples or rotting wood, like the smell of a grandmother's house. Indian Springs Road was a street of cozy, old grandmother houses. Zack wondered how difficult it would be to buy one. A sentimental notion, and Zack knew not to take it seriously, even before he noticed the circle of cats at his feet, lying on the grass with folded forearms, skeptically watching him.

He heard the phone ring inside. He hoped it was Daniel calling from New York. But the door was locked and Zack couldn't get inside. He could only press his ear to the cold glass. He heard the machine pick up, a sharp beep followed by a muffled, mumbled message. He had to imagine what Daniel was saying: Where are you? Why aren't you here? Where did you go? What are we doing?

In almost every couple's life, there comes a time when the partners don't like each other very much. Familiarity really can breed contempt. The couple must work through their dislike and either stay together or go their separate ways. Zack and Daniel were glad to have had their hard, dramatic time early so that they could go on with the rest of their lives, together.

Daniel returned to Williamsburg the next day, and they shared their truths and made their peace. They spent the next year as a two-city couple. This was when they bought Jocko, a solid black puppy with rubbery legs and enormous feet. Neither man had owned a pet since childhood, and a dog is so homey, an old-fashioned emblem of security.

They gave up their New York apartment and Zack moved south. It was three years before they bought the house on Indian Springs Road, as in Zack's daydream. Daniel used the money he inherited from his mother—she died during their second year in Virginia—for the down payment. Almost as soon as they moved in, he and Zack started arguing again. The fights were sudden and noisy, but about nothing important. Neither could figure out why they were fighting. Then Zack understood. They owned a house now. They had the space for arguments, doors to slam, other rooms to shut themselves in. Love can provide an extra room or two, but a whole house is even better, a good, solid structure where you can lose your temper without fear of bringing everything down around your ears.

12

I DON'T NEVER WANT TO SEE YOU AGAIN."

"Do you understand that you've been ill?"

"Did you hear me? I don't never want to see you again."

"Yes, I heard you, Rebecca. But we need to clear up this other matter first. Do you know that you've been ill?"

"Of course I know! You think I'm brain-dead? You been shoving that fucking idea down my throat ever since I got here. That and all your fucking pills and drugs and shit. How could I not know? That's why I don't never want to see you again."

"Good," said Zack. "Very good. We're making progress." He was not being ironic.

Her name was Rebecca Mays, and she was twenty-seven, a seriously overweight white woman who lived with her mother out in Mathews County. She had been brought to Eastern State Psychiatric Center five days ago screaming about rats in her television. They'd been put there, she said, by her mother to drive her out of the house and force her to get a job. She went after her mother with a butcher knife. The police intervened and brought her here.

Here was Building 2, the Admissions Unit, a hospital within the hospital at Eastern State that handled emergency cases. Men and women were treated for anywhere from a week to three months, then transferred back to home care or group homes or sometimes to the long-term placement hospital across the road. Over half of the people who came to Building 2 had been here before. This was Rebecca Mays's first visit.

They were in her room, a single in the women's dorm with bars on the window and no door in the doorway, the only furniture a narrow hospital bed and a steel chair. Mays sat on the bed, her legs stretched over the covers, her arms folded over her breasts, her face hardened in a granite pout. Her hair was coppery red, her skin bad, her cheeks peppered with acne. She wore boys' pajamas, which her mother had brought from home.

Zack sat in the chair, wearing his white clinician jacket, which he wore only at the hospital, holding a clipboard on his knee. Sarah Jackson, the senior nurse, was supposed to be present for the examination, but Sarah had been called away to help Dr. Chadha arrange the transfer of the Lewis girl back to juvenile detention. Zack shouldn't be alone with Mays, but he couldn't wait for Sarah and he needed to confirm their diagnosis before he went home today.

"I don't never want to see you again," she repeated.

"I'm sorry you feel that way, Rebecca. I thought we could work together. But if you'd prefer to work with someone else, I can reassign you to Dr. Chadha or Dr. Aquino."

"No, I want an American doctor. A white doctor."

"Then you have to take me."

"But I don't want you. You stupid piece of shit. You faggot with a beard. Is your beard real? It looks like a disguise, asshole."

Years ago, people like Mays could actually hurt Zack's feelings. He was tougher now, more detached, but the cruelty of the insane still made him appreciate the general kindness of others. Everyone in the world is angry about something, but only a few want to hurt you. The occasional violent cases here could do physical harm, but the more cunning patients hoped to break your heart.

"Rebecca? Do you remember what you did the night that you were arrested?"

She gave her head an irritable shiver, like a wolf shaking off fleas. "I know what they told me I did. I don't believe it."

Zack glanced down at his clipboard. "That you pursued your mother with a heavy knife and called her a cunt and a bitch and said you were going to kill her?"

Zack had interviewed the mother this morning, a frail, frightened, owl-eyed lady in her sixties, a retired schoolteacher.

"If I said those things," said Rebecca, "then I must've been drunk. Because I love my mama. Even when she's a cunt."

"The police report indicates no alcohol in your blood."

"I'd never try to kill her. No matter what I said."

"It wasn't just you who tried to kill her. It was also your illness. But that doesn't mean you're not responsible for your actions."

She shook her head again, an angry shiver. "My illness, my illness? You keep talking about my illness. Why? You need me to admit that I'm mentally ill before you'll let me go, is that it?"

"You need to understand it, yes. But we're not going to release you, Rebecca. Not today. You're going to have to stay here, for a week or maybe two, until everyone involved, including you and your mother, can decide on the next course of action."

She took a deep breath through clenched teeth. "Fuck," she said. "A cig? When can I get a cig? The assholes here won't let me smoke!"

Even in mental hospitals now, one had to go outside for a cigarette, although smoking was one of the few legal things the mentally ill could do to medicate themselves.

"There is a smoking porch," Zack told her again, "but access to it is a privilege. You don't get privileges here unless you cooperate."

"I'm cooperating, ain't I?"

"You are, yes," said Zack. She had refused to come to his office for this interview, so Zack had gone to her. But he wasn't going to use that against her. "I'll write out a pass for you when we finish and put your name on the privilege board."

"So what else do you need from me? You want me to sign something?"

"No, I just need to talk to you for a few minutes. Get to know you a little better."

"You'll never know me," she said with a sneer.

"Probably not. You're very a complicated woman."

He meant to flatter her—he didn't mean to sound sarcastic—but the patient heard nothing.

All Zack really wanted to do was confirm his suspicion that Rebecca Mays was bipolar rather than borderline. The heavy doses of sedative administered when she first arrived had been cut back, and she was more her "normal" self today. He already knew she wasn't schizophrenic. Schizophrenics were the most tedious cases on earth, flat and one-note and too lost in their delusions to respond to other people, not even in anger.

"Your mother told me you were the smartest, funniest girl in your class in high school."

"Damn straight. I'm still smart. Still funny."

"What's your favorite joke?"

She narrowed her eyes at him: hard, mean, blue eyes. "Is that a trick question?"

"I'm just making small talk. Just trying to know you better." She was paranoid, thought Zack, although who wouldn't be in these circumstances?

"I'm not going to answer that."

"Too bad," said Zack. "I needed a good joke today." He glanced back at the clipboard. "You didn't go to college?"

"I went. I dropped out after a year. Fucking waste of time. But I'll go back. When I decide what to do with my life."

She'd been deciding for eight years, while living with her mother, who not only supported her daughter financially but had shielded her, and herself, from any suspicions of mental illness. It was a wonder there hadn't been trouble until now.

"What are some of the careers you've considered?"

"I don't have to answer that."

"No. But the more questions you answer, the sooner you can get rid of me and go out on the smoking porch."

She sucked at her front teeth. "I want to be a teacher."

"Like your mother?"

She gave her head another shake, her personal tic of confusion. "Fuck my mother. She teaches babies, first graders. I'd teach adults."

"What would you teach them?"

"Metaphysics."

"Oh? What kind of metaphysics?"

"All kinds. I never met-a-physics I didn't like." And she laughed, a loud, angry bray. "See, I can be funny. I am so fucking funny. I should have my own TV show. But I wrote Jay Leno and offered myself. For *free*. Do you know what he wrote back?"

"No, Rebecca, what did he write back?"

"Nothing. Not shit. Do you know why? Because he *knows*: I'd take his show away. People would love me and hate him. And it'd be my show, me on TV. That's why I study TV. I'm not some moron watching just to watch. I'm studying it for my career. Or I was until my cunt mother stuck rats inside our TV set to chase me out."

"And you're sure they were live rats?" asked Zack. "Not just rats in a TV nature film?"

"Hey. I was *there*. It was live fucking rats."

"How did an old lady like your mother catch rats and get them inside a television set?"

The eyes widened in a split second of doubt. Then she shook her head again. "Are you calling me a liar?"

"No. But you've been ill, Rebecca. Maybe you imagined rats. You hallucinated rats. You dreamed them."

"Fuck you. It was real rats. I was there and you weren't. When do I get to smoke?"

Yes, she must be bipolar with psychotic episodes, hence the hallucinations. It would be more responsive to medication than a borderline disorder but was still bad news. Bipolars could sometimes manage their disease with drugs, except Rebecca Mays looked like the type who'd soon go off her meds and bounce back here, again and again. In the meantime she'd live in the custody of her mother and terrorize the poor woman. Zack felt sorry for the girl, but he felt far more sorry for the mother.

He wrote out a pass to the smoking porch. "This will be good for today. I'll talk to Ms. Jackson and get your name on the board. But remember, it's a privilege and can be revoked. We're starting you on new medication, which you have to take if you want to keep your smoking privilege."

She snatched the pass from him and greedily studied it, as if it were a check for a million dollars.

"I'll see you again on Thursday. We'll see how you're doing. Okay, Rebecca?"

She didn't answer him; he was already invisible.

"Goodbye," he told her and departed.

Zack put in ten hours a week at Building 2: six hours on Monday and four on Thursday, the day of the general staff meeting. Ten hours were more than enough to throw his outpatient practice into sharp relief. It was such a different world here, so unlike the rest of his life. Here Zack was the adult and everyone else a child. He couldn't treat them as equals. It was all medication and little dialogue, all disease and not much personhood. He was dictatorial in one world and democratic in the other. He tried not to confuse them. Building 2 was a grim world, yet it could also be oddly restful, in the same way that life in wartime must be restful: There were fewer trivialities, ambiguities, and choices. It also felt less emotional. Zack had learned early to shut down most of the sorrow he felt for his mental hospital patients, although he suspected something remained, burning in secret.

He walked down the hall to the pharmacology station and gave the nurse, Ms. Krasic, the prescriptions for Mays's lithium treatment. Then he headed toward his office. It was almost three o'clock, time to go home. He passed the cheerful bumble and buzz of Oprah or one of her imitators on the TV in the common room. A half dozen medicated patients slouched groggily in their chairs. A bony young man in sweatpants and a plaid shirt stood at the door, watching Zack pass. Zack smiled hello: the man jerked back like a startled deer. The unit was locked, of course—all the units were locked—and Zack carried a heavy ring of keys at Eastern State; he always jingled on Mondays and Thursdays. And he wore his white jacket here, which sometimes made him feel tough and efficient, sometimes cold and heartless.

There were three industries in town: the college, Colonial Williamsburg, and the mental hospital. The grounds of Eastern State were a sad echo of the William and Mary campus five miles away, a patchwork of open fields surrounded by scrub pine and scattered with redbrick buildings, half of which were no longer in use. They'd been shut down in the years of deinstitutional-ization. Shuttered brick hulks stood in the tall, yellowing grass. It was already October, and the view from the barred windows of Building 2 was both bucolic and melancholy.

"Zachary, my good friend. How are you?"

"I'm fine, Roy, just fine. Yourself?"

"Oh, I have been worse, but I have been better. You are done for the day? Do you have time for a cup of tea?"

Roy Chadha was the senior psychiatrist at Building 2, a short, dapper man in his fifties with a soft Indian accent. Daniel inevitably called him Dr. Chat. Other units were staffed by newly arrived Russian or Chinese doctors, but the Building 2 patients could be brilliantly, viciously articulate, so the senior, resident, and visiting psychiatrists all spoke excellent English.

"I'm seeing a patient back at the house at five," said Zack. "But sure, I'd love a cup of tea."

Zack followed him into his office, where Roy promptly began to fuss with his tea things: ceramic pot, tea bag tin, mugs decorated with cartoons of cat psychiatrists and mouse patients.

"What a day, what a day," said Roy. "How I hate Mondays. Nobody wants to commit anyone on weekends, so they get crazier and crazier until Monday, and *then* we get them."

"But you transferred the Lewis girl back to the juvenile home?"

"Oh yes. She is not psychotic, only unhappy. I was not afraid for her here, except that she could get bored and do something foolish."

This was a teenage girl who had been brought in this morning, feigning insanity, thinking the hospital would be easier than jail.

Zack told Roy about Rebecca Mays. "I'll write up the diagnosis and have it on your desk before I go. The poor mother. A nice old schoolmarm who got stuck with a psychotic daughter."

Roy passed him a cup of steaming tea and led them to the armchairs in the corner. He sat and sipped. "So how is your home life? Did you have a good weekend?" He was finished with shop talk; he was smiling like a man with a good dirty story to tell.

"Nice and quiet." Zack wondered what Roy wanted to confess.

But Roy's smile was not about himself. "How are things with your boyfriend's new boyfriend?"

"They saw each other again, if that's what you mean." A third time, but who was counting?

"Ah, so it's serious."

"No. It's just steady."

Zack should never have opened his big mouth last week. Roy knew that Zack had an open marriage. They rarely discussed it—there was nothing to discuss—but last week Roy had abruptly asked what the rules were. Roy was smitten with the new Ukrainian nurse, Ms. Krasic. He was happily married and would never act on his desires, but he enjoyed imagining the possibilities. Zack had let slip that Daniel had met someone new and the cycle was starting over. That was all he said; he gave no details about the man being married or Iranian, nothing to identify him. Yet Roy was fascinated. He must have been thinking about it all weekend. As Zack's superior, Roy sometimes acted as his therapist, but the line between consultation and locker room talk could grow awfully thin.

"You boys are such gadabouts. How I envy you."

"They're sex buddies," said Zack. "That's all."

"And you're not jealous?"

"No. I'm glad Daniel is getting laid. Really. He's happier when he's getting laid. I want him to be happy."

"That is what you said last week," said Roy. "And I didn't believe you. But I have been thinking it over. And I suspect you are happy because the door is now open for you. You are free to dip your wick elsewhere."

Zack smiled and shook his head. "I've felt that in the past," he admitted, "but not now. Nobody interests me now. I seem to be taking a vacation from sex."

"You have been taking a vacation for a long time, I think."

"Have I?" Zack tried to remember what he'd told Roy in the past, how much Roy knew.

Roy was smiling, not like a doctor but like a skeptical friend. "How old are you? You are not so old. You could give yourself a prescription. Put some lead back into your pencil."

"Maybe I don't want any blue pills," said Zack with a laugh. "Maybe I don't miss lust. Maybe life is more peaceful without it. Duller maybe. But peaceful."

He wanted Roy to laugh, too, treating his confession as a joke. But Roy only nodded. "It will come back," he said. "It always comes back."

"Lust? You make it sound like Lassie."

"Oh yes. 'Lassie, come home.' " Roy looked more concerned. "You are not afraid you'll lose Daniel?"

"Not at all. It's only sex. We have a hundred other things connecting us. He and his new friend will bonk a few times, for a few months, until their sex loses its magic. The end."

"And if it doesn't lose its magic?"

"It always does," Zack said firmly. "Please, Roy. We don't have to talk about me. I'm aware of the dangers here. The patient is the one with the illness, remember? And I'm fine. Really. This might look dangerous from the outside, but it works."

Roy gave in with a friendly shrug. "I am only trying to understand. But you must get something out of it." He broke into a grin like a naughty boy. "The voyeurism? Knowing Daniel is getting naked with this other man. You find that a turn-on?"

Zack only laughed. "I'm not using them as a masturbation fantasy, if that's what you mean."

"But you do still masturbate?"

Roy was an old-fashioned man at heart, a Brahmin professional, yet he took perverse pride in his American adaptability, his willingness to say anything.

"Yes, I masturbate," said Zack. "Do *you*?" But he promptly regretted asking, since Roy was sure to answer.

"I do," said Roy. "In the shower. And I think about Miss Krasic. Who do you think about?"

Zack groaned again and grinned. "Roy, I'm not crossing that line. Let's keep a couple of secrets, okay?" He stood up to go, chuckling and shaking his head. "I'll see you on Thursday."

13

THE TREES FLEW PAST as Zack pedaled his ten-speed trail bike down the highway. Cold air combed his beard and fluttered the wool scarf around his neck. His white medical coat was left at the hospital, and he wore his old army jacket, so he no longer looked like a doctor but like a local eccentric, an overaged slacker, a middle-aged hippie on a bicycle.

It felt good to escape the locked doors of Building 2, the sad air of chemically neutered lives, the overly warm curiosity of Roy Chadha. Zack knew he'd told Roy too much. One should confide in a friend just to get one's thoughts outside one's head and see what they looked like, but one had to be careful. Zack shouldn't have tattled on Daniel—it felt like tattling now—but what really annoyed him was his confession that he'd said goodbye to sex. Was it true? He'd told nobody else, not even Daniel. It had been years since he and Daniel had had sex with each other, but that was different, that was how they lived. Sex got dispersed in everything else they did. This was not about the act, but about the feeling, the desire. It was a shameful thing for anyone to admit that he'd said goodbye to lust, especially a psychiatrist. Maybe that was why he was happy that Daniel had a new fuck buddy: Daniel was having to screw for them both.

Zack was on Jamestown Road now, starting down the steep hill toward Lake Matoaka. He had to stop thinking and concentrate on the brakes as the bicycle picked up speed and flew downward. The woods on his left fell away—there was the lake, cobalt blue in the October afternoon. Then the slope leveled out and rose again, and he changed gears and pedaled furiously to climb up the other side. He was almost home.

The truth of the matter was their situation neither worried nor excited Zack. Things weren't half as dramatic as Roy imagined. Zack had been here before. Sex might not interest him, but he wanted Daniel to have fun. He knew it wasn't entirely out of love for Daniel; he wanted peace for himself. He had his own full life to consider: patients to see, Victorian novels to read, this beautiful fall weather to enjoy. The trees were starting to change color; the cold air was like soda water. Who needed bodies and orgasms? Well, Daniel did, obviously. Good for Daniel.

Zack coasted on Indian Springs Road and swung into their driveway. He rolled downhill to the carport behind the house. The Toyota was gone—Daniel must have driven to school this morning—but the door to the basement rec room was wide open. Zack leaned his bike against the brick wall, stepped to the door, and looked in.

A child sat on the floor, a little girl of nine or ten.

Zack had never seen her before. She sat cross-legged by the fireplace in a pink leotard and red skirt, watching television. Jocko was stretched out beside her, his head in her lap, happily being petted. He guiltily cut his eyes at his so-called master as Zack entered. Jocko was much too friendly to make a good watchdog.

The girl studied Zack. She had black hair in bangs and large, slightly hooded eyes, like a Hummel.

"Hello there?" said Zack. He never knew how to talk to children. Kids were Daniel's department.

"Maman!" the girl shouted. *"Il est ici!"*

The washing machine churned loudly in the next room. A woman stuck her head around the corner, a beautiful hawklike woman with glasses. Elena Rohani.

She glared at Zack as if *he* were the trespasser.

And Zack thought: She is here to confront me about Daniel and her husband.

"Nobody was home," she said. "But your door was unlocked. So I let myself inside. To do our laundry. As you said we could."

She pretended to be in the right but was clearly flustered.

"You told Daniel you were coming over?"

She frowned at the mention of Daniel. "No. I called, and nobody was home. So I took my chance. Mina helped me to carry it over. We have gone too long and there was too much. Dirty clothes. I hope you do not mind."

"Uh, no. Not at all. Make yourself at home."

"I already have." And she laughed, a disarming cackle.

She wasn't here about Daniel? Good. Did she even know? Zack's relief at understanding this was only about laundry gave way to fresh anxiety. *What* did she know? What kind of game would he have to play not to spill the beans? Damn Daniel. Zack was furious with Daniel for sticking him in this predicament.

Thank God the little girl was here. They wouldn't be able to say anything.

"You seem to have found a buddy," he told the child.

The little girl nodded. "She loves me," she confidently declared.

"Jocko loves everyone," said Zack. "And it's a he."

Jocko looked nervous knowing he was being discussed.

"My name is Zack. What's your name?"

"Mina." She turned to her mother and spoke to her in French.

Elena replied in French, then added, "Speak English. You must practice, and people will think we are keeping secrets." She turned to Zack. "She wanted to know if she could borrow your poodle. I told her no. The poodle is yours and this is his home and we must leave the poodle where he lives."

It sounded like a pointed parable, but maybe not. Zack decided to let sleeping dogs lie, as it were.

"You figured out how everything works?" he asked. "And you have everything you need? Soap and bleach and all that?"

"We brought our own. We are fine. I hope we do not disturb you being here?"

"Not at all. I have a patient coming at five, but we'll be upstairs and can't hear you."

"That is right. You have your office here."

"Yes. Upstairs. Just off the living room."

"I have never seen a psychiatry office. Can you show me?"

Zack was caught off guard.

"The load has another twenty minutes," she explained. "And Mina is watching her television show. What are you watching, *bébé*?"

"Powerpuff Girls."

"Ah. It is her favorite cartoon. She will be fine," she told Zack. "Okay then? I want to see your office."

"Uh, sure."

Damn Daniel, thought Zack again as he led the woman upstairs. He has his fun with the husband and leaves me to deal with the wife.

Elena followed Zack through the living room to the office. She glanced around as she eased herself into Zack's chair. "No couch like Sigmund Freud?"

"I had one for years, but people down here never used it. And it made them nervous, so I retired it to our guest room." Zack sat in the other chair, the chair for his patients.

"You miss your New York sophisticated patients?"

"Sometimes." She wasn't going to talk about it? Maybe she didn't know. "I can't say my New York patients were more sophisticated. But they'd see plays and operas and want to talk about those. Which I enjoyed. Here the common language is TV. But I can work with that, too. It's a different kind of dream, that's all. But now I watch lots of bad TV so I can speak their language."

"I have been watching, too. To improve my English."

"Your English is quite good."

"But I do not dream in English. I cannot write poetry in English. I am still only half here."

She wore no makeup today, but she was still beautiful. Zack had forgotten her odd beauty, like a silent movie star, with her hawklike nose and droopy eyelids—Ross had compared her to Anouk Aimée, but Zack realized with a start that the star she reminded *him* of was young Buster Keaton. She registered more strongly today than she had a month ago, but Zack had more reasons to notice her.

"A new country must be very hard," he said.

"But at least it is not Tehran. I hate Tehran."

She only wants to get to know you better, he told himself. That's why she's here. Zack wanted to know her better, too.

"You and Abbas lived in Iran for a while?"

"Oh no. Only visits. Twice. An impossible country for women. The chador. You know?" She mimed cloth spilling over her face. "I despise it. I hear some women love the anonymity, but I am anonymous already. And they are so hot and smelly. And dishonest. You go about in public dressed like a ghost, then go indoors, throw it off, and you are wearing designer jeans and scarlet lipstick. What kind of lesson is that? The entire country is a school for hypocrites."

"Let's go to the kitchen," Zack suggested. "Would you like coffee?" The fact of the office was turning their chat into a session.

She followed him, pausing by the door to the basement, ostensibly to listen to the washing machine. She sat at the kitchen table while Zack set up the coffeemaker.

"But this is nice. This is homey. You and Daniel? You are happy in Virginia?"

"Very," said Zack. "We have our work. We have our friends." He sat across from her while the coffeemaker began to spit. "It's quieter here. But I don't miss New York."

"I miss Leningrad," she confessed. "Now named Petersburg. I spent my youth working to escape Tashkent, my hometown, a big nowhere city in the sticks. The name is exotic, but it was all ugly new buildings built after the 1966 earthquake. A baking, cement city of parks without people. I burned to go to the university in Leningrad. And I did, and I was happy, but I lost it."

"When the Soviet Union fell apart?"

"Oh no. Long before. When they kicked me out."

"Kicked you out of where?"

"The Soviet Union. First they sent me to prison, then they kicked me out."

Zack hesitated. "You were in prison?"

"For politics. For poetry." She cracked a crooked smile. "I was a zek. Can you believe it?" She chuckled through her nose. "Me? A *zaklyuchenny*. A prisoner. A zek. Three months. The sentence was four years, but Gorbachev declared glasnost and the politicals were let go. Some were advised to leave the country. I took the hint and went to Berlin. And there I met Abbas and lived happily ever after."

Zack could not immediately process it all. She said it so briskly, with such bitter humor, only nothing about it was funny. "You were sent to prison for writing protest poetry?"

She pursed her lips in a plump smirk. "Oh yes. A fine Russian tradition. I wrote a poem about Sakharov. Not a good poem. I was twenty-four. What did I know? The KGB read it, and they are tough critics. They cured me of political poetry. Now I write only about nature. Nature poems and love poems and poems about my children."

Zack was touched, impressed, and a little worried. What would being imprisoned for poetry do to a person's sense of reality?

"I was lucky it was only three months," Elena continued. "A woman's prison. I liked the women very much. Especially the prostitutes. The guards were pigs, but the other prisoners were—genteel? No, gentle. And it was summer, not winter, so we didn't freeze. But it was filthy. It stank. Like a dog kennel. I swore I would always be clean afterwards. So I went straight to Berlin when they exiled me, the clean city. Not so clean as Switzerland, but clean enough. And I wrote my little poems and had my little affairs and lived my little life. Until I met Abbas. Who was a beautiful man, a wonderful painter. We were two refugees from Central Asia, two Caspian cousins come to the West to make our fortune. A countryless man and countryless woman. We hitched our wagons to each other's stars. Poets never make big money, but painters can. Only painters do not know how to sell their goods, but poets have the gift of gab. Better still when one can do the polyglottal gab, like me." She smiled and shrugged. "He will fuck anything, you know. Man, woman, dog. It doesn't matter."

She was looking straight at Zack, still smiling—a cool, rational, bittersweet smile.

Zack had sensed something like this coming; he was not sure why. Maybe it was the steady note of grievance in her bitter humor.

"Why do you say that, Elena? Do we both know the same thing here?"

She held out two open hands with a look of grand innocence. "I do not know how much you know."

"Then we *do* know the same thing."

She shrugged again, the most damning shrug imaginable. She leaned across the table, still smiling. Her smile looked less convincing up close. "I do not mind," she said. "It is only sex. A genius needs his sex. But I did not know if you know."

"I wasn't sure if you knew, but I'm glad you do."

"Good then. We need to say nothing more." And she leaned back and sat up straight, acting quite cool and sardonic. She stole a quick glance at the door to the basement.

"The stairs creak," Zack assured her. "We can hear her if she starts to come up. Or we'll hear Jocko." He wanted to talk about this but didn't know where to begin. He had never had this conversation before. "So this happens regularly?" he said.

"Now and again. And you?"

"Now and again. But not with a married man before."

"Will Abbas be safe?"

Zack was thrown. "Daniel believes in safe sex, if that's what you mean. He gets tested regularly. He's negative." This was such a strange thing to tell someone you barely knew. But their spouses were tricking, which made them more intimate than any family.

"No, I mean—can I trust your lover with my husband? Will he be careful of his feelings? Will he treat him badly?"

"That's not Daniel's style." Zack paused. "Funny. I wanted to know if Abbas would be kind to Daniel but didn't know how to ask."

"It is a concern," she agreed.

"I hope Abbas isn't one of those men who needs to make people fall in love with him just to feed his self-esteem?"

"They fall in love," said Elena. "Men *and* women. But not because he makes them. He doesn't care. They fall in love only because he is lovable. And he *is* lovable. He is so fucking lovable." She thought she kept it bittersweet, but only the bitter came through.

"Do *you* see other people?" he asked her.

She shrugged. "Now and then. When the opportunity arises."

"Men or women?"

She looked surprised. "You're not as innocent as I thought."

"I'm a psychiatrist."

"You're an American. And Americans like everything to be clean and neat. Do *you* see other people?"

He noticed that she didn't answer his question. "I have. But not for a while. It's too much trouble."

She clapped her hands. "Yes!" she cried. "You are right!" Her body language was abrupt and manic, a Russian rhythm. "It *is* so much trouble. Breaking hearts can be fun when you are young. But no fun when you are older and your own heart is brittle."

"True," said Zack hesitantly. Were they still talking about the same thing? "Sex is often a power game for younger people. But we're too old for that. All four of us."

"You think?" She paused. "We have experienced much—me more than him. Too much to sweat the small stuff." She looked at Zack. "What is your reason? Why do you let him do this? Do you love him too much or too little?"

"An interesting way to put it," said Zack. She was not only aware but very precise about her emotional details. He liked her more and more. "I sometimes love him too much, and sometimes too little, and sometimes not at all," he admitted. "But it all averages out by the end of the year."

Elena raised her eyebrows. "I remember feeling like that. Yes. It *could* average out. But no more. Now I never love him too much. Which is a relief. I love his painting. I love his children. But him I love just a little. Which is enough."

Zack didn't believe her. He suspected she didn't fully believe herself either.

There was a loud buzz downstairs like a foghorn.

"Maman!" Mina shouted. *"Le washer!"*

"I hear!" But she remained in her chair, reluctant to get up. "We have said enough for today. I should take care of this."

"But we haven't had our coffee," said Zack.

He followed her back down to the basement. Mina was still in front of the

TV, Jocko sprawled across her lap. The child refused to look at the grown-ups, which made Zack wonder if she'd crept upstairs and heard something. But girl and dog looked as immovable as a statue of two lovers.

Zack watched while Elena shifted a pastel salad of cold, wet underwear from the washer to the dryer. He worried that he'd get much too familiar with this family's laundry in the weeks to come.

"I would like to read some of your poetry," he said.

"It is all Russian. It will be only noise to you."

"You could translate it. Your English is very striking."

She frowned. "Only by accident. I can control my Russian but not my English. I do not always know what I am saying."

"Which is how the smartest, most original things often get said."

The doorbell rang.

"Damn. It's my five o'clock." Fay Dawson, his nervous Christian, which would mean twisting his brain into an entirely new shape.

"I will let myself out when I am done," said Elena.

"I've enjoyed this," he said. "Odd as that must sound."

She studied him a moment with her cool gray eyes. "Yes, we must do this again. As things develop."

"Or even if they don't," said Zack.

They hesitated, unsure how to say goodbye. Then Zack held out his hand, and Elena gripped it, like a friendly business partner.

14

ABBAS MOANED AND KISSED HARDER—his moans buzzed inside Daniel's mouth. He lay on his back on the old studio sofa while Daniel bent over him, one foot on the floor, one knee propped between his legs, kissing and pumping him. The shaft in Daniel's hand felt like stiff rubber. In a second it would turn as hard as hickory. There was already the fresh pollen smell of sperm, but that was Daniel, who had finished five minutes ago. They'd found that Daniel took longer, and so he went first. Abbas, however, came quite easily.

The hands clutching Daniel's head gripped tighter; Abbas kissed deeper. He lifted his hips into Daniel's pumping. And he grunted into Daniel's mouth, a hard, strangled gasp. He broke off the kiss, threw his head back, and let out a cry.

His mouth was wide open, his eyes shut, his face all tongue and palate. And the hickory in Daniel's hand was not only hard but slick. Abbas foamed up like cream soda. His cries jumped from the rear of his throat into the depths of his chest, shifting from treble to bass to treble again, until they ended in a long, low moan.

He fell back, catching his breath like a man who'd just jumped aboard the last train out of a burning city. Then he opened his eyes again and smiled.

Daniel couldn't help smiling, too. He usually treated a partner's orgasm as just a warm courtesy. But it was a thrill to watch Abbas finish, a privilege. Daniel was breathing hard himself, as if he'd come again, too. He absentmindedly wiped his hand off on his own chest, as if to save the scent for later.

Daniel climbed off while Abbas sat up, the two men drawing their humid bodies apart. They sat facing each other on the sofa, stacking their legs together. Daniel wished they had a bed and could lie side by side; the sofa was too narrow. It was after six, and the studio was dark except for the floor lamp out in the middle of the room. The boom box was still playing—the Supremes, which Daniel had brought today as a change from Abbas's Bollywood tracks. The music was meant to cover the sounds of their lovemaking if anyone happened to visit the building on a Sunday afternoon.

There was no guilt afterward, not that Daniel could see. Neither man was ever in a hurry to wash off and get dressed. Once Abbas was naked and satisfied, he liked to stay naked. He sat at his end of the sofa, lean and dark, smoothly crosshatched in body hair. He reached down to his bib overalls for his glasses and cigarettes, put on the glasses, and lit a cigarette. He now smoked unfiltered Camels, the closest American equivalent of Gauloises. He released a harsh cloud in a happy sigh. "Thank you," he said. "Thank you. Yes. I needed that. Very much. This was a difficult week."

"Good. I needed it, too," said Daniel. "Uh, anything in particular?"

"Oh, the teaching. These students are so needy. And I want more time to paint or I go crazy. And this new canvas does not come together." He gestured at the painting that lay flat on the floor under the lamp. "And there are things at home."

"With Elena?" Daniel asked.

"With Osh. I am worried by Osh. He lacks skill in English. He learns everything much too slowly. We are taking him to a specialist to see why he cannot learn quicker."

It never ceased to amaze Daniel that Abbas could bring his family into this room after sex. Another man might be embarrassed or want to use the time to escape his other life—not Abbas. It was a good thing they were only fuck buddies or Daniel might resent it.

Daniel remembered there was something he wanted to discuss himself.

He'd been afraid to bring it up sooner for fear it might stop them from having their fun.

"Did you know," he said, "that Elena talked to Zack this week?"

Abbas shrugged. "Yes. She told me she did a load of wash at your house and talked to your partner."

"About us."

Abbas looked surprised. "He did not know?"

"Oh, he knew. He just never thought he'd have to discuss it with your wife." Daniel couldn't help smiling. Zack had been annoyed, although he claimed he wasn't. It made a great comic situation. Daniel was almost sorry he hadn't been there.

"Good then," said Abbas. "Good. So long as everyone tells everything, all will be fine."

Daniel took hold of Abbas's left foot and began to rub it, just to give his hands something to do. "Does she feel threatened by us?"

"By you and Zack?"

"No. You and me."

He shrugged. "No. She knows you are a couple and we are a couple and nobody is going to run away together."

His bare sole was smooth leather, the toes hard and dry.

"She told Zack she was once a political prisoner."

"Oh yes," said Abbas. "For three months only." As if that made it less important.

"Then it's true?" said Daniel. "She didn't make it up?"

"It's true. Why would she make it up?"

"I don't know. To win Zack's sympathy?"

"Why would she need his sympathy?"

Daniel knew his idea was paranoid, but he went ahead and shared it. "If she wanted to stop us from seeing each other, she'd want him on her side. But if the political prisoner stuff is true, then she's not being manipulative and I shouldn't worry, right?"

Abbas frowned. "Did she ask Zack to stop you from seeing me?"

"No. It's just that Zack got the feeling she's not as comfortable with this as she says she is."

"Oh. That." He already knew about *that.* "She'll get comfortable. She always does. It is none of her business what I do on Sunday."

"But there's no trouble at home?"

"No. Why should there be trouble?"

"Sorry. I've been living with Zack too long."

"Does *he* want us to stop seeing each other?"

"No. He's fine with this." More or less—it was sometimes hard to tell with Zack. "All I meant was, I've picked up his guilt habit. His tendency to worry." Worry was so easy after orgasm.

"There is nothing to worry about," Abbas insisted. "You have an understanding with your partner and I have one with mine."

"You're right," Daniel said and jimmied a friendly foot between Abbas's thigh and genitals. "And it's not like we're doing anything bad. Hey, honey, it's male bonding. Other men go fishing or play golf." He grinned as he stroked the soft black pubic hair with his toes.

Abbas laughed and stubbed his cigarette out in the coffee can. He took hold of Daniel's foot and kissed the sole. "You are a silly man," he said. "A fun but silly man." He released the foot and withdrew his own foot from Daniel's lap. He jumped off the sofa and stepped over to the painting under the lamp.

The bright, wet canvas glowed like a stained glass window in the floor. The silhouette of the painter stood above it, chin in one hand, elbow in the other hand, hips tilted contrapposto, a naked figure contemplating an unfinished task.

Daniel wondered: Did he work on his painting during sex? When Abbas was down on his knees and making love with his mouth—the man gave excellent head—was he also rethinking a brushstroke or shape or juxtaposition of colors? In that case, Daniel was part of the process, a piece of the picture. He liked the idea.

"I cannot get the balance right," said Abbas. "It is too busy. Too unstable. So unstable it is flabby."

It sounded like an invitation to look, so Daniel got up from the sofa and came over.

The new painting featured a life-size shadow of a human body in burnt orange. It was not a realistic body but a soft outline like a gingerbread man against a streaky green ground. The body was decorated with little red and black bodies, Abbas's alphabet people, his ideogram men laid out in lines like the figures of an Egyptian wall painting. A rudimentary penis like a U had been drawn in the wet paint with the pointy end of a brush to indicate that the home body was nude and male. The figures in the stacks of art books on the floor were finally having an effect. Or maybe it was the effect of Sunday afternoons with Daniel.

"I like it," said Daniel. "A city of bodies. A body of bodies. A body full of other selves." He liked it better the more he described it. "Yes, it does look busy. But what's wrong with that?"

"It is too loose. It needs tension to hold it together."

"It's all on the same plane. Did you want to keep it flat?"

"No. Not if flat is flabby."

Sometimes Abbas treated Daniel as a layman, a visual idiot, which hurt. But today Abbas treated him as a fellow painter, and Daniel was pleased.

"Maybe if you suggested a face in the head," said Daniel.

"No, the face must remain blank."

"What looks cluttered is where the figures spill out of the body." Daniel pointed to the right hip, where two lines of alphabet men continued past the burnt orange into the green.

"I wanted to suggest freedom and overflow. But yes. It flattens the body into the canvas. I will take it out." Abbas knelt down, snatched up a palette knife, and without pausing, dug into the green paint covered with beautiful squiggles. It came up in a soft curl like cake frosting. Daniel couldn't help cringing in sympathetic pain.

"You didn't want to think about it more?" said Daniel.

"No. The first thought is always the best thought."

Abbas worked quickly, scraping out a small patch down to the canvas, leaving the burnt orange part untouched. He wiped off the palette knife, then took a tube of paint and a brush and began to lay a light green weave over the open wound.

We must look so weird beside this picture, thought Daniel, like two naked med students examining a cadaver.

Abbas disappeared back into his art, so Daniel went over to the sink to wash off. The porcelain was covered in a black fungus of old paint. There was no hot water, and Daniel scrubbed his crotch and stomach with an icy washcloth. He wondered what the studio would be like next month, when the weather got colder. He glanced over now and then to watch Abbas at work. The man looked quite beautiful stretched over his canvas, one leg extended back, half his weight resting on a locked arm—like a greyhound doing tai chi.

Their spouses talked as if they might be lovers, as if this could turn into a messy, heated affair. No way, thought Daniel. We're just two men who like to jerk each other off and talk about our art. Well, only the art of one man. Yet Daniel found Abbas's selfishness oddly restful. He could imagine one day wanting more from the man, but not now, not anytime soon.

When he finished getting dressed, he came over to say goodbye. Abbas remained squatted by the canvas, delicately painting in the patch with a darker shade of green, seamlessly matching the new brushstrokes with the old ones. The orange body now stood completely free of the ground. There was still clutter, but it was an orderly clutter, a contained busyness. The painting was better.

"You know," said Daniel, "you really should get yourself an American dealer." They had discussed this before.

Abbas did not look up. "If you will give us a few names, Elena can write to them."

"Or maybe I can write to them," Daniel offered.

Abbas looked over his shoulder. "You would do that for another painter? That is very generous."

"Hey. We're generous with our dicks. Why not be generous with other things?" Daniel usually treated his gallery contacts like gold, but he felt he could do a better job of selling Abbas than Elena did. "I should be going," he said before he offered anything more.

Abbas stood up to say goodbye. He didn't touch Daniel—his forearms and chest hair were already flecked with fresh paint scabs—but he held his arms out from his sides and poked his head forward for a friendly kiss. His mouth opened into Daniel's mouth; their tongues lightly shook hands.

"Later," said Daniel.

"Later," said Abbas, and he promptly went back to work.

I5

Canned fruits and vegetables lined the shelves, simple cylinders, solid geometries wrapped in paper. Next came the soups, not just classic red-and-white Campbell's but many brands: Healthy Choice, Pepperidge Farm, Progresso, Pritikin, Amy's organic. Poor Andy Warhol, thought Daniel. He probably never dreamed such variety would ever exist in America.

Daniel visited the Food Lion out on Richmond Road every week, and the supermarket had become invisible to him years ago. The sunless white light was as dreary as the light inside a refrigerator. The place was chilly like a refrigerator, too. But just knowing that Abbas might shop here made Daniel see it through new eyes, foreign eyes. The miles of aisles became very new and pop. Daniel even noticed the Muzak: "You Light Up My Life" at the moment.

"Toilet paper?" said Zack, coming alongside with the half-loaded grocery cart. "One family pack or two?"

"Just one. We still got part of a pack left from last week. We don't seem to shit as much as we used to."

Zack made a face. The doctor disliked talk about feces, farts, and vomit. "Oh, Jane and Jack called today. Their Halloween party is coming up."

"Already? Yeah, it's October. Thank God they don't throw costume parties anymore. Damn, I hate costume parties. Everyone dresses up as who they secretly want to be. It's just too weird standing in a room full of private fantasies."

"You say that every year. And every year you complain afterwards that people are too boring to dress up anymore."

Daniel pleaded guilty with a smirk. "You can't always get what you want."

They came to the air-cooled display of luncheon meats.

"No more liverwurst," said Daniel. "You don't eat it and it stinks up the refrigerator. Get the turkey. It's better for your cholesterol."

Zack tossed a packet in the cart. "Also, Jane wants us to make sure the Rohanis are there."

"Us? Why us? Do people think we *own* the Rohanis?"

"I don't know. Do they?"

Daniel nervously looked around. "You don't have to worry about *that*. Nobody notices a damn thing in the department."

"I'm not worried. I'm just asking. But it's a small school in a small town. Hard to imagine people don't pick up some kind of vibe."

"You underestimate their self-absorption. Their total incuriosity." They continued along the back wall to the dairy section. "Did she come by today?"

"No. Did you expect her to?"

"Wasn't it last Tuesday she came by?"

"No, last Monday." Zack paused. "I don't see her as regularly as you see him."

"You don't have to take that tone."

"There was no tone. I was just being factual."

"I can hear you thinking."

Zack smiled. "You're just hearing your guilty conscience."

Good one, thought Daniel. He couldn't help chuckling. "I'm *not* guilty. Really. Although you must want me to feel guilty, telling me how she was once a political prisoner."

"No. I said only that their lives have been different from ours and you must be careful. They have different expectations. Different priorities. Let's get two things of orange juice."

"I'm bored with orange juice. Let's get a grapefruit juice."

They turned the corner into the produce aisle. The right front wheel on the cart began to wobble and flutter, like a nerve tremor.

And there, ten yards ahead of them, in profile beside the sloping bins of cabbages and carrots, stood Elena Rohani.

It was uncanny. It felt like more than a coincidence, as if Daniel had sensed Elena here and that was why he'd been talking about her.

She didn't see them yet. Daniel saw nobody else. Then he noticed Osh folded up in the rack under the cart, playing some kind of kid game with himself. Mina stood a few feet off, examining the toe of her shiny red shoe, embarrassed by her baby brother.

"Speak of the devil," muttered Daniel.

"She's hardly the devil," Zack said softly.

The kids looked perfectly American, yet their austerely elegant mother was much too exotic for Food Lion. A cashmere scarf circling her neck, she gazed at the milky green cabbage in her hand as if it were a skull.

"Let's turn around," said Daniel. "We don't need to say hello."

"She'll have noticed us," said Zack. "You don't want her to think we're running away."

"All right, all right." Daniel breathed deep. "But keep it short."

They approached, Zack gliding their cart ahead.

Daniel hadn't seen Elena since the dinner party—and certainly not since he and Abbas had started getting together. Yet she was often in his head. He was surprised by how opaque she looked in person, an unfamiliar stranger. He didn't really know her, did he?

She turned. She saw them. She smiled.

"Hello, Elena," said Zack. "Hi, Mina. This must be Osh." He pointed at the little boy under the groceries. Osh grinned up at them, baring his teeth like an upside-down monkey.

"Good evening," said Elena. "Good evening to you both."

She stared straight at Daniel, as if she couldn't quite place him. Then her gaze swung down and up, brazenly inspecting him, Daniel thought, as if she were picturing him naked, the bald little Jew who was humping her husband.

"Where's Abbas?" said Zack. "He doesn't help with groceries?"

"Oh no. Abbas stays home and rests from his busy day."

Zack smiled. "Abbas always gets what he wants?"

Elena smiled with him. "Always."

Daniel grew more uncomfortable. They weren't looking at him, but he could feel them wanting to look. He squatted down to talk to Osh. "What're you doing down here, monkey? Who you hiding from?"

The boy giggled and turned away.

"I have been meaning to call you," Elena told Zack.

"If you need to use our washer again," said Zack, "feel free."

Daniel wished Zack weren't so damn comfortable with her.

"Thank you. We are fine this week. But your friend Ross has been calling and asking us to come to his movie theater?"

"Oh yes. Ross is very proud of his theater."

And he's hot to see *you* again, thought Daniel. He slowly stood up, wondering where this would go.

"But there was nothing we wanted to see," said Elena. "Until this Friday. He is showing one of my favorites, *An American in Paris*."

"With Gene Kelly?" said Zack.

Daniel was surprised. He thought Elena's taste would be more grim and sophisticated, leaning toward Bergman or Tarkovsky. He loved musicals himself, although he hated *An American in Paris*.

"A silly movie," Elena admitted. "A Hollywood extravaganza about artists in a make-believe Paris. But I love the music and the dancing. Ross says it is a beautiful new print. He suggested you come too and we could make it a party. The five of us."

She spoke so cheerfully, so innocently. Daniel decided she was bluffing, daring him to spend a whole evening out with his boyfriend, his fuck buddy, and his fuck buddy's wife.

He waited for Zack to make an excuse, but Zack remained silent, watching Daniel, waiting for *him* to reply. Zack was smirking. He tried to look innocent, but his mouth was pinched in the teeniest smirk.

Elena couldn't be serious. Daniel decided to call her bluff. "I think we're free," he said. "Talk to Abbas. If he wants to see the movie, sure. Why not? We could all see it together."

She looked surprised, but she did not back down. "Good. I cannot wait to tell him." Her smile returned. Even when she and Zack didn't look at each other, they seemed to be smiling at each other.

"Ma-*ma*!" Mina stood ten feet away, arms folded, foot tapping. She did not want her mother talking to these gay men in public—Daniel imagined her thinking *gay* and thinking it nastily. He'd noticed how kids now used *gay* the same way they had used *queer* when he was a kid: "That is *so* gay."

"Patience, my dear," said Elena. "But she is right. We must go. They have school tomorrow. Osh, darling. Out of the wagon. You are too heavy to push."

The boy performed a slow-motion somersault from the rack. He jumped to his feet, holding out his arms—ta da!—as he faced away from the grown-ups toward an imaginary audience.

"Will the kids come, too?" asked Zack.

"Oh no. It will be a treat only for us." She turned to Daniel, her smile more sly and sinister now. "I will talk to Abbas. I think he will be amenable. See you Friday then. See you both. Good night." She pushed off with her cart, much lighter without Osh, who had run off to annoy his sister.

Daniel watched them disappear around the corner. He waited a moment. "Damn that was weird. That was fucking weird. Why didn't you help me?"

Zack tried to look sympathetic. "What did you want me to do?"

"You enjoyed watching me suffer, didn't you?"

"I did not."

"You were smiling."

Zack smiled now. "Because it's funny. And it *is* funny."

"Not when it's happening to you. Did you see the way she looked at me? If looks could kill."

"*She* thinks it's funny."

"Bullshit. She hates me. She's got to hate me."

"Why do you assume she hates you? I don't hate Abbas."

"Do you like him?"

Zack hesitated. "I barely know him. Maybe I'll know him better after Friday."

Did Daniel want Zack to know Abbas? Not really. That was another reason why he disliked the idea of them getting together. "There won't be anything on Friday. He's going to say no."

"You think? Elena can be awfully persuasive."

"Abbas can be awfully stubborn. I wish you didn't like her so much. You do like her, don't you?"

"Yes. She's smart and interesting and honest." Zack paused. "Why should it bother you that I like her?"

"Because I can't always be sure you're on my side here."

"I'm on your side. I'm always on your side." Zack paused again. "But it's not about sides. We're all in this together."

Daniel thought for a moment, then sighed. "You're right. I don't know why I said that. I'm glad you like her."

But life would be easier if he didn't. They wouldn't know the Rohanis as a couple and Daniel could see Abbas in private. Things could just happen in the dark, in a safe, secret compartment.

Zack rolled their cart along in silence, each man disappearing into his own thoughts, until they reached the ice cream section.

"You wanna?" said Zack, in a guilty, apologetic tone. "It might cheer us up." Was he apologizing for ganging up on him with Elena?

"I feel fine," said Daniel, but he opened the dairy case and took out a carton of Turkey Hill chocolate mint chip, Zack's favorite. "But if it'll make *you* happy." He tossed the cold brick into the cart. "At least it's not heroin."

16

Elena called the next day to report that Abbas had said yes to *An American in Paris*. Zack was pleased. If the two couples were going to share spouses once a week, they should meet now and then, all four of them. It was more honest that way, more civilized. We're putting the adult back into adultery, Zack told himself—he didn't share the joke with Daniel. And yes, he wanted to see Daniel and Abbas together, just to get a sense of how the two men behaved with each other. He didn't feel threatened, only curious, and maybe a little voyeuristic. A movie was less dangerous than dinner. A movie would give them something to focus on besides themselves. What could be safer than *An American in Paris*?

"Relax," he told Daniel. "If Abbas can handle it, and I can handle it, so can you."

"Oh, I can handle it. I just can't help wondering if I'm walking into a trap."

"Whose trap? Elena's?"

"Yes. Or maybe yours."

"But I don't want to trap you."

"Not consciously. But unconsciously you might want to punish me. You might want to see me sweat."

"Not at all. I just want to spend time with a family that *you* have made an intimate part of our life."

But when he was alone, Zack asked himself: Did he want to punish Daniel? No. Yet he did feel Daniel was having things much too easy. He should be willing to experience occasional discomfort in payment for his fun.

Friday arrived. It was already dark when Zack and Daniel strolled over to pick up the Rohanis. The house was on the way, and the four could walk to Merchants Square together. It was a crisp, cool fall night.

"How do we do this?" asked Zack. "Do we sit boy-girl-boy-boy?"

"Not funny," said Daniel.

"No? Not a little? And people think *you're* the witty half of the couple." But Zack knew better than to try any other jokes when Daniel was feeling so shaky and vulnerable.

The Rohanis lived on Chandler Court, a cul-de-sac off Jamestown Road. The college did not give their guest artist a whole house but the larger half of a duplex. Zack and Daniel went up to the front porch. Neither had been here before. The breeze produced a long, heavy sigh in the tall cedar trees overhead.

The bell was answered by a red-haired college girl with freckles and a pierced eyebrow.

"Wexler. Hey," she said with a flat tone and sly smile.

"Hi, Maureen. I see you got yourself another babysitting gig. Oh, my boyfriend, Zack Knowles. One of my students, Maureen Clark."

Zack shook hands with the girl. He didn't know how Daniel did it, how he could tell them apart. All college kids looked alike to him, except for the occasional beautiful guy.

"We are nearly ready!" shouted Elena from upstairs.

The floors were uncarpeted wood, and Zack could hear the Rohanis clopping overhead like a pair of racehorses. The living room was small and dark, lit chiefly by the TV set, which Osh and Mina watched while sitting cross-legged on the floor. The furniture was dumpy college-issue, except for a damask folding screen in the corner, full of Arabic or Persian motifs, and a large blue painting propped on the mantel over a cold, ashy fireplace.

"Is that his?" asked Zack.

"Oh yeah. An earlier version of what he's doing now."

It was beautiful, all color and texture, an abstract seascape that slowly revealed itself to be nothing but figures, a dense weave of abstract fish and sea monsters. Zack looked at Daniel with raised eyebrows, as if to say: This is good, isn't it? Daniel nodded: Of course, it's good.

Elena came downstairs, her high heels clattering on the steps, a lemony twist of perfume preceding her. "I hope we are not too late. There will be seats left?"

"There's always seats at the Williamsburg Theater," said Daniel.

Then *he* came down, steadily dropping into view: first legs, then crotch, then a long, lean torso—oddly long, like a swan's neck—and finally a dark, somber face in glasses.

This was the first time Zack had seen Abbas since *it* started. Just a man, he thought. A balding, olive-skinned man with designer eyewear. Zack was disappointed he didn't feel more strongly.

Abbas scowled at Daniel, as if he blamed him for this outing. Then he caught sight of Zack and looked away, embarrassed. If this were a movie, thought Zack, there would be a close-up of me as I begin to suspect something. But it wasn't a movie and Zack already knew everything. Didn't he?

Maybe tonight wasn't such a good idea after all.

Elena turned to Maureen. "You have our cell phone number if there is an emergency. But there will be no emergency, right, Mina?"

"Right, Mama."

"Good night, my dears. We will not be too late."

"And we can have a fire and roast marshmallows?" asked Maureen. "They got a real fireplace," she told Daniel.

"Yes. But you must watch them," said Elena, "especially Osh. Obey Maureen," she told her son. "You must not play with the fire."

"*Oui, maman.*"

It was only two blocks from Chandler Court to the theater. Zack found himself walking with Elena while their spouses walked together a few feet ahead. The spouses barely spoke.

"Abbas does not seem eager to see this," said Zack.

Elena shrugged. "We are always doing what he wants. Tonight we are doing what I want." She lowered her voice. "I am here for the movie. Abbas thinks I am here for something else. But I only want to get out of the house and see a good movie. And you?"

Her directness continued to surprise and please Zack. "Not my favorite musical," he admitted. "I wanted to find out if we could spend an evening together and be normal."

"Normal?" she said, as if it were a peculiar idea. "Hmm."

The college stood inside the *V* formed by Jamestown Road and Richmond Road. Merchants Square was just outside the point of the *V*, between the campus and Colonial Williamsburg, a block-long stretch of Duke of Gloucester Street closed to traffic and lined with shops. Tonight the square was full of tourists strolling in the shadows, the old-fashioned streetlamps no brighter than the watery electric light spilling from the colonial shop windows. There was no marquee over the movie theater—it would have spoiled the ersatz eighteenth-century look—but a poster for the movie hung in the glass case out front. A surprising number of people crowded around the ticket booth.

They found Ross inside, working the popcorn stand as usual. His face lit up at the sight of Elena.

"You came!" he exclaimed. "You *all* came. Great. It's a good night, a good crowd. Here, I saved seats for us."

He eagerly escorted them inside and down the center aisle to a row with a long strip of masking tape across the arms.

"Sit, sit," he said. "Save the aisle seat for me. I'll join you once the movie starts."

They milled for a moment and then filed in: Zack, Daniel, Abbas, Elena, and an empty seat for Ross. They fell into their chain of overlapping couples. Zack was sorry Elena was at the other end of the row and he couldn't talk to her without shouting across the others.

"You have seen this film?" Abbas asked Daniel.

"Oh yeah," said Daniel. "Not great, but it has its moments."

They spoke in a brusque, dry, masculine manner, like two straight men dragged to a movie by their wives.

"The music is great," said Zack. "It has music by Gershwin."

Abbas gazed coolly at Zack but made no attempt to smile, not even as a courtesy.

He feels guilty, Zack told himself.

The theater was half full tonight, crowded by Williamsburg standards, although the extra numbers were not students but older folks, middle-class retirees. Williamsburg had become a retirement center for people who didn't want to go to Florida. Daniel claimed these were people who thought Florida had too many Jews. Zack disagreed, but the locals did tend to be awfully conservative. An old musical might be their idea of a fancy night on the town.

"Hello? Dr. Knowles? Hello?" a woman shyly called out.

Zack looked, and there was Fay Dawson, at the other side of the theater. He smiled and waved at her.

A heavy man with a crew cut grumbled something to Fay—he must be her husband. She lowered the hand she'd been waving and slipped guiltily into a chair beside him.

"Who was that?" asked Daniel.

"Oh, someone I work with."

It was a good thing Fay couldn't guess what was going on over here or the good Christian lady would never trust him again with her own secrets. But maybe she should know. Then she'd understand that nothing she confessed could shock him.

Finally, the lights dimmed. There were no commercials or trailers. The movie began. Ross raced down the aisle and plopped into the seat next to Elena.

The restored Technicolor was gorgeous, the Gershwin score terrific, Leslie Caron exquisite. Zack enjoyed watching Gene Kelly's toothpaste grin and boulder-round butt. The boy-meets-girl story, however, was much too simple, and the thing was paced like a glacier. After half an hour, Zack's attention began to wander. He glanced over at the others. Daniel and Abbas both stared straight ahead, looking skeptical, like two jurors at a murder trial. Elena, however, was enthralled, her face radiant in the kaleidoscopic bath of light. She wasn't kidding, she really did love this movie. Zack pictured her in Leningrad thirty years ago, watching a washed-out print with Russian subtitles. An MGM musical would've seemed as wild and decadent as an acid trip in the old Soviet Union.

Ross appeared to enjoy the movie almost as much as Elena did. Or maybe he was enjoying Elena enjoying the movie. But the three gay men—or two and a half, depending on how Abbas counted—grew detached and bored. Zack sensed Daniel and Abbas getting especially restless.

He wondered how Daniel felt sitting between him and Abbas. Zack remembered seeing movies in college during his closet years when he sometimes found himself sitting beside a crushee. He would let his knee lean against the other man's knee and see what the other knee did. If it withdrew, Zack knew he was barking up the wrong tree. If the knee remained, his heart would fill with hope—he could live off that hope for weeks. But Daniel was beyond the hopeful stage, wasn't he? A knee was superfluous when you already knew the genitals. Nevertheless, Zack stole a sidelong glance down. Their knees were apart, their hands not even close.

He noticed Ross at the end of the row, twisted slightly forward to check out Zack. His face was vague in the movie glow, but he seemed to be smiling. Did he know about Daniel and Abbas? Of course not. He probably thought Zack was wondering about him and Elena. Was anything even going on there? This was ridiculous, like being back in high school. Zack turned away to watch the movie.

They had come to the interminable dream ballet in the last reel: Gene Kelly dances through half-finished paintings by Renoir, Rousseau, and Toulouse-Lautrec until he ends in a splashy, splotchy, crowded street scene like the watercolors that Zack remembered from the waiting room of his dentist when he was a kid. Then Kelly wakes, sees Leslie Caron out his window, realizes he loves her, and runs outside. They dance on a long, long staircase into each other's arms, and the movie ends with the Paris skyline.

The lights came up. Zack shared a look with Daniel, their usual silent exchange after seeing a film with other people.

Daniel screwed his mouth into his nose and wiggled his eyebrows: Bad movie. Now what?

Zack smiled guiltily and sighed: It'll be fine.

17

"Lies, nothing but lies!" cried Abbas as they stepped out into the square. "They were not painters. They were illustrators. Bad commercial illustrators. It pretends to be Paris after the war, but where was Picasso? Matisse? Léger? And it was ugly. I have never seen such ugly colors. Like candy vomit. Candy puke."

"It was a musical!" cried Elena. "A fun, stupid, Hollywood musical. Only an idiot would argue with it."

"Only an idiot would think it pretty."

They were angrily taking out cigarettes and lighting them—not each other's, only their own. Daniel was alone with the Rohanis—Zack was using the toilet, Ross talking with his assistant manager before he joined them for drinks. The old people filing past gave the couple dirty looks, not so much for what they were saying as for their raised voices and maybe their accents.

"It *was* pretty," said Elena. "In an ugly, poison chemical way. Things do not have to be beautiful pretty to be pretty."

"You are blind. That wasn't ugly pretty. I love ugly pretty. That was ugly *thinking* it was pretty. Which is shit."

Daniel was amazed they could say such things to each other. He wondered if it was because they were using English and there was more space between their thoughts and words. He noticed they did not slip into French here, as if French might be too personal.

Zack came outside. "So what did everyone think?"

Leave it to Zack to tap a hornet's nest to see if it were occupied.

Elena declared, "I love it because it is candy. My husband hates it because it is candy. He calls it vomit candy. I married a man with no sense of humor."

"You call it humor? I call it taste. Everything in your movie stinks." Abbas jabbed his cigarette at the air. "The photography stinks, the music stinks, the fashion stinks, the love story stinks."

"Oh, the love story, yes. You know so much about love stories." She turned to Zack and Daniel. "My husband is such a romantic."

Oh yes, thought Daniel, there is *that* elephant in the room.

"You didn't like the music?" said Zack, playing dumb. "But it's Gershwin. Not my favorite movie, but I love the music."

"You see," said Elena. "Dr. Knowles knows how to take pleasure where he finds it. Everything does not have to be great art."

Ross came bounding out of the theater. "I'm free now. Where does everyone want to go? Are we eating or just drinking? Great movie, right?"

"How about the Green Leafe Cafe?" said Daniel, hoping to get them off the movie. "The smokers can smoke at the Green Leafe."

"The movie was shit," said Abbas. "It was lies, it was ugly, it was shit."

Ross laughed. "But what did you really think, Rohani? You're among friends. You can be honest with us."

Ross used this joke often. Only Zack and Elena laughed.

They started up Richmond Road toward the café. The sidewalk was narrow, and they broke up again. Ross walked with Elena, happily chatting with her about this movie and others set in Paris. Daniel walked with Zack, who wanted to talk about Leslie Caron, eagerly analyzing her charms; all Daniel needed to do was nod. Abbas strutted between the pairs, haughtily silent, proudly alone.

Abbas felt different tonight to Daniel. Back at the house, surrounded by others, it was like his sex light had been switched off. Abbas was no longer a body, just a face and clothes. Not only did Daniel feel nothing sexual for him but it was unimaginable that they had been having sex. In the movie theater, however, sitting beside his lean warmth and intimate aromas of hair, tobacco, and soap, Daniel remembered the sex. That was another reason to dislike the movie: it wasn't good enough to keep his mind off Abbas. Sitting with Abbas on one side and Zack on the other, Daniel had felt like a radio tuned between two stations, full of static. Then the movie ended and there was Abbas again, no longer entirely sexless but too cranky and opinionated to be enjoyed.

"I love it most when he and she dance," Elena loudly told Ross. "When Kelly and Caron look into each other's eyes, you can tell: they want to fuck out each other's brains."

The Green Leafe Cafe stood across the street from the football stadium. It was bright and noisy and hectic. There was no music; the noise was all talk. The place had been full of potted plants when it opened twenty years ago—hence the name—but the plants had died. The front half was full of students, the back half—the smoking half—full of faculty. Daniel had forgotten tonight was Friday and most of the English Department would be here. He greeted a couple of friends while he looked for a table. Then he saw Jane Morrison sitting alone with a man who wasn't her husband.

"Daniel!" she called out. "We were just leaving if you need a place to sit."

Daniel cautiously approached. Then he recognized "the other man"—Samuel Clay Brooke from the department, their old-fashioned confirmed bachelor. Hardly a candidate for cheating, but that's where Daniel's mind was tonight.

"Samuel," said Jane. "You haven't met Mr. and Mrs. Rohani."

Samuel rose from his chair and twisted around like a tall tree in a tweed jacket. "Our Purrrr-sians," he cheerfully growled in his rumbly baritone, a cement mixer full of gravel. "So glad to meet you. Are we having a war?"

Elena looked startled. "A war? My husband and I?"

"No, our countries. Our countries!" he shouted through his grin, as if volume could translate his words.

"Samuel, that's Iraq," said Jane. "Abbas is from Iran. They're two different countries." The White House had been threatening war with Iraq ever since August, but it remained only talk. Even the Republicans in Congress opposed a new war so soon after the invasion of Afghanistan.

"Iraq isn't Persia?" growled Samuel, rolling his *r*'s in gravel.

"No, Iraq is Mesopotamia," said Ross. "Iran is Persia. It's right next door."

"We are not the same," Abbas said sharply. "We are so not the same that we fought a bloody war with Iraq. Millions were killed."

"You don't say?" Samuel nodded. "Two different countries, huh? Learn something new every day."

Jane grimaced in embarrassment, then turned to Elena. "I'm sorry I haven't called. Jack and I keep meaning to ask you and Abbas over to dinner, only the semester has been so busy. But I hear that Daniel has been taking good care of your husband."

Jane said it innocently enough—she wouldn't have mentioned it if she'd suspected anything—but Daniel could *feel* a nervous exchange of glances around him, like the snapping of tiny mousetraps.

"He has," said Elena drily. "He and Zack have made us both feel very much at home."

"Good then. Very good. Well, I better be going. Did you want a ride back, Samuel? Good night, all. Have a good weekend. See you on Monday, Daniel. Abbas."

"Damascus?" said Samuel as Jane led him away. "Is that Iran or Iraq? All I know is the *Arabian Nights.*"

They sat down at the big oak table—the Rohanis on the outside, Zack and Daniel on the inside, Ross at the end—and they ordered their drinks—Elena wine, Abbas scotch, the Americans beer.

"Good old Samuel," declared Ross. "Just when you think the absent-minded professor is ancient history, along comes Samuel Clay Brooke to bring the stereotype back to life. But talk to him about something he knows, Hogarth or Blake, he can be brilliant."

"Dead white men," said Abbas with a sneer. "That is no surprise. He is a dead white man himself."

"Darling, don't be an ass," said Elena. "You are very fond of several dead white men."

He gave her a cold, hard look. Then his mouth broke into a thin smile like a crack in plaster. "No, I prefer *live* white men." And he stared across the table at Daniel.

They all noticed the stare. Only Ross didn't know what it meant.

Daniel was glad that Jane and Samuel were gone. Abbas was in a strange, unpredictable mood. He could feel Zack beside him, watching with his usual warm, wary concern. Part of Daniel wished that Zack weren't here either.

Elena turned to Ross. "Another movie about Paris I love? *Last Tango in Paris*. Do you know *Last Tango*?"

"Know it?" Ross laughed. "Lady, I've lived it. Everything except getting shot while chewing gum."

"Yes. I can see that. You are like Brando," she teased. "But you are much nicer than Brando. Who would want to kill you?"

"Nobody at this table," said Abbas.

Their drinks arrived. The Rohanis had not eaten dinner, but Abbas said he wasn't hungry.

"It is your funeral," said Elena, and she ordered a hamburger.

Abbas knocked back his scotch and ordered a beer. Daniel decided it was a good sign that he switched to beer.

"So you served in Vietnam?" Elena said to Ross. "You seem much too quiet and civilized to make a good soldier."

"I was a terrible soldier," said Ross. "But no worse than I am at half the stuff I try."

"What was it like? I am curious. How long were you there?"

Ross began to tell his stories about being an officer in Vietnam. They were good stories, without false heroics or false modesty—he had been a supply officer in Danang yet everyone experienced some kind of combat over there—but Daniel had heard the stories before and he knew what Elena was doing: she was flirting with Ross, trying to make her husband jealous. Daniel waited for Abbas to turn away and talk with him or even Zack to let his wife know that he saw through her and didn't care. But Abbas just sat there looking at Ross while Ross told stories.

Elena's burger arrived. She intently followed Ross's tale about a terrifying mortar attack while she ate the burger and bun with a knife and fork.

"Very interesting," she said when he finished. "I have friends who lost brothers or fathers in Afghanistan. I cannot help but compare the two experiences."

"Yes," said Ross. "Two very brutal, unnecessary wars."

Abbas jumped in. "With the Americans killing Buddhists and the Russians killing Muslims," he said nastily.

Ross did not take offense. "We were supposed to be killing Communists, but yes, other people got killed. Buddhists and Catholics and anyone else who got in the way. It was a vile war."

Elena was staring at her husband, reading more in his words than the others could. "Do not play Third World with us," she said. "You are First World, Abbas. You are the West. You and your brother and your wealthy family. Do not play the victim. It isn't pretty. Now that the Second World is dead, I am more Third World than you are."

"Yes, the Soviet Union is dead," Abbas shot back. "Goodbye and good riddance. They cannot kill Muslims anymore." He glared at her, already thinking about something else. "My wealthy family is not so terrible when you need them to put bread on our table."

Elena kept her temper. "I was not attacking your family. I was only saying you cannot pretend to be Third World."

"Because only *you* are the victim, only *you* have that right?"

Daniel glanced at Zack and Ross, wondering if they understood this better than he did. The surface argument was in a foreign language, although the deeper argument seemed clear enough.

"Please," said Elena. "We will not play haves and have-nots tonight."

"You started it," said Abbas. "You sit here, surrounded by admirers like a queen bee, everyone giving you homage, and you claim *you* are neglected, *you* are the victim." He shook his head. "You are ridiculous."

"I am not the one playing victim," said Elena. "Besides, *you* are the queen bee here. You have more admirers than I."

"Guys!" cried Zack. And he laughed, a deliberate, professional, intervention laugh. "You're not alone tonight. You're with other people. I don't know what you're trying to act out, but it's not good."

"See!" said Elena. "You make us look ridiculous to our friends."

"Me?" said Abbas. "Yes. It is always my fault. Always me." He closed his eyes and scowled. "I have a headache. A terrible headache. Daniel, my friend? My muscles are in knots. Can you rub my neck and shoulders?"

He said it so naturally that Daniel innocently got up and came around the table. Only when he saw everyone look at him did he realize what a meaning-ful request it was.

"Rub-a-dub-dub," he joked as he began to knead Abbas's shoulders. The skin was warm under the shirt, the muscles like rope; there was a delicate feathering of untrimmed black hair on his neck.

Daniel stood behind the husband and wife. He could not see Abbas's face, but Elena had turned her head just enough to look at her husband—she had a profile like a bird woman by Grandville, the nineteenth-century cartoonist, beautiful yet spooky. Daniel wondered what the other people at the Green Leafe thought. This probably looked perfectly harmless outside the intimate circle of their table.

"Hmmm, nice," said Abbas. "You are so nice. You cannot believe what a nice, warm, affectionate man Daniel can be."

The words were as startling as a tongue kiss in public, yet Daniel's first re-action was to be pleased. Fear and embarrassment followed, but first he felt flattered, touched. He saw Ross looking wide-eyed, finally understanding. He saw Zack looking worried, his attention focused on Elena. He couldn't guess the expression on Abbas's face: triumphant, indifferent, innocent?

A pack of girls at the front of the room began to shriek like parrots, but they were laughing at a boy who danced by their table with both wrists perched on his head, fingers wiggling like antlers.

"Thank you," said Abbas, and he reached up and clutched Daniel's left hand and warmly squeezed it. "I feel much better."

Daniel came back around and sheepishly sat down again, afraid to look the others in the eye.

"What do we owe?" asked Elena, snapping her purse open. "It is late and I am tired. We should be getting home."

"It is early!" said Abbas. "Stay. We are not going."

"You stay. I am tired. I am going."

"Do you know the way?" asked Ross. "I can walk you back."

"Thank you, I can find my way." She paused. "Unless you were intending to go, too."

"Let me walk you. Please. I can take you across campus. It's shorter and you won't get lost." Ross made the offer sound chivalrous and harmless.

She turned to Abbas, as if to ask his permission. But Abbas refused to look at her. He lowered his head and lifted his shoulders, blocking his view of her.

"Yes, Ross. Walk me home," she said and stood up. "What do we owe?" she repeated.

"That's okay," said Zack. "We'll take care of this. Our treat." He was watching Ross, trying to read his intentions or signaling him to be careful. Ross only smiled.

"Gentlemen," said Ross. "I can't thank you enough for coming to my theater tonight. We had a great time, didn't we?"

Elena told Zack and Daniel good night, then faced her husband. "You will not stay too late, Abbas?"

"I will stay as late as I please."

"Fine then. It is your funeral. Let us go," she told Ross. "Ah, thank you," she said when Ross offered her his arm. She took hold of the arm in both hands and strolled toward the door, swaying along with the fierce, old-fashioned grace of a woman in high heels, never looking back at her husband.

18

ABBAS BLANDLY WATCHED THEM GO. He took another swallow of beer. "Is your friend going to fuck my wife?"

Daniel was too startled by the question to reply.

Zack, however, remained calm and reasonable. "I doubt it. I know he likes her. But Ross is too gentlemanly to try anything. He'll probably just talk with her, flirt with her, then say good night."

Zack was trying to keep the peace, but Daniel didn't want peace. He wanted everything out in the open.

"Why? Are you afraid Elena *wants* to fuck him?"

Abbas glared at Daniel. "She can fuck who she pleases. I do not care." He shook a cigarette from his pack, stuck it in his mouth, and lit it. "You will be coming to the studio on Sunday, yes?"

Why did he mention this in front of Zack? "I was *planning* to," said Daniel, wanting to suggest that he wouldn't if Abbas continued to be an asshole.

And then, as if to prove the point, Abbas turned to Zack. "You know about our Sundays, don't you?"

Zack cautiously nodded. "I do."

"And it doesn't bother you?"

"No. Should it?"

Abbas smiled. "That is right. You *are* a psychiatrist. You can only answer questions with questions."

"It's a bad habit, I admit. But sometimes questions are the best answers." Zack paused. "You haven't answered mine. Do you *want* me to be upset that you and Daniel are seeing each other? Does it make it more exciting for you?"

Daniel was surprised to hear Zack being quietly confrontational, gently tough. In all their years together, however, they had never had a scene like this, where he and Zack sat down with the third person to thrash things out. But there had been nobody like Abbas, who actually wanted this scene.

"Yes, I want my life exciting," said Abbas. "I don't want it too civilized. I need excitement or I go dead inside."

"But you're a husband and father," said Zack. "You can't get too uncivilized. You don't want to lose your family. You love your kids, I know. A self-contained excitement isn't such a bad thing."

Abbas narrowed his eyes at Zack. "What are you saying? You do not want me to run off with your boyfriend?"

"It never crossed my mind. I was thinking about your family. You need to be careful for their sake," said Zack. "You're feeling very dissatisfied and restless tonight. You're trying to fix it with a little drama. You want to get the people around you all excited and upset. But dramas have a way of getting out of control."

Abbas slowly nodded to himself, taking the words in and weighing them. "He is very smart," he told Daniel. "Very smooth. Now I know why you paint the way you do."

Daniel stuck his head out at Abbas. "What?"

"You are a passionate, sensual man. Your painting is too tight. It is like this." He held up a fist. "It should be like this." He opened his hand and caressed the air.

"My life with Zack doesn't make me paint the way I paint," Daniel said angrily. "I've always painted the way I paint."

"So you prefer mess in your life and order in your art? It should be the other way around."

Daniel snorted. "Like you? Your life is so damn orderly?"

Abbas smiled and shook his head. "You are such a pair. You play your little games and think you are taking great risks. But you are so safe, so American. Even your love is safe."

"Unlike you and Elena?" said Daniel. "You really love each other and that's why you're always at each other's throats?"

"Yes. Maybe. Why not?" said Abbas, trying out different replies. "But it is better than what you have. You are not lovers. You are only friends. Only chums."

The accusation hit Daniel like a slap. It left him too angry to speak.

Zack had listened to their exchange with one hand cupping his beard, pressing the hair around his face like insulation. He lowered his hand. "Abbas, why are you striking out like this? Are you bored? Or do you feel threatened?"

"Threatened? What could threaten me?"

"You spend the evening with two people you're involved with, your wife and Daniel. And your wife starts flirting with another man. She wants to make you jealous. She wants to push your buttons."

Abbas scowled. "My buttons are not pushed."

Daniel jumped back in. "Ross finds Elena very attractive," he taunted. "He could be putting the moves on her right this minute."

"Daniel, don't," said Zack. "We don't need to get angry with each other. This doesn't need anger."

But Abbas remained cool and controlled. There was a mean look to his eyes, but that may have been only his rectangular glasses. "Who is angry? I am not angry. My wife loves only me. Nobody else. She loves me and my children. That is all. She thinks she can make me jealous, but I know not to believe her."

"So you can fuck other men but she can't?" said Daniel.

Abbas gritted his teeth. "She is none of your business."

"But Zack and I *are* your business?" Daniel shot back. "You can say we don't have a real marriage, but we can't say anything about *your* marriage?"

Abbas resumed nodding to himself, more slowly this time. "You are idiots. Both of you. You do not know how easy your lives are. You do not have children to worry about. You do not have a crazy wife. You live in the nation where you were born, in a big house where you can make roots and keep things, where you don't have to always throw things away because you are always moving. And so you can take your time and paint slowly and feel things slowly. I do not have that luxury. I must feel everything quickly and intensely. Because I do not have so much time."

He leaped so rapidly from subject to subject that Daniel couldn't follow him.

"Your wife is anything but crazy," said Zack. "I find her admirably sane. Especially when one considers her circumstances."

"Her circumstances?" said Abbas. "You mean me? I am her circumstances?"

"You and a dozen other things. A mother with two children. A woman without a country. A poet without a language."

"A wife without a husband?" Abbas charged.

"I never said that. And neither has she. Is that what *you* feel?"

"No. Never. We are man and wife. We fight like man and wife. Other couples fuck. We fight. What do you and Daniel do?"

None of your damn business, Daniel wanted to say.

But Zack said, "We talk. And we fight, although more quietly than you and Elena. And we love each other—in our fashion. As I'm sure you and Elena love each other in yours."

"Pretty words," said Abbas. "Very pretty words." He turned to Daniel. "So will you be coming over Sunday?" he asked again. "Or have I spoiled that for you?"

Daniel was amazed at the man's blunt way of cutting to the point, of leaving him with no wiggle room. "Maybe we should forget our Sundays. For a while." He wanted to leave a door open. "I think we need a break from each other."

"You want a break?" said Abbas, nodding to himself. "Fine. Yes. Good. I am tired of you. I am bored with your body. I am bored with sucking your cock and jacking you off. I need a younger, better, braver lover. You have become nothing but a hassle." He spoke flatly, drily, as if these were facts, nothing more. But he must be infuriated that Daniel could even think of ending the sex, which was why he ended it for them. He stood up. "Good night. Goodbye. Good riddance." He turned and walked away, his steps quickening as he passed through the café to the front door.

None of the students noticed his exit, but adults are invisible to students. Realizing how public their argument had been, Daniel nervously looked around: only townies remained at their end of the café—the faculty were gone.

Abbas's cigarette was still burning in the ashtray. Zack reached over and carefully stubbed it out. "Let's pay the check and get out of here." He was taking deep breaths, as if he'd just climbed a long flight of stairs. He had been so calm and detached during the scene, yet now he was breathing like a man who'd been in a ferocious quarrel.

"Zack?" said Daniel. "Honey?"

"I'm fine," said Zack. "Really." He produced a thin, embarrassed smile. "It's all just catching up with me, that's all. Let's go. Okay?"

⁓ ⁓

"I'm sorry. So damn sorry you were exposed to that," said Daniel when they were outside and walking home.

"Not your fault. Or rather, it's as much my fault as yours. I'm the one who insisted we get together. Well, I *wanted* to get to know them better."

They were cutting across campus toward Jamestown Road, already performing their postmortems on the evening. They had to keep their voices down. The old mansard-roofed dormitories stood asleep around them like fat brick prison ships.

"It *was* your idea," Daniel conceded. "But I don't think either of us could guess how crazy he would get when we were all together."

"He's not crazy," said Zack—it was a word he did not let anyone use lightly. "He's just unhappy and uncertain."

"He sounded drunk at times."

"He did, only I suspect that's the language difference. The brakes are off when you speak a foreign language, so he sounded uninhibited and tipsy. I assume he believes everything he said."

Daniel wondered if Zack were referring to Abbas being sick of sucking Daniel's cock, et cetera. Or was he thinking about the accusation that he and Zack were only friends, only chums?

"And he was jealous of Ross, right? I didn't just imagine that?"

"Oh yeah, Elena certainly knows how to make her man jealous," said Zack. "We should give Ross a call as soon as we get home. To make sure he didn't have a run-in with Abbas."

Daniel felt oddly indignant that Abbas had been jealous, as if he still owned his wife no matter whom he was fucking himself. It seemed dishonest and fake. Only why should that matter to Daniel? It didn't. Not at all.

"You mess around with a guy a couple of times and you think you know him," he admitted. "But I feel like I don't know him. I'd never seen his mean side before. He's a little crazy, a little nuts."

"He's not crazy," Zack repeated. "He's complicated, conflicted. Like he said himself: he's had a difficult, scattered life. He has no core identity. He needs to be the center of attention. He wants everyone to love him. And when they don't, he gets anxious and angry and he lashes out."

Daniel suspected there was a diagnostic name for this condition and Zack didn't want to use it. But Daniel didn't want to hear Abbas defined as a disease, not even now.

"It sounds like his family helps them financially," said Daniel.

"Yes, I've been wondering how they live the way they live. We both know how badly painting pays."

When they got home, Zack took Jocko out for his walk and Daniel called Ross. He called first at his house—no answer—then his cell number. Ross answered from his car.

"Confrontation with a jealous Iranian husband? Hey, sorry I missed that. No, I left a half hour ago. Nothing happened. We had a nice walk and chat. She did the old you're-not-my-type-but-I-enjoy-flirting-with-you number. And I did the old if-you're-feeling-lonely-and-want-to-flirt-again-I'm-your-handyman bit. Besides, the babysitter was there. What about you? Looks to me like *your* hands are full." He laughed. "I thought *something* might be up. That's why I thought there might be room with me."

"It's not as interesting as you think," said Daniel. "I'll tell you later. Just wanted to make sure you got out in one piece. Good night."

Zack returned, and Daniel told him that Ross was fine. They got ready for bed and ended up in Daniel's room, lounging on the covers with Jocko and continuing the postmortems.

"They are their own country," said Zack. "Like any couple. But they're more their own country than others. Well, they have to be."

"It was fun while it lasted," said Daniel, "but I'm glad it's over. I knew it'd end sooner or later. But better now, when it was just a little nutty, than later, when it got really nutty."

"And we got to visit another country. You more than me. But we got a close look at other lives without going too far from home."

Zack was his usual calm, easy self, and Daniel was glad. This calm sometimes annoyed him, but not tonight. Daniel noticed Zack was careful not to say anything that might smack of I-told-you-so.

Back in their younger years of threeways, they often found that they enjoyed analyzing the evening afterward more than they enjoyed the event itself. As a result, they had a good time even when they struck out. Tonight felt as good as the old days, maybe better.

19

THE NEXT DAY WAS SATURDAY, and Daniel went to the pool for his swim. He was relieved that Abbas and the kids weren't there. In the afternoon he worked with Zack in the yard, raking and bagging leaves. He wished they could burn the fallen foliage—he loved the smell—but open fires were no longer allowed. On Sunday he and Zack took a long walk after breakfast in Colonial Williamsburg. It was a beautiful day with everything in warm shades of brown, orange, or yellow: trees, bricks, grass, and sunlight. They could not hold hands here, and it was never in their body grammar anyway, but twice Zack bumped shoulders with Daniel as they walked down Duke of Gloucester Street, as if to say hello. Not until the afternoon, when Daniel used to visit Andrews Hall, did he think about Abbas again. The fucker must be happily painting away. Oils or semen, it didn't matter to him how he made his mark. Daniel was glad it was over.

That evening, however, a sadness fell over him like the drab sadness of Sunday nights when he was a teenager and Sunday was a school night. It had been only sex, but sex can't help promising something beyond itself, a new and different life. The habit of hope still clung to sex. Now hope was gone. Daniel reminded himself that sex might start out as fun but it always ended badly, in pain or boredom, sorrow or resentment. He fixed a good dinner for

Zack and himself that night—steak and salad—and afterward they watched a new DVD of Chaplin two-reelers and Daniel felt better.

He woke up the next day, Monday, feeling exhausted, barely able to get out of bed. He wondered if he were coming down with the flu. Luckily, Monday was Fundamentals of Form, which he could teach in his sleep. Two hours of student conferences were scheduled for the afternoon, but his energy had returned by then.

Daniel gave each student fifteen minutes, which colleagues found overly generous, but his students enjoyed talking about their art—"processing"—more than they enjoyed doing it, and Daniel indulged them. The two hours passed painlessly. He thought he was done for the day when Maureen Clark stuck her head in the door.

"Mr. Wexler? You got a minute?"

Maureen wasn't scheduled, she wasn't even taking a class with him, but Daniel told her to come in. He always enjoyed chatting with Maureen.

"Do you mind if I close the door?" she asked.

That surprised him. "Uh, no. Go ahead."

She closed the door and sat down. "Mr. Wexler, you're cool, right? I'm not making a complaint or anything, right? I just want to talk about this with someone I can trust. Can you promise this won't leave the room?"

"So long as it's a private matter, not a legal matter, sure."

"I don't *think* it's a legal matter."

Daniel was very nervous now. He should have known something was up: Maureen never called him *Mr.* Wexler.

"All right," she began. "Friday night. I was babysitting for the Rohanis on Friday night."

"*Yes?*"

"But first let me say how much I like them. Really. The husband and wife and kids. All of them. But especially Elena. Mrs. Rohani, I mean. She is so beautiful. And she flirts with me. I never had a grown-up woman flirt with me. I like it."

He should tell her that Elena Rohani flirted with everyone.

"All right," Maureen continued, and she described everything she'd done with the kids that evening: how they built a fire and roasted marshmallows and played Candy Land. She was one of those Southern storytellers who had to include every detail. Then she put the kids to bed. She was sitting at the fireplace, warming her sock feet, reading art history, when Elena came home, alone.

"She was so pleased I had a fire going. She begged me to stay and sit with her. 'It is cozy, yes?' " Maureen did Elena's words without imitating her voice today—this was serious. "And she said we should have some absinthe, only there was no absinthe, would I like some brandy, and I said sure, I never had brandy. And when she came back from the kitchen with two big old glasses like goldfish bowls, she said she was feeling all achy and tense. 'If I promise to give you a back rub after, will you give me a back rub?' And the next thing I know, we have a quilt and an exercise mat spread in front of the fire and she's lying on her stomach and I'm doing her back."

"Was she dressed?" Daniel hadn't spoken in five minutes; he was surprised at how angry he sounded.

Maureen made a goony face, as if this were the dumbest question imaginable. "Well, at first! But she took off her blouse and then her bra, and she said I'd probably be more comfortable if—"

"The kids were in bed?"

"Oh sure. They were upstairs asleep. And her husband wasn't supposed to come home until late, she said, so we had the house all to ourselves."

Daniel wanted to cut to the punch line, the kicker, because he knew where this was going. Elena was so angry with Abbas that she was determined to make him jealous, first with Ross Hubbard, then with a woman, a young woman, *a student*.

"It was nice," Maureen insisted. "All warm and friendly and nice. She's almost old enough to be my mother, but she has a beautiful back, you know. Like a cello. And the smoothest skin. She just lay in front of the fire, telling me where to rub. Promising she would do the same for me. But you'll never guess what happened!"

"No, what?" Daniel muttered.

"I heard footsteps outside, and suddenly the door opened and there was Mr. Rohani! Her husband! And he just stood there, looking at us, staring. I was so scared. I didn't know what he'd do." She drew a deep, frightened breath, remembering the experience.

"Did he hurt you? He didn't hit you, did he?"

"Oh no. He was sweet. Really." She bobbed her head around, looking goony again. She was unsure what the appropriate response might be. "No, he just closed the door and came in and said, 'Pretty. Very pretty. The children are sleeping?' And his wife looked over her shoulder, and they spoke in French. Which made me kind of nervous. But then he said to me, 'Here, I will show you how to do it.' And *he* began to undress."

Daniel said in a stunned whisper, "The three of you had sex?"

"No way!" Maureen grimaced. "Just them. I only watched."

Which was even stranger, maybe worse. Daniel could feel his stomach knot up, as if he were in the room with Maureen, watching Abbas and Elena put on a show for her or each other or whomever they wanted to prove themselves. What were they trying to prove?

"It didn't start as sex," Maureen was saying. "It started as a massage and them naked, just talking, and me just sitting there, watching and talking with them. They said I could stay or leave, it was up to me. I took off the rest of my clothes, mostly to be polite but also so I wouldn't feel like a dirty old man. Or woman. But they forgot I was even there and got totally into each other. I couldn't take my eyes off them. I was fascinated. I've watched porno before, but nothing live. Have you ever seen straight people make love?" She rolled her eyes up into her head. "*Incredible.* They really got into it. I was afraid they were going to wrestle each other into the fire."

Abbas and Elena had involved a student in their kinky sex game? Daniel was stunned, hurt, disgusted. It had been different when he was in college. Weirdness happened all the time between faculty and students, and everyone treated the affairs, pot parties, and orgies as simply part of their education. But times had changed. This was an age of awareness, responsibility, and lawsuits. Abbas had exposed a student to something obscene and brutal, and not just any student but one of Daniel's favorites.

"And when they finished, they looked so satisfied. I was envious! So much so that when Elena apologized and said she hoped I wasn't shocked and was there anything she or Abbas could do—" Maureen broke into giggles. "But no, I said no, thank you kindly, I've had enough new experiences for one night. I pulled my clothes back on and told them good night. And they remembered to pay me for babysitting—I forgot. But I went back to my dorm and had the damndest time falling asleep."

Daniel studied Maureen, with her freckles and short red hair—she looked like a farm girl despite her pierced eyebrow—and tried to imagine her sitting naked in firelight, watching a husband and wife fuck. And he couldn't, not in a hundred years.

"How do you feel now?" he asked. "Do you feel guilty? Confused? Do you need to talk to anyone else?" Did he actually want to involve Zack?

"I feel fine," said Maureen. "Really. Very fine right now. I needed to talk with someone, because keeping this a secret was making me feel like a pervert. I couldn't talk about it without getting people in trouble. But telling you, I don't feel like a pervert anymore. It was a privilege, wasn't it? An adventure. Not every day that you get to be part of a primal scene like that."

She was tough and cool. She was an art student, for chrissake. She should be fine. "You're right," said Daniel. "You can't tell anyone else. We don't want to get the Rohanis in trouble."

"Oh no. Absolutely not. But if anything else happens, I can come back and talk to you, right?"

The idea that this could continue produced a new knot in Daniel's stomach. "Do you think something else will happen?"

"I don't know. I have him for painting, you know. I babysit for them. And I really like her."

"Maureen, how old are you?"

"Twenty-one."

She seemed sixteen, but she was old enough to know her own mind. She was certainly legal.

"It's not my job to tell you what to do," he said. "*But.* I think you should cool it with them. Keep your distance. For now anyway. Because things like this can get out of hand."

"I like her *a lot.*"

"But you have him for a teacher. This could get him in trouble. More important, I think you can get hurt emotionally."

"Really?"

"They're a married couple. They're working out their own shit. You don't need to be drawn into it. I can't tell you what to do—and please, come talk to me if anything else *does* happen. But I think you should keep your distance."

"Yeah, I see your point. It's no good for me to have a crush on a married woman." She sighed once, then again. "But yeah, I'll keep my distance from her. But I got him for Advanced Painting. Where, in fact, I gotta go next."

"Today?" She was taking a class with a teacher whom she had seen fuck his wife?

She looked at her watch. "Oh shit, I'm late." She jumped up. "But this has been a big help, Wexler. Really. Thanks loads. I'll let you know what happens. Bye." She opened the door and flew out.

Daniel got up and went into the hallway, but she was already turning the corner. He did not call after her.

She'll be fine, he told himself. She's a tough little cookie, a curious cat who can experience all manner of things without curiosity killing her. He returned to his desk, shaking his head over Maureen, trying to be amused. He must have displayed the same improbable combination of innocence and ruthlessness when he was her age.

But he was furious with the Rohanis, both of them, for using Maureen. Elena had wanted to make Abbas jealous, and it was no skin off her nose if she did it with a man or a woman. Abbas had wanted to prove to Elena that *he* was the center of her world, that she craved *his* dick, no matter where his dick had been. So he fucked her in front of the babysitter, wanting a witness to make their fuck more real. Daniel didn't picture the scene—he hadn't pictured it when Maureen told her story; he refused to picture it now—yet his stomach continued to twist and churn as if the experience had gone straight into his body without being seen, not even in his mental eye.

He had been right to tell Maureen that this couple was crazy and she should keep away. But he couldn't just leave things there. He could not go home with his moral indignation still stewing in his gut. He needed to confront Abbas and set the selfish bastard straight.

Daniel left his office and headed down the hall. He would look into the studio class and tell Abbas that they needed to talk today. Then Daniel would be committed to confronting him.

The classroom door was closed. Daniel didn't bother to knock. He opened the door and walked into a sunny studio and the eerie silence of painters painting, a concentrated stillness accompanied by a soft, wet scratching. A dozen students sat behind a dozen easels, copying something at the front of the room. Daniel turned to look. It was not a human model but an old-fashioned terra-cotta torso. Lopsided and life-size, it sat on a low stool like a mutilated corpse.

"No, no, no. You do not understand. My words are going inside one ear and out the other."

Abbas was scolding a student, Derek Sinclair, at his easel. Then he saw Daniel—and his face brightened. His eyes actually lit up, as if he were happy to see Daniel. He raised one finger, asking him to wait.

Daniel felt like he'd been hit in the chest. Just seeing the man after Maureen's stories was as startling as a blow to his rib cage. Daniel almost said, Ooof. It wasn't hate, it wasn't even lust, but Daniel was not indifferent. No, anger did not leave him cold to Abbas.

"You think you know everything. But you know nothing. Scrape it off," Abbas told Derek. "Take your turpentine and cloth and scrape your canvas clean and start all over."

He's a terrible teacher, thought Daniel, impatient and arrogant. I'm a much better teacher than he is.

Maureen sat in the back of the room, only mildly curious to see Daniel here so soon after her confession.

Abbas came out from the forest of easels. He was smiling at Daniel, a warm, confident, welcoming smile. He turned to the class. "I will return in five minutes. Save your questions until then." He directed Daniel back into the hall. It was as if he'd arranged this meeting. "I must show you something."

Daniel was too confused to speak. He followed Abbas around the corner to his private studio.

Abbas unlocked the door and turned on the light in the room where they used to trick. He went straight to a new canvas on the floor, a big square of stretched material that looked empty except for a few curved lines drawn in charcoal. Abbas pointed at it, shook his head, and began to chuckle.

"Look!" he said. "Just look!"

"I don't see anything."

"Exactly! I could not paint this weekend. I could not even begin. I set up my canvas, I set out my colors. And nothing. I could not even lay down a ground. I could not decide what color it should be. My mind was a total blank."

"It happens to us all."

"Not to me." Abbas continued to chuckle, finding his failure weirdly funny. He seemed like a different man from Friday night, but he was always different away from his wife.

Daniel couldn't see his point. He plunged ahead. "You realize, don't you, the school has very strict rules regarding sexual relations between faculty and students."

Abbas looked puzzled. "Oh? What did the girl tell you?"

Too late, Daniel realized he might turn Maureen's teacher into her enemy. "It wasn't her fault. It slipped out. I made her tell me the rest of what happened."

But Abbas was neither angry nor guilty. "So she will have told you we did not have relations with her, only each other. We did not force her to stay." He smirked. "She got quite the eyeful."

And Daniel lost it. "Dammit, Rohani! What you and Elena do to get your kicks is none of my business. But when you involve a student, you involve the school. Maureen is someone I've known for a long time. Luckily for you, she's not someone who's going to flip out. But you and Elena were using her, and I don't appreciate it."

Abbas remained calm. "What is this really about, Daniel? This is not about your student. This is about me." He was still smirking. "You are jealous. Terribly jealous. You talk like a man in love." His smirk softened into a smile. "That is so sweet."

Daniel was stunned, embarrassed, furious.

"That's ridiculous!" said Daniel. "You don't know what you're talking about."

"Oh, but I do," said Abbas. "Because I'm in love with you."

And Daniel was stunned in a whole new way.

It's only his limited vocabulary, he thought. Abbas used the word *love* too easily. It had too many meanings.

"Bullshit," Daniel finally said. "You're not in love with me. You want me to want you. That's all. You want everyone to want you."

Abbas looked pained, almost contrite. "I am sorry," he said. "I know you cannot believe me. I was an asshole on Friday night. I said so many ugly things. But I was an asshole because I was in love."

"You were an asshole because you were jealous," said Daniel. "First of Elena with Ross. Then of Elena with Maureen."

"Yes, yes, a little. In both cases," Abbas admitted. "But I was most jealous of you and Zachary."

"Me and Zack?" Daniel hesitated. "Because you're in love with me?" He tried to put a sneering spin on his words.

Abbas nodded. "Which I began to understand on Friday when I fought with your boyfriend. Then when I made love to my wife."

Daniel tried to stay skeptical. He needed to remain skeptical to protect himself. "You wished you were making love to me?"

"No. I wished it was you and not the girl who was watching. So I could hurt you. So I could make you jealous." He raised his eyebrows at Daniel: Do you get it yet? "And I wanted to make you jealous because I loved you."

Yes, that sounded right. Daniel had been hurt just knowing Abbas still fucked his wife, so hurt he couldn't picture it. He pictured it now, not their bodies but Abbas's face: the Iranian husband always looked so happy during sex.

"I am jealous of many people," Abbas confessed. "I fall in love too easily. I love my work, my children, and sometimes my wife. But now I am in love with you. And the others must bear with it."

Was he sincere? Or was he only manipulating Daniel? Was he even aware how manipulative he was? Daniel resisted, but under his disbelief was a silly feeling of joy. It was fun to be loved, exciting to be wanted. Elation ballooned in his chest. Nothing Daniel said or thought could pop that feeling.

"If you fall in love so easily, it doesn't last long, does it?"

"Oh no. This is only body love. Love-affair love. With a beginning, middle, and end." He gestured again at the blank canvas. "But that is why I couldn't paint on Sunday. I was too busy thinking about you. I thought I could forget you and work on my work, but no. I could only smoke cigarettes and pace around and feel frozen."

The man was such a painting machine that he thought a failure to work proved his sincerity. The square at their feet looked like a great white bed.

"I thought this wasn't going to be about love," said Daniel.

Abbas smiled again. "Too late."

He really did seem like a different man today, sheepishly amused with himself, as if being in love were such an absurd experience that he found it funny.

Here was where they should embrace and kiss and declare that love was mutual. But they didn't.

"So what did you want to do about this?" Daniel said curtly.

"I think we should resume seeing each other. And let love happen. Let it have its beginning, middle, and end. But we cannot see each other's spouses again, because they only make us self-conscious. They make us jealous and unhappy."

"I'm not jealous of Elena."

"No?" said Abbas in surprise. "Not a little?"

"Not a bit." Daniel studied the empty canvas again, as if it could tell him he should say no to Abbas, declare this over, and walk away. "I'm going to have to think about this," he finally said.

"And you want to discuss it with Zack?"

"Probably."

Abbas studied Daniel for a moment, as if wanting to talk him out of it. "I suppose you must." Then he shrugged and sighed. "I should go now. I must get back to my class."

He went to the door, and Daniel followed. Then he twisted around, as if to kiss Daniel.

Daniel jumped back.

And Abbas laughed. "Ah! You do care. Good! I will leave Sunday open. Goodbye." Abbas grinned and strolled away, with the easy, rolling gait of a man who was confident he'd won.

20

Daniel walked home in a confused stupor of guilt and excitement. He felt as if he'd done something terrible, but he hadn't done anything yet, and it wasn't like he wanted to do anything new. He simply wanted to do what he'd been doing all along, only under a different name—maybe a more honest name than the one they'd been using. Nevertheless, the word *love* changed things, didn't it?

The sky was a dusky enamel blue over the playing field next to PBK Hall. Daniel crossed the street to Indian Springs Road, where it was night under the trees, with a spicy smell of woodsmoke in the crisp, cold air. He was walking down the center of the road—there was no sidewalk—when he saw a pair of headlights coming toward him. The car did not swerve to one side as most cars did for pedestrians but continued straight toward him, even as it slowed. It came to a dead halt. Daniel walked past on the driver's side. The window was down and Elena Rohani sat at the wheel.

He was surprised that the Russian woman drove, but why not? It was a nice car, an old model Saab, maybe secondhand, but it had clearly cost money. The car gave off a rich, baked aroma of clean laundry. Two baskets of hot, folded clothes sat in the backseat.

"Good evening," Elena said happily. "How are you?"

"Fine. Just fine." Did that sound sarcastic? Would she think he was lying? Did she even know about the latest turn in her husband's emotions? "I see you got your laundry done."

"Oh yes. And I wanted to talk to Zack and apologize for Friday. Many harsh things were said. I wanted to apologize to him. *And* you."

No, she didn't know, did she? Good. Let's keep it that way, he thought, at least for tonight.

"No apology necessary," he assured her. "Beautiful evening, isn't it? Give my best to Abbas. Bye." He strolled into the red glow of the taillights. The glow pulled away and she was gone.

Daniel followed the curve of the road home. The front of their house was dark, but inside the kitchen lights were on. The kitchen was empty. Daniel saw two dirty coffee cups in the sink. Zack and Elena must have drunk coffee here while the Rohani family clothes tossed in the washer in the basement. He could hear Zack downstairs now with the evening news. He began to fix dinner, a good, practical action to assure himself that life was the same, everything would be fine, nothing had changed. He was frying bacon for spaghetti carbonara when Zack came up the stairs.

"Hi, love. How was your day?"

"Fine. Just fine." They kissed each other hello, and Daniel was tempted to say nothing about Abbas.

"Need any help?"

"No. Go back down and finish watching the news. Dinner won't be ready for another ten minutes."

"Not much happening in the world today," said Zack. "Thank God." He went to the refrigerator, got himself a Diet Coke, and sat at the kitchen table. He looked so solid and reasonable.

"I ran into Elena outside. She came over to do her laundry?"

"Oh yeah. And she wanted to apologize for Friday. For needling Abbas and putting him in such a bad temper that he said the things he said. They were having a messy fight and she was sorry to involve us. But they worked things out."

Daniel could pretend he knew nothing. It would save him from having to tell the long, involved story of his double-feature afternoon. But he was fixing dinner, and that made him feel safe.

"Well, I got to hear from their babysitter *how* they worked things out," he began. And he told Zack about Maureen's visit, giving him the short version of everything she'd reported.

Zack listened with a look of surprise and growing concern. When Daniel finished, he was too confused to speak.

Daniel used Zack's silence to tell the second half of the story, about his meeting with Abbas and how he went to confront him about Maureen but they ended up accusing each other of jealousy. "And then he said *he* was jealous because he was in love with me."

"In love with you? In *love*?" Zack looked stunned.

"You think he's lying? You don't think I'm lovable?" They were getting too serious and it was time for a joke.

Zack didn't laugh. "No. I just— I believe it. So quickly that I don't know why I didn't suspect it before. In love? Of course."

"Yes, well, he falls in love all the time, he says, and this year it's my turn." Abbas hadn't really said that, but it was true to the spirit of his confession. "And he thinks we should resume seeing each other. Until we get each other out of our systems."

Zack was silent again. His eyebrows were down. His beard stuck out to one side—he had been pressing it around his chin while Daniel told him Maureen's story.

He was silent for so long that Daniel wondered if he should go back to cooking. He had stopped after finishing the bacon.

Then Zack calmly said, "I think it's a bad idea for you to see each other again."

"Why? It'll be the same as before. We just call it what it is."

"It's not the same. It's different now."

Well, of course it was different, but Daniel didn't want to hear that. "Why are you fighting this? Why do you suddenly want to play Dr. No? You were fine before."

"But then it ended. And I realized how glad I was it ended."

Daniel had been glad, too, but now he wanted it to continue. He had thought talking to Zack might change his feelings about Abbas, but as soon as Zack said no, Daniel understood he wanted to continue.

"You're not just fuck buddies anymore," said Zack.

"No. We're not."

"Are you in love with him?"

Daniel could have flatly said no, but he wasn't sure what he felt, so he told the truth. "I don't know. I like having sex with him. I like that he's in love with me. But I don't know if I love him."

"But he loves you. That's dangerous enough."

Daniel took a deep breath. "Do we have to talk about it? We always talk about it. If we just let it happen without talking about it, this thing'll run its course like the others and that'll be the end of it."

"No. This one is different. It's more complicated. There's more people involved."

"Yeah, he's married with kids. You don't have to tell me."

"And he hates me," said Zack.

"He doesn't hate you."

"He's jealous of me. He said so himself. And I have to say: I don't like him much, either."

Daniel didn't know how to respond to that.

"I can't help feeling that he's using you," said Zack. "As some kind of weapon in his marriage. As part of his fight with Elena."

Daniel wanted to feel insulted, but he'd heard a similar charge earlier today. Oh yes, he had told Maureen that the Rohanis were using *her.* "Maybe he's just using me for sex," he told Zack.

"But you agree? He *is* using you."

"Maybe I want to be used. It's fun to be used. It doesn't happen often when you get to be our age."

And Zack's expression relaxed. The fight went out of his eyes. "Is that what this is really about? One last fling while you're still in your forties? Your last chance at fun before you get old?"

"No. Yes. Maybe. *I don't know!*" Daniel hadn't even considered it, but of course it was a possibility. "Is that so damn bad?"

But before Zack could answer, the telephone rang.

There was caller ID on the extension in the kitchen, in case a patient called. Zack got up and went to the counter to look. "Oh shit," he said, but he picked up. "Elena, hi. Yes?"

He listened to her—Daniel could hear only the seethe of an angry voice across the room. It seemed that Elena and Abbas were having another argument. Zack frowned—it was a different frown from the one he'd worn during *their* argument. And he and Daniel were having an argument, too, weren't they?

"No, Elena. I wasn't lying. I thought things were fine. I just now heard about it myself. I also heard about you and your babysitter. No, I'm not accusing you. I'm just saying that we can't talk innocent parties and guilty parties here. It doesn't help."

Zack continued to face Daniel, wanting him to experience as much of this conversation as possible through his squints and scowls and grimaces.

"No, I won't talk to Abbas. This is between you and him, and myself and Daniel. Each couple needs to resolve this on its own. It's difficult enough with two people. Four is impossible. No, you don't want to give him an ultimatum like that. You can't throw him out, and you can't keep him a prisoner, either. Let him take a walk if he needs to blow off steam. Why don't you both take a walk? Take it outside, away from the kids. Remember them. You both love your kids. And it takes two, it always takes two. Ask yourself why you're so angry now when you weren't angry before."

Zack lifted an eyebrow at Daniel, admitting his words might also be about them.

"That was him going out? Good. Let him get his cigarettes. He'll be back. You feel calmer now? You sound calmer. Wait until the kids go to bed. Then you and Abbas can have a good long talk. If there're any problems, you can call here. Okay? Talk later. Bye."

He hung up and let out a long, amazed sigh. He was not only the "husband" here, he was the best friend *and* the psychiatrist. Daniel admired him for being able to handle so many different roles, even as he wished he might fumble one.

"She's really pissed off?"

"Like you wouldn't believe. Hell hath no fury like someone who thinks something's fixed when it isn't."

Zack looked shaken, confused, less righteous. Her anger had upstaged his anger.

"How did she find out?" asked Daniel.

"He told her."

"Honesty *is* the best policy," said Daniel drily.

Zack responded to the sarcasm with a tiny wince. "Where were we?"

"No place good," Daniel admitted, although he couldn't remember what they had been saying.

"But you see," said Zack, nodding at the phone. "That's another reason to break it off. There *are* other people involved. Not just the kids but Elena."

"She was fine before, she'll be fine again."

"She's not an easy woman."

"I thought you liked her."

"I do. But she's in the most difficult position here. She manages to keep everything in balance, but it's got to be hard."

Zack liked Elena too much. Daniel did not want to fight him about Elena. "Now I remember where we were," he said. "We were going to have dinner."

Zack hesitated. "Yes. You're right. Want me to do the salad?"

"Sure. That'd be nice."

They stopped discussing "it" and quietly fixed dinner. They worked without words, washing vegetables and boiling pasta, silently stepping around each other in their familiar kitchen dance. They didn't speak again until Daniel brought the two steaming bowls of eggy carbonara over to the table.

"All right, the situation *is* complicated," Daniel admitted. "But it's good it's complicated. It's good there are so many people involved. If it were simpler, it'd be dangerous. But he's not going to leave his family. I'm not going to leave you. Nobody will get hurt. Do you feel hurt now?"

Zack frowned. "I'm not hurt. But I'm worried."

"You identify too easily with other people," Daniel chided.

"No," said Zack. "I identify too easily with you."

Which surprised Daniel; it touched and confused him.

"Is it him you don't trust or me?" he asked nervously.

"He's selfish, reckless, and unpredictable. He's not a kind man."

Daniel paused again. "Neither am I."

"No, you are," said Zack. "Usually."

And that hurt, but in an affectionate, accurate manner.

"Look," said Daniel. "Every affair has its duration. Let's let this one run its course. It's my last fling. Right? Like you said before. And then you and I can be two nice, *kind,* old men together."

"And that's what you think will happen?"

"I know it's what will happen."

Zack thought a moment. "So go on a trip," he said wearily. "Go up to New York or down to Puerto Rico for a week. Fuck each other's brains out. Get each other—"

The phone rang again.

Zack irritably got up to read the caller ID. "It's the college."

"Must be a student. Let the machine take care of it."

"Get each other out of your systems," Zack continued as he returned to the table. "And leave the rest of us in peace."

The machine clicked, their recorded message played. An angry voice came on. "Daniel? Are you there, Daniel? Talk to me, Daniel!"

Daniel jumped up and snatched the phone. "Abbas?"

"She is making me crazy, making me mad. I must see you tonight or I will go nuts."

"Where are you?"

"The art building. If I did not get away, I was afraid I would hit her. I am so full of poison. Please, please, come over."

"I'll be right there." Daniel hung up. He was excited, frightened, amazed. He found Zack staring at him.

"What does he want?"

"He needs to see me right away. He says it's an emergency."

"To talk?"

"I don't know." And he didn't. He was so excited that Abbas wanted him that he didn't need to know his purpose. "I told him I'd go over right away. Don't worry. I'll be back."

"I don't care. Fuck it. Just go." Zack turned away. "I'll enjoy this delicious meal without you." And he dug into his pasta, as if he were upset over eating alone, nothing else.

Daniel knew he should say something to acknowledge Zack's anger or hurt. But words would lead only to more words. He grabbed his coat and left.

〜〜 〜〜

It was cold outside. Daniel did not run down the street. He walked—quietly, steadily. He did not know if Abbas wanted him for talk or sex or a punch in the nose, but he wanted to go to him. He knew he was making other people unhappy—he was making himself unhappy—yet he still wanted to go. He must be in love.

〜〜 〜〜

The lights were on in Andrews, but the first floor was deserted. Daniel went upstairs to Abbas's studio. The door was wide open. The room was dark except for the gooseneck lamp on the floor. The sofa was empty.

Then Daniel saw Abbas behind the sofa, angrily pacing in the dark, his face flaring up behind a cigarette. The confident, humorous lover of this afternoon was gone. "I have no time. Close the door," he commanded and ground out his cigarette on the concrete floor. "No talk. I have had enough talk today."

"Fine," said Daniel. "Me too." And he went straight to Abbas and got his tongue into his mouth before either could say another word.

〜〜 〜〜

What does sex feel like with someone you're in love with? Is it so different from sex with a friend or a stranger? Maybe love isn't sex. Maybe love happens only in the time between sex, when you are anticipating sex or remembering it. Or so Daniel told himself as he ran his hands over a muscular back and hairy ass and sucked on a thick, Camel-flavored tongue.

Both men were eager, rushed, careless, trying to pack an hour into five minutes. Neither had shaved since this morning; they kissed through thin masks of sandpaper. Abbas never broke into his usual smile, but he began to sigh like a man sinking into a hot bath, over and over. And Daniel found himself thinking: If I touch him here, will that express my love? Or if I get my finger here or my mouth there? He was sorry he hadn't brought condoms, but there are other obscene things one body can do to another to prove that love is shameless.

21

WHY ARE PEOPLE AFRAID? People are so afraid nowadays. Not just me, but everyone. But life is good. Life is comfortable. In America anyway. But people are so nervous. We live out at Kingsmill. It's a gated community. There's security guards and electric fences, and friends have to call ahead just to visit us. But this is Virginia. What's to be afraid of? There're no terrorists here. Or drug dealers or prostitutes or people like that. And I don't mean black people. You know my feelings there. We talked about race already."

"Yes, we have," said Zack impatiently.

"The Rock Church is very good about race."

"I know it is. Continue."

Fay Dawson paused. "Are you angry with me today?"

"Not at all. I'm just waiting to see where you're going with this." He carefully softened his tone. "Do you include yourself in this fear, Fay? You have a different understanding of your panic attacks now that they're over?"

"Oh yes. I'm not so afraid of being afraid," she replied. "I see now that everyone is afraid. So I don't feel petrified by fear. But it's not like the drugs have made me fearless."

"Good. They shouldn't."

Zack was not feeling as easy and empathetic this week as he liked to be with his patients, not even with Fay Dawson, his favorite. But Fay was doing better. She was off of Xanax, although she still carried a single emergency pill in a vial attached to her key chain like a lucky charm. She was still a Southern good girl, but not as nervously polite as she'd been six weeks ago. She still asked good questions about herself and the world.

"But everybody is afraid," said Fay.

"Of the same thing?"

"I don't know."

"Do you have any theories?"

She shook her head. "But I wonder if their being afraid is what makes me afraid. And that's why I don't love my children. Because I'm too busy being afraid."

Zack was surprised by how annoyed he felt. "Fay. I thought we were finished with that. You do love your children."

"I don't love them enough."

"What's enough?" he snapped. He paused and swallowed his irritation. "You love them enough to worry. You even love them enough to get angry. You can lose your temper and a few hours later feel full of affection again."

Fay noticed nothing odd about *his* temper today. "Which is easy to do with Melissa but much harder with Malvern."

"Oh? And what did Malvern do this week?"

Malvern was her sullen ox of a teenager, an angry boy who tried to burn off his hormones in bodybuilding and Bible study. The Rock Church did not allow dancing or dating, but their adolescent males behaved no better than secular boys did.

"I was so petty," said Fay. "So silly. He got home from football all upset. His coach was putting him back on second string after the last game. I tried to comfort him, telling him there were worse things in the world. And he turned on me and said, 'Yeah, like being a nut job, like being a psycho.' *And I wanted to strangle him.*" She quietly emphasized each word as if to prove her crime.

"You weren't being petty," said Zack. "That was an awful thing for him to say. You were right to be angry."

"I wasn't just angry. I hated him for it. I still hate him."

"Let yourself hate him," said Zack. "A little. But don't forget. He's a teenager. He doesn't always know what he's saying." The kid was a complete asshole, but with his own sexual and Oedipal issues, which they didn't need to get into. "He's much too self-conscious and self-absorbed right now to remember that anyone else exists."

Fay was studying Zack, frowning. Before he could ask what she was thinking, she said, "You expect very little of people, don't you? Is that because you're always seeing the worst in them?"

Zack was taken completely by surprise.

"What a curious statement, Fay. Would you prefer me to say your son *is* hateful and you should get rid of him?" He tried to deflect the remark back to her emotions. But it was true, wasn't it? He saw so many terrible things in people, so much hate and meanness, that he looked at everyone with lowered expectations. He cut the human race a lot of slack. Did he cut them too much?

"I didn't mean Malvern," she insisted. "I was thinking about me. You judge me far more gently than I judge myself."

"Fay. I repeat: I'm not here to judge. You already judge yourself plenty. You don't need my judgments on top of your own."

What would Fay say if she knew what was going on in *his* life? Two weeks had passed since Daniel declared that he and Abbas were not just fuck buddies but lovers. They were going to New York this weekend, with Zack's blessing, to visit galleries and museums and hump each other like dogs. That would shock her, wouldn't it? But it didn't shock Zack. Should it?

"With Melissa it's different," Fay was saying. "I can want to kill Melissa, but I always love her again five minutes later. But with Malvern, and Yancy too, once I'm angry, I stay angry for days . . ."

Was he cutting Daniel too much slack? Did he expect too little from him? Zack had been telling himself all week that Abbas was not a threat, that they were all being adults about adultery. And yet, it must be eating at Zack if the subject could pop into his head at such an inappropriate time as now.

"I'm not the tolerant, understanding wife that I should always be with him."

"Is he always the tolerant, understanding husband?" Zack said automatically, even as he understood too late that he'd missed a key sentence. He needed to give his full attention to Fay. He wasn't helping her, or himself either, by using her concerns to think about his own.

He spent the last ten minutes of the session fully focused on Fay. They discussed Yancy at length, his virtues and faults, her mother's dislike of him—he made a note to talk more about Fay's mother next time—and how his work as an attorney intimidated her.

"I worried for the longest time that I wasn't smart enough for Yancy. But then we joined the church and I saw he had his spiritual side, his frightened side."

Zack scribbled in his notes: "fear of Gd makes hsbnd lovable?"

"You don't like me talking about religion, do you?"

She must have seen Zack frowning. "Not at all. It's just that I can discuss religion only as psychology, not theology. I'm afraid I don't do it justice."

"Well, theology only confuses me," Fay admitted.

They finished for the day, and he walked her to the door.

"That was Yancy at the movie theater with me."

"Oh yes. Of course." The night seemed like months ago, but it was only two weeks.

"I'm sorry I didn't come over and introduce him."

"You don't have to apologize. It's a tricky social situation." Zack remembered feeling that the husband didn't want to be introduced.

"Did you and your friends enjoy *American in Paris*?"

"Some of us enjoyed it very much. I love the music."

"They don't tell stories like that anymore," said Fay. "All innocent and sweet. But times have changed."

"They have. But the big change is we can tell *all* our stories now. Back then, we had to keep most things a secret. And life looked simpler." Zack paused. Who was that for? "Goodbye," he told Fay. "See you next week."

Her crabby son sat in the Jeep Cherokee parked out front. They had agreed that Fay wouldn't resume driving until after Thanksgiving. Zack watched her get into the car, and he closed the front door.

He assumed his mind would immediately fill back up with the thoughts he had fought off during the session. But no, his mind remained calm. He couldn't understand where the sudden questions had come from today. He was fine about Daniel and Abbas—for the most part. He was perfectly fine about them going to New York this weekend. After all, he was the one who'd suggested it. If they spent forty-eight hours together, they might get their fill of each other. They could pack into a single weekend what otherwise would take months to learn. They could finish their affair—or run off together. Whatever. Zack was looking forward to the break, its peace and quiet, the long walks with Jocko.

He was back in his office now, sitting in his chair, holding the notebook with the Fay Dawson notes in his lap, but he didn't read them. He set the book down, opened his address book, picked up the phone and dialed.

"Elena? Hi. Zack here. I just had an idea. How would you and the kids like to come over for dinner this weekend? What? I could come over there. Yes! That's much better anyway. I'm a terrible cook. Will you let me bring dessert?"

22

D RAW ME A PICTURE!"
The boy slid the paper and crayons across the table.

"Sorry. I draw badly."

"He cannot make pictures," declared Mina. "Only Papa can make pictures."

"Many people make pictures," said Zack. "But not me."

It was Friday night, and he had just finished dinner with Elena and the children. While Elena washed the dishes—she refused Zack's help—he sat with the kids at the dining room table, trying to get to know them better.

"Why don't *you* draw a picture?" he told Osh.

"Picture of what?"

"Whatever you like. How about your family?" Which was what psychiatrists always told kids to draw, but Zack didn't know what else to suggest. "You, too, Mina. There's plenty of paper and crayons."

"I'm too old for pictures," said Mina, sounding absurdly haughty. She went up on her elbows, however, and watched while her brother began to sketch and scribble.

They were lovely kids, both of them. Osh had delicate fingers and the most beautiful eyes, large and dark, with heavy lids above and below. It would take years for him to grow into those eyes. His sister's eyes were dark, too, but less spooky, more at home in her face. A pair of silver hoop earrings emphasized her righteous dowager side, yet the sleeves of her sweatshirt hung sloppily over her hands like any little girl.

"You're very old, aren't you?" Zack told her. "How old?"

"Ten," said Mina.

"A good age. What do you want to be when you grow up?"

She shook a hand from her sleeve and counted off fingers. "A young woman, a mother, an old woman, a corpse."

Zack smiled uneasily. He hoped this was a nursery rhyme translated from Farsi or Russian.

"I cannot reach," Osh announced. "I must sit in your chair. No!" he commanded. "You stay." And Osh climbed into Zack's lap, dragged the paper over, and resumed coloring. Zack was flattered that the boy trusted him enough to use him as a seat, even though the little bird-boned butt jabbed his crotch.

Like father, like son, thought Zack. The Rohani men were the physically affectionate ones, the women wary and careful.

The evening had been pleasant, the food good—a spicy lamb stew that could be either French or Uzbek—the conversation harmless. Zack forgot how the presence of young children simplified emotional life, reducing it to crude outlines: emotions could only be indicated without getting fully expressed. But the family seemed content, the dark apartment felt warm and cozy. A fire burned in the fireplace, dishes clattered in the kitchen.

He looked over Osh's shoulder at the picture taking shape: a house like a tent under a green mass of threatening clouds. There was a family of four: two parents, two children, all with red faces. Did the red indicate blood or shame or racial difference? The four figures were all touching each other. They were connected and smiling. The green cloud turned into a great sheltering tree. The family looked safe. Whatever was happening in the strange world of grown-ups did not appear to worry the boy.

"Give them a dog," said Mina, pointing to a blank spot.

"We have no dog," said Osh.

"But we want one."

Osh took a purple crayon and drew a dog with five legs. Or was the fifth leg his tail?

Zack was sorry he hadn't brought Jocko.

Elena came out of the kitchen, drying her hands and tugging the sleeves of her cashmere blouse back down. She was not dressed like a housewife tonight. *"C'est l'heure de coucher,"* she said, clapping her hands. "Both of you. Your father is not here to overrule me. I want a rest from my many, many excellent hours with you. Say good night to Dr. Knowles."

"They can call me Zack," said Zack.

"Not Uncle Zack?" said Elena.

"Uh, sure." Was she being sarcastic?

"Good night, Uncle Zack," sang Osh.

"Good night, Dr. Knowles," said Mina.

Elena herded the children up the stairs—they were surprisingly obedient despite the presence of a guest. "Don't go yet," she told Zack. "I will be back."

He lingered at the table, examining Osh's drawing, then got up and went over to the fireplace—the notorious fireplace. He knew only Daniel's version of the babysitter's story. It was hard to imagine this elegant mother behaving like that. Yet Elena was full of surprises. Zack wasn't entirely sure why he had come tonight, what he had expected to find. He had come mostly for himself, of course, for company. Part of him thought Elena might need help, but Elena seemed fine. They all seemed fine.

He looked around the big downstairs room, with its white plaster walls, dark oak trim, and drab college furniture. The chief personal notes here were the children's toys and Abbas's paintings. The ethereal blue canvas that Zack remembered from his first visit still stood over the fireplace with its dense pattern of geometric fish and sea monsters. Propped in front were several small framed pencil sketches of Mina and Osh. They looked sweetly old-fashioned against the abstract painting; family life brought out the realist in Abbas. The pencil strokes were light and delicate, as if blown upon the paper like breaths. Osh looked lively and impish, Mina soulful and regal. Zack noticed no pictures of Elena.

Elena came back down the stairs. "Coffee or wine?" she said. "I will be having wine."

"Wine sounds good," said Zack.

Elena went into the kitchen and returned with two glasses of burgundy. They settled into the pair of chairs on either side of the fire. Elena lit up a cigarette, sank back into the cushions, and growled. It was a soft growl, but Zack braced himself for a question about Abbas and Daniel, a statement, a charge.

The two men had driven to Richmond this morning to catch a flight to New York. They had been together all day. What were they doing now?

"You have wonderful children," said Zack. "Lively but very well-behaved." He would not be the one to bring up their spouses.

"They are wonderful, aren't they?" And Elena began to speak Russian, a backward-running gobble of syllables with a soft cadence underneath. She was quoting poetry.

"That sounded lovely," said Zack. "Is that one of your poems?"

She nodded.

"What does it mean?"

"I do not translate well. But it means, roughly, you break my heart and I break yours, but it does not matter, because one day you gave me two beautiful roses."

"Nice," Zack said hesitantly. "I'm sure it's even better in Russian. But it's a concentrated thought. Both sad and tender."

Elena was gazing at the ceiling with her steel gray eyes, listening for her son and daughter. The children had their father's eyes, not hers.

"Do you miss Russia?" Zack asked.

She glanced down at him. "I miss the language but not the people. Russia is no longer a land of poets. It is a land of gangsters. I have not only lost my homeland but my homesickness."

"Do you miss Europe?"

"Yes. Paris especially. Berlin a little. But I was young and wild in Berlin. We are all fond of our wild times. Even though I was often unhappy there. I was poor and lonely and always falling in love. I was thirty-two—not so young—but making up for lost time."

"You met Abbas in Berlin."

She looked at Zack as if to say: Do we really want to talk about this? "Oh yes. *Une belle histoire.*" She took a gulp of wine. "We met at a gallery exhibit of his paintings. In the Turkish quarter. It is the gay quarter, too, but I thought he was Turkish. Except he spoke beautiful French. Much better than mine. I liked his paintings and he liked me and we agreed to meet for coffee. He told me right away that he liked girls *and* boys. I told him I was the same. He said he did not know which he liked better, but boys were more plentiful in Berlin. He was seeing a boy at the time. We became good friends and saw each other often. I would help with his letters and applications and catalogs. He would help with my French. Meanwhile my heart was being hurt by girls and his by boys. We were a safe house for each other. Until one cold October day, when he was miserable over a pretty Dutch boy, we were walking in the Tiergarten and he said, 'I want to have children. Do you want children? My family will give me all the money I need whenever I marry. Does this interest you?' And it did. Very much."

"His family has money?"

"Oh yes. They are rich. The parents are dead now, and Hassan, the big brother, has gone back to Iran. He is a banker, but he works with the mullahs, representing them overseas. He does not approve of Abbas's art. But he still sends the money that his father promised."

Zack had suspected something like this. He wasn't surprised about the family money. He just wasn't sure what it meant.

"Do I shock you?" said Elena. "I did not marry for the money."

"I wasn't thinking that."

"But the money made it possible. We were to be a white marriage. *Un mariage blanc?* You know the phrase? But we did not stay white. Not only because we wanted children but because Abbas is often horny. He is ten years younger than I. He doesn't care who he screws, he will even screw his wife. We still have sex, you know. Even now."

"So I heard."

"Oh yes. Little birds." She smiled, slightly embarrassed. "Many little birds. The town is full of little birds." Her lips parted for a sigh. "As he grows older he does not want the sex with me so much. Which is fine. I do not love the sex. But I do love him, and I enjoy the sex as a coin of his affection. I never fell in love, but one day I woke up and understood I loved him. Does this sound crazy?"

"Not at all."

"This love can be like pride. Like jealousy. It can be as bad as romantic love. I want to have him to myself. I do very stupid things. What is happening now is all my fault."

"What's your fault?"

She looked at him as if he'd insulted her intelligence. "Our husbands. What is happening between our husbands."

Here they were. They could postpone it no longer.

"I pushed my luck," she admitted. "Such a curious phrase. Pushing my luck. I should not have forced things by bringing everyone together. I thought I could break them apart by making Abbas jealous. I was in a devilish mood that night. I rubbed it in my husband's face. I did not care who got hurt. Not your friend Ross. Not even that sweet-faced college girl. And I succeeded— for a bit. I won—for a bit. But in the end I made things worse. I threw them into each other's arms."

Her words were strong and melodramatic, yet she delivered them with dry amusement, as if she didn't fully believe them.

Zack said, "So it's no longer just sex? They really are in love?"

Elena shrugged. "I suppose. But what do you mean by love? There is love and there is falling in love." She shook her head. "A man falls in love because there is something wrong with him."

Zack laughed and nodded, and she smiled. She was pleased he understood.

"Abbas has his work and his family," she explained. "And he has sex. Daniel and I are both giving him sex. Why does he need more? What lack must he fill? I do not know. I cannot guess. What is wrong with Daniel? Are things missing in his life?"

"Little things. Human things. Nothing major." Zack was reluctant to get into Daniel's dissatisfactions for fear of betraying him.

"How does he behave at home? Does he act like a man in love?"

A good question. But Daniel was not a kid anymore. He did not moon around the house humming love songs. "To tell the truth, he's the same as always. A little gentler, maybe. More considerate. Distracted but not irritable. What about Abbas?"

"Abbas is gentler, too. So long as I and the children do not get in the way.

He is like he is when a painting is going well. Not until love falls apart does he become difficult."

Oh yes, they had that to look forward to. Whether it ended in a bang or a whimper, the participants would be miserable.

"What do the children know?"

"Nothing. Only that their father and his friend have gone to New York on business."

"Have they seen their father go off with other friends?"

"Oh yes."

"Osh seems fine about it. Mina doesn't look happy."

"Mina is being Mina. She likes to play everybody's mother, everybody's conscience."

There was a soft crunch from the fire as a log broke in two. A new flame rose up; the gold light illuminated their knees and faces.

"How long do you think it'll last?" asked Zack.

"I was going to ask you."

"In the past," he began, "the bad flings lasted a couple of months. The good ones lasted years. But the good ones were chiefly sex and friendship. The bad ones were unrequited love. Although Daniel didn't call any of them love."

"What does he call this one?"

"He calls it love. He says it's a love affair and asks me to bear with him because, like all love affairs, it will have a beginning, middle, and end."

"Of course it will end. Everything ends. Most things end badly."

She was only being rhetorical, but Zack could not leave the statement unanswered. "Not in my experience. In my experience most things go on and on. But when they end, they usually end for the better."

"That's a very American perspective."

"Maybe," said Zack. "Or a psychiatric one. But it's not as sunny as it sounds. We want things to end, we want to start over. But what looks like a bad ending is often just a bad middle."

"Except for death."

"Except for that," Zack agreed. "But even there, our end is always somebody else's middle."

There's something about English as a second language that fills an exchange with first principles, turning any conversation philosophical.

Elena lit up a new cigarette. She noticed Zack watching her. "Does my smoking bother you?"

"Not at all. I used to be a smoker myself. I still enjoy the smell."

"Ah, so you are a vicarious smoker *and* a vicarious adulterer."

Zack frowned. "I'm not getting any pleasure from this affair."

"None?"

"No."

"Not even in talking about it with me?"

She was very acute, very keen. He trusted her, but he might trust her more if she were a little less quick and knowing.

"I enjoy our conversations," he admitted. "I like our friendship. I want to think we'd be friends even if our spouses weren't seeing each other. But they've certainly accelerated the process."

"Very true. They have thrown us together. They have made us family." She examined her cigarette, then took a deep drag and released a luxuriant, silky cloud.

Zack couldn't help breathing in a taste, even though he knew she was watching.

Elena smiled. "You once told me you had said goodbye to sex. Is that true? You are seeing nobody?"

"It's true. I've said goodbye to sex but not goodbye to love."

"And you always slept with men, never women?"

"I was a late bloomer. I liked women, so I went to bed with a few in college before I understood liking them wasn't enough." He was both amused and worried by her questions.

"Do not look at me like that," said Elena. "I am only thinking aloud. I often think in symmetries."

For a second he thought she'd said "cemeteries."

"But we know that making Abbas jealous doesn't help. I like you better as a friend. And *I* prefer to keep the high ground."

"So you won't be seeing your babysitter again?"

She laughed. "Oh no. She is sweet. But I feel bad that she likes me more than I do her. I cannot encourage her. What is the time?"

"A little after nine. I guess I should go?"

"Oh no. I am only wondering what *they* might be doing now."

She wasn't completely cool or detached about this, was she?

"It's early for New York," said Zack. "They're probably just sitting down for dinner." If he were alone, he could forget about Daniel, but he couldn't with Elena. He refused to picture Daniel and Abbas enjoying the city he knew so well.

"You once told me that you never loved Abbas too much anymore."

"I said that?" She looked surprised. "And you believed me?"

"Well, yes."

"Sometimes I believe me, too. But peace comes and goes." She nodded to herself. "You are the doctor. Which of us is crazier? Me for marrying a homosexual? Or Abbas for marrying a woman? Or your lover for loving a married man? Or you for letting it happen?"

"You think this is partly my fault?"

"You are no more guilty than I. We are both letting it happen. But what else is there to do?"

"A patient the other day told me that I'm tolerant only because I think too little of people."

"Too little? What is too little? One cannot think less of people than I do. But yes. That is maybe my philosophy, too. Which makes me want to try to be kind to others." She smiled at him. "We have much in common, Doctor. We are in this together. All four of us." Her smile grew into a wide, defiant grin. "So which of us will have the big nervous breakdown before it is over?"

23

Their plane landed at La Guardia just before noon, and they caught a cab into Manhattan. It was a clear, cold, crystalline day in November. Daniel sat beside Abbas in the taxi, watching him watch the city skyline as it came into view: a jawful of needlelike teeth against a chalk blue sky. Abbas gazed, readjusted his glasses, and gazed a little more. He'd been to New York before, but a man has to be awfully jaded not to enjoy this distant panorama of Oz. Daniel, too, loved the sight, although he still saw the gap where the World Trade towers once stood, like a little hole in the sky. Friends who lived here reported that they also noticed the hole, even a year later, seeing it all over again with each new change of season and light.

The taxi dove into the tunnel under the East River and came up again in the middle of the city. Manhattan towered overhead, tall, impossible buildings defying gravity. Daniel's hometown never ceased to amaze him, but seeing it with Abbas made it seem even more fresh and startling.

They checked into the Larchmont, a small European-style hotel on West Eleventh Street in the Village. "Welcome to New York, baby," said Daniel up in their room, and he threw his arms around Abbas. He hadn't dared kiss or touch him on the plane. Abbas timidly kissed back and asked if Daniel would mind waiting in the lobby while he used the toilet. "Uh, sure," said Daniel.

The room was small, the bathroom door thin. Daniel understood perfectly even as he realized again that they'd never been together for so long as they would be this weekend. "Meet you downstairs," he said.

This was not just a sex weekend, a love weekend. They were here on business. They were here for art. They had appointments at galleries, or rather Abbas had appointments, set up by both Daniel and Elena. Tomorrow they would go to Daniel's favorite paint store and maybe a few art shows before they finished at the Metropolitan Museum, which was open on Saturday nights. In between, they'd spend hours and hours in bed, or so Daniel hoped. He and Abbas had never shared a bed before.

"You will not be seeing any important painter friends or collectors this visit?" Abbas had asked on the flight up.

"No, this trip is all for you," said Daniel. "I'm just along for the ride." Daniel didn't know any collectors, and seeing his New York painter friends, important or otherwise, only depressed him.

He waited in the lobby for half an hour until Abbas came down in a handsome green overcoat with a cashmere scarf, carrying his portfolio case. Daniel proposed they walk to the appointments. New York was a great town for walking, he said.

They headed up to Fourteenth Street and west toward the Hudson River. Daniel was glad to be back in the city, delighted by the variety of faces, the wealth of features. He saw more people walking one block in New York at lunch hour than he saw in an entire month in Virginia. There were all manner of noses and hats, skin tones and hairstyles. Colors were drabber in cold weather because of the winter coats, yet the people remained vivid. Daniel led Abbas north into Chelsea, the new art district. SoHo was almost dead, the galleries replaced by designer outlets and fancy shoe stores. The dealers had moved uptown to this transitional neighborhood of auto shops and warehouses. The overpass of an abandoned train track spanned a cross street like a black gate to Art Land. Most of Daniel's experience with dealers had been in SoHo, yet his stomach still knotted up as they passed through the gate.

Their first stop was S. R. Bernard, in the same building as Mary Boone and a half dozen other galleries. Dealers tended to clump in one location like vultures. The exhibition spaces were identical: white walls and blond floors. Only the art changed from gallery to gallery, although it didn't change enough.

Daniel buzzed at a frosted glass door on the fifth floor, and they were buzzed in. A male assistant came out from behind his desk. "Can I help you?" Abbas was already frowning at the pictures on the walls—sinister black-and-white photos in the style of Joel-Peter Witkin. Daniel introduced himself and said that he'd brought an important Iranian painter to meet Simon Bernard.

"Yeeeees?" went the assistant uncertainly. "Simon has stepped out. I'm not sure when he'll return."

"We have an appointment," said Daniel.

The assistant marched back to his desk. He was as blond as the floor, and remarkably tanned for November. He opened a notebook. "You don't have an appointment."

"We do," said Daniel. "For two o'clock on Friday."

"Today is Thursday."

"No, it's Friday."

The assistant pointed his chin at Daniel as if to say, Prove it. He let out a sigh, turned a page, and said, "You're Abba?" He pronounced it like the Swedish pop group.

"Abbas. Abbas Rohani," said Abbas with a stern, regal air. He knew how to treat servants, and the boy was clearly a servant.

"Uh-huh," went the boy. "Simon has you down. So he should be back any minute. Can I get you anything? Coffee? Bottled water? Fruit juice?" It was as close as he came to apologizing for his mistake.

Simon Bernard arrived fifteen minutes later, a large, pink, shiny man in his fifties with a black leather jacket and martini breath. He was profusely apologetic and thoroughly insincere. "Daniel Wexler? Yeeeees? Haven't seen you in ages. How are you?" He pretended to remember him but clearly didn't.

I must be in love, thought Daniel, if I can introduce Abbas to a dealer who forgot that he gave me my first show twenty years ago. Yet Daniel felt no pain for himself, only anxiety for Abbas.

"And you are—?" Bernard asked Abbas. His tongue poked the inside of one cheek as he looked him up and down. He seemed to like what he saw: a dark, handsome man who stood with his coat open, like a male model, displaying a zigzag-patterned ski sweater. "Rohani. Uh-huh. Come into my office. Did you send slides or CD-ROM?"

Daniel had instructed Abbas to send both, so that dealers couldn't claim they looked only at the medium he *hadn't* sent.

Bernard sat at his computer and rummaged through the debris on his desk: magazines, diskettes, loose slides, a phone bill.

"We brought a fresh copy of the catalog from the Paris show," said Daniel, handing Bernard the booklet. "And the CD-ROM."

"The Pompidou?" said Bernard, examining the booklet. "Hmm? Good printing job?" A habit of uncertainty turned the simplest statement into a question—one saw where his assistant had learned how to speak. Bernard took the disk and fed it into a slot. He began to open files. "Yeeeees? Now I remember. Very pretty. Egyptian? No? Iranian. Whatever. Deserty. But nice, elegant." He opened and closed images, refreshing his memory. "Too bad it's abstract. That was hot ten years ago. Now everyone is getting back to figurative."

Which was bullshit and it infuriated Daniel, yet Abbas remained smooth and courtly. "But it is figurative," he said. "Do you not see the bodies? The torsos and sex organs?" He leaned closer, keeping his tone low and husky; his French accent didn't hurt. "Growing up Muslim, I learned to hide the erotics of my imagery. But they are there, I assure you."

"Yeah?" Bernard clicked back through the pictures. "Very subtle. Very . . . visceral." He frowned. "Reproduction never does justice to this kind of work, however. I'd need to see the real thing. But you're out in Pennsylvania, right?"

"Virginia," said Daniel. "He's a guest artist at William and Mary."

"Even worse," said Bernard. "That's a weekend trip, right?"

"Come for a visit," said Abbas. "It is a dull town, but I know I can make it interesting for you." He was shameless.

Bernard winced. He disliked being tempted. "Sorry. No. My schedule is locked tight for the next six months. There's no way I can visit until next summer."

"I can wait," said Abbas. "In the meantime, let me show you this." He bent down and slowly unzipped his portfolio. Daniel was impressed—the man could eroticize anything. He lifted out a small framed canvas, one foot by two, and set it on the desk.

It was a smaller version of Abbas's orange gingerbread man, his body of bodies, but with Arabic mixed with his little alphabet men. The picture suggested a cross between a Persian miniature and a 1920s European abstract. It was more concentrated than the big canvas, delicate and exquisite, the portable Rohani.

Bernard frowned again. He'd been looking for a safe, noncommittal way of saying no, but Abbas wasn't giving it to him. One never knew how a dealer would respond when cornered like this, if he'd turn nasty or propose marriage.

"Beautiful," he finally said. "Abstract, but it has figurative sensuality. I presume that's the Muslim influence? I've never seen anything quite like it."

He must not know Klee or Miró; the ignorance of dealers never ceased to surprise Daniel.

"But I don't know how to sell it," said Bernard. "Beauty is out of fashion. This kind of beauty. People want their art raw and edgy. But fashions change. Maybe next year." He returned the canvas to Abbas. He didn't want this temptation either. "Can I keep your CD and your catalog? Let me show them to a friend. I'd like to hear what he thinks. You are in New York for how long? Pity. But I can reach you in Virginia, can't I?"

He was on his feet now, leading them toward the door. He had finished the meeting and was getting rid of them.

"This has been a pleasure, Abbas." *He* got his name right. "Thank you for thinking of us. If you don't hear from us in the next week or so, feel free to give me a call."

"Thanks for your time, Simon," said Daniel at the door. "It was great to see you again."

"It was good seeing you, David. It's been too long. Goodbye."

They rode down in the elevator in silence and came out on the street. "Asshole!" declared Abbas. "Big asshole! I come to him with a show in Europe and good work in hand. I even flirt like a whore with the fat pig. What else does he want?"

"Welcome to New York," said Daniel. "At least he didn't say no."

"They never say no. Not in Paris or Berlin either."

They started down the street toward their next appointment.

"But you handle yourself well," Daniel told him. "You were cool and confident and never lost your temper. I like the new piece." He pointed at the portfolio. "You work well when you work small."

Abbas accepted the compliment with a shrug. "One does what one can. Short of sexual intercourse."

"You might have come on a bit strong in that department."

"You think? I was afraid I was not strong enough."

"I thought you made yourself clear."

Abbas frowned. "But you are not objective here. You are more tuned to my body English than they."

Daniel couldn't argue with that.

"But yes, maybe I scared him. Only sometimes you can scare them into saying yes. Have you ever gone to bed with a dealer?"

"Uh, not since graduate school."

"Exactly! Only when one is young does one make *that* mistake."

The next gallery was Eye Wash, a large space over a restaurant by the river. It was run by a beautiful young woman named Sophie who wore T-shirt and jeans. She was better organized than Bernard and actually expected them. Nevertheless, there was a briskness about her, a know-it-all tone that didn't go away, not even when Abbas turned on the sexy smile. He was even smoother with a woman than he was with a man. This time, however, Daniel was not amused but worried, uneasy. Not because he thought Sophie would succumb but because she was so pretty that Abbas *should* want her. Bernard was a joke, but this girl was something else. If she had a sensual bone in her body, she should want Abbas. She made Daniel see again how handsome Abbas really was. So why did this Middle Eastern hunk waste his time with a middle-aged art teacher? Was it because Daniel was the only game in town back in Williamsburg?

He was relieved that Abbas got no more from Sophie than he had gotten from Bernard: a promise to consider his work. Which wasn't very promising since there were no paintings in her gallery, only sculptures and constructions.

One corner was filled by a piece called *Chance*: thousands of Lotto tickets were stacked in several houses of cards, high-rises of luck—two of which had already collapsed. It was fun, but was it art?

That was how things went for the rest of the afternoon. Nobody said no, but nobody said yes, and it didn't matter if the dealer was smart or dumb, polite or rude, attractive or ugly. Elena's contacts were as useless as Daniel's. They visited only six galleries, yet it felt like six hundred. None of the art on display elicited either envy or scorn. Daniel had forgotten that his joke about painting being what the dinosaurs did wasn't a joke. The work was all gimmicks, sometimes with craft, sometimes without, yet nothing was so absurd that one could dismiss it with laughter. Too often, the piece was already laughing at itself.

When they finished, it was after five o'clock and pitch dark, the bleak early dark of November. What now? The Dia Center had an opening tonight, but there's nothing like an afternoon of art dealers to kill all love of art. Another man might have felt angry, but Daniel was only depressed.

"Want to get something to eat?" he asked Abbas.

"It is too early. I'm not hungry." His face was tired and blank, worn out by all the insincere expressions that had performed there.

"We could go over to Eighth Avenue and look at pretty men."

Abbas lifted his eyebrows. "That is what you want?"

"Not really. But I thought you might enjoy it. Not something you get to do in Virginia."

Abbas thought a moment, then shrugged. "Oh, why not?" he said, and they headed over toward Eighth.

What Daniel really wanted to do was to go back to their hotel and take Abbas to bed. But he was feeling too sad right now, too vulnerable. The autumn darkness poured straight into his soul. He felt like he'd failed Abbas this afternoon. He needed to put some time between failure and sex tonight. It wasn't as if he believed he had to *earn* sex with Abbas—although success could brim over in carnal gratitude. No, what Daniel feared was that he needed sexual love so badly right now that it would break his heart if he didn't get it, or overwhelm him if he did.

They found a table at the Big Cup, the hangout for Chelsea boys who didn't drink alcohol—it seemed like nobody in New York drank anything but coffee anymore. They sat with their cappuccinos and looked around at the young men—young for Daniel but peers for Abbas. Why was Daniel doing this to himself? What did he hope to prove by coming here?

"Hmm. They are prettier than the men in Berlin," said Abbas. "They take better care of themselves."

The bulked-up bodies of a decade ago had been replaced by leaner, lighter builds, rangy, tattooed physiques that suggested a cross between swimmers and heroin addicts. It was all males behind the steamed-up plate glass windows, only a few in conversation. The others were reading books or magazines or working at laptops, so the café looked like study hall.

"Why do you need to look at sexy men?" Abbas abruptly asked. "You no longer find me sexy after I flop?"

Daniel was stunned. "You? How could I not find *you* sexy?" He never guessed that Abbas might feel *he* had failed Daniel. "I'm the one who flopped. I thought I could help you. I love your work. I thought they'd love it, too. I figured a man who had a show in Paris could make a dent in the thick skulls here in a way that I never could. I was wrong. I'm sorry."

"I was to be your revenge on them?"

Daniel was stunned all over again. "I don't think so." He wanted to dismiss the accusation, but it made sense, didn't it? "No. I was feeling virtuous and selfless today. Sharing what I couldn't have. Without envy," he insisted. "Believe me. I wasn't using you. I didn't mean to humiliate you."

"I am not humiliated," said Abbas quietly. "I am disappointed. But I am not angry. And I do not blame you. I am not with you because I think you will help my career."

The man could say absolutely anything. Daniel didn't really think he was using him for his career. So why *was* he with Daniel?

"But I am disappointed," Abbas repeated. "New York is as shitty as Paris. Shittier than Berlin. I do not know what I was expecting." His face looked extremely long tonight, his eyes cold and dead; Daniel had never seen him look so forlorn.

"Sorry," Daniel repeated. "I'm sorry to put you through that. But we'll forget about today. We'll have fun the rest of the weekend."

Abbas nodded. "How far is the hotel?"

"A twenty-minute walk. What? Did you want to go back and rest before dinner?"

"No, I want to go back and fuck."

His dry tone made it sound like a grim necessity. Failure was not an aphrodisiac for Daniel, but maybe it was for Abbas. Or was sex a consolation prize?

"And we can go out and eat later?" asked Daniel, pretending dinner was his chief concern.

Abbas shook his head. "I do not want to go out again. Can we buy some food and take it back? Bread and cheese. Some wine?" His face remained glum, yet more life came into his voice as he talked. "And maybe a nice dessert? We can stay in for the rest of the night."

"We could," said Daniel worriedly. "Yes. We could try that."

24

Outside in the cold again, walking toward a warm, promising bed, Daniel waited for his melancholy to lift, but it didn't. He wondered if he were too depressed for sex tonight. Maybe sex would only take him and Abbas out of their sadness for a few minutes, then throw them down again deeper than ever.

They went to the Jefferson Market on Sixth Avenue—it had leaped across the street since he and Zack lived nearby—and they purchased plastic tubs of cubed cheese, baby tomatoes, cold fried chicken, and various salads, as if for a picnic. Picking out different foods made Daniel feel better. They debated over dessert—flan or rice pudding—before they chose a small chocolate cake. They got a bottle of good red wine at the liquor store next door. They borrowed a corkscrew at the front desk of the hotel and went up to their room.

They set the bags of food on the dresser, took off their coats, and began to kiss. Their faces were cold, their hands colder; the room was warm; their skin began to thaw.

Abbas broke away to use the toilet. He returned with a box in his hand. "Look what I brought." Condoms.

"For you or for me?"

"We shall see."

The hotel room was much smaller than Abbas's studio, homier, cozier. There was not only a bed here but a carpet, a chair, a mirror. They left the room dark except for the soft light from the bathroom.

Abbas's look of grim need slowly gave way to his sex smile. It was different from the coquettish smile he had used with dealers or the tender smile he gave his son and daughter. This was a happily lewd smile, a toothy, selfish smile. Daniel enjoyed seeing it even more than he enjoyed the sight of Abbas's erection.

Daniel was pressed against the wall, both of them quite naked, when he noticed that the shade was up and a pattern of bright windows watched from the other side of the courtyard.

"We forgot to pull the shade," he murmured.

Abbas continued to grind softly against him. "Let them look. I am proud of being like this."

Daniel laughed. "Where's your famous Muslim modesty?"

"I am such a bad Muslim that I am hardly Muslim. But I am Muslim enough to enjoy the blasphemy of nudity."

They tried this and that with each other, in front of the mirror and in the chair and finally on the bed, saying such things as "Oh *yeah*," or "Oh, you feel good." Neither ever said "I love you" during sex. They'd had sex three times in the two weeks since they declared they weren't just fuck buddies but lovers. They used the word *love* occasionally in conversation, but always hedged with other words: "I still think I'm in love with you" or "Being in love can be a distraction at work." Daniel avoided saying it plain for fear it would sound fake. He could say "I love you" to Zack, but they had twenty-one years to give the phrase weight. This was different, more intense and elusive. He assumed that Abbas must feel something similar, although words in English wouldn't have the same superstitious meaning for him. Still, actions speak louder than words.

Daniel worked his lips and tongue against the bare root of him; he eased in his middle finger and pressed the testicles in his palm. But it wasn't enough. He wanted new thrills tonight, fresh obscenity. He came up for air. "I want you to come in my mouth," he said croakily. "Would you like to come in my mouth?" It had been years since he'd let anyone do that.

Abbas was squinting down at him, watching with stunned, rapt, prurient curiosity. He eagerly nodded and took Daniel's head in both hands, and they resumed. His hands seemed to love Daniel's head, the bald scalp and close-cropped hair.

Then his sphincter gripped Daniel's knuckle, clutching it like a wedding ring. Daniel removed his finger; it was like uncorking champagne. But there was no pop, no spurts, just a series of happy groans from the other end of the bed, and a sudden fullness in Daniel's mouth.

After he finished, Daniel opened his mouth and let it dribble out. He spat at what remained even as he tried to catch the taste for old times' sake. The bitter flavor was enough to remind him that sperm was not only a symbol but could be poison, even Abbas's sperm. The idea of it was more powerful than the fact. The fact of it was just thick saliva. It hung like gesso in the black tufts of pubic hair. Abbas remained flat on his back, legs spread apart, joyfully catching his breath.

Daniel abruptly thrust his face into the wet crotch, rubbing his lips and nose and eyebrows in the stuff. He clambered up the bed. "Kiss it off," he said. "Lick it off."

"Crazy boy!" cried Abbas, laughing. "You are crazy." He wiped Daniel's mouth with the back of his hand and kissed him there.

Daniel rolled off and lay beside Abbas, laughing with him, pretending he'd done nothing strange. What was that about? What did he really want? He wanted to do something extra to show his love, but there was nothing else, was there?

"I bet I know what you want right now," he told Abbas. "You want a cigarette."

Abbas looked down at Daniel's hard-on. "You do not want me to finish you?"

"Later," said Daniel. "I'm saving it for later. We got all night, remember?" He felt so close that his orgasm seemed a matter of no importance. He was still afraid of how he might feel once desire was removed and he would have nothing else to look forward to. And maybe, just maybe, he wanted to prove that his love for Abbas was not only sexual.

"If you are sure. Yes. I would love a smoke."

Abbas turned away, found his pack of Camels, and lit one. Daniel remained alongside, watching. They were spread out on the bed in a way they couldn't spread out on the couch in the studio, two hairy men, although Abbas was so much hairier that he made Daniel look almost Waspy. Daniel's skin was lighter, too, but not as light as he expected. He wondered if that would change in the summer, when they tanned. He assumed Abbas would tan much darker. Would they still know each other this summer?

There was no new painting here for Abbas to work on after sex, no home for either of them to return to. In Williamsburg they seemed to have sex to make a private, secret space for themselves. Here they were already alone, already private. Now what?

"Did you want to take a shower before we eat?"

"Oh yes, I forget," said Abbas. "We have hot water here. We do not have to rough it."

But the bathroom was small, the shower not big enough for them to wash together. Daniel sat on the lowered the lid of the toilet and watched while Abbas went first. His body was a reddish brown silhouette in the clear shower curtain. Daniel formed a tent of fingers over his nose for one more whiff of Abbas—a musky scent of semen and fishy smell of anus—before he washed him off his hands.

"You are serious when you say you like the little painting?" asked Abbas from under the spray.

"The portable Rohani? Yeah. I like it very much."

"Hmm. That is what Elena thinks, too. I wonder if I should do more pictures like that."

"Only if you want to." Daniel was surprised to hear that he and Elena agreed on something.

Dinner that night was a picnic in bed. They smoothed down the covers and spread out a towel so they wouldn't get crumbs in the sheets. They drew the shade and turned on the table lamp. "It is chilly in here," said Abbas. "I am sorry, but I must put something on." He wiggled into his ski sweater, but nothing else. He left his glasses off. Daniel pulled on his long-sleeve jersey, and they sat cross-legged on the bed, naked from the waist down. They ate everything with their fingers, including the rice salad and tabbouleh.

"Very Arabian Nights," said Daniel.

"I am thinking the Roman Empire," said Abbas.

Their penises hung in their laps like two droopy flowers.

They praised the food, recommending the items they passed back and forth. They opened the wine and poured it into two plastic cups from the bathroom.

"Did you know," said Abbas, "that our spouses are having dinner together tonight?"

"Uh, yeah. Zack told me."

"What do you think? Are they talking about us?"

"I hope not. But yes. Probably." What else did Zack and Elena have to talk about?

Abbas was eating a chicken breast, nibbling the breading, then biting the meat. "I trust Elena to speak well of me. She is a good egg. I know I call her crazy, but she is smart, she is tough. Other women are weeping machines, but Elena is tough."

"She doesn't like me, does she?"

Abbas shrugged. "I presume Zack doesn't like me."

"He doesn't dislike you. But he doesn't trust you."

"Oh? Why?"

"He doesn't think you know what you want."

Abbas looked surprised. "But I do. I want success and happiness and love. All kinds of love. I am not always sure how to get those things, but the things remain the same."

Daniel was just one more item on the menu, which should have pleased him, but it made him anxious.

"Why are we talking about our spouses?" he asked with a laugh. "We get away from them and we talk about them. Why? We have to remind ourselves what we're escaping?"

Abbas chuckled, too. "I talk about Elena only out of habit. I am not guilty. Not tonight. Because I paid her in full last night. She has no reason to complain."

Daniel blinked. "You had sex with your wife last night?"

Abbas nodded. "It was only fair. Since you and I were going off." He wiped his mouth with a napkin. "And I thought about you the whole time, so you should not feel jealous. Did you have sex with Zack before you left?"

"I've told you. We don't have sex anymore." Daniel's mind jammed shut on the image of Abbas fucking Elena while thinking about him. It was too confusing. "You know," he said, "Zack hopes this weekend will cure us of each other. That we'll fuck each other's brains out and I'll get you out of my system."

Abbas laughed. "I like the fucking-our-brains-out. But I don't want to get out of your system. Not yet."

"Good. I want to keep you there, too. For a little longer."

What Zack meant, of course, was that they would learn all there was to know about each other, replace mystery with banal reality, and become bored with each other. Daniel didn't want to mention that idea to Abbas.

He held out his plastic cup for more wine. Abbas obliged him.

"So does Dr. Zack have an outside friend? Who does he see?"

"Nobody. Not for a while anyway."

"And he is not jealous of us?"

"No. But he's not the jealous type."

"I am, you know."

"I know. So am I. A little." Daniel worriedly sipped the wine. "But I'm more selfish than Zack."

"It is human to be selfish."

Daniel nodded. "Sometimes I wish that I were even more selfish. Because then I'd feel less guilty. But that's something else I love about you. Your happy selfishness."

Abbas winced. Over the word *selfishness* or the word *love*? "You should talk to my brother. He calls me selfish, too, only it is not a good word for him. He believes all artists are selfish who do not work for God or their people."

"We are," said Daniel. "The good artists and the bad ones. Although there's no telling which is which until we're dead."

Abbas let out a loud belch. *"Excusez moi,"* he said disdainfully. "I often revert to my roots when I speak of my noble elder brother. The great Islamic statesman."

"Are you out to your brother?"

"Out?" He laughed. "Such a decadent, Western concept," he said with mock solemnity. "Hassan would never understand. And he's the family banker, so it behooves me not to confuse him."

Daniel knew there was family money, and compromises were probably required, but he was hardly one to judge here.

Abbas looked down and frowned at the tubs of chicken bones and leftover rice. "Are you finished? Did you get enough? I suggest we clear off the bed and take a nap."

"But I'm not sleepy."

Abbas smiled. "Neither am I."

He'd rather fuck than talk. Daniel didn't blame him.

They got up and collected the remains of their picnic. They threw most of it in the trash but set the cake on the dresser for later. Abbas bent over the covers, swatting at crumbs, exposing the long ovals of his beautiful ass. He turned around and tossed back his glass of wine. His erection had returned, sticking out like a little animal below the skirt of his sweater. Then he peeled off his sweater, and his erection was part of his body again. He climbed under the covers. Daniel pulled off his jersey and joined him. The warm, heavy blankets buried them up to their ears.

"So," said Daniel. "Feel better? Less depressed?"

"When was I depressed?"

"About art dealers."

"Oh, them. Fuck dealers. Fuck art." He put his arms around Daniel and drew their chests and erect cocks together. "What are the most orgasms you have ever had in one day?"

"Three," said Daniel. He didn't have to think about it. "You?"

"Six. When I was young and in Berlin and going to the baths."

"Six different men?"

"Three men at the baths and a woman at home."

"Hmm." He assumed the woman was Elena.

"Those were my rabbit years, my donkey years. But I enjoy sex so much more now. Especially sex with you." He put a hand on Daniel's bottom and kissed him on the mouth. "This time I want to see *you* have an orgasm," he whispered.

"Deal," said Daniel, and he stretched up and closed his eyes and fell into a warm, open kiss.

25

THEY WENT BACK TO BED around ten but didn't get to sleep until one. There was none of the postcoital funk that Daniel had dreaded. He was in his late forties now, and his orgasms were milder, less profound. The only odd note was when Abbas wanted Daniel to fuck him. That's who the condom was for: the married man. Daniel put it on, but he couldn't stay hard enough to get inside. It'd been too long since he'd fucked anyone. If he'd thought about it earlier, he could've gotten some Viagra from Zack—but no, he was glad he hadn't.

It didn't matter. That was a symbol, too, and there were other ways they could bring each other off. Afterward, they talked some more, finished the wine, and ate the chocolate cake. Then they did it again and Abbas fell asleep. He snored, yet so softly that Daniel soon drifted off, too. He slept through the night without a single dream.

When they woke up the next morning, Daniel hoped they would loiter in bed, but Abbas promptly jumped up to take a shower. "This is my one total day in the city. I cannot waste a minute."

Daniel loitered alone, feeling very sober without another body beside him, his own body thoroughly sated and oddly indifferent. Maybe he wasn't in love after all. But then a heroin addict doesn't feel like an addict when he's just had his fix.

Abbas came out of the shower, dried himself off, and did a few stretch exercises, as shameless as a cat. Daniel had never seen him naked in broad daylight, only in the drab electric light or twilight of his studio. The body in its delicate scribble of curly black hair was no longer opaque but translucent, luminous. Daniel wished he had a camera so that he might keep this image for later, when he'd forgotten everything else about Abbas.

They ate breakfast at French Roast on the corner, which was hardly Paris, although the café did allow smoking. They headed east to buy presents for Elena and the kids.

"You disappoint me," said Daniel. "You're my selfish ideal, remember."

"Oh, but I am selfish," said Abbas. "I am buying back their affection. Aren't you going to buy something for Zack?"

"I wouldn't know what to get. Whenever he wants something, which isn't often, he buys it himself."

Daniel waited for thoughts of Zack to make him feel disloyal and guilty. But no, he felt fine. Maybe he really was falling out of love with Abbas.

They worked their way down lower Broadway, buying glow-in-the-dark ceiling stars for Osh and a Hello Kitty knapsack for Mina. At Shakespeare and Company, Abbas picked out two recent volumes of poetry for Elena—Daniel was impressed the faithless husband knew what his wife had and hadn't read. Daniel then took him to his favorite paint store, Soho Art Materials on Grand Street, a holdover from SoHo's age of art. They entered a dark, musty, atticlike space lit by a trio of bare lightbulbs dangling from the ceiling. Fresh lumber and rolls of unsized canvas leaned against the back wall. Stacked on the floor or set on tables were flat, narrow boxes filled with tubes of paint—oil, acrylic, watercolor—neatly arranged like shotgun shells. Paint sticks filled other boxes. There were metal trays full of camel hair brushes, little drawers full of pen nibs, and shelves stacked with all varieties of paper. The place was like a candy store for artists, yet it only made Daniel sad.

Abbas stocked up on Old Holland oils, which were too expensive for stores in Virginia to carry. The colors bore magical names like Van Gogh yel-

low, Pompeii red, or Caput mortuum—an ashy purple of death. The bill came
to $425; Abbas put it on a credit card.

"Money is never a problem, is it?" said Daniel outside.

"Elena watches our budget, but now and then I splurge."

Walking up Lafayette, they approached a young male couple who wore
sunglasses and were holding hands. Abbas twisted around and looked over
his shoulder as they passed.

"Men didn't hold hands back in the old days when we lived here," Daniel
explained. "It wasn't cool. But gay men are more sentimental now."

"Take this," said Abbas, and he gave the bag of boxed oils in his right hand
to Daniel—his left hand carried the bag of gifts. He reached down with his
newly free hand and took hold of Daniel's free hand. His fingers were long
and slim, like a basketball player's.

They walked down the street like that for a full minute, while Abbas
looked at passersby, checking out reactions. The gesture did not feel romantic but exploratory, experimental. He didn't resist when Daniel gently withdrew his hand and slipped it into his pocket. The day was cold, and neither of
them was wearing gloves.

We are both only playing at love, imagining what love would be like,
Daniel decided. But we're not really in love.

They returned to their hotel room to drop off the purchases. Daniel proposed a quick nap—love might be only a myth, but lust was back. Abbas said
no, there'd be time for naps later. He wanted to get up to the Metropolitan
Museum, even though Daniel assured him it stayed open late on Saturdays.

⌒ ⌒

Abbas had wanted to visit MoMA, the Museum of Modern Art, but it was
closed for renovation. Daniel preferred the Met anyway. It was friendlier,
more varied—cheaper, too—and there was always a lively crowd on Saturday
evenings.

They caught a train uptown—Abbas had never ridden the subway—and
arrived as the afternoon sun began to sink into the bare trees of Central Park
behind the museum. The coppery light cast a huge blue shadow over the

monumental stairs out front. They went inside and checked their coats. "It is like a giant bank," grumbled Abbas in the Great Hall. "Why are there so many flowers?"

They went upstairs to the permanent collection, which was another thing that Daniel liked about the Met. The art here tended to be older, quieter. He found the past simpler than the present. He could admire work up to 1866, say, without needing to compete, without feeling judged by it.

Abbas, however, responded differently.

"Courbet? Ugh. I hate Courbet. Every government building in Paris has one. The only painter who is worse is Millet. And there he is. Disgusting. And Ingres. So overrated. His women look like shiny dinner plates. These are all French painters. Do they have nothing here but bad French art?"

They started in the nineteenth century and worked backward. Daniel thought Abbas might become less talkative, less competitive as they got further from their own century, but it didn't happen.

"The Dutch. Which means Rembrandt. Boring old Rembrandt. And Vermeer. There he is. Two, no, three Vermeers? I like Vermeer. Sometimes. I might like him more if stupid people didn't love him so much. Steen. Hals. Cuyp—the cow man. He paints cows over and over, the way that Bonnard paints naked women in bathtubs. I wonder if he ever fucked a cow."

Daniel tried to be amused by Abbas's chatter—some of it was funny—but the man suffered a bad case of the anxieties of influence. He appeared to be in competition with the entire history of art, trashing everyone in a nervous attempt to clear a space for himself. Daniel had met others like this, but they were usually bad artists, fakes. Abbas was a wonderful artist. He could afford to love *someone*.

There was a Thomas Eakins show in the American wing, which Daniel wanted to visit, but Eakins was a guilty pleasure and Daniel didn't dare expose the earnest, repressed American to this anxious, flippant Iranian. He might come away hating both men. He proposed they visit the Islamic gallery. Let him kill his own, he thought.

"No, Islamic art is all boring ornamentation," said Abbas. "Where are the moderns? I want to see the moderns."

Suit yourself, thought Daniel, and he led them toward the Lila Wallace collection in the back.

"I was wrong," said Abbas. "This place is not like a bank. It is like a train station. A train station full of terrible art."

They walked into a room full of Picassos.

And Abbas came to a halt.

He looked around, frowning. Daniel braced himself for a new string of jokes and insults. There are more bad Picassos in the world than good ones, but these were pretty good. A couple were great. There was the portrait of Gertrude Stein and a few bold, beige Cubist works. *Three Musicians* was here, jagged and colorful, apparently on loan from MoMA. Next to it hung *Harlequin.*

"Good old Pablo," said Daniel. "The man just shitted paintings."

He only wanted to get in the first wisecrack, but Abbas turned to him, looking insulted.

"Kidding," Daniel chirped. "I love Picasso. He's a giant. You think you know him, you think he's old hat, and then he goes and surprises you all over again."

Abbas took a deep breath and nodded at the paintings. "These are here?" he whispered. "I did not know. I have seen only copies."

"Yes, well, half are on loan, so we're lucky to catch them."

Abbas nodded again, in silence, struck dumb by great art. Daniel couldn't help feeling a gush of love for a man who could love an old warhorse like Picasso.

Then Abbas said, "He depresses me."

"He makes you sad?"

Abbas shook his head. "He got *his* foot into the door." He was angry. "*He* succeeded. Why can't I?"

Daniel didn't know what to say in response. Because he's Picasso and you're not? Because he was doing this a hundred years ago? Even then it was forty years before he got a break?

"Look at this." Abbas passed his hand an inch in front of *Harlequin,* a figure like a checkered playing card with a small head. "So simple. A pattern on a pattern. You see it in a book and it looks like magic. But it is only paint. A little sloppy. A little handmade. Is it so much better than my work?"

"I love your work," said Daniel. "You know I love it." What else could he say?

Abbas didn't seem to hear. "What am I doing wrong? I work hard. I give it everything. I paint the best I can. And what do I have to show for it? Not shit."

A young Japanese couple entered the room and went over to Gertrude Stein. They wore headphones and were cocooned in audio; they didn't hear the painters arguing in whispers. Daniel and Abbas were as invisible as ghosts.

Daniel pointed at *Harlequin*. "Why let this get you angry? This is great work. Can't you just enjoy it? We saw all that crap yesterday, and it didn't bother you."

"Because it was crap. It is not what I am doing. But this is good. I think I am better, but anyone can see I am almost as good."

Daniel admired and envied such confidence, even if it sounded slightly insane. But if you're going to be competitive, why not compete with the great dead?

"No, it is not enough to do good work." Abbas sneered. "You must sell it. I have nobody to blame but myself. I should have tried harder yesterday. I had my chance and I blew it. And we go back tomorrow and I have wasted this entire weekend."

Daniel felt like he'd been slapped.

"What am I? Chopped liver?"

The hoary old punch line elicited nothing from Abbas but a blank stare. "You are fun," he said. "Our affair is fun. But I have been too busy having fun. I need to work harder."

But an affair is work, thought Daniel. Especially with you.

"Bullshit," he told Abbas. "You work very hard. I saw you yesterday. You worked those dealers like crazy. You did everything but offer them your firstborn male child." But that might not sound like a joke to Abbas. "You don't need to beat yourself up."

"Easy for you to say. You have given up being an artist and care only for the other things."

Again Daniel felt slapped. "Yes. Maybe. Why not?" he replied. "There is art and there is life and a man has only one heart." He was automatically quoting someone but could not remember who.

"Well, I have three hearts," said Abbas, and he counted them on his fingers. "For my work, for my family, and for men."

Not for Daniel in particular, but for men in general. Fine.

"I think you're spreading yourself awfully thin," said Daniel.

"You think that? Yes. You would." He spoke softly, drily, sadly. Then he noticed the Japanese couple. They watched from the corner with a passive, connoisseur gaze. Abbas abruptly lifted his arms and shook the backs of his hands at them: go away.

They could not have looked more startled if a painting had made a face at them. They turned and hurried out.

"Degas," said Daniel. "It was Degas I quoted." He pretended that that was all that was troubling him, the source of his quotation.

Abbas bowed his head, as if to say, Sorry. Or, Things are fine now. Or simply, Let's not talk about this anymore. "What else is there? Show me some bad art. Bad art makes me feel better."

They spent the next hour wandering the Wallace wing, looking at everyone from Matisse to Rothko to Jasper Johns. It wasn't a great collection, but Abbas said little, making none of the larky, unfunny jokes that he'd made about the Old Masters. Both men remained in a mild sulk, although Daniel assumed Abbas wasn't sulking about love but about his artistic future. The Iranian resented not being part of this collection. Which might be nuts, except Daniel felt Abbas really did belong here. He could be hurt by the man but still admire his art.

When they decided they'd had enough, they returned to the Great Hall to get their coats. The hard space echoed like a high school gym. Packs of people passed over the floor like schools of fish.

"Danny? Oh my God. Danny! *Daniel Wexler!*"

A shockingly familiar face floated forward. A middle-aged woman like a Long Island soccer mom surfaced in front of him.

"What the hell are *you* doing in town?"

It was Daniel's sister, Amy, who *was* a soccer mom on Long Island. Her face looked leaner, her hair grayer. He'd just seen her in August, and she hadn't changed, but he was always surprised now by how much his older sister resembled their late mother.

"Hello, Daniel," said the short, jowly man by her side, Daniel's brother-in-law, Tony.

"Holy shit!" cried Daniel, and he covered his embarrassment by giving Amy a fierce hug. "Sorry. I came up on business. I would've called but knew there wasn't time. Uh, this is a colleague at school. Abbas Rohani."

"Pleased to meet you," said Tony.

Abbas gazed at the husband and wife as if from a great height, but he was a head taller than both.

"Where's Zack?" asked Amy.

"Back home. He couldn't get away."

Amy studied Abbas from the corner of her eye, then let out a nervous laugh. She knew her little brother well enough to have her suspicions.

"Your name is Abbas?" said Tony. "You're Palestinian?"

"No. Iranian."

Daniel asked Amy, "How about *you*? What brings you to town?" Great Neck was a good two hours away when the traffic was bad.

"Oh, we had to bring pillows and things to Simone"—his niece who was a freshman at Barnard—"and I wanted to see the Eakins show, which got a great review in the *Times*. Have you seen it yet?"

"Are you free for dinner?" Tony asked. "They opened a new restaurant here, which we wanted to try. Can you join us?"

"Sorry, no. We're meeting people downtown. And then we have an early flight tomorrow."

Daniel stopped any further questions by asking about his nieces, which Amy was happy to answer. She asked about Zack. Tony asked Abbas if he were visiting America or in residence.

"Isn't the new Palestinian foreign minister named Abbas?"

"I do not know. I am Iranian," Abbas repeated.

Finally Daniel kissed his sister and brother-in-law goodbye—Tony was one of those straight men who give and receive a kiss on the cheek—then hurried Abbas into the line to get their coats. They spilled down the stairs to the dark, windy street, flagged a cab, and jumped in. Daniel fell back against the seat and began to laugh.

"Damn! I sure the hell wasn't expecting *that*!"

Abbas nodded but didn't smile. "Your family are Jews?"

"Uh, yeah."

"Your brother thinks you are sleeping with the enemy."

Daniel grimaced. "He's not my brother. Brother-*in-law*. And you're hardly the enemy. They don't know we're sleeping together."

"No? Then why did they keep asking about Zack?"

"Only three times." Which was too often.

"Your brother-in-law is totally hung up on Muslims."

"No, he isn't. He's just curious. He's a corporate attorney and very liberal, very open-minded."

Abbas thought a moment. "I see. Still. That must have been very uncomfortable for you."

"It was. But I'm not embarrassed to be seen with you."

"No? I would be embarrassed if my brother saw me with you."

"You would?" Daniel didn't want to explore that. "But I told you. Tony isn't my brother."

They ate dinner downtown at the Cedar Tavern. It wasn't the original Cedar, where Pollock and de Kooning went, but Abbas didn't need to know that. He was silent for long stretches of the meal. When Daniel asked if anything were wrong, he said he was tired, that's all. Daniel couldn't guess if he were fretting about Picasso or Jews or something else entirely. He looked forward to sex that night as a way of being with Abbas without having to talk.

They got back to the hotel early, around ten, and Abbas said, "Do you mind if we only sleep tonight? I am not in a frisky mood. Maybe we did it too much last night."

"Really?" said Daniel. He felt hurt, then angry, but was too proud to show it. "Poor baby. I didn't mean to wear you out. Anything I can do to change your mind? All right. I won't beg."

Abbas slept in his underwear—French briefs and a guinea T-shirt—which looked sadly dingy to Daniel's bitter eye. Daniel got into bed naked, hoping his body would change Abbas's mind. Abbas didn't even look at him before he turned off the light.

Daniel slid over and held Abbas from behind.

You think one thing in your mind, then put your arms around the other person and think something different with your body.

Daniel's anger turned into sympathy, concern.

"Is there anything you need to talk about?" he asked.

"No. I am tired, that is all. I have had a very long and full day."

"Tired or depressed?"

Abbas thought a moment. "Tired," he said. "I apologize. Maybe I will feel frisky again in the morning. Good night." He took the hand that Daniel held on his chest and kissed it goodbye. Daniel withdrew his hand and rolled away.

It was as bad as being married.

Abbas soon began to snore—maybe he really was tired—and Daniel just lay there, thinking.

He'd spent the entire day naming and renaming his cluster of emotions: I'm in love, I'm not, I am. He seemed bent on turning his feelings into whatever he wanted them to be. But what did he want?

It felt silly and pointless to lie naked alongside a sleeping man. Daniel considered jerking off with his back to Abbas, the ultimate fuck-you, only that felt even sillier. He got up, fished a clean pair of boxer shorts from his travel bag—he hadn't brought his pajamas—put them on, and got back under the blankets.

If he could have sex without orgasm, why not love without sex? Sex is often strange, but love is even stranger.

His sister tonight probably assumed this weekend was all about sex. He'd told Amy a little about his open marriage. She was more amused than shocked. She already thought male sexuality was a raunchy, loveless free-for-all. Which made Daniel wonder what kinds of fantasies Tony had confessed to her. She didn't know half of it. But being seen by his sister with his lover couldn't help making this trip feel more important to Daniel, more like love.

So was he in love?

When you're in love, your expectations are often so high that you feel only disappointment. Or boredom. Or anger. There *is* love, Daniel told himself, but the emotion happened yesterday or might happen tomorrow. You're almost never *in* the emotion. You're so busy being around the person that you don't have room to be in love with them. Maybe you can feel in love with someone only when you're apart.

Abbas was here and not here. He was asleep. Sleep didn't count. The man had been here and not here all day, but especially since the museum. He remained half hidden in his silences, his family, his ambition, his English-as-a-third-or-fourth-language. He'd always be here and not here.

And yet, Daniel was in love with him. Admit it, he told himself. Only when you're in love do you constantly ask yourself if you're in love or not. You *are* in love. You're hooked. Now what?

Daniel suddenly felt homesick for Zack. The emotion was a soft sadness, without guilt or pain. He was glad he was going home to Zack tomorrow. This other love was a foreign country, and Daniel was only visiting. He did not intend to renounce his homeland. He did not want to emigrate. He'd be going home for good, eventually.

26

Zack was home on Sunday night, sitting in the basement rec room, watching the new *Forsyte Saga* on *Masterpiece Theatre*. There was no fire in the fireplace, only the space heater clicking on and off like a giant toaster. Zack never thought to burn wood when he was alone; Daniel was the one who loved real fires.

Jocko suddenly lifted his head. Then Zack heard it, too: a car on the street. When it rolled down the driveway toward the carport outside the rec room, Jocko went wild. His toenails clattered over the glazed brick floor; he looked back at Zack, slinging his long tongue out of his mouth, wanting Zack to confirm: Yes. *He* was here. *He* was back. Jocko loved both of his humans, but he loved Daniel more.

Zack opened the door, letting cold air in and Jocko out. The Toyota filled the carport, and Daniel was stepping from the car. Jocko leaped at him. Zack remained in the door, smiling. There was no way he could compete with such raw canine affection. He was glad to see Daniel, surprisingly glad, as if he'd feared Daniel might not return.

"Calm down, sweetness. Calm down," sang Daniel, swinging his travel bag around the dancing dog. He dropped the bag and threw his arms around Zack. "Oh, but it's good to be home."

Daniel felt wonderful in Zack's arms, lean and solid. Then Zack caught a peppery whiff of tobacco.

"Oh yeah, I let him smoke in the car on the drive back from the airport. I hope you don't mind."

Zack lightly laughed. "If you really love him, you'd get him to quit. Like you did me."

"I don't love him," said Daniel, "like that."

For a split second, Zack thought it was over. But that'd be too easy, wouldn't it?

"What're you watching?" Daniel asked.

"New episode of the Forsytes. Don't worry. I'm taping it. We can watch it later together."

"Keep watching. I'll dump my gear." He started up the stairs.

"There's meat and cheese in the refrigerator if you're hungry."

"Great. You need anything from the kitchen? No? Back shortly."

Jocko eagerly followed Daniel upstairs, still delighting in his other human.

The last fifteen minutes of *Forsyte Saga* passed quickly. Soames continued his bitter war with his wife, Irene: he loved her but she hated him. It was just ending when Daniel came back down in his flannel pajamas and leather slippers, carrying a cutting board loaded with cheese, turkey, and crackers. He brought two glasses of dark beer.

"Thanks," said Zack, taking a glass and turning off the TV.

Daniel set the cutting board on the coffee table and sliced off a piece of cheese. "That's a sweet kid's picture on the refrigerator."

"Osh drew that for me. When I was over there on Friday."

"I thought so. Pretty picture of a pretty family." Daniel smiled. "Is it supposed to make me feel guilty?"

"No. Just a kid's picture. I like the way kids see things." In fact, Zack wanted to remind them both that there was another family involved, one with children. "So? How was it? Did you have fun?"

"We did. I did. To a point."

"Oh?"

"We flew up on Friday, caught a cab into town . . ." Daniel began with his usual we-did-this-we-did-that list of things, not so much storytelling as a download of data: the hotel where they stayed, the art dealers they saw, the shops they visited. It was an elaborate way of clearing his throat. Zack became impatient.

"You'll never guess who we ran into at the Met. Amy and Tony. Amy asked after you. She said to say hi."

Zack was thrown to hear that Daniel's sister had met Abbas. "How's she been doing?"

"Fine. They were in town to see Simone."

Zack liked and trusted Amy but was surprised by how much the brother and sister told each other. He told his own family very little about *his* private life. "What did she make of Abbas?"

"I don't think she made anything of him. I introduced him as just another art teacher. Tony asked if he were Palestinian."

But Zack shouldn't feel upset if Daniel's sister knew Daniel had an outside boyfriend. It was between the brother and sister. It had nothing to do with him.

"You said you and Abbas had fun only to a point."

"Did I say 'only'? I don't think I said 'only.' But we had fun. Yes. It was a good weekend." Daniel appeared undecided over how much to tell.

"Did you learn anything new about each other?"

Daniel smiled, a guilty, hesitant smile. "He snores. But not half as bad as you do."

Sleep was an intimacy *like* sex, but it wasn't sex. Zack didn't need to hear about the sex. "What else?"

"What else? Not much we didn't know already. He's hungry for success. So hungry he couldn't enjoy the Met. He hated everything there. Even the stuff he loved he hated. Because he resents the fact his stuff isn't there yet." Daniel shook his head. "He's a real piece of work. You should've seen him with dealers. Very smooth. I was impressed. Although he didn't get any further than I do."

Daniel spoke with a dry, amused, detached tone, like a man looking back on an old folly. Yet the detachment didn't feel sincere.

"He's good company, perfectly charming for forty-eight hours. But totally self-absorbed. He never asked a thing about me the entire weekend. It was always about him. But maybe that's them. Does Elena ever ask you about you?"

"No. But I'm not sleeping with Elena."

Daniel didn't miss a beat. "Thank God for that. Because there's no telling how Abbas would react. What's good for the gander isn't good for the goose here."

Zack decided to come right out with it. "But you're still in love with him."

Daniel nodded. "Oh yeah. Infatuated. Smitten. Whatever we want to call it. Even now."

"Why now?"

He sighed. "You wanted us to fuck each other out of our systems. Remember? Well, I didn't fuck him out of mine but he fucked me out of his. He's already tired of me. One night was enough." He sighed again, then smiled. "He was never in love with me. He tricked me. He told me he was in love only so I would fall in love with *him*. And now that he's proved himself, he can move on to his other loves. His art and family and future and the rest of it."

Daniel wanted sympathy, and Zack was tempted to give it, but not yet.

"We've gone as far as we're gonna go. The fun part is over. It's all downhill from here." He gave Zack a sad, hurt, Jocko-like look. The real Jocko lay at his feet, head resting on his forepaws, studying the tip of Daniel's slipper. "Sorry, dear, but I'm afraid you're going to have to bear with me for a few more weeks."

Zack frowned. "I thought the fun part was over when it went from sex to love."

"I don't blame you for being angry."

"I'm not angry. But I'm beginning to get bored."

"Not as bored as I am."

Zack was annoyed with Daniel for insisting on the role of chief sufferer here, especially when Zack wanted to show sympathy.

"If the fun part is over," said Zack, "you can break it off. You have no reason to continue. You're not a masochist."

"It doesn't work that way and you know it."

"No, I know. But it worries me when it's *not* fun. Fun makes sense. This doesn't."

"That's love for you. Love never makes sense."

Zack grew more irritated with Daniel's easy chatter, his complacent suffering. "So what made you realize he doesn't feel so strongly about you?"

"Last night, he didn't want to have sex," said Daniel. "And he didn't want it this morning either."

Zack waited for more. "And you got into an argument? After hearing him and Elena go at each other, I'd hate to get into an argument with Abbas."

"No. There was no fight," said Daniel. "We just didn't have sex. Last night or this morning."

Zack stared at him uncomfortably.

"I know it doesn't sound like much. But it proved to me what I was beginning to feel. He wants to be in love but he isn't. He loves his work more than he loves me, and now he wants to get back to work. He knew we were returning today and we can't get together again until next Sunday. He should have wanted to make me happy. It's not like he can show his love any other way, in conversation or favors. So that made it clear to me: He doesn't care. It's over."

Zack couldn't argue with that. He didn't want to argue with it. "Fine then. Good," he said. "If it's over, let it go."

Daniel nodded, calmly and wisely. Then he bared his teeth and screwed his cheeks up to his eyes, pretending to be a child throwing a tantrum. *"But I don't want it to be over!"* he cried.

Zack almost broke out laughing.

But Daniel was serious. His face remained twisted in an ugly grimace of folded skin, his eyes close to tears.

Zack automatically leaned in to embrace him.

And Daniel leaned away. "Dammit to hell! This is my last chance! I'll be forty-eight in February! I want love! Dirty, dangerous love! Not the dull, safe, friendly love I have with you!"

Zack stared at him, stunned.

Daniel stopped, amazed at his own words. "I didn't mean that."

"Yes, you did."

"All right. Maybe I did. But I shouldn't have said 'dull.' That was wrong. I'm sorry it slipped out."

"I am too." The word had startled Zack like a slammed door. His expression remained calm and controlled, yet he felt stung, angry.

They sat on the sofa, afraid to look at each other, then stole one look, then another.

Jocko remained on the floor, head raised, alertly watching.

"Zack. Listen. I don't blame you that I'm in love with another man. I'm not that self-centered and hypocritical."

"That's nice to hear." You asshole, he thought. How dare you even *think* of blaming me for falling in love with this guy.

"But the body was always more important to me than it is to you. This is a different kind of love. It's already ending. Please bear with me. One last fling. It's almost over. I'll be my old self again. I'll be kind again. I promise."

"Fine then. Good." Without noticing what he was doing, Zack had shifted to the far end of the sofa. "But leave me out of it from now on. You don't have to report each and every little thing you feel or don't feel. Like you want me to be part of it. Because I *don't* want to be part of it."

Now it was Daniel's turn to look hurt and confused.

"Let's not talk about it anymore," Zack declared.

"Isn't that my line?" Daniel smiled, wanting Zack to laugh.

Zack kept his cold, dead, stone-faced look.

"Suit yourself," said Daniel. "If that's what you want. Because talking about it only makes *me* feel worse."

"No. Talking makes you feel better. It gives you permission to feel whatever you're feeling."

Daniel glared at him. "You don't have a clue what I'm feeling."

"Not anymore, I don't."

They sat in silence again. Zack waited for Daniel to apologize, to back down, to be kind. He hoped he wouldn't, because an apology would make *him* apologize. He didn't want to apologize yet. They owed it to themselves to go to bed angry tonight. He wanted Daniel to suffer, even if it meant he would suffer, too.

"We can continue this tomorrow," said Daniel. "Or *not,* if that's what you want. I'm exhausted. I've had a long, confusing weekend."

"And I didn't?"

"Oh, please. I can't open my mouth now without you arguing? Not tonight, Zack. Don't make me feel worse than I already feel." He stood up and set the beer glasses on the cheese board. "Uh, can you take Jocko out for his walk? I'm already in my pajamas."

Zack slowly raised his eyes and stared at Daniel.

"All right!" Daniel snapped. "I'll put on my fucking shoes and coat if it's too much trouble for you!"

But Zack didn't intend to look angry or righteous. He'd only been wondering what they would say to each other tomorrow. "Stop making a fuss. Of course I'll walk Jocko."

"You're the one making the fuss. If looks could kill."

"That's not what I was thinking. The look was all in your guilty imagination."

"The hell it was. Good night." He went up the wooden stairs, which groaned and squealed beneath him.

"Good night," Zack finally called out.

No kiss, no pet names, no apology, nothing but an agreement to walk the dog. Which *was* something.

Now that Daniel was gone, Zack wanted to apologize for losing his temper. It's hard for a psychiatrist to remain angry. He's too aware of the different meanings of anger. Daniel was no doubt right: Zack's look probably could've killed. But why was he so angry? Because Daniel called him dull and safe. But he was dull, he was safe. Were they really such terrible traits?

Jocko had followed Daniel upstairs but returned as soon as he understood Daniel wasn't going to walk him. He trotted over to the door, then trotted back to Zack and sat squarely in front of him, watching with his melancholy black button eyes.

"What's the matter, Big Dog? Feel abandoned? Unloved?"

Zack capped his hand over the coarse, woolly topknot on Jocko's head. The compact skull felt so angular and fragile. Zack carefully scratched him behind his ears. Jocko closed his eyes.

The dog was happy to hold his bladder a little longer if he was going to get some affection. Maybe he was thinking: If the fun human won't pay attention, there's always the dull human. Or maybe he thought nothing at all but was lost in contented doggy stupor, stoned on animal chemistry.

Zack could only imagine what Jocko felt, of course. He didn't have a clue what a poodle's emotional life might be. But could he really know what Daniel felt? Or his patients, for that matter? He could only guess, only hope. Who are you? What are you? What do you dream at night? How can I help you?

You think you know somebody, thought Zack, and you don't. You think you know yourself and you lose your way. People want to believe that love makes them clairvoyant, that it enables them to see into the other person and deep into themselves. But romantic love is an illusion, its oneness all mirrors, a narcissism for two, nothing more. And maybe not just romantic love but domestic love as well.

Jocko twisted his head out from under Zack's hand and moved toward the door, whining.

"Sorry, Big Dog. I didn't forget." Zack got up, put on his coat, and took down the leash. "One of us has got to pee. I know it isn't me."

27

The next day was Monday, a hospital day, and Zack drove out to Eastern State in the car. The weather was too cold and rainy for his bike—he would stop bicycling altogether after Thanksgiving.

There were the usual routine crises at Building 2 that morning. Not one but two different outpatients had been rehospitalized over the weekend. Both had gone off their medication. The first, a man, stripped to his waist outdoors at Monticello Shopping Center and began to rant about Jesus and lawyers; the other, a woman, locked herself in a bathroom, cut off her hair, and then tried to cut her wrists. There was also a teenage boy, brought in by the police on Saturday night, although it soon became clear to everyone, including the cops, that the kid wasn't psychotic, only the victim of some strong LSD. By then, however, it was too late to uncommit him until Monday, when the visiting psychiatrist, Zack, arrived. Zack had a long talk with the boy to set his mind at ease—he was terrified to come out of a bad trip of acid into the bad trip of a psychiatric ward—then explored why he'd been doing drugs in the first place.

But the day's chief event was Zack's meeting with Rebecca Mays, his "bipolar I with psychotic features," and her mother. Mrs. Mays had requested that Rebecca be released into her care. Zack wanted to talk her out of it. He invited Rebecca to his office so the three could talk together.

"Mommy!" Rebecca cried and threw her fat arms around the tiny, gray-haired, elementary school teacher. She towered over her mother. "I miss you so much! I cry myself to sleep every night just thinking about you."

Rebecca "played" at being well and she overdid it, but she actually was doing better. She was on a milder regimen now, so there was more Rebecca and less chemistry. She'd taken great care in dressing herself today, wearing a grown-up cardigan and a necklace, although she also wore her usual pink sweatshirt and her hair was tied back in a scrunchy.

The mother sat very still, a good Southern lady like a pale ceramic doll. She said almost nothing while her big, overanimated daughter talked and talked. Zack assumed she was remembering how difficult life had been with Rebecca at home.

"As you can see, Rebecca *is* improving," he said.

Rebecca sat up in her chair, proudly, smugly, as if she'd pulled a fast one on them both.

Zack went on. "Which is why I think she should stay another month. We can continue the treatments, fine-tune the medication, and try more serious counseling."

He expected the mother to look relieved, but her face became sad and pathetic. "She can't come home?" she said plaintively.

"Let's give her another month. That's not very long. What do you think, Rebecca? Another month won't hurt."

Rebecca's eyes went dead. Her sunny, vinyl pink face grew red and thick. She slowly turned to her mother.

"You idiot," she said with a sneer. "He sees right through you. He knows you don't want me. You shoulda practiced more. You coulda faked him out. But you want to leave me here. You want me to rot. You don't want me home. You lying sack of shit."

And the mother burst out crying. She bent forward to hide her sobs, holding two open hands under her face as if to catch her tears.

Zack remained calm. "Why do you say that, Rebecca? Why do you attack your mother? Your mother's not to blame here."

"No, you're the one to blame," she snarled. "You stupid shit. You ass-eating pill monkey. Don't act all kind and loving with me. I read you like a book. You and her are in this together. You both want to keep me locked up forever!"

The habit of anger was still strong, despite the medication. The drugs reduced her manic states without killing her rage. Zack let her spew, wanting to see how long this would last, where it might go. He also wanted her mother to see that Rebecca was not ready to go home. Her violence was all verbal. She gripped her chair with both hands while she shook her head at them, jiggling her heavy lips and flinging spittle in all directions. She excoriated them for a full minute, calling Zack a greedy quack and her mother a selfish pig.

And then, like a thunderstorm, it stopped. Rebecca was silent, scowling, catching her breath. The color faded from her cheeks. Her face became less swollen, less raw. She looked confused.

Her mother stopped crying. She kept her eyes down, her lips pinched; she seemed petrified with embarrassment.

"Are you finished, Rebecca? You get everything off your chest?" Zack kept his voice low. "Did you hear yourself? What was that all about? Do you know? Can you talk about it? So what do you think? Another month here might not be such a bad idea after all."

Rebecca remained perfectly still. "Right," she said with an uncertain smirk. "Right. I heard myself. I don't get me either. I don't know where that came from. Too late to erase now."

Zack said, "It's not you, Rebecca. It's your illness. Your illness is not yet under your control." Especially when she was around her mother. These poisonous tirades were part of their life together. It wasn't just the drugs that had helped her but the absence of her mother. Rebecca resented Mrs. Mays as much as she loved her. She hated the mother whom she couldn't live without. It was sadly logical, yet mental illness can be an extreme logic. Zack wanted to help Rebecca, but he also needed to protect her mother.

"Right," said Rebecca. "Right. So can I just go back to my room and try this again next month?"

"Visit with your mom," Zack suggested. "Here in my office"—where he could watch them—"or out in the reception area."

Rebecca's look of confusion changed into a sour grimace of self-disgust. "No. I screwed up. I don't deserve to be with my mommy. I should go to my room. Sorry, Mommy. I'll do better next time." She wanted to punish her mother as well as herself. Zack decided not to fight her decision.

She stood up, kissed her mother on a tear-glazed cheek, and departed.

Mrs. Mays watched her go, then turned to Zack. "She's like this only when she's unhappy. She'd be happy if she were back home."

Zack put on his toughest, most concerned look. "Mrs. Mays? You don't really believe that. This is not unhappiness, this is illness. You need to think about it as a chronic condition, like MS or cancer. We might be able to control it eventually, but even that will take time."

Zack laid out the best possible future for Rebecca, emphasizing the importance of altering her habitual use of anger and getting her into the routine of taking medication. She needed to learn to be content while medicated, a state that most bipolars found boring, so they went off their meds, with dire results for all concerned. He said nothing about the likelihood of Rebecca's condition worsening.

Mrs. Mays finally gave in. "Another month," she agreed. "But I want her home. Soon. She's all I have in the world." She gazed at Zack with her ghost gray eyes. "The house is too quiet. I miss her. I don't miss her screaming or throwing things or sometimes hitting me. But I miss her good days. Because she is very good company on her good days." She tried to smile. "I'm not going to be around much longer, Dr. Knowles. I'd like to have her home before I go."

Of course, thought Zack. The woman was in her seventies. She did not have much time. No wonder it was so hard for her to admit her daughter was ill. There was no happy ending here, only difficulty for Mrs. Mays until she died, then difficulty for Rebecca afterward. Because what would become of Rebecca without her mother? She could end up on the street or a permanent resident of the hospital; she'd be at greater risk for suicide during her depression episodes.

"I understand," said Zack. "We'll see what we can do."

When he stood up to open the door for Mrs. Mays, his body experienced a sorrow as physical as vertigo. He felt both heartsick and stupid. You do what you can and it's never enough. The families of the chronically mentally ill, and the mentally ill themselves, can be so terribly, painfully human.

"We'll see what we can do," he repeated, touched her birdlike shoulder goodbye, closed the door, and returned to his desk.

There are far worse things in life than an extramarital affair, he thought. He could not begrudge Daniel his little sex drama, especially now, when it was winding down.

So why was it still at the back of his mind this morning, in the presence of real catastrophes? Zack often forgot about home at the hospital and the hospital at home, although he knew his unconscious freely mixed the two. Yet last night's argument still hung behind his thoughts, unfinished, unresolved. There was nothing for him to do except ignore it and get on with his work. But it was still there, wasn't it?

The bulk of the afternoon was wasted in an emergency staff meeting where Roy Chadha struggled to make peace between the nurses and the orderlies—they were at war again over the division of duties. Zack didn't get home until three. He found a car parked out front, a secondhand Saab, the Rohanis' car. Of course. Today was Monday, Elena's laundry day. Zack was surprised by how glad he was that Elena was here. He always enjoyed seeing her, but today was different, his happiness stronger. It took him a moment to remember that they had news to share, notes to compare.

He opened the back door and caught a fresh aroma of baked, clean clothes. Jocko guiltily looked up from his spot on the rec room sofa, hopefully beating his tail against a cushion, wanting Zack to be pleased he'd "caught" a guest for them to play with.

Zack patted Jocko and called out, "Elena?"

"In here!"

He found her around the corner at the laundry room table, solemnly folding clothes. "Sorry," she said. "I am almost done. I was hoping to be gone." She sounded sad, even tearful.

"I'm glad I caught you. Where's Mina? She still at school?"

Elena nodded and continued to fold what looked like pale blue underpants—Zack was too shy to glance again and find out whose. Her beautiful beak of nose looked more beaky than usual, with more color than the rest of her face.

Then Zack understood. "You have a cold."

She sniffed. "It is only starting. But you must keep away. I do not want to share."

He'd been around too many sobbing women today, and his mistake was natural. "Would you like some tea? Come upstairs and I'll make us some hot tea with lemon and honey."

"Yes? You sure? Oh, why not? When I finish here. But I cannot stay long. I promised Mina I would take her to get new shoes."

Zack went up to the kitchen and put the kettle on, feeling nervous, almost guilty. It wasn't as if he were going to tattle on Daniel. He just wanted to know what Elena knew about the weekend, if it were good news or bad news or meant nothing at all.

By the time Elena joined him in the kitchen, two heavy mugs were set out on the table, a bright yellow lemon had been cut into sections, and the tea was steeping in its glazed clay pot.

"My cold is not so terrible," she explained as she sat down. "It looks worse than it feels. I am careful not to sneeze on the laundry."

"I could give you something for it," said Zack, "but I've found it's usually best to let colds run their course."

He poured out the tea. They puffed away the steam and sipped. Zack waited to see if she would bring up the subject, but all she said was "I cannot taste a thing. But the heat is good."

"Just plain old Lipton with lots of honey and lemon. So how have you been doing? Besides the cold. Abbas get back okay? Did he say anything about their trip?"

Elena shrugged. "Only that he had a good time but he is glad to be back."

"Nothing else?"

She shrugged again. "He says he needs to work harder on his paintings. That is all. Why do you ask?"

"Daniel thinks it's over. Their thing."

Her black eyebrows arched upward. "Oh?" She took another sip of tea.

She rolled it around in her mouth before swallowing. "Over for him or for Abbas?"

"For Abbas. He's still interested but he thinks Abbas isn't."

"Hmm." Her eyebrows went down and she sat very still, thinking.

"Abbas indicated nothing like that?"

"No. But he wouldn't. He would never tell me such a thing because it might give me satisfaction."

"Really? Daniel is the opposite. He'd tell me right away. Not just to make me happy but to get a little sympathy."

"Then you are nothing like us." She nodded to herself. "What makes him think it is over?"

Zack was reluctant to confess something so private and possibly trivial. "Uh, maybe Daniel's reading too much into it. But Abbas didn't want to have sex with him on their last night together. Or the next morning either."

Her eyes grew very wide. And she began to blink.

"Does that sound like Abbas?"

She shrugged—she had a very eloquent shrug today. "Abbas is always wanting sex, but when it suits him, not the other person."

"So it means something he didn't want it their last night?"

She shrugged again. "I have given up trying to understand what will and will not give my husband a hard-on. He can want the other person only so long as the other person doesn't want him more. He is a taker, not a giver."

"Are we talking about just sex here or love too?"

"There is no difference with Abbas."

But Zack felt there was a difference. "Daniel thinks Abbas was never in love with Daniel but only wanted Daniel to be in love with him."

"Of course," she said, as if they'd been fools not to realize this sooner. "He wants people to want him. He needs people to want him. And one or two are not enough. He wants drama, frisson. Which means rubbing?"

"Or friction," said Zack.

"Yes. Friction. Action. Trouble. He enjoys trouble. But he gets his fill and moves on. He loves to be loved, but finds it difficult to love back. What is surprising here is he has had his fill so soon." She poked out her mouth in a thoughtful pucker. "But Daniel is older than most of Abbas's boyfriends. Maybe he is less trouble, less friction."

Zack frowned. "Daniel won't want to hear *that*."

"You are telling him we spoke?"

"I don't know. Maybe not. It's bad enough having a love affair fizzle out without thinking that the spouses are gloating."

"Are you gloating?"

"No, but he might think we are."

She considered that for a moment, tapping her lips with her index finger. "If it is over, that is good news, yes?"

"It will be. But Daniel's going to be miserable for a while, especially if he thinks there's a chance it's not over yet. I wish there were a way to hurry it along."

"To punish him?"

The idea startled Zack. "I don't want to punish him. I just want this to end. Sooner rather than later."

She looked skeptical but continued. "I want it to end, too," she said. "But I learned my lesson last time. I say we let sleeping dogs lie. Or fuck. Or not fuck. Or whatever it is they are doing. Because to fight with Abbas only excites him. He loves the fight. The friction. I am not going to give it to him. I think we should let things go as they are. I am going to be Zen. I am going to play dumb. He will not know that I know. I *am* curious, I admit. But I will not ask him. I will not give him that satisfaction. But you are still talking about it with Daniel?"

"Actually I'm not. We had a fight about it last night. I told him I didn't want to talk about it anymore. Not another word."

"A fight? You are angry? You are jealous?"

"Not jealous, but—fed up. Bored. He gets to have his fun and I have to hold his hand afterwards. Which makes me feel dull, safe, boring. Which I resent."

She smiled. "So the doctor is human after all?"

"You thought I wasn't?" Was that how she saw him? "I admit that, as a psychiatrist, I don't have much sympathy here. Daniel wants a great drama in his life, one last big drama. My job is to help people avoid big, unnecessary dramas."

She nodded. "Yes. My feelings exactly. Life is difficult enough without people making big ugly dramas for their amusement."

We are such a pair, Zack thought: prudent, rational, detached. Yet underneath, Elena was more passionate and emotional than he was. "Do you really think you're strong enough to say nothing and let this finish out naturally?"

"You think I am too impatient? You think I am not so Zen?" She laughed. "Maybe you are right. But we shall see. Maybe because I am tired with a cold, the Zen will be easy."

28

Daɴiel weɴt iɴto school on Monday morning with a guilty conscience. He regretted last night's words with Zack and knew he should apologize, but he couldn't yet. He didn't want Zack's pity just now; he didn't even want his understanding. He also wondered if his affair with Abbas were really over. Talking about something makes it so, which was another reason to regret having said so much to Zack. The change may have taken place only in his imagination, although so much about this kind of love is just half imagined anyway.

Nevertheless, when Daniel encountered Abbas in the upstairs hall of the art building that morning, something felt different, something had changed. He looked so handsome, foreign, and aloof.

"Get home okay?" asked Daniel, even though he'd dropped him off at his door. "Elena and the kids happy to have you back?"

Abbas blinked distractedly inside the black-framed squint of his glasses. "Of course. They missed me. Didn't Zack miss you?"

"Not really. I think he was glad to have me out of his hair."

That was a cue for Abbas to say he already missed their weekend or had enjoyed being in Daniel's hair or something suggestive. But Abbas only nodded and murmured, "Good," as if he wasn't listening. "If you will excuse me, I must get to my studio."

He was preoccupied, scattered, distant. Daniel remembered how Abbas used to greet him with an eager, overjoyed smile. Had he only imagined that, too?

Daniel decided to forget about Abbas and concentrate on teaching. The end of the semester was approaching, and he had a full week ahead of him. He could be patient, he could wait. For the next few days, however, he found he needed to see Abbas daily, just to say hi. He didn't want to get into a serious conversation, not yet, and he couldn't, not with students and faculty floating around. No, all Daniel wanted was a daily glimpse, like a fix, to assure himself that Abbas was still here, that Abbas still liked him. It felt painfully adolescent. It'd been different when they were having sex, he told himself. One orgasm was the equivalent of six hellos and he could forget Abbas in between. But New York had spoiled him, a weekend of sex ending in a night without it. Now Daniel hunted down Abbas in the hall and even his classroom, just to look at him and say hi. Which didn't seem to bother Abbas. He didn't appear to notice that anything was wrong. Which was another indication it was over.

Daniel was still in love, of course, only this wasn't love as an obsession but love as a worry, an obligation, a grudge. Zack was right: he should just let it go. Yet Daniel refused to drop it, just as he refused to confront Abbas and ask: What's going on? He was afraid Abbas would tell him. Plus, it was difficult to catch Abbas alone. The Iranian spent most of his time between classes in his studio with the door closed, his music playing loudly. He was busily painting, and Daniel knew better than to interrupt.

Friday afternoon arrived, and Daniel was in his office, finishing up for the week, filling out student evaluations, when there was a knock. He looked up: Abbas stood in the doorway, leaning lazily against the jamb.

"I am sorry to disturb you. But are you coming by on Sunday?"

Daniel couldn't help smiling. "Did you want me to come by?"

"Absolutely. I want you to see my new work. I have been very busy since we got back. I think you should be the first to look."

The smile faded. Lucky me, thought Daniel. "And that's all you want? My eye?"

Abbas frowned and turned to peer down the hall toward the other office doors. He spoke softly, as if to himself. "First your eye. But the rest of your body might be nice after."

Daniel's heart swelled, rose, floated. He didn't trust Abbas, but he wanted to be pleased. "Sure. I got nothing planned on Sunday."

Abbas must have heard the note of resistance because he quickly added, "I am sorry if I have been unfriendly since our trip. But I have been working very hard and had no time for personal matters." He made *personal* sound like a synonym for *trivial*. "But now I need to get out of my head and down into my body again. For a brief visit." He grinned: his old eager, openly sexual display of teeth. "Are you interested?"

They were only sex buddies again, fuck buddies, not lovers. Which should be fine—it was certainly easier—yet Daniel felt disappointed. "So it's just my eye and dick you want. You don't need the rest of me?"

Abbas laughed. "Your tongue would be nice. And your liver and pancreas, too. But first I want your eye." He lowered his voice to a sensual whisper. "And your dick is still one of my favorite animals."

"Sure. Why not?" said Daniel, as coolly as he could pretend.

~~~

Daniel said nothing to Zack about getting together with Abbas that weekend, but Zack didn't ask. On Saturday Daniel began to change his mind. First he considered not going. Then he decided he would go but he'd tell Abbas, "It's over. Let's just be friends." He'd say it as soon as he arrived. Or maybe he should wait until after they'd had sex. Which was more important, his pride or one last orgasm? He decided to let his body set the tone and see what happened.

Sunday arrived, and he took the car. If he walked over, Zack would know where he was going. They were continuing their game of don't ask, don't tell. "See you at dinner," was all he said.

The day was cold and overcast, the sky oyster-colored, the wintry grass of PBK field like brown suede. Andrews Hall was deserted and spooky, like it was every Sunday. Daniel heard music playing upstairs, a chanting buzz accompanied by a patter of drums. It was the *Lagaan* soundtrack again, no longer exotic, coming from the wide open door of Abbas's studio. Daniel walked down the hall toward the music, trying to feel casual and aloof despite the warm fist forming in his crotch. The sounds of Bollywood and spicy smell of oil paint were all it took to give him an erection.

Inside the studio, framed by the door, a figure in blue overalls and a dirty thermal underwear shirt performed stretches beside a canvas on the floor, applying paint in long, steady strokes. He held one brush in his right hand and three in his left.

Daniel remained out in the hall, wanting to appreciate this image of Abbas a moment longer, so graceful and self-contained.

Then a small voice called out: "Can I have more cocoa, Papa?"

"If you have more now," said Abbas, "there won't be more for later. And we don't want to bust your tummy."

Daniel peeked around the doorframe. Osh and Mina had taken over the sofa: Osh lay on his stomach at one end, working in a coloring book; Mina sat at the other end, reading a picture book, her long legs in pink tights just reaching the floor.

Daniel stepped back, surprised and embarrassed.

Abbas heard him and looked up. "Daniel! My good friend Daniel! What a surprise!" He straightened up, grinning—the fakest grin imaginable. He sounded like the host on a TV show for kids. "Look, children. It's our good friend Daniel Wexler. What brings you here today? Did you just drop by your office?"

"Uh, yeah," said Daniel. "Hi, kids."

"Hi." "Hi." Their greetings were simultaneous and mechanical, like a jangly piano chord.

Abbas came toward Daniel, shifting the lone brush from his right hand into the hand full of brushes. He lowered his voice. "Elena has a terrible cold. She needs her sleep and asked me to look after them. It was easier for me to bring them here, where I can work, than to look after them at home."

"Didn't you take care of them yesterday?"

"Yes, but her germs pay no attention to our deal. I am sorry. There was nothing else I could do."

You could have said no, thought Daniel. You didn't have to give in to her. "So did you want me to go?"

"Oh no. Not immediately." He glanced over his shoulder at his son and daughter. "I still want your eye. But we will have to wait for later for *us*. You understand?"

"No problem. I get it." Right in the neck, he got it. "You guys having fun visiting your daddy today?"

"Fun fun fun," chanted Osh, looking for a fresh crayon. "It *stinks* in here." He curled his lips out, delighting in the new word.

"It does not!" said Mina.

"It stinks *nice*," he explained.

They looked so small and innocent sitting on the big sofa where their daddy and Daniel liked to get naked. Daniel hated thinking that, but he couldn't help it. In front of the sofa stood the electric radiator that he'd brought from home. The studio got cold on weekends, when the college turned the heat down; sex was less sexy when you had to do it tangled up in blankets and sweatshirts. Now the radiator was keeping two children warm.

"They are fine," said Abbas. "They amuse themselves. Let me show you the work. Mina, will you turn off the boom box?"

"I like the music," said Daniel.

"No, I would rather you look in silence. Music gives too much information."

Mina shut off the CD player and turned her back on the men, facing the corner of the sofa to concentrate on her book.

Daniel followed Abbas to three stretched canvases that lay flat on the floor. They were good-size paintings, four by six—Abbas had been very busy since he got back. Two were nearly finished, the third solidly started. They looked like shiny Oriental carpets, the wet paint luminous. Abbas had been right about the music: it hung in the air even after it was turned off, making the pictures look Indian if not Persian.

Daniel half expected a Picasso influence—he remembered their night at the Met and how aggravated Abbas had been by old Pablo—but no, the new work was a continuation of Abbas's previous work, except plainer, more abstract. The alphabet men and ideogram figures were gone, and these paintings were all about color, with dark, twisty lines like the bones of paisley forming skeletons in each picture. Color fields hung on the bones like skin, each canvas dominated by a different color: one was apple green, the other Vermeer yellow, the newest work Pompeii red. The colors were gorgeous—Abbas had made excellent use of the new paints he'd bought in New York. It took Daniel several minutes before he understood the bones.

"This is Arabic lettering?"

"These two are Arabic. From the Koran. That one is Farsi."

Abbas had used text before but only the idea of text, the suggestion of writing. These were real letters magnified, so one saw only pieces of letters, portions of words.

Abbas pointed at the green painting. "This has a piece of 'In the name of God, the compassionate, the merciful.' " He pointed at the yellow canvas. "This one includes 'Anyone male or female who does what is good will enter the Garden.' " He pointed at the red. "And this one is Farsi. It has a portion of 'Margbar Omrika.' "

"Which means?"

Abbas smiled. "Death to America."

It was ironic, of course. All three were ironic, only where did the jokes land? Daniel couldn't guess. "Will Arabic or Farsi speakers recognize the quotes despite what's missing?"

"Not unless I tell them."

"Will you?"

"I do not know yet."

It was a gimmick, a postmodern art trick: You find your meaning and then hide it—painting over it or putting it in a foreign language. You know it's there and it influences you while you work, but mostly it just makes you feel you're actually saying something. Daniel had used this schtick himself. Today it only annoyed him. The new paintings annoyed him. They were beautiful, yet cold and austere, with or without their text.

"So what do you think?" said Abbas.

"They're beautiful."

Abbas heard the other thoughts under the words. "But?"

But Daniel wasn't the most objective judge here, was he? He was jealous of the paintings. Abbas believed in them, giving his work more attention, emotion, and time than he gave anything else in his life, including his children. Daniel was jealous of Mina and Osh, too, but he also identified with them.

Daniel decided to come out with it. "They're a little too cold for my taste. Cold and impersonal."

Abbas considered this. "Maybe that is just me. Maybe you find me cold and impersonal?"

It was as if Abbas were reading his mind. "It's possible."

"But what is bad in people might be good in art," said Abbas. "A little coldness is often better than sloppy warmth."

"You find me sloppy?"

Abbas pursed his lips together, a kind of shrug of the mouth. "I wasn't talking about you. Only me." Were they even talking about the same thing?

Daniel stole a look at the kids, wondering what they made of this exchange. "I prefer your warm side. Which sometimes comes out with your family." But never with Daniel.

Abbas followed Daniel's eyes to his children. He looked back down at the green painting, the merciful God painting. He set his chin in his hand and thought a moment. "Osh, darling? Could you come here? I need your help."

The boy jumped off the sofa and happily bounced over.

"You are right," Abbas told Daniel. "They are too cold. They need a human mark or touch or something. Do you love me, Osh?"

The boy giggled. "*Oui,* Papa."

"And I love you." He knelt on one knee beside his son. "Hold out your hand. Give me your arm." He pushed back the boy's sleeve. "You must keep very still." He reached down and picked up a stubby tube of paint. He squeezed it into Osh's palm: a fat jewel of carmine red. "We will clean it off later, but first we will have fun." Cupping Osh's little hand in the saucer of his paw, Abbas used his thumb to smooth the cold, oily redness over the palm and tiny digits.

The boy stared in amazement as his hand turned the color of horror-movie gore. He began to laugh as if being tickled.

Abbas laughed, too. "No, no," he said and hugged him. "Keep your hand open. Don't get it on your clothes. Your mother will be furious." He wiped his own thumb with a rag. "You are my brush," he whispered and gripped the boy's wrist. "You are my crayon. Hold your fingers so." He demonstrated with his free hand. "I am going to put you in my painting."

Mina had come over and crouched down in her pink leotard, looking fretful, as if watching two boys do something nasty.

Osh held his mouth wide open as his father took his hand and pressed it on the wet canvas. Then he peeled it off, as delicately as a stencil, leaving a small red handprint on the feathery swirls of apple green paint.

"There!" Abbas promptly took the rag and began to clean off the boy's hand. "That is you. You are in my art. You are immortal. What do you think?" he asked Daniel.

Daniel was confused seeing Abbas use his son so cheerfully, so callously. Yet the handprint was effective, even beautiful. "It works," he said. "It changes things. It makes it look like a cave painting."

"Hmm. I like that." Abbas laughed. "You hear that, Osh? You are a caveman. You are the first human. You are Adam." He hugged his son again. "Here. I must wash your fingers with turpentine or it will dry and your mother will kill us both." He led the boy to the sink.

Daniel continued to study the handprint. It looked not just primitive but primal, tragic, a small bloody hand pressed against the name of God. A grown man's hand wouldn't be half as disturbing.

"What about you, Mina?" Abbas called out while he cleaned off his son. "Would you like to go next? Can I have your foot?"

She stood beside Daniel, scowling at the painting. "No! It looks yucky. Dirty."

"Oh, please? A blue foot on yellow? Won't that be pretty?"

"No, Papa! If you make me, I'll tell Mama!"

Abbas only laughed. "Forget it. I wanted to make you immortal, too. But never mind." Still holding Osh's hand, he looked around the sink. "Where is the soap? There is no soap. Darling Mina? Take your brother to the ladies' room down the hall. See that he washes with the good-smelling soap. I have made him smell like an old motor. That's a good girl."

Heaving a sigh of daughterly exasperation, Mina took the grinning boy by the arm and led him out.

Abbas returned to the painting and examined it. "Yes. It is more mysterious like this," he told Daniel. "*And* more human."

"You can put anyone and anything to use, can't you?"

Abbas looked up, startled.

Daniel too was surprised by what he'd said. He'd been thinking it but didn't know he'd say it. He didn't know what he could do with the accusation.

"Well, I *am* cold and impersonal," Abbas calmly admitted. "Like my art. I will use anyone. Even my children."

"That's not what I meant."

"Yes it is. You have been angry with me ever since you arrived." He watched the door, listening for his kids. "What else do you want from me today? I am sorry we cannot mess around, but can you not see my hands are full?"

Daniel could've apologized, he could have backed down. But no. He'd postponed this long enough.

"I want to finish this today," he said. "I want the truth."

Abbas signaled with two open hands that he couldn't guess what Daniel meant.

"You don't love me. Just say it. Please. You love your children. And your painting. And maybe your wife. But not me."

Abbas frowned. "Fine. If that's what you want to hear, I will say it. No, I do not love you. I have no time or room in my life for another love."

Daniel was stung by how quickly he agreed. "You once said you *were* in love with me."

"I thought I was. But I was wrong. That doesn't mean we still cannot be friends."

Daniel added it together. "Friends who sometimes fuck?"

"Why not?" Abbas glanced back at the door. "We cannot be having this conversation today."

"So when are we going to have it?"

"When my children are not down the hall," Abbas said sharply.

Daniel looked at the door, too. "Do you really love them, or do you just hide behind them?"

Abbas stared at Daniel, not furiously but blankly, puzzled. "Of course I love them. How could I not?"

Daniel was shocked with himself for saying such a thing.

"What is it?" Abbas demanded. "You think because I don't love you I can't love them? Is that it?"

"No, of course not."

"Good. Because I do love them. I may not be the world's best father. But they are my pride and joy."

"Sorry," said Daniel. "No. I shouldn't have said that." He was blindly striking at the man. Of course Abbas loved his children, even if it were in the mindless, selfish way that a man loves himself. They really were his pride and joy. "I'm just disappointed and a little pissed off. I'm not thinking clearly today." Or maybe he was thinking too clearly. "I think we need to break this off completely."

"You think? Yes. I think so too." Abbas looked straight at Daniel, more confused than angry, maybe even hurt. It was as if he were still translating to himself the many things they'd said to each other. He suddenly turned away, walked over to the boom box, bent down, and hit a button. *Lagaan* came back on, a jangly polyrhythmic song of bongos, voices, and sitar.

Daniel didn't understand why he did that—until Osh ran in from the hall followed by Mina. Abbas must have heard them coming. He didn't want his children returning to a room full of the electricity of their father quarreling with his lover.

Osh began to hop around to the music.

"No, like this!" cried Abbas, and he lifted his arms over his head and gently spun around.

Osh copied the movement exactly, a willowy shadow of the grown man.

Abbas showed him a set of hand gestures—like hula hands—and Osh repeated those, too. Father and son began to dance in swaying, twisting movements that were more about arms and torso than they were about feet. The dance looked too loose to be traditional, but like a mix of things picked up from movies and weddings. Osh did not stomp around like a little boy but moved with eerie, precocious grace. His face took on the solemn pout of a child deep in make-believe.

Abbas did not even glance at Daniel, but he seemed to be saying: Look at me. See, I love my children. His dance wasn't entirely spontaneous, but it was sincere. Daniel was both moved and disturbed to watch Abbas dance with his son, wagging his ass in a shameless way no Western father would ever move around a child. Daniel eyed the shape swinging in the seat of overalls and couldn't help remembering its look and feel. He still wore the memory of the sphincter around his finger like a wedding ring. It was an obscene thing to think about a man in the company of his children, yet Daniel insisted on thinking it. He didn't want the kids to make him feel guilty, but they did.

Mina stood by the sofa, watching with her big eyes and pinched sparrow face, a small version of her mother, as disapproving as Elena. She was always odd man out here, wasn't she? Then Daniel realized: She doesn't disapprove, she feels excluded. Was this her choice or her father's or Muslim tradition? But they weren't devout Muslims.

He stepped over to Mina. "I don't know how to do this dance. Can you show me?"

She looked up at him with a sour, skeptical squint.

"Like this?" He held his arms straight out on either side of him.

"No! This," she declared and lifted her hands over her head with her elbows at right angles.

He did the same—it was a surrender gesture—and began to dance with her, snaking his hands in the air the way she snaked hers. He tried smiling at her, but Mina wouldn't smile back. She wouldn't even look at him.

What did she know? Nothing, he hoped. But she must feel the change that Daniel brought to this family, the tension he produced in her parents, the silences and bad moods.

"Mina. Like this," cried Abbas, and he performed one of his pirouettes for his daughter, which she duplicated.

Daniel did it, too, like a do-si-do done by a telephone pole in an old Disney cartoon, but then he realized the movement was for her, all her, and he had no business taking it for himself.

Soon Mina was dancing with her father and brother, drawn by their gravity away from Daniel. Which was only right. Daniel had brought her into the dance, but it was her father she wanted, her father she loved.

Abbas smiled at her and at Osh, but not at Daniel. He seemed to forget about Daniel. He concentrated on dancing with his children. Which made him look even more beautiful, more lovable.

Daniel wanted love from Abbas, but all Abbas could give him was sex. Just sex. Daniel had no business confusing this family or himself for the sake of just sex. He should go elsewhere for sex. It was that simple. He should leave these people in peace.

"I got to go," he called out over the music.

"Goodbye," said Abbas indifferently. He didn't stop dancing.

Had Daniel hurt his feelings? He hoped so. "Bye, kids."

"Bye," said Osh.

"Bye bye," said Mina, more warmly, but she was probably just happy to see him go.

Daniel went out into the hall, *Lagaan* still playing at his back. He hurried to the other side of the building and his office. He unlocked the door, turned on the light, and switched on his computer. He found a chat room almost immediately.

Just sex, he told himself, the sooner the better. Bad sex would be preferable to good sex, since bad sex would get the virtuous taste of sacrifice out of his mouth. He loved Abbas and he loved the man's children and he was walking away from them. He felt very moral right now; he didn't trust the sensation. There had to be somebody in town on a Sunday afternoon who just wanted to get his rocks off. But no, everybody must be watching football on TV. The few names that popped up on the screen were mostly in D.C. The best he could do was Richmond, an hour away, and it was Sugar Bear 13, whom Daniel had met a year ago and did not care to see again.

～⁓　⁓～

"It's over. You'll be happy to hear. We did it with a minimum of fuss. We couldn't say much. We couldn't do much either. He had the kids with him today. Elena has a cold, *he says.* I think he was just hiding behind them. He's afraid of what I'd say if we were alone."

Zack sat at the kitchen table with a paperback in his hand, another Victorian novel—he was still doing Elizabeth Gaskell. He looked more surprised than pleased, and strangely worried. "What makes you think Elena *isn't* sick?"

"I don't know. I just felt he was lying. It was his choice to have the kids there. They made me feel guilty. They're sweet kids. I like them. But I didn't appreciate him using them as a secret weapon."

Zack looked more worried. "You really think he brought them to make a point?"

"Oh, I don't know. I don't care. It doesn't matter. Now that it's over." He laughed. "Gimme a break. I don't need the how-does-it-make-you-feel patter tonight, because I feel fine. I'm glad it's over. I said it was ending, didn't I? And I was right. Better sooner than later. Don't look at me like that."

"How am I looking?"

"Like you're sorry. You should be glad. You gave me plenty of space and I had my fun and now it's over. The end." He opened the refrigerator. "What do you want for dinner? I'll cook."

"That's okay. It's my turn."

Daniel snapped his head around. "I said I'd cook, dammit! Just let me cook dinner, all right!"

Zack froze. "All right," he replied after a moment.

Daniel took a deep breath. "All right," he said more quietly and turned back to the refrigerator. "We got chicken, we got beef liver. There's plenty of tomato sauce if you want to do pasta. And yes, I do feel a little blue right now. Not angry, just blue." Daniel addressed the freezer furred with frost. "Give me a few days and I'll feel fine. I don't want to talk about it yet. All right?"

"All right," repeated Zack. There was the usual sad uncertainty in his voice that sounded like guilt, but Daniel knew it was probably love. Daniel wasn't entirely sure he deserved to be loved right now. Maybe he was only projecting both his guilt *and* his love onto Zack.

29

"M Y NAME IS ZACHARY KNOWLES. I'm a doctor here in town—a psychiatrist to be exact. But that's not why I'm here tonight. I'm here as a gay man. Bill has asked me to tell you a little about my life as a gay man. And to answer any questions you might have."

Once a year, toward the end of the first semester, Zack spoke to the gay student group that met at St. Bede's Church just off campus. This was a Homo 101 gathering—there were hipper, more political organizations for later—and it attracted the just-out or not-quite-out kids, all freshmen and sophomores. It had been started five years ago by Bill Kelly of the Italian Department, a good gay Catholic—an ex-monk, in fact—who somehow convinced his priest to let a queer support group meet in the church basement. Roman Catholics were a minority in town and could be surprisingly progressive. It didn't hurt that Bill was a jovial force of nature, so wholesome that not even Mother Church could refuse him. He was fifty and single and probably celibate. Daniel called him Sponge Bill behind his back, in allusion to the fiercely optimistic cartoon character.

"I'll start the ball rolling," said Bill, with a big gap-toothed grin. "The rest of you can jump in with your questions whenever you like. Zack, you grew up here in Virginia, right?"

Zack began with a few tales about Norfolk, the Boy Scouts, and high school, while he took in his audience. The kids looked younger than ever. Daniel saw college students all the time, but Zack got them only in doses. If he didn't know better, he'd say this batch was still in junior high. The girls outnumbered the boys, but Zack found both genders equally sexless, like puppies. They dressed like ads for the Gap or Old Navy, which this year meant their jeans were improbably low, their torsos so long they resembled otters.

"How old were you when you first told yourself: I'm gay?" asked Bill.

"Not until my senior year in college. Until then I was falling in love with guys but going to bed with women."

"You had sex with girls?" one kid asked indignantly.

"That's right," said Zack calmly—he was used to the indignation. "I liked women and I was curious about sex. It seemed only natural to try combining the two. I didn't know any gay men. But it didn't work. I only made people unhappy, including myself. It's something we all have to explore and discover on our own. I told myself at the time that I was bisexual, which I'm not. But there are real bisexuals out there."

They always hated hearing that. They wanted people to be one way or the other. They wanted to believe that once they made their choice, they would never have to choose again.

"But now you have a boyfriend," said Bill, happily changing from a subject that made him uncomfortable to one he loved to talk about. "How long have you been together?"

Zack told them. There were no gasps—they were too young to be surprised. Or maybe they were too worried about the present to think about any kind of long-term life. Zack was here as a role model, a promise of happiness, an assurance that everything would be fine. Well, things were fine, although real life was much messier than these kids were ready to hear.

He was glad that Daniel had broken off with Abbas. But he felt guilty, too, since he was partly responsible—secretly responsible.

A girl raised her hand. She scrunched up her face to ask her question. "Uh, how long had you known each other when you first went to bed together?"

"We did it the night we met."

There was an uncomfortable tensing around the room.

They were so priggish. They thought sex was the dirtiest, guiltiest, most important thing in the world.

Zack had talked on the phone with Elena today. Yes, she did ask Abbas to take the kids to the studio on Sunday. No, she didn't push or plead or lie. She was ill, but Abbas gave in immediately. Which proved to her that he was ready to end it. The quiet approach is often the best. You go to a door thinking you'll have to break it down, but first you knock and the door swings open: it wasn't locked, it wasn't even closed. Ah, the Zen of the common cold.

A scowling boy in a classic backward baseball cap raised his hand. Zack expected a follow-up question about meeting Daniel, but the boy said, "Aren't you angry you and your partner can't get married?"

All they could think about was sex, but all they ever wanted to talk about was marriage. Most of them didn't even date yet.

"No, I'm not angry. Legal marriage was never an option for gay people until recently. I'm used to being excluded. It is unfair—I don't deny that. But exclusion has made me question marriage. What is it? Why do we have it? What does it mean? My partner and I have had to reinvent marriage for ourselves. We've been making it up as we go along. But I think that's true for more couples, including straight couples, than most people realize."

Zack had given this little speech a hundred times. He always believed it, although on some days it felt more valid than others.

"But rules are a good thing!" the boy insisted. "They show us how to behave. If we could have marriage, we'd be better off. We wouldn't always be— *fucking around*!"

So his question was about sex, too. Of course. Zack wondered if the boy were angry with himself for fucking around or with the idea that everybody else was. He was a bony kid with bad skin, his hormones in full eruption; he was away from home for the first time, and instead of enjoying his freedom, he was lonely, horny, guilty.

"But lawful marriage doesn't automatically make people monogamous," said Zack, carefully keeping to generalities. "Just look at the straight people around you, including the fictional ones in movies and TV shows. They have marriage and still get in trouble."

"If they weren't so selfish," the boy righteously declared, "and didn't go running off wherever their gonads took them, they could stay in love, and marriage would do what it's supposed to."

Zack suspected a recent divorce in the family—the boy's father leaving for another woman? Homosexuality wasn't the problem here. But Zack couldn't explore that in front of the others.

"Sex isn't always a bad thing," he said gently. "Don't think of sex as the enemy. It's part of being human. It's a good way to let off steam. It's a great way to meet people. And it's the best way to fall in love. I mean, the genitals *are* sometimes attached to the heart. Even male genitals."

The last observation often got a laugh at conferences, although never from Bill's group.

"But there's more to gay life than sex," said Bill with a nervous smile. "Just because our guest is a psychiatrist doesn't mean he can't talk about other topics." Bill disliked all talk about sex, especially promiscuity, which he considered the shame of gay life. He *was* an ex-monk. "Kimberly? You had your hand raised?"

"You and your, uh, spouse equivalent," began a pretty girl with braces. "When did you come out to your families?"

"Later than we should have. More of you are probably out to your parents than people in my generation were at your age. You're braver than we were." Which wasn't entirely true, but it didn't hurt to compliment them. Zack spoke for the next ten minutes about coming out, which was easier to discuss than sex. In fact, it was usually the first question at these sessions. The kids, too, preferred family, forgiveness, honesty, and other moral issues to the icky stuff.

Should he have told Daniel about his conversation with Elena? Probably. It felt too late now. He kept forgetting and remembering his secret, but telling Daniel now, several days later, would make his talk with Elena seem more important than it was. A confession might make Daniel think that Sunday had been all Elena's doing and Abbas hadn't really fallen out of love. Now that the sleeping dogs had stopped fucking, why wake them up again?

A boy raised his hand. "Do you have children, and if not, did you ever consider it and do you miss not having any?"

Questions about babies ran a close third to questions about coming out and marriage.

"No, we don't have kids. But it was never an option until recently. We didn't know if love between two men was possible, much less raising children. So we never considered it. Now that all kinds of gay people have kids, either by adoption or other means, we're too old to try. But as a psychiatrist, I see again and again just how difficult being a parent is. It's not for everyone. So I can't say I miss it. And I like the life I have. I can't imagine any other."

Another girl raised her hand. "To what do you owe your long and happy marriage?" She spoke with a giggliness that made the question, which was probably sincere, sound smarmy and false.

"Luck," said Zack uncomfortably. "Pure luck."

"And you really love each other," said Bill. "His partner, for those of you who don't know, is Mr. Wexler in Fine Arts."

"But all couples love each other," said Zack. "At one time or another. Even couples who break up often still love each other." That was for the boy whose parents may be divorced. "Love is only the beginning. It's what follows that counts. What you do with it. How you handle it."

"What would you say is the next most important trait in a long-term relationship?" asked Bill. "Honesty?"

Bill didn't have a clue, did he? No wonder he was single.

"Honesty is good," said Zack. "One should *try* to be honest. But more important than honesty is trust. Since complete honesty is not always attainable or even desirable."

He looked around the circle of faces: sweet, doughy, unbaked faces sprinkled with pimples and doubt.

"You have to trust yourself *and* the other person," he explained. "There are no guarantees here. The world is an unreal place. You want someone with you to make it feel less unreal. You want to keep them there, and you think you can do it with a few magic words, a marriage contract, a wedding. But it doesn't work that way. Love is always difficult. With or without lawyers. With or without psychiatrists. There are a hundred trade-offs. A thousand possible mistakes. You're going to make lots of mistakes. And you won't always know which are the mistakes and which are the right things you did, until years later."

He looked around the room again, at the amused, petulant, confused, or skeptical faces. He took a deep breath and smiled.

"Sorry. That's not what you want to hear tonight. That's for the advanced course, for who you'll be ten years from now. Tonight I should say just: Be patient. With yourselves, your family, your friends, your boyfriends and girlfriends. Take a few chances. Risk making a fool of yourself. Give yourself time. Because most things eventually work out for the best. If you let them. If you're lucky."

30

For the first week Daniel felt fine. It was a relief to know that the affair was over. There was some pain, of course, but that was only hurt pride. Life was suddenly easier. Daniel didn't have to worry if Abbas were going to be kind or cold the next time they met. He didn't have to fret about two kids. He could stop being guiltily angry with Zack for being so damn patient. After feeling so many contradictory, conflicting emotions, it was good to feel nothing.

Then, during the second week, Daniel began to miss the old atmospheric pressure. He'd be doing an irksome chore at school or home and think, Damn, this is dull. I'm glad I can look forward to—only to remember it wasn't there anymore. There was nothing to look forward to. This was it, this was his life, until he met his next outside lover or fuck buddy. Only he didn't want to meet anybody new. He had thought he could lose himself in recreational lust, hooking up through chat lines or masturbating to porn. But no, sexual desire died on him. He only wanted to get through the semester and then the school year, but what did he want to do this summer? Not paint. He no longer believed in painting. There was nothing for him to look forward to except bad things: illness, accident, old age, death.

He fell into a funk like a bad cold, as if the Rohani kids had infected him with their mother's hypothetical virus. His deep fatigue remained in his muscles and bones, however, without ever turning into congestion or even a runny nose.

Thanksgiving was coming up, and he and Zack were invited down to Norfolk, as always, for turkey dinner with Zack's father, sister, brother-in-law, and twin nieces. One night Zack asked if Daniel knew what Abbas and Elena were doing for the holiday.

Daniel stared at him in disbelief. "What the hell, Zack? You want to take them with us? Are you nuts?"

"I was just asking. Just curious." Zack made another one of his guilty faces. "You're right. We can't. For a number of reasons. It was just sad picturing them all alone on Thanksgiving."

Daniel wondered if Zack were testing him. Didn't he see how much Daniel was hurting? Maybe he did and couldn't help wanting to poke him in his sore spot. Passive aggression was not a new concept for either man. But Daniel didn't want to confront Zack about his hurt feelings. He did not want Zack's I-told-you-sos; he did not want his sympathy. He preferred to enjoy his self-pity in private.

Daniel was relieved to hear from Jane Morrison that she and John were having the Rohanis over on Thanksgiving Day. "I've been meaning to invite them to dinner all semester. Also, John's mother is coming, and she's on her best behavior when there's company. Are they strict Muslims? Can we drink in front of them?"

Daniel and Zack drove down to Norfolk on Thursday morning, taking Jocko with them. A dog was the perfect social accessory for dealing with the Knowles family. Zack himself joked that if his family couldn't talk about dogs, they probably wouldn't talk at all.

The day was painless but dull. Zack's dad was his usual gruff, aloof Southern gentleman, his sister chipper and well-meaning, the brother-in-law butch yet friendly. Zack also had a brother, but he and his family lived down in Texas, and they did not visit often. Everyone was on his or her best behavior, hiding in courtesies, total Wasps, Daniel included. Only the twins—two very spoiled five-year-old girls—and Jocko were their authentic selves.

"Down, Jocko, down!" cried Daniel when Jocko jumped into his lap to lick Chee-to crumbs off his face. "Show some manners."

Mr. Knowles laughed. "Whadja expect? He's a *French* poodle."

The food was good, the meal perfectly pleasant. Nevertheless, once he'd eaten and there was nothing else to want here, Daniel found himself thinking: This is so sad. How could Zack live with these people for so long? He has so little in common with them. They are so unappreciative of who he is. I'll be glad when we get back to Williamsburg and I can visit— But he couldn't, could he?

Finally, he and Zack said good night and thank you and headed home. Zack drove. He'd had a glass of wine with dinner but nothing afterward, while Daniel had finished off a whole bottle of Merlot watching a football game. Football actually became interesting if you had some alcohol in your system.

The interstate was nearly deserted as they flew over the James River, a wide black emptiness on either side of the bridge's long arc of orange sodium lights.

"Another year, another Thanksgiving," said Zack. "Thank God, it's over."

"But it was peaceful," said Daniel. "Not like my family. Where everyone has a grudge or grievance or score to settle. You can't say no to Aunt Leah's crumb cake without getting your head bit off for not coming to her husband's funeral ten years ago. But at least everything is out in the open."

"We can't all be hot-blooded Middle Eastern types."

Daniel was surprised by the edge in Zack's voice. "I wasn't criticizing your family." Although he was, wasn't he? The choice of geography confused him until he recognized the other connection.

Zack drove in silence for a minute, an endless minute. "Tonight *was* peaceful," he admitted. "But it's a fake peace. What we're faking is Mom's absence. We miss her, but we can't talk about her death. Well, Sissy and I did while we did the dishes, but we couldn't mention it in front of Dad. It's been six years. I don't often miss her. Except at Thanksgiving."

"Of course," said Daniel sadly. "Sorry. I should have thought of that. I forgot."

"Yes, well, you got other things on your mind these days."

The bitter tone hung in the air after the words faded.

"Forgive me. I shouldn't have said that," said Zack. "I have no business using my mother's death like that. It's just— She was in my thoughts today, and I wanted to have it acknowledged."

"Fine. I acknowledge it." Daniel tried to remain cool and tough, but other thoughts spilled out. "Look, I lost my mother, too, and I loved her very much. Our mothers have nothing to do with this."

"No, they don't. I apologize." Zack resumed his silence for a moment. "But I have to say: I'm losing patience with your broken heart."

"I'm not heartbroken. I'm just feeling—I don't know—old."

"Well, it's getting tired. Especially when you don't talk about it."

"There's nothing to talk about."

"Then what are we talking about now?"

"I don't know. You're the one who started it."

Zack took a deep breath. "I should know better than to try to discuss any-thing with you when you've been drinking."

"You certainly should," declared Daniel with mock righteousness. "Hey, I'm a bear of little brain and great thoughts hurt me." He hid in a joke, hop-ing to make peace with the joke, even as he reached for the car stereo to end this conversation.

There was already a CD in the machine, Mahler songs, more of Zack's nerd music, high-toned and lugubrious, but Daniel let it play, a conciliatory gesture.

"Your mother was a good lady," said Daniel. "I miss her, too."

Zack sadly nodded, accepting the change of subject. "She was a wonder-ful lady. Loving and tolerant and curious about people. Supportive of each of us, different as we were. But not without faults," he added. "She was always giving in to Dad, just to keep the peace. She didn't always have the courage of her convictions. She had her limitations. But don't we all?"

⌒ ⌒

Thanksgiving weekend was a long weekend, of course, but they stayed home, sharing a kind of peace. It was a fake peace, like the one Zack described at his father's house, yet they went about their separate chores and shared pleasures, even watching a couple of DVDs together—*Nosferatu* one night, *Romy and Michele's High School Reunion* the next—as if it were only their shadows who were unhappy with each other. Daniel was relieved when Monday arrived and they both returned to work.

It was exam time at school, and everyone was off the usual routine. Daniel did not see Abbas in Andrews Hall, which was surprising, since it's a law of nature that you inevitably run into any person you want to avoid. Daniel gave no exams, but he used the two weeks before Christmas break for private meetings with students to discuss their studio work. None were terribly interesting, except Jonathan Stuart, who'd put together a clever construction featuring a cartoon sculpture of himself—a photo collage pasted on a small piece of foam core—sitting in a dollhouse like a college dorm, all mopey and afraid, while outside loomed giant editorial cartoons of President Bush and Saddam Hussein, also pasted on foam core. The UN had passed its resolution against Iraq at the beginning of November and the inspectors were now over there, hunting for weapons of mass destruction. It was assumed war had been safely averted, despite the sword rattling by the White House. The crisis had come and gone without ever really mussing the hair of college life.

Maureen dropped by Daniel's office to chat before she went home for Christmas break. She had no new gossip to report.

"No more babysitting for the Rohanis?"

"Nyaah, I think they're too embarrassed to invite me back."

"Do you know if they're staying in town over Christmas?"

She didn't think they were. Mr. Rohani had asked their class if anyone knew the art scene in Toronto. She got the impression that he and his family were going up there to see relatives over the holidays.

"I didn't know he had family in Canada."

"Don't quote me," she said. "But that's the impression I got."

On the final day of the semester, the school began to clear out at noon. By five it was like a ghost college, a school of the dead. Daniel took a long walk around campus to soak up the melancholy. The winter dusk provided a good, thick, familiar sadness. It was like being back at the George School, a Quaker prep school in Pennsylvania that Daniel had attended in tenth grade, where he was alone and miserable and often in love. He crossed Jamestown Road to Chandler Court, walked through the gate, turned right, and strolled toward the duplex rented by the Rohanis. If Abbas or Elena saw him out here, so be it. Let them think he was a stalker, a prowler, a pervert. But the house under the tall stand of cedar trees was pitch-black. The car was gone. Daniel went up on the porch and saw two or three days' worth of mail jammed into the box.

So Maureen was right. The Rohanis had left town. No wonder the college felt so empty, not just a ghost college but like a haunted house after the ghosts had been exorcised. No wonder his sadness felt pleasant, not like real pain but like the first love of adolescence, when you're pleased to discover you're not heartless after all.

When he got home, he asked Zack if Elena had said anything about visiting Canada.

"No. But we're not in constant contact. Despite how it might look." He hesitated. "If it were a long trip, I would think she'd tell me. It must be a short visit." He sounded worried.

"I'm sure they'll be back. I'm actually glad they're gone. I'm just surprised neither of them said anything to anybody."

Over the next few days Daniel noticed that he and Zack were gentler with each other. Daniel didn't do anything deliberately: it just came out differently. He was on vacation now and used his free time to read in the morning and do errands in the afternoon. He bought a tree and set it up in the living room while Zack was at the hospital. Daniel loved the novelty of evergreens in the house, the fresh, sappy outdoor aroma. The smell only depressed Zack, who reported that Christmas trees looked especially grim at Eastern State. He might've ruled out having a tree at home except he'd learned that the absence of decorations in the house made his patients nervous. They didn't care if their shrink were an atheist or Jew or Buddhist, so long as he celebrated Christmas.

One night there was a special screening of *Orphans of the Storm* on Turner Classic Movies. Daniel and Zack watched it together, transfixed. A silent melodrama, as shameless as Dickens, it told the tale of two sisters, one of them blind, separated by the French Revolution. The climax was the rescue of the sighted sister, played by Lillian Gish, just as she sticks her head under the guil-lotine. "What a movie!" Zack said afterward. "It plays your emotions like a harp. When Lillian hears her blind sister crying in the street, you're so deep in the scene you hear the voice yourself, even though it's silent."

Daniel adored him for responding so strongly to the movie. We still can't talk about love, he thought, but we can talk about movies. Which wasn't a bad thing, was it?

31

Z ACK? ZACK? WAKE UP, ZACK," a voice whispered. "Zack, baby. You're gonna love this."

Zack opened his eyes. He was surprised to find Daniel in his room, on his bed, still wearing his sleep sweater and red plaid boxers. The light on the ceiling was odd, a pale, clear, shadowless glow. Zack sat up in his nightshirt and looked out the window over his headboard. Everything was blank outside, vacant, white.

"Oh shit," he said and laughed. It was snowing.

Snow is rare in this part of Virginia, and never before January. It was a week and a half before Christmas. Snowfalls were still a treat for Zack, despite his years in New York.

Daniel the Yankee enjoyed his pleasure. "I knew you'd love it. Isn't it beautiful?"

It fell out of the sky like feathers and silted up the backyard in soft, peaceful drifts. It was a silence made visible, a sweep of quiet, until the wind changed and there was a sudden ticking like sand grains hitting the windowpane.

Jocko sat on the floor, looking confused and excited, hearing and maybe smelling the cold new element outside.

Daniel knelt beside Zack, parked one elbow on the windowsill, and leaned into him. And Zack wrapped two arms around Daniel, one across his sweatered chest, the other over his shoulder, holding him in a warm box of arms.

"No day like a snow day," said Daniel, gazing outside.

"And today's Sunday," said Zack, his eyes fixed on the backyard. "So we don't have to worry about canceling anything."

Daniel settled more snugly against Zack. "Winter fucking wonderland."

Daniel was back. He'd been gone for several weeks, maybe months. It was good to have him back again, even if Zack wasn't sure how much of him had been missing. Did Daniel even know he'd been gone? The humiliation and self-pity of a failed love affair had stood between the two men like a tall, unacknowledged elephant. But the elephant had moved on, and here was Daniel again.

⁓   ⁓

They ate a quick breakfast and took Jocko for a walk in Colonial Williamsburg. The snowfall was already tapering off, but stray flakes still floated in the gray air. The entire mile of Duke of Gloucester Street, from the Wren Building to the Capitol, was covered in white. New snow lined the bare trees and quilted the rooftops. It crunched and squeaked underfoot, compacting like Styrofoam. Jocko strained on his leash and pounced in the foot-deep powder, high on the stuff, intoxicated. His black coat was beautiful against the whiteness.

Everything looked new and interesting this morning. Threads of eighteenth-century woodsmoke climbed from chimneys along the street. A man on horseback ambled by, lifting his tricornered hat at Zack and Daniel as his snorting beast dropped several pounds of warm, wheaty dung into the fresh snow. There were no cars except for a handful parked outside Bruton Parish Church, where the early service was just beginning. An organ chord rolled from the high windows over the village green, which was now white. Only a few people were out walking around, residents and college students delicately stepping over the silence.

"Beautiful. Just beautiful," Daniel whispered.

"It's like a time machine," said Zack. "Only the snow doesn't take us back in time but outside it."

"Everyone looks like Brueghel's *Hunters in the Snow*," said Daniel. "He got that right, how figures turn dark against the white."

And to illustrate his point, a family of five came up the street from the Governor's Palace around the corner. Three adults and two children, they were dark silhouettes until the eye adjusted and added color and features. The two men and the boy wore Russian fur hats. The mother and daughter had identical burgundy red scarves looped around their faces. A severely cropped row of pollarded trees stood along the snowy street like the columns of a ruined temple.

But the woman was staring at Zack. And he realized: We know these people. It was the Rohanis plus one, the Rohanis and a stranger.

And his first concern was for Daniel, wondering what *he* felt running into Abbas and his family. But Zack couldn't look at Daniel, only at Abbas.

Abbas gazed back at them with remarkable calm, a dry, evenhanded indifference, his face darker than Zack remembered.

Elena suddenly broke into a grin. "Zachary! Daniel! And Jocko, too! What a surprise. It is a most beautiful day, yes?"

Jocko leaped at Mina like an old friend, pulling Daniel forward on his leash. Mina was promptly joined by Osh, the two kids petting the poodle, who loved the attention. Mina's scarf looked like a costume, as if she were in a children's production of *Fiddler on the Roof*.

The new figure, the stranger, stood by and watched, a stylish gentleman in a camel hair coat and neatly trimmed silver beard.

"You must forgive me," said Elena. "Hassan Rohani. Abbas's brother. From Tehran."

The man smiled and bowed but did not offer his hand.

And Zack remembered Elena's stories: the brother was an important man in the Islamic Republic of Iran. Many Muslims do not shake hands with infidels. The head scarves took on a new meaning.

"This is Daniel Wexler," said Abbas in a low, gruff, manly voice. "My colleague at school. And his friend, Dr. Knowles."

Hassan increased his smile. "Ah, the male couple, yes. I've heard good things about you. You've been very kind to my brother and his family." He compensated for his inability to shake hands with the sweetest smile imaginable.

"You're here in the U.S.?" said Daniel, sounding faintly alarmed. "For how long?" Zack wondered what Daniel knew about the brother that he didn't.

"Not long, sorry to say. Only two weeks. But I wanted to visit my brother and his family while there was still time."

Hassan's accent was different from Abbas's, less French, more neutral, even American, with occasional Middle Eastern notes.

"We were taking a morning hike to your Capitol," he said. "Would you like to join us?"

Zack wanted to accept, hoping to learn more about the brother, but this was Daniel's call, not his.

"Sure," said Daniel, with surprising ease. "That's where we were going." Maybe the elephant really was gone.

Abbas looked neither pleased nor annoyed but benignly poker-faced, blandly aloof.

They began to walk toward the fat brick building in the distance, Zack falling in alongside Elena, Daniel strolling with "the men"—he passed Jocko's leash to Mina.

"Who is your new friend, my dear?" Hassan asked Mina.

"Jocko!" she said proudly. Both kids looked happy to be with this uncle, who clearly adored them.

The kids plunged ahead with the dog over the powdery drifts. The adults walked more carefully, keeping to the center of the street, where there was less snow. Elena slowed her steps; Zack did likewise; they fell behind the others.

Her dark red scarf was wrapped around her neck as well as her head, concentrating her face to a pair of elegant glasses and a pretty blade of nose. Her cheeks were bright pink in the cold.

"You've been out of town?" said Zack.

She tugged the scarf back from her jaw: she was not used to wearing it. "Oh yes. We drove up to Toronto. To see what it's like in winter. Since we will be moving there. And to pick up Hassan. He sometimes has trouble at airports. The Canadian border is easier."

"What kind of trouble?"

Elena shrugged as if the answer were obvious. "He is from Iran. He travels on a special visa, and they sometimes let him through, but they sometimes hold and question him. Which can mean as much as twelve hours. They hold him most often at airports. He asked that we come pick him up in Toronto."

"That's a long drive just to save him a possible inconvenience."

She shrugged again and smiled. "Abbas loves his brother very much. And Hassan handles the family finances. So it is well worth any inconvenience."

Zack watched the three men walking ahead, Hassan in the middle, pointing at buildings and asking Daniel about them. He was a tourist, not a terrorist, and Zack wasn't really suspicious. His real concern was Abbas. Yet there were many unanswered questions.

"What did he mean when he said he wanted to visit you while there was still time?"

"Oh, different things. He thinks there might be a war. But there always might be a war. More important, next month he is being brought into the government. They are making him their minister for economics. The position is important, and he'll be very busy. Also, they will not let him leave the country, for fear he could be seized. They are very protective of their best people. So this is his last chance to visit. And he loves Mina and Osh very much. He has no children of his own."

"He's a bachelor?"

"Oh no. He is married. Extremely married. Two years ago he took a second wife. But still no children." She lowered her voice. "We cannot discuss it, but we think he is sterile."

Hassan looked about ten years older than his brother, maybe around Zack's age. He was smoking a cigarette in an old-fashioned, European manner, cupping his hand around it. He appeared to be talking intimately and forcefully with Abbas, who was also smoking. White clouds of breath and smoke drifted overhead. Daniel gestured goodbye to the two men and stopped walking. He let the brothers move on while he waited for Zack and Elena.

"What happened?" Zack asked.

"Nothing. They began to talk about private matters. There was no place for me. Plus they were speaking Farsi."

"Oh yes. The brothers are often like that," said Elena. "As thick as thieves and indifferent to others."

Zack sensed Daniel and Elena exchange a look—he was walking between them—but he couldn't tell if it was friendly or unfriendly.

"I have a very big favor to ask," she suddenly declared. "Will you invite us to dinner again?"

Zack turned to Daniel, wondering what he made of the request. Daniel looked equally surprised.

"Hassan wants to talk with Americans," Elena explained. "He wants to meet our friends. Not to worry, he knows nothing about his brother's private life. But I would enjoy the dinner, too. Hassan is looser when he is a guest in other houses. I can actually sit down with the men. We live very differently with a mullah in the house."

"You mean he's like a Muslim priest?" said Daniel.

"Oh no. I was speaking hyperbolically. He is a businessman, one who found God and politics. But more Catholic than the pope, if you know what I mean."

"And that's why you and Mina are wearing scarves today?" said Zack. "He demands it?"

"Oh no. He never demands. He offers, he suggests, he *gives*. 'Here is a beautiful scarf. It will keep you warm. It will give me pleasure to see you wear it. And not to be a fuddy-dud, but it will make me feel better knowing strange man can't see your hair.' " She let out a heavy sigh. "It's easier to say yes than to say no."

"And Abbas goes along with this?" said Zack.

"What can he say? He becomes very quiet around his brother."

Zack turned to get Daniel's reaction, but Daniel was looking down, watching his boots crunch over the snow.

"He does not punish or threaten," said Elena. "Do not think that. He is like a too-loving mother-in-law. With God on her side. But after three days of Islamic love, I want to be a grown-up again."

Zack's immediate impulse was to say yes to dinner. He wanted to help Elena, and he was curious, very curious. But he had to discuss it with Daniel.

"We'll have to check our calendar," he said. "I can't remember what this week is like."

"I can't either," said Daniel, still looking down. "I think it's full."

No, he wouldn't want dinner, would he? Zack understood, although he hoped he could change Daniel's mind.

"You do not have to tell me today," said Elena. "You can call later in the week. But I need a night out. Desperately. And maybe we can remind Abbas who he really is. He is only playing a part around his brother, but he plays it too well."

"You mean he believes that stuff?" said Daniel.

She shrugged. "Who knows? He acts skeptical yet respectful. He says he is humoring his brother, but I think it is more." She paused. "If you invite us to dinner, you can see for yourselves," she concluded with a smile. Then she hurried ahead to join the others—they were entering the yard of the Capitol.

Zack turned to Daniel, but Daniel looked away with a frown that suggested he hated the idea of dining with any of them.

They caught up with Elena, the brothers, the children, and Jocko under the arcade of the Capitol. The building was open despite the snow, although the first tour wasn't scheduled for another fifteen minutes. There were no other tourists in the covered area.

"Built in 1753," Hassan cheerfully read from the painted wood plaque fixed in the wall. "So it's a brand-new building. More than a century younger than the most recent mosques of Isfahan."

Hassan was still not the man whom Zack expected to see. He had removed his hat and unbuttoned his coat and stood there in a handsome blue suit, which he wore without a tie, as bald as Daniel and bearded like Zack. He was stockier than his brother. He did not look like a mullah or politician but like a doctor, maybe even a psychiatrist. He looked more like a shrink than Zack did.

Zack took Jocko back from Mina. "We can't take a dog inside," he told her. "We'll just say goodbye here."

"Abbas!" Daniel's voice sounded loud and abrupt in the brick chamber. "Would you and your brother and Elena like to come to dinner this week?"

Abbas stood up straight, almost at attention. "What day?"

"I don't know. I'll check our calendar."

"Good. We will check ours."

Both men spoke curtly, coldly, like two boys challenging each other to do something dangerous.

"Wonderful!" cried Elena. "That would be lovely. You are such a fabulous cook. Let us know what we can bring."

"Do not go to any trouble on my account," said Hassan. "It is honor enough to be invited to your home."

Zack wasn't entirely surprised by Daniel's change of mind. He was often like this, sullen and resistant one moment, then abruptly generous. Zack just hadn't expected the change so soon.

"Hassan. Abbas. Elena." Zack gave a little bow to each but shook hands with Elena. "We'll give you a call."

"Yes," said Daniel. "We'll call you. Tonight or tomorrow. Goodbye. You too, kids. Enjoy the snow."

They headed out the gate with Jocko and back down Duke of Gloucester Street. They did not speak for the first fifty yards. The only sounds were the crunch and squeak of snow and a subdued canine panting.

"All right," said Daniel. "You first."

"Me? I'm primarily a spectator here. You're in the thick of it. What was it like for you?"

Daniel took a deep breath. "Painless. Weirdly painless. Almost painfully painless. I was amazed at how little I felt. I kept looking at him, waiting to see something. I saw nothing. I almost didn't recognize him. Whatever was there is gone. You'd think I hadn't seen him in months instead of just a few weeks."

"And that's what was painful?"

"Plus he never looked at me. Which pissed me off. It was like he didn't want to see me, not even as a friend or colleague."

"So why did you invite them to dinner?"

"Because I was sure he'd say no."

"It was a dare?"

Daniel twisted his mouth into a smile. "He was acting so damn butch and pious around his brother. Like he had nothing to fear from me. Nothing to feel ashamed of."

"You think he should feel ashamed?"

"You know what I mean. Do you want me to uninvite them?"

Zack hesitated. "Not really. Because I *want* them to come. I'm curious about his brother."

"Curiosity killed the cat," said Daniel. "Well, I'm curious too. I don't know who this brother is. I don't know who Abbas is anymore. What do you think Elena has up her sleeve?"

"Nothing. Why should she be up to something?"

"I don't know. Except I would think she'd be overjoyed to have a mullah in the house. If it kept her husband in her bed."

"Elena is more enlightened than you give her credit for."

"Well, she's your friend, not mine."

His tone of voice surprised Zack. Was Daniel jealous of his friendship with Elena? "Look, if having them over for dinner is going to be too weird for us, maybe we shouldn't."

"But I want to. Because it feels over. Really. It began with a dinner. Let's let it end with a dinner. Don't worry. I'm not going to pull out the blow job painting this time."

Zack turned and stared at him.

And Daniel laughed. "That was a joke, Zack. Can't I make jokes about it? Now that it's over?"

"Yes. You're right. Sorry. Of course we can make jokes." Jokes proved that they were still alert and open and fully aware of what was happening around them.

They came out of the restored area into Merchants Square, where a chorus of shovels harshly scraped the pavement. It was a noise Zack associated with New York, not Virginia. A half dozen store owners were out clearing paths to their doors.

Ross stood in front of his theater, bundled up in an old army coat and digging away with a pointy-bladed garden shovel. "Hey, dudes. Look at this shit. So pretty when it comes down. But then you got to clean it up and you find it's nothing but mess. So what's new?"

Nothing, they told him. Nothing at all.

32

The future cabinet minister of the Islamic Republic stood in their living room on Wednesday night, gazing skeptically at the fire in the fireplace, the simply dressed Christmas tree, the pictures by friends that hung on the walls. Daniel had forgotten about the art and wondered if he should have taken some of it down. Peggy Hoffman's nude photo of her hypermuscular husband, like an Edward Weston pepper, did not look so abstract or innocent tonight. Fuck it, this is our home, he thought. It was too late to change anything anyway.

Hassan Rohani solemnly nodded. "A lovely house. Very cozy. Very all-American. Speaking of which, I brought you this. Something very all-Iranian." He handed Daniel and Zack a square wrapped in pretty paper and a ribbon.

Elena groaned satirically.

Daniel pulled the paper off. Inside was what looked like a dark red vinyl tile sealed in plastic. A label in Farsi ran along the top.

"Dried salted cherries," said Hassan. "An Iranian *treat*." He bared his teeth on the last word and began to laugh.

"Like eating cherry rubber," said Elena. "*Salty* cherry rubber."

"It is not to everybody's taste," grumbled Abbas. "If you do not want it, you can return it. Osh and I like it very much."

"I'd like to try it," said Zack. "Just a taste. Maybe later."

This was hardly the first time that Daniel had socialized with an ex–sex partner, but tonight was different, stranger. Abbas let his brother take center stage, falling into the background, becoming a shadow of his brother, opaque and sullen. Daniel caught none of the ghost notes that one sometimes feels with an old trick: desire, regret, anger. No, Abbas felt like only a shadow, a mannequin, an effigy of what he'd been. Which was depressing.

Daniel hurried back to the kitchen to finish fixing dinner, leaving Zack to handle the guests. He couldn't understand why he'd agreed to this, what he hoped to prove. Well, he wanted to prove to Zack that things really were over between him and Abbas. And by proving it to Zack he could prove it to himself. But the brother was an odd ingredient, not just an excuse for tonight's dinner but a strong new color that changed the entire picture.

"Can I help with anything?"

Daniel almost jumped at the sound of Elena's voice. She stood in the kitchen doorway.

"No, we're fine. Just checking up on the chicken. Uh, you could serve the wine. Uh, can you and Abbas drink with his brother here?"

"Absolutely. 'When in Rome' is one of Hassan's favorite slogans. Here. Show me where the glasses are."

Elena acted as if they were buddies: first on the walk on Sunday, now in the kitchen. Daniel suspected she was just happy that he and Abbas were no longer fucking. But maybe the presence of the brother made her desperate for allies.

"Is that why you're not wearing a scarf tonight?" he asked. "When in Rome?"

She mockingly stroked her exposed hair. "Oh yes. This is a private dinner, and the rules are different. He is not a complete hard-ass. He grew up in Europe, remember, and he still does business there." She set out five glasses.

"One for him?" said Daniel. "He drinks when he goes out? I had grandparents like that. They kept kosher at home but loved to eat bacon whenever they visited us."

"You will see," said Elena. "You do not have to worry about Hassan in your house. Iranians are famous for their selfless courtesy. 'I am your slave.

Please step on my eyes.' " Her accent was brutally cartoony. "They do not mean a word, but it helps to keep the peace."

~

A half hour later, everyone was sitting at the dinner table, eating Daniel's roast chicken, garlic mashed potatoes, winter squash, and spinach.

"But I love America," said Hassan. "Your government says we hate you, but it isn't true. The entire Muslim world loves and admires America."

"Everyone?" said Zack. "There's a lot to dislike."

Zack and Hassan had started talking politics before dinner, Zack exploring with friendly questions, Hassan answering amiably. Abbas continued to say little.

"We love the idea more than the fact," Hassan admitted. "The fact is a different story. But the idea is beautiful. Freedom, safety, prosperity. Who could not love that?"

Daniel suspected this was the chief reason why Zack had wanted to have the Rohanis over: so he could sit with a real Muslim and indulge his intellectual curiosity. Daniel still couldn't get a fix on his own agenda for tonight. It was strange to sit directly across the table from the brother of a man whom he'd kissed and brought to orgasm. Hassan looked enough like Abbas that Daniel couldn't help thinking: This is Abbas with religion and no hair. This is Abbas ten years from now, a bald businessman with graying eyebrows and a gray beard. I don't want to have sex with *him*. But then, he didn't want to have sex with Abbas again either.

"The Iranian dream is similar to the American dream," Hassan was saying. "They are both about freedom. Which means freedom of conscience, which is the freedom to choose what is right. Which should mean the freedom to choose God. Despite what one hears, Islam is not a monolithic dogma. It is a variety of beliefs. Much more various than your Catholic Church. There is no Muslim Vatican. Iran offers the kind of religious freedom that one finds in the U.S. You would be surprised to know how much open religious discussion takes place in our mosques and universities."

"But only religions with God," said Elena. "They cannot talk about religions with no God. Or even a God with no Mohammed."

"True," said Hassan. "Quite true. But only because we are a new country and still learning how we can agree to disagree." He pointed his fork at his plate. "Excellent food. Very tasty. Delicious."

"We do what we can here in the Great Satan," said Daniel.

Hassan laughed again, a hearty, friendly laugh.

The man was personable, charming, often humorous, not at all what Daniel had expected or wanted. He did not look all that foreign either, although he came to dinner wearing the same combination of a tailored blue suit and white shirt with no collar or necktie that he had worn on Sunday. Was this Islamic corporate drag? He accepted the glass of white wine that Elena poured for him, but he didn't drink it. He left it untouched by his plate.

Daniel's curiosity got the better of him. At the next lull in conversation, he pointed at Hassan's glass. "Is that for Elijah?"

Hassan glanced down, understanding exactly what Daniel was referring to. "Oh no, it is just something I do. To remind me who I was and who I am now."

"You've been through something like Muslim AA?"

Zack loudly cleared his throat.

But Hassan wasn't offended. "My old life was one of chaos," he admitted. "I was never an alcoholic, but alcohol was part of my chaos. But I found my way to God and God provided order."

"This is not so recent," Abbas told them. "It happened long ago, when my brother was in his twenties."

"But I need to remember my old life," said Hassan. "So I can appreciate who I have become."

Elena rolled her eyes. "Hassan had a wild time as a young man in Paris, with whores and cocaine and rock and roll. Now he can spend the rest of his life being good."

Hassan smiled, as if at a harmless joke. "Yes, the seventies were wild, in Paris *and* Tehran. I went back and forth between the two cities, a sensuous businessman, a playboy accountant. I still cannot believe my excesses. Then the revolution came and Tehran stopped being fun, so I stayed away. Our father was first *with* Khomeini, then *against* Khomeini, and the family permanently joined me in Paris. I was twenty-six, so Abbas was—?"

"Fourteen," said Abbas.

Daniel noticed Zack listening attentively.

"We were a family again, stranded in the wicked West, exiled in Babylon. You would think I would rein in my appetites, or save them for trips to Amsterdam. But no. They became worse. I will spare you the sordid details and say only that the disorder of my sensual life began to spill into my family and business life. A confused accountant is a terrible thing."

"You made inappropriate use of funds?" said Zack.

"Oh no. I was tempted but didn't. There were other low points, however, which might be called turning points. The most shameful was when I was *seeing* our new maid"—he bared his teeth in another little smile—"a lovely Haitian girl who lived in our attic. Late one night I was up in her room and the door fell open and there stood my little brother, listening. Did I send him away? Did I cover my shame? No. I told Abbas to stay and watch. I wanted him to see. I wanted to show off. For the rest of my life I will burn with shame whenever I think of that."

Daniel was amazed he could tell such a story in front of strangers, especially if it shamed him.

"I was a horny little teenager!" said Abbas. "I *wanted* to watch."

"It was a disgusting deed for a man to expose his younger brother to. You were my responsibility and I failed you."

"But then you changed your mind and sent me away."

"Because the look on your face made me understand: I was acting like an animal."

Abbas let out a sigh. "It did not upset me. You always say it did. But I found the spectacle"—he searched for the right word with two open hands— "illuminating! The two of you looked so beautiful together. Disturbing yet beautiful. Not *traumatique*. Perhaps it is what made me into a painter."

The story was too personal, painfully private. It made the brothers seem terribly intimate and close. They were so close, in fact, that they didn't even notice the other people listening.

Elena only looked amused. She'd clearly heard this before. "Your guilt is very sentimental, Hassan. I am sure you have done worse things in your life."

"I have. This was only the first sin. It taught me to recognize sin. Blood is thicker than water, especially with brothers." He turned to Zack, as if a psychiatrist would understand. "I began to recognize the other sins, the whores and drugs and the rest. And I felt ashamed of them, too. The great change in my life began in shame. I slept with a good friend's wife and felt shame. I was angry with my father and felt shame. I walked past beggars on the street without giving them money and felt grievous shame. It took a year or more, but shame made me feel very naked in the world. Exposed and alone. I was alone with my sins. I saw that I had no inner life, only an outer life, a material life. I was all matter and no spirit. I felt so alone that I began to miss my country. Not God. My country." He now turned to Abbas. "Isn't that interesting? I was a man without a country. I wanted my country back. So I went looking for it in the mosques of Paris. I didn't want God, I only wanted to hear Farsi or Arabic or see a veil or turban, things I once found backward when we lived in Tehran. I used to think Islam was narrow and confining. But the secular world drowns in choices. Whores and cocaine and Haitian girls. It is like Sartre said, We were never so free as under the German occupation." He paused, then loudly cleared his throat and addressed everyone. "To make a long story short, I found God, or rather God found me, and I came home."

There was silence around the table, nobody certain what to say next. Abbas was staring down at his plate—in embarrassment, guilt, or worry, it was hard to guess.

Then Elena said, "A very pretty story, Hassan. I always enjoy hearing it. Not least because its purpose seems to change from telling to telling."

33

Wнen тнеy finiѕнed eатinɡ, Zack helped Daniel clear the table, eager to compare notes with him in the kitchen.

"The brother is not what I expected," he said as they loaded the dishwasher. "Very worldly, very open. A Muslim businessman who quotes French existentialists? And not without a sense of humor."

"I'd say he wants to impress us," said Daniel. "Only he barely notices we're here."

"You feel that, too? Yes. It's all between the two brothers, the older sib out to prove something to the younger sib, while Elena keeps getting in her two cents. How are you holding up? Is this too strange for you or is it objectively interesting?"

Daniel frowned. "Don't worry about me. It's interesting, but not *that* interesting."

They came back out with the coffee and cake and found their guests in the living room, all three using the fireplace as an ashtray for their cigarettes.

"Our smoking does not bother you?" asked Hassan.

"Oh no. Go ahead. I used to be a smoker myself," said Zack.

"So polite," said Elena. "Almost Iranian. 'Please step on my eyes,'" she said in a thick, parody accent.

The Iranians laughed, and Zack automatically laughed with them. Daniel looked guilty, as if embarrassed for Zack.

They took their seats on either side of the fire, Daniel, Abbas, and Hassan on the sofa, Zack and Elena in the love seat facing them. While Daniel handed out the cake, Zack introduced a new topic, something he'd been wanting to explore. "I apologize for my ignorance, Hassan. But I know almost nothing about Islam. Not even the basics. For example, do you actually pray five times a day?"

Hassan was happy to discuss his religion. The rules and rituals were not strictly enforced, he said, but provided order when order was needed. He usually prayed twice a day, in the morning and the evening. The calls to prayer back home were the most beautiful sounds imaginable, lovelorn chants from all over the city, but one did not need to answer every call. He took a prayer rug with him on his travels, a lovely kilim that he'd purchased in London. He would pray alone in his room—he did it here in the house on Chandler Court—but he tried to visit a mosque every Friday, even when abroad.

"Is there a mosque in Williamsburg?" asked Zack.

"In Newport News," said Elena. "In an old car dealership on a highway, between a Burger King and a filling station." She took nasty pleasure in the location.

"You should have gone there during Ramadan," Hassan told his brother. "If not for your sake, then for Arash. It is good for a boy to have such memories for later, when it is time for him to choose or not choose religion. It was invaluable for me."

"No," said Abbas quietly. "We did not observe Ramadan. Nor did we observe Death to America Day."

Hassan chuckled. "November fourth," he explained to his hosts. "The day the American embassy was seized after the fall of the Shah. We stopped celebrating it years ago. It was never very popular. We did not have Death to America trees in the home"—he pointed at the Christmas tree—"or send Death to America cards to each other."

Daniel gazed at their tree. "It's sometimes odd being a Jew at Christmas. It must be hell to be a Muslim."

Zack examined Daniel, wondering where this was going.

Hassan only smiled. "Not at all. Christmas is charming. Exotic. You must feel something similar when you read Greek mythology or visit the ruined temples of Rome."

"All religion is like chemotherapy," said Elena. "It does more harm than good."

"I couldn't agree with you more," said Daniel.

The others were instantly silent, as if two guns had just been fired in the air. Zack was surprised to find Daniel and Elena on the same side—he wondered if he'd have to step in and keep the peace.

Hassan remained calm and confident. "Yet true religion, in the end, does more good than ill. Like successful chemo."

"And who is to say which religion is true?" said Elena.

"The one that does the most good. That gives solace and unity to the most people."

"Ah, majority rules?" Elena spoke lightly, playfully, as if this were a game she and her brother-in-law often played together.

"Yes, majority rules. Democracy is good. It dilutes and smoothes away personal error." Hassan addressed Zack. "Iran was thrown too quickly into the future. We became lost in modernity." He made the word sound very foreign: *mo-dare-nity*. "We needed God. We needed Islam. Because people must believe in something larger than themselves. We could believe in race and be like the Nazis. Or in the State and be like the Communists. So Islam is better. We are bringing back the good, old, moral Iran of our ancestors."

"The old Iran was not so moral," said Abbas, looking down at his coffee cup. "It was about cruelty and riches, sensuous painting and freethinking poetry." He said something in Farsi, a lovely singsong of syllables, then translated. " 'We go to the tavern to make up for all the time we have wasted in the mosque.' "

Hassan waved the quote aside and laughed. "That is the old Persian cynicism. Omar Khayyam and the rest. Maudlin drunks. There are other Persian poets."

"Yes, there are erotic poets like Hafiz." Abbas spoke again in Farsi, but didn't translate this quote.

Hassan hesitated, then frowned. For the first time tonight, he seemed at a loss for words. He glanced over at Zack, then looked away, embarrassed. Then he found his words.

"You misread him. That is divine love. He is a Sufi, and the Sufis are often misread. Hafiz's love of boys is only a metaphor, a dangerous yet beautiful metaphor. Otherwise it is *vicious* pederasty."

His harsh tone startled Zack. He looked at Daniel, who appeared similarly startled. Abbas continued to face his brother, defiantly poker-faced, coolly silent.

"Erotic love is divine in its own right. It doesn't need to be a metaphor."

Everyone turned. It was Elena who spoke.

"Hafiz writes so grandly about men loving boys," she said, "that it is absurd to pretend he means something else. Why not say that American movies where men and women kiss are only metaphors and allow them in your theaters? Pornography, too, is a divine metaphor. Naked bodies are only similes for hungry souls." She spoke slowly, carefully, with the tiniest smile.

And Zack understood: she found her husband's sexuality less of a threat to her marriage than she found her brother-in-law's religion. She was on her husband's side here. Would she come right out and spill his secret? What did Hassan know? Surely he knew something. He wasn't stupid. He knew he was visiting the home of two gay men. Did he know his brother had been seeing one of them?

Hassan studied Elena, as if weighing and judging her threat. He turned to Daniel. "You are an art professor. What do you think of my brother's paintings? Are they good?"

The change of subject confused Daniel. "Sometimes. Often. Yes. They can be quite good. Beautiful, in fact."

"I like them, too," said Hassan. "But I am in finance and he is my brother, so what do I know? I presume I am prejudiced."

"You know only the old work," said Abbas, seizing the subject. "The new work is very different."

"When can I see the new work?"

"Whenever it is convenient."

"How about tonight?" Hassan turned to the others. "Let us take a walk. It is not too late. Your studio is nearby, yes? It would be fun to look at your work with people who know art."

Abbas frowned. "The studio will be freezing. The heat is turned down during the holiday."

"Then we won't stay long. We will have a quick look and go home. Since your daughter is babysitting your son, we cannot stay out late anyway."

"I want to see it, too," said Elena. "It has been months since I've been to the studio. I have not seen the newest things."

Abbas exchanged a long, uncertain look with his wife. "Fine then. Suit yourself. It is your funeral," he told his brother. "You will not like it. You will find it too strange and modern."

"Maybe. Maybe not," said Hassan. "I am a man of many worlds. Nothing my brother does will ever strike me as *too* strange."

They quickly put on their coats and hats. Elena knotted a scarf around her head, but then, as if to prove it was only for warmth, she squeezed a beret on top. They went out the front door and down the street toward the campus. It was cold, yet most of the snow was gone. All that remained were a few lacy patches of ice on the lawns.

Zack walked with Daniel, letting the Rohanis get ahead.

"What does Hassan think he's going to see?" he whispered.

"Beats me. But he won't see anything sensuous or pornographic, that's for sure."

"Maybe it's just his way of changing the subject." Yet Zack felt there was an exact purpose to everything this politician said or did.

Abbas had been right about the art building. The heat was turned down, the interior freezing. Daniel flicked on lights as they went up the stairs. They came to a door and Abbas unlocked it. The cold darkness gave off a resinous stink of paint and turpentine. As the fluorescent lights fluttered on, Zack's eyes darted around a big room, taking in stretched canvases stacked like stage flats against a wall, then other canvases lying on the floor. The place was total chaos, far messier than Daniel's studio at home. A massacre of squeezed paint tubes covered a table. Underneath were coffee cans full of dirty brushes, and a black boom box slapped all over with blue fingerprints.

Zack saw the sofa in the back, a long green vinyl sofa. Which was where Daniel and Abbas must have spent every Sunday this past fall. Which didn't matter now that it was over, although it must matter or Zack wouldn't instantly know that they'd fucked here. It looked like such a plain, simple, harmless sofa.

Zack wondered if Elena noticed it, too, but no, she already stood over one of the paintings on the floor, frowning at it.

Four stretched paintings lay flat on the floor. They hadn't fallen there but were deliberately set out to be worked on. The visitors strolled around the canvases as if they were Abstract Expressionist flower beds. Everyone remained wrapped in his or her coat, their breaths visible in the cold, their arms folded disapprovingly. Zack didn't know if the others disapproved or not, but he had no love for abstract art. Oh, he could admire colors and textures and technique, but he wanted people in his pictures, figures, even abstract figures that could be misread as people. He looked and looked, trying to will some kind of appreciation. Out of the mess of this room and the mess of his life, Abbas had produced a series of austere, beautiful abstractions, swirling fields of concentrated color, with large spermy squiggles embedded inside.

"These are new," said Daniel, pointing at the floor paintings. "I've seen the others but not these."

"They are all different from the old work," said Elena. "Very—" Her hand stirred the air without finding an answer.

Zack noticed a stack of library books in the corner, fat art books on artists he knew and liked: Hockney, Degas, Bacon, Balthus. He resisted the impulse to open a volume just to give his eye something solid to look at.

Abbas was circling the room, keeping his distance from his paintings. He approached Zack. Zack pointed at the books.

"I see you're not completely indifferent to the human figure."

"What?" Abbas looked. "No. But the figure was only a phase I was doing to get where I was going. Now I am done with the body."

Daniel stood close enough to hear. He turned to Zack with raised eyebrows and a snarky, what-did-I-tell-you smirk.

Abbas joined his brother and wife, who stood in front of a large green painting tilted against the back wall.

"Abbas, I do not know," began Elena. "These are heavy. Maybe too heavy?" It was hard to guess if she meant the adjective in its old, slangy sense or something else.

Hassan, however, was intrigued by the paintings. "I love the colors," he said. "So rich. And the bits of Arabic are suggestive." He aimed a finger at his brother and smiled. "It is the Koran, yes?"

Abbas shrugged. "I began with Farsi, but Arabic is better. The samples of calligraphy from the Koran are quite beautiful."

So the squiggles weren't sperm but the word of God?

Elena looked alarmed, Hassan delighted.

"The new work is about color," Abbas insisted. "But I needed something for the colors to hang on." His voice took on the self-conscious drone of most artists describing their art, an anxious mumble that Zack knew primarily from Daniel's comic parody of it. "I tried numbers, but numbers are too solid. Arabic is softer, more various. And the bits of Koran offer a second layer of reference. The passages I quote can also be used as titles." He pointed at the green painting. "This one, for example, is called 'In the name of God, the compassionate, the merciful.' "

Hassan began to smile. "And it is green," he said. "The favorite color of Mohammed."

Abbas frowned. "That was an accident."

"There are no accidents in God's universe," Hassan teased. "What is this one called?" He pointed at the pale orange rectangle on the floor.

" 'Surrender to God and you will be safe.' "

"And that one?"

Dark blue with waxy white lettering.

" 'Shall we believe as imbeciles believe?' "

The grin faded a little, but did not disappear. "I see. Your titles are also jests. I have no problem with that. Because a jest is serious, too." Hassan readjusted his smile, renewed it. "You think you are a great rebel, a liberated nihilist. But you are working out your feelings for God. Which includes a great love of Him."

Abbas stood up straighter. "Not at all. I am only working out problems in shape and color. I don't care about God."

"You say that, and maybe you think it. But you don't really feel it. Not in your heart of hearts. Otherwise, it would not express itself so clearly in your paintings. And I would not find them so beautiful."

Abbas kept his defiant posture, yet the look in his eyes seemed to change, softening then rehardening. He felt flattered by his brother, and he didn't want to be flattered.

Elena stood off to the side, watching her husband defend himself. Zack expected her to jump into the argument. But she noticed something new in the painting that leaned against the wall.

"Is that a hand?" She pointed at a red mark on the bright green canvas. "A child's hand?" She leaned in closer. "Is that Mina? No, it's Osh!" She glared at her husband. "You put his hand in your painting!"

Abbas looked confused. "So?"

"He isn't dead!"

He stared at her in disbelief.

"It looks like blood!" she cried. "You make it look like somebody killed him." She barked at him in Russian, or maybe it was Farsi with a Russian accent.

Zack had never seen Elena so furious. He'd seen her angry with her husband, but that had been about pride and self. This was more raw and out of control, this was about her children.

"She does not like you quoting the Koran," said Hassan.

"Bullshit!" She switched back to English. "Who cares about your Koran! He can quote the Koran or the man in the moon, I don't care. So long as he doesn't use *my* children as his metaphors."

"*Your* children?" said Abbas. "They are my children, too."

"Not when you use them as symbols! Not when you use them as signs!" She pointed at the handprint. "This is asking for trouble, Abbas! This is tempting fate!"

"Elena, you are talking like a superstitious old woman," said Hassan. "Our friends here will think you are a crazy mother."

She twisted her face into an ugly scowl. "Zack and Daniel know I am an excellent mother! A better mother than Abbas is a father!"

"Stop this immediately!" Zack declared, holding up both hands. "No more. Be silent. Before anyone says anything they can't unsay."

And they were silent, much to Zack's surprise. This was his other half speaking, his professional half, which he often forgot when he was with friends or family.

"Elena," he said quietly. "Relax. It's only a painting. Abbas meant no harm. Did you, Abbas?"

Abbas took a deep breath. "No. Of course not. I put him in the painting only because he was there and we were having fun."

"Hmmm." She was nodding and staring at him. "I am sorry I flew off the handle." She turned to take another look at the painting but couldn't. "Let's go home. I am tired and it is late and I do not like this new work, Abbas. It will take me time to digest. But you cannot tempt fate. Maybe I *am* a superstitious old woman. But if Osh gets hurt next year or later, I will not be able to stop myself from blaming you."

They all trooped downstairs and parted outside.

"Thank you for an excellent evening," said Hassan. "This has been very enlightening. For everyone."

"Call if you need anything," said Zack, pretending to address all three but looking only at Elena.

The Rohanis cut across the playing field toward Chandler Court while Zack and Daniel made a beeline across the lawn toward their street. The frozen grass crunched underfoot like gravel.

Daniel spoke first. "I saw him put Osh's hand in the painting, you know. It seemed innocent but still made me uncomfortable."

"Well, Elena's anger was fed by lots of things tonight," said Zack. "But that handprint does look sinister."

Here we are, thought Zack, finishing another evening where we looked at the same events from slightly different angles, as if through a pair of binoculars. It was always interesting to put together the stereoscopic vision afterward.

"Do you think Hassan really loves art?" Zack asked. "Or does he only love his brother?"

"Are you kidding?" said Daniel. "He knows nothing about art. He might love his brother, but it's a bossy, possessive kind of love."

"I give him the benefit of the doubt. I think his love is genuine. But tricky."

"I'll say it's tricky. The man's a Muslim fundamentalist. Any love he gives is going to be like a ton of bricks."

They walked down the middle of Indian Springs Road, between the sleeping houses, keeping their voices low.

"Does he know his brother's gay?"

Daniel was silent for five paces, then ten paces. "He must. Don't you think?"

"He's smart. But smart people can surprise you with their blind spots. He might know without knowing that he knows."

"Whatever," said Daniel. "It's not our fight anymore. It's none of our business now."

No, it isn't, thought Zack. Yet it could be again. Their households were too tangled together for them to pretend otherwise. But they didn't need to get into that now.

"I can't say I liked his paintings," said Zack.

"Honey, you don't get contemporary art."

"I get some of it. But this work is too abstract, too dry."

"I prefer the earlier stuff," Daniel admitted. "It was more playful. Now he's gone from Klee to Rothko. But I like his grandeur."

"I like your work so much more. And I'm not just saying that. Even when it's an empty room or a landscape, one can sense people have just left and we know something about what you feel about those people."

"Uh-huh," said Daniel, without interest.

Zack had praised Daniel's work before, and Daniel never seemed to believe him. Tonight he didn't even seem to hear.

"Like the man said," Daniel continued, going back to *his* subject, "the body was only a phase he was working through. And now the phase is finished and he's going to get really abstract."

34

On Saturday afternoon Daniel went with Zack out to Eastern State for the annual Christmas party. He hadn't gone in the past few years, not because the party was too weird but because it wasn't weird enough. He wasn't entirely sure why he went this year, although he had his suspicions.

"Anybody I should be warned about?" he asked in the car. "Exciting manic-depressives? Dangerous nymphomaniacs?"

"No, it's a pretty tame bunch. Just watch out for family members. They can pump you for pity like there's no tomorrow."

The party was held in the day room, a large, open, sunny space with no visible bars on the windows, hardly *Marat/Sade* but more like a 1960s nursing home. People sadly sat or moved about with the slow, self-conscious uncertainty of the elderly, yet the median age here was only forty. Few patients wore robes and pajamas, and it was difficult to tell patients from visitors, at first. The chief decoration was an artificial tree like a big green scrub brush wrapped in chains of construction paper. Christmas music played over the P.A. system, songs from fifty years back, but then Christmas music, like mental illness, is stuck in its own time outside of time.

Daniel spotted Mrs. Chat, the senior shrink's wife, and went straight to her.

"Hello, Daniel. So good to see you. You are here like me, to offer an example of normal?"

"If we count as normal, the world gets a lot of wiggle room."

"You're telling me, brother," said Mrs. Chat with a laugh. She was a lively, bosomy Indian lady who reminded Daniel of his aunt Louise in Brooklyn, frank, funny, and just a bit nosy. They stood side by side, watching their spouses work the room.

Dr. Chat was chatting up an African American family, laughing with them in forced amusement over something said by the stiff, white-haired scarecrow who must be a father or uncle.

Zack crouched in the corner, talking to a large young woman with a face like a troll doll who sat moping in a chair. He coaxed her up and across the room to a little old lady beside the tree.

"How have you been keeping yourself?" Mrs. Chat asked Daniel. "Keeping out of trouble?"

Her question might be just friendly noise, but there was no telling how much Zack told Dr. Chat and what Dr. Chat told his wife. "Oh, you know what they say," said Daniel. "No rest for the wicked."

The troll doll began to shriek, "I love you, Mama! I love you, I love you, I love you!" and threw her arms around the old lady.

The old lady looked terrified.

Zack gently drew the two women apart, calming the troll doll, whispering to the old lady.

The whole room was staring—you'd think the daughter had shouted an obscenity, which was exactly how she'd used the words.

Zack remained remarkably calm and professional. A nurse came over to help, but Zack gestured her away: they were fine.

Daniel couldn't understand how he did it. So few things seemed to upset Zack in his work. Which might be why he often appeared to experience everything from a slight distance. Zack seemed to want too little from life. Selflessness was a virtue, but not necessarily a pure virtue. It might also be a fear of self.

Daniel found himself admiring Zack today, but he also envied him. There was a tinge of resentment in his envy. If only he could be more like Zack, if only he could lose himself in other people's troubles, then he might get into less trouble. Next year he would do better. Yes, next year he would be wiser.

~~~

Christmas Day fell on a Wednesday, which poked a hole in the middle of the week. They did their usual morning of a big breakfast and gifts: Zack gave Daniel a boxed set of Murnau on DVD, which was actually for them both. Daniel gave Zack the BBC adaptation of *Wives and Daughters,* also on DVD, which he wanted to see, too: he knew he'd never read Elizabeth Gaskell but he was curious about where Zack had been these past months. They gave Jocko a knotted piece of rawhide as big as a dinosaur bone, which was solely for Jocko.

At noon they drove out to Ross's house on the Chickahominy for a midday dinner. The scenery was classic. A gray glaze of ice covered the river. The woods around the old farmhouse were still lightly salted with snow. The hot tub steamed threateningly out back.

The only other guests were Jane Morrison, her husband, John, and their teenage daughter, Artemisia. "I invited the Rohanis, but they couldn't come," said Ross. "Something about a visiting relative from Iran who's not very good company."

Zack said, "That's funny. We had them over for dinner the other night, and Hassan was fine. Perfectly charming."

"Charming *enough,*" said Daniel.

"Well, we had them for Thanksgiving," said Jane. "And *she* was charming but Abbas was a total pill."

The roast goose was different yet tasty, the wine excellent, the conversation nicely restrained by the presence of a fifteen-year-old: departmental shop talk and gossip were kept to a minimum. Artemisia also meant everyone had to wear bathing suits if they used the hot tub after dinner. Zack and Daniel begged off anyway, claiming they were getting over colds and should be heading home.

It was not yet seven when they drove back to town. The highways were eerily deserted. Traffic signals changed over empty intersections. Swarms of gaudy lights covered the stores and houses along Jamestown Road, but on Indian Springs only discreet pairs of electric candles stood in the windows. Daniel took Jocko for his walk as soon as they got home. When he returned he found Zack laying wood for a fire in the rec room. "I thought maybe we could watch one of our Christmas presents. *Faust* or *The Last Laugh*?"

The doorbell rang. They looked at each other worriedly.

"Better not be a patient," said Daniel, and he went upstairs to get the door. Emergency visitors sometimes changed their minds when they saw Daniel and remembered their doctor had a life. Daniel turned on the porch light and peered through the little window.

Abbas stood on the porch, wearing no coat, only a heavy sweater. His Saab was parked on the street, the motor running.

Daniel threw open the door. "Something wrong?"

Abbas was breathing smoke; his hands were pressed into his armpits. "I need to talk. Come ride with me."

Daniel was too surprised to answer.

Then he heard Zack. "You can come inside and talk, Abbas. If you need to talk privately, I'll make myself scarce. It's a big house."

Zack was standing behind Daniel, at the end of the hall.

Abbas looked offended by the invitation. "No. I need to drive. I need to be moving. I need to go somewhere for a drink."

"You can drink here," said Zack.

But Abbas was adamant. "Thank you, no. Will you come?"

Daniel turned around, intending to face Zack and speak to him. But he kept turning and opened the closet door to get his coat before he looked at Zack. "I won't be long," he said. "All we're going to do is talk."

"Fine," said Zack. "Then go." His tone was dry and dismissive. "Just be careful driving. If you *do* drink."

When Daniel got outside, Abbas was already striding across the yard, and Daniel followed, not looking back, not wanting to see Zack standing in the door. He climbed into the car. It stank of cigarette smoke. He watched Abbas put the car into gear and let out the brake. He had never seen Abbas drive before.

Abbas kept his eyes locked on the street, his hands set rigidly on the wheel. "I am crazy horny tonight," he said. "Angry horny. So horny I cannot think clearly."

He had come to Daniel for emergency sex? Daniel couldn't help feeling insulted, excited, and touched. "All right," he said. "Where can we go?"

Abbas remained stone-faced. "I don't know. The art building was locked up today—I could not get in. It is freezing anyway."

"You want to try a motel?"

Abbas nodded. "But I do not have much time. I have to be home by ten. Before my brother goes to bed."

"Where does your family think you went?"

"I said I needed to be alone and think about my work. And that I would pick up milk and eggs on the way back."

Daniel chuckled. "You sure are romantic, baby."

Abbas didn't even smile. "This is not romance, it is physiology."

Daniel directed him east, where the cheaper "family" motels were located. There was a big, impersonal Hampton Inn he'd used last year when he was seeing a young architect with a boyfriend.

"So things are crazy at home and you had to get out?"

"Like you wouldn't believe."

"Oh, I can believe. And you need some tension-easing nooky."

Abbas gritted his teeth and nodded. "I want to come and come and come until I bleed."

Daniel was too stunned to answer. "Uh, let's try here," he said.

They swung into the parking lot of the Hampton Inn. Daniel went inside alone, stepping into heated air and sugary music. He tugged his coat down in case his boner was showing.

"Merry Christmas, sir," chirped a pretty young woman at the front desk. "What can I do for you?"

"My friend and I have been driving all day. We need a place to crash. What's your cheapest room?"

"I'm terribly sorry, sir, but we're full up this evening."

"On Christmas Day?" Didn't all good Christians stay home today?

"The Yuletide is a very special season here in Colonial Williamsburg. You should have made reservations."

Daniel went back to the car. "This might be harder than I thought. Let's drive out toward Busch Gardens and see if we have better luck further out of town."

Abbas twisted around to back up the car. His face looked dark and gloomy in the light from the motel lobby. He hadn't shaved today. Daniel could feel the whisker burns just looking at him—the sensation excited Daniel. When they were on the highway again, he wanted to kiss Abbas to cheer him up and encourage them, but he couldn't, not while Abbas was driving. He reached over and rubbed his thigh, but the gesture felt only chummy, not erotic.

Then Abbas said, "Hassan wants us to come to Tehran."

"What?" Daniel looked at his face again. "For a visit?"

"Forever. He says I belong in Iran and they need their artists and I will have a great future if I come home."

Daniel was confused, alarmed. "You said no, right?"

"Yes. Of course I said no."

Daniel resumed looking for motels, as if a motel would solve this. The smaller motels were totally dark, as if closed for the week. The larger ones all bore "No vacancy" signs.

"Does Elena know about his invitation?"

"Oh yes. She was there. And she said she would be miserable in Tehran, and I would be miserable, too. She has seen their art and it is all kitsch. I will be a cultural prisoner, she said. 'You will celebrate him one month, and censor him the next. You will change your mind and call him an enemy of God. Like you did Salman Rushdie.' And Hassan said, 'Oh no. That was a big mistake. Nothing like that will happen again.' "

None of it made sense to Daniel. "Why would he want you there? Is it to control you?"

"No. He loves me. He loves his niece and nephew. And he is afraid we will be separated if there is a war. But I told him: if there is a war, we will be safer here than next door in Tehran."

"Your brother really thinks there'll be a war with Iraq?"

Abbas shrugged. "He doesn't know. Nobody knows. But I made myself clear: Elena and the children and I will not go to Iran."

"Here, this one looks good," said Daniel. "Let's try this one."

It was a Motel 6 between the highway and the railroad tracks. The place was open, although only a few cars were parked out front. Inside the office was a big silver wreath like an aluminum foil life preserver, and an immensely fat young man like a baby elephant playing a video war game. "Yeah?" he grumbled.

"Can I get a room for me and my friend? We've been driving all day and we're exhausted."

Daniel felt the elephant scowling while he signed the credit card voucher, but the guy was probably only pissed to have his game interrupted. "Uh, what time is checkout?" Daniel took the plastic room card—nobody used keys anymore—returned to the car, and told Abbas to drive to the end of the building. One last car was parked there, an SUV. A television flickered behind the curtains.

"You could not get a room without neighbors?" said Abbas.

"I didn't ask," Daniel snapped. "Does it matter?"

The lock clicked open, and they heard muffled laughter from the TV next door. The room smelled of cold and mildew, like an old refrigerator. Daniel turned on the overhead light; it was so dim and bleak that he immediately turned it off. "Get the bathroom light," he barked at Abbas. He couldn't understand why he was angry. He drew the curtains and turned on the heater under the window. "It'll warm up soon," he said, trying to sound friendlier. "Let's use this bed. It's closer to the heater."

Abbas grabbed his shoulders, turned him around, and kissed him hard. His tongue pumped in and out. His whiskers bit like tiny teeth. His hands were cold and clumsy. They hadn't done this in weeks and were starting all over. Sex had lost its continuity. It was no longer smooth and frictionless but awkward, bumpy, grabby.

Abbas stopped kissing, stepped back, and yanked his sweater over his head. "Hurry up. We don't have much time."

Daniel undressed quickly, like a man who was going to jump into a river and save a drowning swimmer. He watched Abbas, wanting to enjoy the sight of him undressing, but Abbas looked so serious sitting at the foot of the bed, grimly struggling with a shoelace. Daniel whipped off his own undershirt and shorts: the air was freezing. He leaped under the blankets: the sheets were like ice. He wiggled there, trying to warm the bed. Then Abbas stood up, a nude silhouette, and he climbed over the covers and under them, his warm body joining Daniel's body. He promptly got on top and resumed kissing, opening Daniel's legs with his knees, holding Daniel's head in both hands.

Daniel ran his own hands over a muscular back and oval ass and sinewy thighs. How had he convinced himself this didn't matter? A hairy chest rubbed a hairy chest; a hard tongue filled his mouth. Daniel hooked his legs around Abbas's legs and hung on happily.

Then Abbas withdrew his tongue and lifted his head. He let out a short, sharp sigh. "It's not working," he said.

Daniel laughed, thinking he was kidding. "What isn't working?"

Abbas unwound his legs and rolled off. Daniel reached down. He found a warm squash of genitals, the penis barely distinguishable from the scrotum.

"Oh, baby," Daniel whispered. "Here. Relax. I'll get us in the mood." He set Abbas's hand around his own erection, as if to set an example. He resumed kissing, more slowly now. He cradled testicles in his hand, as gently as eggs; he stroked with his thumb.

But it was no good. The thing remained a loose handful of skin. Its softness was as contagious as a yawn. Daniel needed the other body to want his body, and when the other body didn't, his body died. The laughter from the TV next door became audible again.

Daniel scooted under the covers to use his mouth.

"No!" Abbas stopped him. "It is no good. Forget it." He turned as if to get out of bed.

Daniel grabbed his shoulder. "Hold on. It's not even nine yet. We still got time. Maybe our bodies just have to get used to each other again. Relax. Have a cigarette."

"My cigarettes are in the car. If I get dressed to get them, I won't come back." But Abbas remained in bed, sitting up with his knees raised under the blankets, his body folded around his genitals. He rubbed his face in the blankets. "I thought I wanted this. I thought it would help. It would make things clear. But it doesn't."

"Help make what clear?"

"My future. My choices."

Oh shit, thought Daniel. This was why he needed sex tonight, not because he was horny but to finish his argument with Hassan.

"But you already said no to your brother."

Abbas frowned. "But I will have to say no again and again. Not only to him but to myself."

"Why? You don't want to go to Iran."

"Most of me doesn't. But part of me does. And why not? I am nobody in America. Painting is dead here. But my brother says Iran needs artists. Iranian art for the Iranian people. I could have success. I could be useful. My brother says. And I am Iranian. I am a foreigner everywhere else. I would be foreign there, too, but maybe less so. Still, there might be a war. So I can't even consider it."

"Does your brother know you're gay?"

Abbas remained sitting up, facing forward. "He knows. He does not understand. It is a childish thing, he says, a schoolboy thing. I have children now, he says. My children love me, my wife loves me, he loves me. He says I must listen to their love and forget about sex with men."

"Poor baby. No wonder you can't function. You got a helluva lot on your mind tonight."

Abbas nodded. "And I wanted to get out of my mind and into my body, but my body is useless to me. My body is dead." He grabbed the blankets and pulled them to his chin as he scooted against the headboard, keeping his nudity covered. "This was a mistake, a big mistake. But I was angry at home and making everyone else angry, and Elena said, 'Go get laid. Get sucked by your American. Get fucked by your American. Maybe that will make you feel better.' But I can't and now I feel even worse."

Daniel lay on his side, staring up at Abbas. It was *Elena's* idea that Abbas come see him? "*She* sent you?"

"Yes. She wanted me to take my edge off. I was so impossible to be around."

Daniel was amazed by how angry this made him. He tried to cool his temper by chuckling. All he produced was a dry, mirthless noise. "You people. You're crazy. You're all crazy! And you keep dragging me into your craziness!"

"You are angry?" said Abbas. "Why are you angry?"

"*You* tell me. Or no. I'll tell you." He took a deep breath. "I'm angry because you don't know what the hell you want. You don't know if you want to be a gay man or a good father or a great painter or a good brother or what.

You have to have your wife tell you that you're horny before you even come looking for me."

Abbas closed his eyes. "I am sorry to bring you out on such a cold night and not deliver. But I am even more frustrated than you that I cannot get hard."

"Yeah, because that's the only way you can see me: with a hard-on. Otherwise I don't exist." The bed was too warm now, too confining. Daniel threw back the covers and got up. "Hell, Elena is more aware of my existence than you are." He walked around the bed, looking for his boxer shorts. "She thinks a roll in the hay with me will guarantee you won't want to run off to Iran? She doesn't have a clue, does she?"

Abbas was scowling. "Why are you talking like this? You are talking like a man in love. You are not in love with me."

Daniel found his shorts and flipped them open. There are few acts more awkward than pulling on your undershorts after failed sex. Daniel stepped in and pulled them up before he answered. "No, I'm not in love. This isn't love talking. This is just ego. It's just pride. I have my pride, you know."

They were only words, of course, but they felt right, they felt true. Daniel was relieved to have stumbled upon them.

Abbas seemed to consider their accuracy. He lifted his arm and pointed. "Give me my clothes."

"Get them yourself."

"I don't want you to see me like this."

"Like what? Like I haven't seen you naked a hundred times? Like I haven't seen every inch of your body?"

Abbas closed his eyes. "I feel very ashamed right now. *Please.*"

It was such a desperate request that Daniel gave in. He gathered Abbas's clothes off the floor and dumped them on the bed.

"Why the sudden modesty? Is it your guilty conscience? Or your brother? Or do you suddenly believe in God?"

Abbas glared at Daniel. "You are an American fool. You know nothing about family or homeland or God. And a guilty conscience is a Western concept. Turn around."

"Don't flatter yourself. I don't need to see your dick."

Daniel turned away and sat on the other bed to get dressed. He heard the slither and snap of clothing behind him. Their bodies were as angry as their voices, confused to have been naked without getting any pleasure or relief.

Daniel finished first and stood at the door, waiting for Abbas. He opened the door and stood back, careful not to touch him. Fifteen minutes ago they'd been able to grope or poke anywhere. Now the slightest brush of a hand seemed like an insult. Abbas walked past with his head held high, acting proud that they hadn't had sex.

He was getting into the Saab when a pair of headlights swung by, illuminating him from the waist up. He raised his arm to shield his eyes, like a man having a vision in a biblical epic. Daniel covered his eyes too and saw a small white sedan cruising the front of the motel, apparently lost.

The sedan came back again as they were pulling out. Abbas slammed on the brake. Both vehicles paused, motors running, each driver waiting for the other to roll down a window and speak. Then the white car lightly tooted its horn, as if to say "Sorry," and drove on.

They said nothing on the drive back into town.

When they pulled up outside the house, Daniel declared, "I think we need to avoid each other from here on out."

"Absolutely," said Abbas.

Daniel waited for details, but Abbas offered none. Daniel got out of the car and carefully closed the door, not wanting to slam it.

In the house, the living room was dark, and Daniel was afraid Zack had gone to bed. Then he heard music downstairs, a sinister pipe organ. Zack was watching a movie.

Daniel came down the stairs. Zack only glanced at him. "I went ahead and started *Faust.* Since we both already know the plot."

A Gothic maiden stood in flickering light that might be hellfire or heaven, it was hard to tell in black-and-white.

Daniel sat on the sofa. "The man's a total mess," he said. "It was never about love. It was about pride and sex. Ego and sex. Although it wasn't sex tonight. It was just a Jew and a Muslim sitting naked in a Motel 6 and snapping at each other. That was my Christmas."

Zack pressed the pause button on the remote. The image on the screen froze, not perfectly but shakily. Zack remained turned toward the TV. "Your face is red with whisker burns," he said.

"Yeah?" Daniel nervously touched his cheek. "I must look like I've been rimming a porcupine. I know you don't want to hear about it, but nothing happened tonight. He couldn't even get an erection."

"No, I don't want to hear about it," Zack said drily. "I'm tired of hearing about it."

"It's no good trying to jump back into something that's over."

"*I told you,* I'm tired of hearing about it."

Daniel ignored the plea. "Do you know why he wanted to get laid tonight? You know whose idea it was? Elena's."

That got Zack's attention.

Daniel backtracked and filled him in on Hassan's invitation to Iran—"I can't say I'm surprised," said Zack—then explained Elena's role and how upset he'd been when Abbas told him.

"So it was Elena's fault the two of you went off to fuck?"

"I told you, we tried to fuck but couldn't."

"You get no points there."

"Why are you angry?"

"Because I thought it was over. I was sure it was over. I was *glad* it was over!"

Zack losing his temper made Daniel lose his. "But *some* people won't let it be over! They keep throwing us together! Socially or sexually! You're the one who invited them to dinner the other night."

"I didn't! You did! Remember?"

"But you wanted me to invite them!"

Zack was silent for a moment. "So where did you leave things?"

"We're not going to see each other again."

"Where have I heard that before?"

"Look. There's nothing we want from each other now. We can't have sex. We can't talk. I think he's getting religious."

He thought that last item might interest Zack. Instead Zack said, "How do you know you won't want sex again? After his brother leaves town, maybe he'll be able to perform again."

Daniel hadn't considered that. He didn't like considering it now. "No. I know him too well now. Sex has gotten too complicated. It's not fun anymore. It wasn't fun tonight. I'd have to be a total masochist to want to go back to bed with him. I'd have to be obsessed or in love, and I assure you, I'm neither of those things."

"That's good to hear," Zack said softly. "I'm glad to hear that." So softly that Daniel barely caught it, the whisper of sarcasm.

He was angry with Daniel, coldly angry. Which was his right, of course. Yet Zack's cold anger made Daniel indignantly angry with Zack. It was an unjust emotion, yet Daniel felt it.

"You're really pissed with me tonight, aren't you?" said Daniel.

Zack paused. "Yes. And with myself. And with them. We're much too involved here, too tangled up in Rohanis. I wish we could wash our hands of the entire family."

"We can now," said Daniel. "If you want to. I made a start."

"I think it's too late for a total break. But maybe we can cool it."

"Fine with me."

They were both silent, as if waiting for someone to admit or deny blame, or offer ground rules for breaking off with the family.

"Want to watch the movie?" said Zack. "I could return to the beginning." He was backing away from the argument, offering peace.

Daniel stood up. "No. Finish it without me. I'm going to bed." And he started up the stairs.

It was a petty blow against Zack, a peevish poke. He knew how much Zack disliked seeing a movie without him, sorry they couldn't discuss it afterward. Zack could be such a baby. Which Daniel wanted to remember tonight. He was tired of always being the greedy, guilty, neurotic, needy one.

35

D r. Kπowles? Hassaπ Rohaπi here. I would like to buy you coffee. Today or tomorrow. I am leaving on Sunday. I do not know your schedule, but I am at the Barnes and Noble Superstore in Merchants Square every afternoon between one and four. You will always find me upstairs, drinking their good American coffee."

The message was on Zack's answering machine, the "Dr. Knowles" number used by patients. Zack checked it regularly in case someone called with an emergency. Today was the day after the day after Christmas. Zack suspected Hassan wanted more than a friendly chat; he knew he should ignore the invitation. Both he and Daniel needed to keep away from the Rohanis. Yet he was curious—very curious—and Daniel was out for the day, gone to Richmond to look at wallpaper for the dining room, his home project for the winter. Zack knew he was still angry with Daniel but decided that his anger had nothing to do with his desire to see Hassan. He'd be very careful, and would tell Daniel about the meeting later.

Zack walked over to Merchants Square that afternoon. The day was cold and overcast. The bookstore was full of tourists. Upstairs, however, the café along the balcony was nearly deserted. This was a hangout for students, and they were all home for the holidays. Christmas music still played over the sound system: "Santa Claus Is Coming to Town."

Hassan sat at a corner table with an open laptop and a loose heap of magazines and newspapers. He wore his usual blue wool suit with a collarless shirt. He looked very solemn, typing away with two fingers. He saw Zack over the tops of his half-glasses. He broke into a grin and stood up.

"Doctor! So good to see you. I was afraid we would not get a chance to talk before I left." He closed his laptop and took off his glasses. "Sit, please. The news is not good." He gestured at the magazines, mostly business-related, plus the *Times* and *Wall Street Journal*. "Your president does not trust the UN inspectors to do their job. We hate Saddam Hussein even more than you do. But war is not a good idea." He continued to smile in his silvery beard. "War is vile. Which we learned for ourselves when we fought an eight-year war with Iraq, back when they were *your* allies."

Zack thanked Hassan for the offer of coffee but said he'd already had too much caffeine today. "I assume you didn't just want to drink coffee with me. There was something in particular you wanted to discuss?"

"What? No small talk first?" Hassan laughed. "I am a bit that way myself. Which is not a good way to do business in either Tehran or Paris. No problem. I already sense that one gets what one sees with you, Doctor. Your *batin* and your *zahir* are the same. Your inside and outside." Still smiling, he carefully placed his hands on the table, side by side. "So. I will cut to the chase. I am concerned about my brother. I am trying hard to convince him and his family to come home to Iran."

"Really?" said Zack, feigning surprise. "Right away?"

"As soon as possible. In case a war closes your borders."

"But Abbas wants to stay here?"

"No, he would like to come home. Part of him. But yes, part of him wants to stay. And that part listens to his wife. They've made common cause against the part that's on my side."

Zack pretended to think about it. "I'm sure they have perfectly good reasons for wanting to stay out of Iran."

Hassan nodded. "Some better than others. Which brings me to your *mate.*" He lightly smacked his lips on the word: it made them sound like Adam and Eve. "Who has a very special friendship with my brother."

"Yes, well, yes." Zack kept himself detached from his sudden nervousness. "They have a lot in common. They're both painters. They both teach. You saw them the other night. All four of us have become very good friends over the past few months."

Hassan chuckled. "Doctor? You do not have to fib. I know my brother. I know the nature of his friendships."

Zack glanced at the other tables along the balcony, not because he thought someone might hear this but to give himself time to think. The only other coffee drinker was a thirty-something law student poring over a textbook. He must be a married man who had come here this afternoon to get away from his family.

"Do not misunderstand me," said Hassan. "I do not care that this friendship is sexual. I certainly do not care that my brother's friend is an American or even a Jew. No, what matters is that this friendship could be keeping him from coming home."

He knew more than Zack anticipated, yet he clearly knew nothing about Christmas night. Maybe he was just guessing at things and hoping Zack would spill the beans.

Zack said, "Sorry. But I can't speak for either Daniel *or* your brother here."

"I understand. You are loyal and discreet. I respect that. You do not have to speak for anyone. But may I describe the situation from my point of view? You can agree or disagree and tell Daniel or not. The choice is yours."

Zack told him to go ahead; he was willing to listen.

Hassan cleared his throat. "I love my brother. Very much. Not only as a brother but now, since the death of our father, I am the head of our family. I want to bring him and his children home. For selfish reasons, I admit. I love my niece and nephew as if they were my own. But I also want to make my family whole again, in a way they have not been whole since we left Iran in 1979. And I want to help my brother, who is very unhappy here. He is quite lonely, despite his wife and children. But if he came home to Tehran, he could be part of something larger than himself, a solid growth of self and family and country and God. A beautiful unity. I need him. His country needs him. He needs us. Everyone will benefit."

Hassan maintained a serene cheerfulness during his speech, a jovial confidence that made Zack uneasy. His charm made his words sound cynical. The man was a charmer, a game player. His belief in God was sincere—Zack granted him that—yet people were only means to an end for him; he didn't care what they thought or wanted for themselves.

"We all dream of coming home," said Zack. "It's a common desire. But it works best as a tool, a metaphor. I assume Abbas is going to be a little lonely no matter where he lives. For a variety of reasons. Including the fact that he's gay."

Hassan laughed. "He is not gay. Not really. Gay is a Western concept, a European thing. Have you not read Foucault?" His cynical smile made Zack think he was joking, at first. "He has a very strong sex drive, my brother, and can satisfy it only with men. Which sometimes leads to obsession. Not love but sexual obsession. If he had not seen me with our maid all those years ago, he would have developed proper sexual feelings. So it is partly my fault, which is another reason why I feel responsible for him. If he had married more wisely, he might have outgrown these habits. But his Russian wife is too old and bossy. She would put any man off the female sex."

There were so many knots to undo here that Zack didn't know where to begin. He was indignant for Elena's sake. He decided not to discuss her for fear of losing his temper.

"Your brother is his own man," he said. "Which you should know better than anyone. He makes his own choices. Nobody can change his mind for him, not his wife or brother or lover." He hesitated: Yes, he should go ahead and say it. "He and Daniel were never lovers. They were fuck buddies. Briefly. Do you know the term? Then they were just friends. Now even friendship is winding down. Abbas's decision not to go to Iran has nothing to do with sexual obsession."

Hassan kept his smile; his smile never broke. "You are certain of that?"

Zack hesitated. He was not completely certain about anything with Daniel, much less Abbas. "I am. Yes. I get regular reports, whether I want them or not."

Hassan's eyebrows went up. He looked surprised, amused. "So I cannot blame your mate? Alas. I was hoping to find my solution there. I thought maybe you could ask him to cut off the juice and that would be the end."

Zack faked a smile. "Daniel would be flattered to hear that. But there's been no juice for some time. They're just friends now."

Hassan kept his look of amused surprise. "And this buddy-fucking was okay by you? It did not make you angry or jealous? I was about to say you must be the wife in your marriage, until I remembered women in your situation, and they are often furious."

It was intended as a put-down, and not a subtle one either. "Every marriage is its own country," said Zack. "With its own laws and customs."

Hassan shook his head. "You secular Americans. Everything is only lukewarm for you. All in shades of gray. There is neither love nor hate, good nor evil, hot nor cold. You are so gray and civilized. Which is hard for us hot-blooded people to understand. We are a yes-or-no people. You probably don't even think of yourself as an atheist but as only an agnostic. Am I right?"

"Actually, I am an atheist," said Zack. "Although I tell people I'm agnostic. Just to keep the peace." He hated this kind of I-am-more-passionate-than-you, passion-is-truth line of talk; he refused to be pulled in. "But there are plenty of good reasons for Abbas and Elena not to go to Iran. Reasons that have nothing to do with Daniel."

"Such as?"

"Iran cannot be an easy country for a man who sometimes has sex with other men—"

"There should be no problem if he is discreet."

"Or for an independent woman who prefers life in the West."

"Then she can stay in the West."

Zack hadn't digested the first answer when he heard the second. "You'd break up their marriage?"

"If necessary. It's a bad marriage. It deserves to be broken."

Zack was so startled he didn't know how to respond. "Who would take the children?" But he already knew the answer.

"The children belong to the father."

Zack felt paralyzed, his brain numb. "But Elena loves her kids. She loves your brother, too. And he loves her, in his fashion."

Hassan dismissed the possibility with a flip of his hand. "If he loved her, he would not go to men for sex. In Iran he could get a good young Iranian wife, or two, and his loneliness would end. I do not deny Elena's heart would break to lose a son and daughter. But she has nobody to blame but herself. For marrying into our family for money and not love. She knew what she was getting. I have no qualms about telling my brother to leave her." He took a deep breath—ruthlessness was tiring. "Which is neither here nor there, since he said no to Iran under any circumstances, with or without his Russian woman. He would rather stay here in the Great Satan"—he laughed again—"even if he is getting no ass. Do you know if he's buggering someone else now that he no longer buggers your mate?"

Was this why Hassan wasn't shocked by his brother's sexuality: he assumed Abbas was a top? As if anybody ever stayed in one position for long. "I don't really know," said Zack. "I don't think so."

Hassan nodded to the left, then to the right, as if talking to himself. "So that's our story? Very well. I tried. Nothing for me to do but accept defeat and go home to Iran." He stood up, declaring the meeting over. "This has been very interesting, Doctor. Thank you for coming to talk. I hope I didn't say anything to shock you?"

"Not at all. You're a very reasonable man." But Zack couldn't just leave things there. "Going back to your statement about agnostics and shades of gray? You should talk to some of my patients. The ones who see everything in primary colors. *They* believe in good and evil, love and hate. They feel they are good and other people are evil. They love, other people hate. And so on. It makes life easier. They don't have to think. Their categories do their thinking for them."

Hassan only smiled. "You are calling me crazy?"

"Not at all. I'm not attacking your point of view. I'm only defending mine. We're all a bit crazy. But a little gray is good now and then. It gives us space to maneuver in. Have a good trip back to Iran. Good luck there."

"And good luck here, Doctor. You're welcome to visit us, you know, you *and* your mate. You would find much that's appealing, despite what you've heard."

"I don't doubt it. I'm sure there's a lot to love in both the country and the people. Goodbye."

Zack lifted his hand in a casual salute, remembering Hassan didn't shake hands. He trotted down the steps and out into the cold, pleased that he'd spoken in praise of gray, sorry he hadn't made a more passionate speech. But righteous passion would only make *him* feel better; it would not change Hassan's mind.

Zack was surprised at how tired he felt, as if he were walking away from a bitter argument. Yet neither man had raised his voice once during their conversation.

He was crossing the beige cobblestones in front of the Trellis Restaurant when he noticed a female figure sitting on a bench. It was too cold to sit outside. Zack looked again and saw the burgundy scarf around her head. She was smoking and watching him. It was Elena. She put out her cigarette and stood up. He noticed other cigarette butts under her bench. She came over.

"You've been waiting?" he asked. "For me or for him?"

"For you," she said curtly. "And now you are here and I can go. We are walking the same way, yes?"

She looked tired and sleepless inside the hood of her scarf, with dark circles under her eyes. He wanted to offer her his arm but didn't. They strolled toward Jamestown Road.

"You met with him?" she said. "What did he want to tell you?"

"Do you really need to hear?"

"If it's about my husband and our future, yes."

He gave her the short version: how Hassan wanted him to get Daniel to break off with Abbas so Abbas would go home to Tehran.

She curled her lips back from her teeth, as if to deliver a horse laugh. But she didn't laugh. "He is such a fool. He does not know Abbas loves nobody but himself. Other people are only minor. Hassan is very clever, but very stupid too."

"But he knows about his brother liking men. And he knew he'd been seeing Daniel."

Elena shrugged. "He figured out the liking years ago. Now he assumes that any man, gay or straight, who spends time with his little brother must be hot to get into his pants."

"The two of you really dislike each other, don't you?"

"What did he say against me?"

Was this why she waited for him? So she could protect herself against new charges? Zack decided not to mention Hassan's words about taking away her children: they would only feed her anger. "Nothing you haven't heard. That you married a gay man for money, even though 'gay' is only a Western concept. And you never loved him."

"Love?" She sneered. "What does Hassan know about love?"

"He says he loves his brother."

"He loves him like a pet. He wants to take him home like a pet. 'I want to make you happy. I want you to find peace in God. I want our family whole again.' " Her voice dropped an octave for an ugly grumble. "Blah blah blah. But Abbas is being strong. Abbas has said no. Again and again. Which confuses Hassan. He cannot believe his brother is not a puppet. Of me or a lover. I have been proud of him. And relieved. When I heard Hassan was going to meet you today, I was afraid he had a new trick up his sleeve. But no. He was only barking at the moon. Good. It is almost over. He is leaving the day after tomorrow, and we will be safe."

"You'll drive him back up to Canada?"

"Oh no. He can fly. It is easier to leave the country than it is to enter." She was more relaxed now, convinced that things were fine. Zack wanted to be happy for her, but he felt confused and irritated with Elena. It took him a moment to remember why.

"I understand it was your idea for Abbas to come see Daniel the other night?"

She didn't even blink. "Why not? I like Daniel. He is a known property. And better that they see each other than that they each meet a sweet young thing they might run off with."

Which was the sort of thing Zack had once believed himself, but no more. "Things are different now. Daniel is finally getting over Abbas. This could've reopened a wound."

"You think?" She looked perturbed. "I'll be more careful next time." She took a deep breath and sighed. "You feel you must protect everyone, don't you?"

The question threw him. "Not everyone. I wish I could, but I know I can't." She'd caught him in one of his chief guilts: not his failure to protect everyone but his arrogant belief that he should. "I do what I can, which isn't much, and then hope for the best."

Elena shrugged. "Well, my family is all that matters to me. And now they are safe. Hassan will fly back to Iran and Abbas will go back to being his old self. Maybe I will encourage him to find a new boyfriend. How does that sound? Do you approve of that?"

Zack frowned. "I don't know. It might make Daniel jealous. Which could make the whole thing start over again."

Elena laughed. "Then we will do nothing. We will actively do nothing and hope for the best. There is nothing better than doing nothing, is there?"

36

I HEAR A NOISE OVERHEAD. It starts out like a jet plane. Then it sounds like a baby. A crying baby. And I see it. It's an angel. An angel of God as big as an airliner. It comes down out of the clouds. And I'm so happy. Because it's an angel. Who wouldn't be happy to see an angel? Then I hear people screaming. I can't understand why they're screaming, until I see what the angel is doing. As his shadow runs over the ground, it squashes things, crushes things. Houses and schools and shopping malls. And people. It crushes them like bugs. Leaving tiny spots of blood like when you slap a mosquito."

"You're no longer happy in the dream?"

"Oh no. I'm terrified. And confused. This is an angel of the Lord, and these are His people. Why is He destroying them?"

It was Friday morning, two weeks into the new year, 2003, and Fay Dawson's anxiety attacks were back. Her usual appointment was Monday afternoon, but she'd needed to see Zack immediately. She connected the return of her panic to a dream she'd had on Wednesday night.

"Then what happened?"

"I woke up. I was shaking. Like a leaf." Her face turned chalky pale as she remembered. "I couldn't breathe, I couldn't catch my breath. But Yancy held me—he was very good to me this time—and I could breathe again. But I couldn't go back to sleep. I just lay there, terrified. And ashamed. I've been anxious ever since."

"Why were you ashamed?"

"For dreaming what I dreamed. For being afraid of God. For being angry with God."

Fay had never come to him with an overt dream about God or heaven or even damnation. As if religion were all in her conscious, not her unconscious. Or maybe she didn't trust Zack enough to share her nakedly religious dreams.

"I've told you, Fay. You can't feel guilty for your dreams. Your dreams are outside your control."

"That's an easy thing to say. It's not an easy thing to feel."

"You said you were angry with God? Why?" He usually tried to avoid anything theological, but this might lead into the personal.

"Oh, stuff. Don't you know?" She had to take a deep breath before she could say it. "They tell us God will protect us if we love Him. And we do love Him, my whole family does. But He doesn't protect us. He keeps letting terrible things happen. Like Melissa almost dying. And now He's filled the world with terrorists who want to hurt us for no good reason. It isn't fair. Reverend Donald says it's not for us to judge God, but one can't help feeling—cheated."

It was a war dream. Of course. Zack should've recognized sooner that Fay's angel was a bomber or a missile. "Have you been watching a lot of news since Christmas?"

"Yes. Well, I don't. Yancy does. He keeps cable on all evening, even while we're eating dinner. It's awful what that Saddam can do to us." She pronounced his name "Sodom." "He has all those terrible germs and chemicals and things. Ugh. It's too awful to think about."

As soon as the holidays ended, the media had started talking up Iraq again. The weapons inspectors were finding no weapons of mass destruction, which the administration said only proved Saddam Hussein wasn't cooperating and the United States would have to invade. A few politically aware patients—all leftists or liberals—began to come to Zack with war dreams, variations on the old nuclear nightmares of the Reagan years: booms of blinding light, fiery conflagrations, black rain. Zack didn't recognize the war dressed up in angels, but the H-bomb dreams were religious, too, weren't they? The end of the world, the end of time.

Fay feared Iraq would do to us the very things that we would probably do to them. After all, we were the ones with bombers like destroying angels. It was a classic case of projection, but Zack couldn't get into that without discussing world politics. No, he needed to bring this back into her life, her private concerns.

"What's happened since Monday? I remember we had a very good session on Monday."

Nothing had happened, everything was fine, Fay said. The kids were back in school. And not a moment too soon, since Malvern was being a pig again. He used to be such a lovable kid, but now he was mean and hateful. "Which is an awful thing for a mother to say about her own flesh and blood."

Zack heard the front door open and close. Daniel was teaching today, so it must be a patient. Nobody was scheduled this morning except for Fay. Maybe it was someone else with an emergency.

"In your dream," said Zack, "where were you? Up in the air with the angel? Or on the ground with the people being crushed?"

"Oh no. Not on the ground. I'm not afraid I'll be crushed. I'm with the angel, I think. Just watching."

Like TV, thought Zack. Or maybe she identified with the angel. She wanted to kill her bratty son—who wouldn't?—yet could imagine such a thing only by killing *everyone*? Zack didn't want to pursue that idea either.

"You don't think my dream is about God?" said Fay abruptly. "Only about stuff on the news?" She sounded hurt, indignant.

"It doesn't have to be one thing or the other, Fay. Your dream could be about several things: God and Iraq and your family too."

"My family and I are fine. My fears are all about God. And maybe the war." Her button nose twitched. "All this war talk makes me wonder if He's really there. If He really knows what He's doing."

She talked about God the same way that Zack and his friends talked about George Bush.

"Let's forget about God for a minute," said Zack. "Let's just talk about the war. What are you afraid will happen if there *is* a war? Let's focus on real things that could happen to you and your family."

Fay went through a list of terrible hypothetical acts: hijackers crashed a jetliner into Colonial Williamsburg, a car bomb exploded outside the office where Yancy worked, poison gas or anthrax was released in the school that Malvern and Melissa attended. Zack let her talk, helping her with questions but only so she could flesh out her scenarios. It was Fay herself who asked, "But why would terrorists attack Williamsburg?" The town was a symbol of American liberty, but weren't there better symbols to destroy? Fay wasn't stupid. She knew her atrocities were highly improbable yet couldn't fully accept it until she'd gone through her list aloud. She slowly talked herself out of her fears, all but one. A friend had a brother in the army, she said, with an airborne unit down at Fort Bragg. They were afraid he'd be sent to Iraq.

"A justified fear," said Zack. "You should keep that fear."

She was calmer now, more focused, but Zack went ahead and wrote out a prescription putting her back on Xanax.

He wondered how many talks about the war he'd have with patients in the weeks to come. How long would it take for war worry to reach the wards at Eastern State? Once a subject got into hospitalized heads, it was hard to get out. They were still obsessed with the burning towers of 9/11, but so was the rest of the country. A national tragedy can be like a mass dream dreamed by millions. Therapists could use the upcoming war to explore inner lives in the same way they used individual dreams. Yet Zack knew that one person's anxiety projection in Virginia would be another person's bombed-out home and dead family on the other side of the world.

"I'll see you Monday," he told Fay. "If there are any problems, don't hesitate to call." He opened the office door and saw a stranger sitting in his living room. He'd forgotten someone had come in. There she was, a pretty African American woman in a tweed suit. She held a trench coat over her lap, shifting it aside as she stood up.

"Right with you," Zack told her and escorted Fay to the front door. He wondered if the stranger were a new patient and he'd forgotten to mark her appointment. He saw the SUV parked on the street, with Fay's husband at the wheel. "Yancy drove you over? Good. You said he was being more sympathetic." He lifted his hand in a wave but couldn't tell if Yancy saw him or not. "Until Monday. And remember the words of good old FDR. 'We have nothing to fear but fear itself.' " Zack was embarrassed quoting the line, but it really was the great American mantra.

He closed the door and turned to the newcomer. "Good morning. I'm Dr. Knowles. What can I do for you?"

"My name is Whitehurst," she said. "Justine Whitehurst." Her hair was straightened, parted in the center, and pulled back tight, positively nineteenth century. She took out a little wallet and showed him a badge, just like in the movies. "I'm with the FBI."

Zack brought a hand up and began to smooth his beard. He knew his own body language and understood this was a nervous gesture, a guilty gesture. But who doesn't feel a little guilty talking to the police? Zack dealt regularly with cops, especially out at the hospital, yet the self-consciousness remained.

"This is not about you. This is an unofficial visit, a friendly visit. I'd like to ask a few questions." She did not sound friendly but spoke with cool, hard quickness. She was young, in her early thirties, and appeared to be overcompensating.

"You realize, don't you, I'm a doctor and have a confidentiality agreement with my patients? Who did you want to talk about?"

"Mr. Hassan Rohani."

Zack's mind went blank for a split second. "Is he in trouble?"

"No. Not that I know of. Not with us. He's no longer in this country. We just want to learn more about him."

Zack found himself stroking his beard again. He stopped and said, "Let's go in here. I don't know how much I can tell you." He led her into his office and indicated the chair vacated by Fay.

Whitehurst irritably glanced around the room as she sat down. Zack realized she was nervous, too. She was as intimidated to be talking to a shrink as he was to be talking to the FBI. Nervousness made her seem more human. Otherwise she was a robot.

She took out a notepad and faced Zack. "Do you know why Hassan Rohani was in Williamsburg?"

"Yes. He was visiting his brother."

"His brother? He has a brother?"

"Yes. Abbas Rohani. Who's artist in residence here at the college." Zack was surprised she didn't know that.

"Do you know how we can reach him?"

"Abbas? He's in the phone book. He works at the school. He shouldn't be hard to find." Zack didn't mean to sound sarcastic, but it came out that way.

"He's Iranian too?"

"He was born there, yes. They *are* brothers. But I think Abbas has a French passport."

She glanced again at her notepad. Zack realized she wasn't writing anything down.

"What's this about exactly?" said Zack. "I'm not comfortable talking to you without knowing what it is you're looking for."

"We just want some information," said Whitehurst. "All we know is an important Iranian official visited the U.S. and didn't go anywhere except here. We want to know why."

"I told you. His brother and his brother's family are here. He came to visit them."

"How do you know that?"

"Because we're friends with the family. We had them over for dinner one night while Hassan was in town."

"Who's we?"

"My boyfriend and I."

"Okay." She did not appear surprised to hear he was gay.

"But Hassan flew back to Iran two weeks ago," said Zack. "You're investigating him only now?"

"These are busy times and we are badly understaffed. What did you talk about at dinner?"

"Religion, Paris, abstract art." Zack tried to remember what else. "Sufi poetry."

Again, no sarcasm was intended, but Whitehurst didn't notice. "Did Mr. Rohani ever indicate he'd be meeting anyone else while he was in the country?"

"No. He spoke to me only about his brother and his brother's family and his concern for their welfare. He really did seem to be visiting this country only to see them."

"What were his concerns?"

"Uh, personal matters." Zack paused. "I assure you it was nothing political or potentially criminal."

Whitehurst looked back down at the notepad. "Is that what you and Mr. Rohani were discussing at Barnes and Noble two days before he flew home?"

Zack froze. And he understood: She didn't need to write anything down because her notepad was already full of notes.

She was looking straight at him now. There was a pinched, attentive look to her eyes, like she was a lab assistant watching a lab rat make a choice.

"Yes," Zack finally said. "That's what we discussed." His mouth was dry; he swallowed. "How did you know that? Did Hassan tell you?" He had to swallow again. "Has Hassan been arrested?"

She remained very still, as if surprised by the question.

"Tell me!" said Zack. "I've been cooperating with you. I'm happy to cooperate. I work with the police all the time. You can at least tell me if he's been arrested or not."

She sat a little straighter, trying to stay stone-faced, poker-faced.

"Look. If you won't level with me, I'm ending this conversation right now. I won't say another word without an attorney present."

Whitehurst relaxed her expression a little. "Oh, all right. No. He has not been arrested. He flew straight back to Iran. If he were still in the country, we'd be talking to him and not to you."

Zack nodded while he put it together. "So how did you know we met at the bookstore? Somebody reported us? Or you were already following him?"

"I'm not at liberty to disclose that."

"But you already knew about him visiting his brother, right? You were just playing dumb before."

"We knew the two men claimed to be brothers, yes."

Zack hesitated. "What makes you think they aren't? No, I've seen them together. They're definitely brothers." Just talking to the FBI ate away at one's certainty. If Zack hadn't had experience dealing with the delusional, he might have fallen for her doubt game.

She glanced at her notes yet again, pretending to refresh her memory. "Why are you being so loyal to the Rohani brothers? Not everybody would. I know I wouldn't be if I were in your shoes."

"What does that mean?"

"Oh? Maybe you don't know." She'd gone back to being a robot, not a nervous robot, just a robot.

"Maybe I do know." But did they know the same thing? What if she knew something worse?

"I probably shouldn't tell you this—" A faint hint of smile appeared at the corners of her mouth. "Did you know your boyfriend and the brother went to a Motel 6 on Christmas night?"

Zack stared at her, trying to guess why she'd said this, if she wanted to bargain or threaten or simply hurt him. "You've been following them?"

"No. We only stumbled on that. But we have been asking around. It's widely reported on campus that Mr. Wexler and the artist in residence are having an affair."

Zack was disturbed but not surprised to hear other people knew. He was surprised only by how disturbed he felt, a cold panic in the pit of his stomach, as if *he* were suddenly naked in public.

"Why're you telling me this, Ms. Whitehurst? Do you think I'll feel grateful? Or do you just want to hurt and humiliate me?"

"I just want you to understand that you have no business protecting these people. They're not your friends. I want to make sure that you're on our side and not theirs."

She was black and she was female, which suggested a kind of innocence, condescending as that sounded. Only now did Zack see the righteous bully under the mechanical courtesy. If she'd been white and male, he would've recognized it sooner. She was the classic other-directed good girl, black division, like Anita Hill or Condoleezza Rice. She'd sacrificed a lot to get where she was. She'd lost a lot of imagination and flexibility along the way.

"I *was* on your side," said Zack. "*They* were on your side, too. But you're turning us against you. You're not very good at this."

The robot didn't even blink. "Does the wife know about Christmas night?"

"Yes. She does. In fact, we all know what's been going on. We have no secrets here, hard as that must be for the FBI to understand. It's a private matter. It has nothing to do with national security. It's our own private, personal matter. You can't use it to bargain or blackmail us into getting more information. You must already know that, yet you still want to play the bully. It feels good to be a bully, doesn't it?"

Whitehurst remained stone-faced. Then she said, in flat, measured tones, "I am not one of your pathetic patients, Doctor. I'm an agent with the FBI. We don't care about the fun and games you and your friends indulge in. All we care about are the threats to our country, which we have to fight while you have your fun and games." She stood up. "I've wasted too much time here." She pulled on her trench coat and reached into a pocket. "Here's my card. If you change your mind and decide to cooperate, you can call me at this number."

Zack understood she was more upset than she let on. Upset to be in the wrong? Or upset to have stumbled into this mess of open marriages? He followed her to the front door.

"But I *have* cooperated," he said. "I told you everything I know. There's nothing else to add."

"It's your country, too," she said. "If you change your mind, call me." She walked across the lawn to her car, a simple white sedan.

Zack slowly closed the door. He immediately wanted to call Elena and warn her but feared he was too agitated and wouldn't be coherent. He decided to call Daniel first, so he could talk away some of his agitation. But as he dialed Daniel's number, he realized he was angry with Daniel, furious with him. Look at what he'd exposed them to. The whole campus knew he and Abbas were screwing around, which didn't disturb Zack as much as knowing the FBI knew. The college was full of friends; the FBI was all strangers. Zack didn't want the FBI watching and judging them like a clumsy, imitation God.

Daniel didn't pick up, only his answering machine. Zack left a message: "I just had a disturbing conversation with an FBI agent, an African American woman named Whitehurst. They're investigating Abbas's brother, which means they've been watching us. *All* of us. They know about you and Abbas. I don't know what this means. Call me as soon as you get this message. You should probably warn Abbas. I'm going to call Elena. But be careful."

He wanted to sound supportive, he did not want to sound humiliated. And he wasn't humiliated. Was he?

He clicked the phone off and back on again and dialed Elena's number.

37

"Big gray elephant, little red mouse," said Daniel. "Big gray elephant, little red mouse. Mass and color balance each other. Size *doesn't* matter, despite what people say"—there was one lone snort—"when the color is strong. Big gray elephant, little red mouse."

This was the second semester of Fundamentals of Form, and they'd moved on to color, which they were exploring in pastels. Daniel strolled around the room, looking over shoulders. The class was down to a dozen students. A few worked at tilted worktables, but most held drawing boards in their laps. Daniel enjoyed the return to teaching after the holidays. It was a bit like busywork, but relaxing, productive, sane. He looked forward to a cozy if boring winter. Boredom should help him get back to his own art. He had gotten all the drama he needed last semester.

He stopped beside Nancy Mereen. Not content to stick to the exercise, she'd gone ahead and turned the assignment into a full-fledged landscape: a gray mass of water under a tiny red sun.

"Nice. Very nice." He heard the door open and close behind him. "Forget the assignment," he whispered. "You get the principles. Go ahead and add some blue or purple to your gray. There's color in colorlessness." He turned to see who'd come in.

Maureen Clark stood just inside the door, bundled up in a swollen down coat. Daniel hadn't seen her since Christmas break.

"Hey there, Clark," he called out. "What can we do for you?"

She cringed, embarrassed by the attention. She performed a rapid dumb show with her hands to indicate she couldn't talk in front of everyone.

Daniel came over. "What's up?" he said softly.

"Can we step outside? I need to tell you something."

"It can't wait?"

"I got a class across campus at eleven, and this is really important and I should tell you right away."

"Okay. Right back, everybody," he announced. "Big gray elephant, little red mouse."

Daniel's office was at the other end of the building, so he led Maureen out to the stairwell. "What's up?"

She squeezed herself into a corner, her down coat puffing up around her. "I don't want to worry you," she began, "but something really weird happened last night. I was at the Campus Center, and two people came up, a man and a woman. They were dressed like church people, and I thought they were Mormons. But they said they were federal agents and they wanted to talk to me. They wanted me to tell them all about Mr. Rohani. What kind of teacher he was, what the kids said about him, who he hung with. Stuff like that."

A dozen questions instantly filled Daniel's head. He didn't know which to ask first, but he remained calm.

"What kind of agents? FBI or something else? Did they show you a badge or ID card?"

"They showed me badges, and the badges looked real. But I can't remember which agency it was. They said something about the Justice Department. The man was white, but the woman was black. They were both middle-aged."

"What did you tell them?"

She looked frightened. "I shouldn't have talked to them, right?"

"I didn't say that. I'm sure you were discreet." Had she been discreet? "And they were the police. You had to talk to them."

"They weren't pushy," she confessed. "They were very friendly. We just sat at the gedunk stand and drank sodas. I told them nothing but good things about Mr. Rohani. How some students thought he was too tough but others thought he was great. How having him on campus was a real education, since he made us see there were all kinds of Muslims. But we never talked about politics in class, only art."

"You didn't say anything about your little adventure back in the fall with him and Mrs. Rohani?"

"Oh no! Never." She looked startled, as if she'd forgotten it. "They never even asked about her."

Daniel relaxed again. "So what do you think they wanted?"

"I don't know. They said they only needed information. If there's a war, they said, we need to know who our friends are."

"You haven't told Mr. Rohani about this yet?"

"No. Should I? I don't know what to say."

Daniel thought a moment. "Maybe *I* should tell him. I won't mention your name. I'll just say it's a trustworthy source. But I don't think it's anything to worry about. He just needs to be careful."

Maureen looked relieved. "It *is* nothing to worry about, isn't it? Good. I wasn't sure. But I needed to talk about it with someone I could trust, and you're the only one."

Daniel didn't know if there was or wasn't cause for alarm, but he assured Maureen things were fine and no harm had been done. "I should get back to my class. And you have to cross campus, right?"

She thanked him and hurried off. Daniel returned to the classroom. He was surprised at how calm he felt, as if he'd convinced himself as well as Maureen they had no cause for panic. There was another ten minutes before the hour ended and he could go find Abbas. He drifted among the students, pretending to give his full attention to their exercises.

He and Abbas had seen little of each other since their Christmas night fiasco. They'd been keeping their distance, which seemed to work. They could greet each other in the hall now without warmth or pain. What would Abbas think when Daniel came to him with a wild-ass story about the feds nosing around? Would he think Daniel was trying to fuck with his head? Or would he think Daniel was a nervous Nellie who was upset about nothing? Maybe it would be better if he kept mum. But Abbas might really be in trouble. Better to do the wrong thing than nothing. Daniel ran both hands over his hair and scalp, assuring himself his head was still firmly on his shoulders.

When the first student began to put away his work, Daniel looked at his watch. "Right then. That's all for today, gang. See you next week." He went straight down the hall to Abbas's studio.

The door was closed. Nobody answered when Daniel knocked. He heard nothing inside, no music or movement. He went around the corner to Abbas's office, which Abbas never used, but Abbas wasn't there either. Finally he went to the classroom for Advanced Painting. The door was wide open. There was nobody in the turp-smelling room, only a dozen easels, each bearing a small canvas with a different version of the same male nude in boots. For a moment Daniel thought the figure was Abbas. Did he pose naked for his students so he could point out anatomical details more easily? Then Daniel saw a canvas in a more advanced stage and realized the model was Ted Dean, an old student turned slacker who still lived in town.

Suddenly Abbas strolled in. "Oh?" he said when he saw Daniel. He was wiping his hands on a paper towel. He looked neither pleased nor unhappy to see him. "I thought you were a student. I told them I would be here Friday mornings for anyone who needs help. Big waste of time. Nobody ever comes. Only one person came today."

"Well, they have other classes," said Daniel.

"If they were serious about their art, they'd let their other classes go hang. But they are just hobbyists."

Daniel was tempted to defend them, just to postpone saying what he'd come to say. His mouth was dry. He moistened his teeth.

"I don't mean to worry you," he began, "but I thought you should know"—he sounded as flustered as Maureen. "There are federal agents on campus asking after you."

Abbas lowered his eyebrows. "What kind of agents? Immigration?"

"I don't know. I didn't talk to them. A student talked to them and came to me, so I could warn you."

"Immigration visited me two months ago. And before that was someone from the CIA."

"So you're used to this?"

Abbas shrugged. "Yes, no. Whatever country I go to, there is always somebody asking questions."

"I assume this was FBI, but I'm not sure why. Sorry. I didn't know this was normal. I shouldn't have bothered you with it."

"No. It is good to know people are snooping. So I can be prepared. Thank you for the warning."

Abbas looked different: quieter, darker, sadder. Daniel wasn't sure if he were different from Christmas night, or different from their good times together, ages ago. Daniel had seen so many different personalities in this body. No wonder the man seemed slightly worn out.

Daniel turned to go. Two strangers stood at the door, a young white man and a young black woman. Both wore overcoats and suits.

"Excuse us," said the man, pink-faced, with a crew cut that added to his boyishness. He towered over his partner. "We're looking for Mr. Abbas Rohani."

Their timing was disturbingly perfect. Daniel was stunned, but Abbas said simply, "Speak of the devil."

"You're Mr. Rohani?" said the woman, short and bug-eyed, with some ocher in her skin color. She turned to Daniel. "And you're—?"

"Daniel Wexler."

"Oh," she said, as if disappointed. "My name is Whitehurst, this is Parker. We're with the Federal Bureau of Investigation." They flipped open two badges and snapped them shut, like soft castanets. "If you'll excuse us, we'd like a minute alone with Mr. Rohani."

A chill ran up Daniel's back, making him stand straighter.

"Go on, Daniel," said Abbas. "I will be fine." He sounded cool and confident and slightly condescending.

"You sure?" But what could Daniel do here? "All right. But if you need anything, I'll be in my office. Nice to meet you," he curtly told the agents and stepped outside. He considered lingering there, but Abbas gently closed the door. Daniel headed down the hall.

These were the people who'd talked to Maureen Clark? They looked too young to be dangerous. If the FBI intended to nail Abbas, wouldn't they send someone older and more experienced?

Daniel entered his office, intending to call Zack and tell him what was going on. His message light was blinking. He promptly played the message:

"I just had a disturbing conversation with an FBI agent, an African American woman named Whitehurst . . ."

Zack's voice remained calm and reasonable. Daniel was surprised he gave the race of the agent—usually Zack refused to mention race, on principle. Daniel played the message once, then played it again, feeling more worried the second time. The FBI had spoken with Zack, which suggested this was more serious than they claimed. And they knew about him and Abbas, which unnerved Daniel more than he thought possible. Only what did they know? That they'd been lovers or fuck buddies or nothing at all to each other? Daniel didn't even know the answer there.

He got up to close the door and call Zack, but he heard footsteps approaching. Abbas came to the door in his winter coat.

"The FBI is taking me to lunch," he announced. "They want to ask me about my brother and his visit to the U.S."

Whitehurst and Parker stood a few feet behind him.

"We're just gonna talk," said Parker amiably as he held out a business card. "Is there a place you'd recommend for burgers?"

"Uh, the Green Leafe?" Daniel took the card.

"It has my beeper and cell phone numbers," Parker explained. "And our office in Richmond. So you'll know how to reach us. But this won't take long. Only an hour or so."

Daniel felt more intimidated than ever. He could read malice and judgment in their deadpan faces now that he knew they knew he and Abbas had fucked. They weren't so innocent after all. They understood more than they let on.

"Do not worry," said Abbas. "I do this often. I will be fine."

"He'll be fine," echoed Parker. "We're just gonna eat and talk."

"You'll see your pal soon enough," said Whitehurst in a flat, tired, dismissive tone.

And they left, the agents leading the way.

Daniel waited for Abbas to look back and indicate with a facial expression or gesture what he was really feeling, but he only looked down, buttoning his coat.

38

THE PHONE FINALLY RANG, and Zack got it. Daniel was calling from school to report that Abbas had just left with a man and woman from the FBI. "They said they wanted to talk to him over lunch."

Zack felt his entire body turn cold. "Maybe you should come home." He promptly called Elena and told her the news. She responded much as she had to Zack's first call about the FBI: with instant dismissal and long silences.

By the time Daniel got home, it was snowing again, white flakes tumbling from the sky like ashes. The winter before the Iraq War was full of snowstorms, even in Virginia.

Zack and Daniel sat at the kitchen table with cups of hot tea.

"There's no cause for alarm," Zack argued. "They'll just ask their questions and send him home. But I've been thinking of people we can call in case we *do* need help. Roy at the hospital should have a few ideas about the international law involved. And Jeremy"—Jeremy Edwards, their own attorney, who did malpractice work—"might be able to recommend a good lawyer in criminal law."

"You think Abbas will be charged with a crime?"

"I don't know. I'm just trying to think ahead. I don't like being surprised like I was this morning."

They tried to remain calm and talk about other things, but there were no other things.

"What exactly do they know about me and Abbas?" said Daniel.

"They weren't specific. But they knew about the night you checked into a Motel 6."

Daniel smirked and shook his head. "A person can't sneeze in this town without somebody offering them a handkerchief," he said in his best *Last Picture Show* voice.

"You're being awfully cavalier."

"How else am I supposed to react? To be honest, my sex life seems pretty innocent right now, compared to everything else."

Zack couldn't argue with that.

At one o'clock, two hours after Abbas went off with the agents, Daniel called the number on the business card. He got a machine. He left a message and then called the Green Leafe to ask if Abbas Rohani were there. "You know, the Iranian artist in residence?" They knew who Abbas was, but he hadn't been in today.

Daniel set the cordless phone flat on the table, very gently, very carefully, as if it were a mousetrap that might snap off a finger.

"Maybe they went somewhere else," said Zack. "Maybe he's already home." He snatched up the phone and dialed Elena.

"I shouldn't have let him go off with them," Daniel muttered unhappily. "I should have told him to wait."

Elena answered. No, he had not come home. He hadn't called either, and she was getting worried. She didn't sound panicky, however, but curt, irritable, impatient.

"You want to wait with us over here?" Zack asked her.

"I cannot. The kids are coming home. I must be here for them."

"Then I could go over there. If you think company will help."

Daniel gave him a confused, blinking look.

"Or we could both come over," said Zack. "If that's okay?"

"Yes. Thank you. I need the distraction. Until the kids get home. Then I will be myself again. I am always myself around the kids."

Daniel was frowning when Zack got off the phone.

"Sorry. Did I misunderstand you? You don't have to come if you don't want to."

"It's not that. I'm not afraid of being around Elena." Although he must be if he could think it. "I'm just— I'll go. There's no real cause to worry. But if I stay here alone, I'll just sit and worry."

Zack made a few calls requesting advice before they went out. Nobody answered; it was all machines. He left his cell phone number. He hated carrying his phone with him and did it only in emergencies, which today clearly was.

Daniel remained sitting across from him but did not look at Zack once while he left his messages. Then Daniel asked, "So what's the worst possible thing that can happen here?"

"I don't know. To be honest. My biggest fear right now is that it's Friday. If they're holding Abbas, we won't be able to get him out until Monday." There were other fears beyond that, of course, but Zack didn't want to think them.

⌒ ⌒

They drove over. They could've walked, but Daniel pointed out that they might need the car later. The snow continued to fall but stuck only in the grass, like a heavy frost.

When Elena opened the door, the TV was blaring behind her: a talk show. She wore jeans and a sweatshirt and no makeup. Zack realized with a start that he'd never seen her dressed so casually, not even when she did her laundry. Her face looked dry and pinched. She turned the TV off. "I left it on while I cleaned," she said. "I needed the noise."

She led them to the big table just outside the kitchen. "I am making cupcakes for the kids. A special treat when they get home." She sounded distracted, that's all, mildly preoccupied, nothing worse.

Daniel remained standing. He looked terribly uncomfortable to be in this house. "I'm sorry. You don't really need us here, do you? Everything will be fine, right? We're overreacting, right?"

She stared at him as if she didn't understand a word he'd said. "Oh no. Terrible things happen in other countries. Why not here?" She told them to sit. She would make coffee.

Daniel lowered himself into a chair and looked around at the toys on the floor, the paintings on the walls. Zack was trying to think of something to say to put Daniel's mind at ease when his cell phone buzzed in his coat pocket. He took it out. "Hello?"

It was Jeremy, their lawyer. A displaced Yankee in his mid-thirties, Jeremy was quick and to the point. Why did Zack need a criminal attorney? Who was this Iranian? Were they sure it was FBI? He was in extreme lawyer mode, so he was highly melodramatic, with a terse, macho, TV masculinity.

"You're right," he declared when Zack finished. "I can't handle this case. There's a couple of good lawyers I can call, but I probably won't hear back from them today. Let me lay out the menu of possible events. So you'll know what you're in for."

Zack signaled for pen and paper, which Elena brought over. She and Daniel sat on either side, watching him write it down.

First, the FBI could do exactly what they said they were doing, talk to this man over sandwiches, take their sweet time but return him home safe and sound.

Second, they might want to hold him as a material witness. In which case they could actually arrest him or, more likely, issue a subpoena and release him on his own recognizance.

"As a witness to what?" said Zack. "Doesn't there need to be an actual crime for a man to be subpoenaed?" Zack had testified in court on several occasions and knew a little law.

"Don't you watch the news, Doc? The war on terror? Under the Patriot Act, the feds can do whatever they like. They don't have to charge anyone, not if they think it's terror-related. Which brings us to the third possibility. They arrest your man, hold him a few weeks while they investigate. Then, if they don't find anything, they deport him. They don't need cause. They don't need a public hearing. They just ship him back to his homeland.

"Or the fourth possibility, they do charge him with a crime and the case goes to trial. Which is a good thing, since it means he gets legal representation and can communicate with his family while he's in jail.

"Because there's a fifth possibility, a worst-case possibility, where they label him a suspected terrorist. 'Terrorist' has become a very broad category.

If you're friends with a terrorist, if you give money to one, if you tell him the time of day, then you're a terrorist, too. They could hold you in this country without charges or bail. They could even send you to Guantánamo in Cuba, where they're holding the al-Qaeda suspects seized in Afghanistan."

Jeremy thoroughly enjoyed playing the omniscient know-it-all today. He loved politics, but his vocation was civil law and his cases were rarely exciting. He was glad to have a chance to show off his insider knowledge. He didn't intend to be cruel, yet he expressed no compassion, no pity. Zack had never treated him, but he couldn't help wondering if Jeremy had had a bad experience with another shrink and was taking it out on him.

"Your man has an Iranian passport?"

"No, French, I think." Zack looked at Daniel and Elena. They nodded eagerly. "Yes. A French passport."

"That's good. The French aren't too popular nowadays, but they are legal. You might want to get the French embassy involved once we know what's going on."

"And when do you think we'll know?"

"We could know by the end of today. Or tomorrow. Or next week. Or not for months."

Whatever the story, Jeremy wanted to help. He'd make a few calls and there'd be a qualified attorney involved by Monday. "And you'll need him. Because if your man hasn't been released by Monday, we'll know he's in big trouble."

Zack thanked Jeremy, promised to report all developments, said goodbye, and snapped the phone shut.

There was a warm, sweet, absurd smell of cupcakes coming from the kitchen.

Zack looked down at the sheet of paper covered with his jagged hen scratch—art paper torn from a sketchbook. "All right," he began. "You heard my end. Let's go over my notes and see where we stand."

He went down the list, item by item, pausing repeatedly to warn all three of them that this wasn't Jeremy's area of expertise but the man appeared to have some idea what he was talking about.

When he finished, Elena was leaning forward on the elbows of her crossed arms. "It is not so bad," she said. "It could be worse." She shrugged. "I admit I expected better in the Land of the Free. At least here it is a surprise. It was sadly ordinary in the Soviet Union."

"You were arrested more than once?" said Zack. "Not just the time you were sent to prison?"

"Only the once. But it was enough. I told you about my arrest?"

"Just that you spent a few months in prison. For writing a poem about Sakharov."

She frowned. "The poem was only part. What can I say? I was young and stupid, a hick from Tashkent. We don't have to discuss it." She got up and went to the kitchen, where she opened the oven and removed the fragrant cupcakes, setting them on the stove to cool.

"Actually, I'd like to hear about it," Zack called out. "If you don't mind talking about it." He wanted to know how *she* had dealt with arrest. She had far more experience here than they did, and her ordeal should put this one in perspective.

"You are sure? You really want to hear?" She returned to the table and sat down. "Very well. Where to begin? I grew up in Tashkent but always dreamed of going to Leningrad. You could not live just anywhere in the Soviet Union; you had to win your place."

It was a rehearsed story, one she'd told many times, to herself if not to others, and she had to begin at the beginning.

"I studied hard and went to different schools and finally got to university in Leningrad. Where I met a smart set of pretty young Russians, the children of bureaucrats and colonels. They were a spirited bunch, and younger than I, in spirit as well as age. Gorbachev had come to power and he promised change, and we wanted to test him. It was, what? 1987. We went by train to Moscow for a small demo in Pushkin Square. There were a dozen of us. We wanted to celebrate poetry. That's all. We had a banner to hang over the library steps. A pack of boys would play guitars and sing while the rest of us passed around mimeos of our poetry. That is the word? Mimeos? No big deal. We wanted to test the ice. To see how open the new openness was. A poetry party in Pushkin Square.

"So we arrive, the banner goes up, the boys take guitars from their cases. But before we can sing a word, we are surrounded. By a mob of pigs from the KGB. They were waiting. They knew we were coming. They herded us together, then separated us. Suddenly I was alone and pushed into the backseat of a big black Volga automobile, surrounded by smelly fat men in heavy coats, all old enough to be my father. And they were laughing like it was a game. They were drunk, and there was so much vodka on their breaths that the car stank like a surgery. I was terrified. I was sure they would rape then murder me. They'd dump my corpse in the scrap yards. But I couldn't let on I was scared. I had to laugh and joke with them, which was exhausting. It was the longest day of my life.

"We finally got to the police station, and I saw my friends again. The boys were beaten into pulp. They had such bloody faces I didn't recognize them at first. The KGB pigs made the girls get a good look, and they shoved us into our cages. And let us all rot for three or four days while they decided what to do with us. There were no visitors, no lawyers, no telephone calls, nothing."

Elena began to smile, a strange, sad twist of her mouth, as if she could not believe such a thing had ever happened to her.

"I was nobody. A hick from Tashkent. But my friends were the children of bureaucrats and colonels. The police loved rubbing their noses, like bad dogs, in the dogshit of their helplessness. Our trial was a joke, but also a relief. Being sent to prison was a relief. Because I knew where I was going. I knew where I would be. I had solid ground beneath my feet. There were walls all around me, but the ground beneath my feet was solid."

A very deliberate story, a tale like a parable. Zack felt badly shaken by it. He turned to Daniel, expecting to see a face full of sorrow and pity. But Daniel was frowning, as if annoyed with Elena for sharing her experience, as if angry with her for confusing them with *her* story, *her* suffering. Zack was surprised and disappointed.

Then Daniel reached across the table, grabbed Zack's cell phone, opened it, entered a few numbers, and turned away.

"Agent Parker? This is Daniel Wexler again. We still haven't heard from you." He was so coolly indignant that it took a moment to realize he was talking to a machine. "There are people here who are terribly worried, a man's wife and children. Can you *please* do us the decency of letting us know *what* is going on?" He beeped off and snapped shut the clamshell of phone.

"You didn't leave our number," said Zack.

"They know our number," said Daniel. "You can be damn sure they know *all* our numbers."

There were footsteps on the porch, and Zack's heart jumped into his throat. There were happy squeals outside, and the door flew open. Osh and Mina spilled in, two children drunk on falling snow. Osh covered his face with his mittens while Mina tried to stuff whiteness down the back of his snowsuit. She saw the two men and snapped to attention, instantly sobered by their presence.

"We have company, darlings," Elena sang out and switched to French, the family language. Zack wondered if she were telling them things he and Daniel shouldn't know, but she pointed at their red galoshes and he caught an English word, *cupcakes.*

Osh immediately became obedient, doing everything asked of him. He and Mina set their galoshes by the door, hung up their coats, and tromped up the stairs in their thick wool socks.

"You are free to go," declared Elena. "Now that they are home, I will be fine. I will not worry. I will be too occupied. Their noise will drive out worry. Oh shit."

"What?"

She made a face. "I was going to go to the store this afternoon. There's no food for dinner. I remembered while I was baking but then forgot."

"Write out a list," said Zack. "We'll pick up whatever you need."

"Or you can go with Zack and I'll stay with the kids," said Daniel. "In case somebody calls."

Zack exchanged a look with Daniel. Neither wanted to leave, both of them wanted to help. And Elena was happy to accept. They were all in this together, weren't they?

39

THE SNOW CONTINUED TO FALL, but the roads were still clear when Zack drove Elena up to Food Lion. He was glad to get out of the Rohani house, which had begun to feel like a hospital waiting room, a limbo zone where time stood still—Zack was usually on the other side of the door in hospitals. The afternoon was cold and crisp, the snowfall lovely. Not until they were in the aisles of the supermarket did the strangeness of the day catch up with him again. Here we are, he thought, buying milk and eggs and toilet paper while a woman's husband is being questioned by the FBI, or locked into a jail cell, or even loaded onto a plane to Cuba. And not just her husband but other husbands, fathers, and sons. The banality of everyday life carried him from hour to hour while his own government performed its cruelties in secret.

He could not share his fears with Elena, and his hopes would only sound pathetic to a woman who'd been through so much. Zack didn't know what to say to her.

"Here, let me pay for this," he said at the checkout counter.

She waved away his money and paid with a credit card.

Out in the parking lot, they loaded the groceries into the Toyota and got in. "You do not have to feel guilty," said Elena. "It is not your fault these things are happening."

"I'm not doing this out of guilt. I just want to help."

"And Daniel? Why is he doing so much?"

Zack was silent while he backed the car out. "You're our friends. He'd do the same for anyone."

"Whether he had been to bed with them or not?"

He hesitated again. "I think he would. Yes. Although I don't see how it changes anything. I know you've had a harder life than ours, Elena. It's natural for you to think everybody's out for number one. But sometimes people do things just to do them. Not because there's something in it for them."

"That is not what I meant. I do not know what I meant."

They were on the road now, and he couldn't look at her while he drove. He was a very careful driver, especially in bad weather.

"You are right," she agreed. "It changes nothing. Sorry. I say such things only because of my state of mind. I am worried. I do not like being worried. Especially when I do not know if my worry is appropriate. I mean, this isn't the Soviet Union. This is a land of *some* laws, *some* rights. And Abbas will not get raped. Although he might enjoy thinking he would. The idea, not the deed. Do not take that expression with me."

Zack couldn't guess what his face was expressing.

"I know Abbas and I love him," she explained. "And yes, I am angry with him. I am often angry with him. But an arrest does not change love or anger."

~~~   ~~~

When they got back, the house felt different, less like a waiting room, more like a home. Daniel had built a fire—he loved a good fire—and he sat on the floor in front of the hearth with Osh and Mina, playing a game on a dimpled metal board. A few dimples held marbles. It was Chinese checkers, a game Zack had forgotten existed.

"Nobody called," Daniel said quietly. "We've just been sitting here, having a good old time. Haven't we, kids?"

He and the children looked quite content, perfectly peaceful. It was an imitation peace, of course, a charade of normalcy, yet when Daniel looked up at Zack, he appeared quite pleased with himself, as if this white lie were a major accomplishment.

And Zack thought: Who am I kidding? He's still in love with Abbas. He cares about him enormously. That's why he's here today. That's why he's putting himself through all this. And Zack couldn't help admiring Daniel. A different kind of man would've shut down his emotions, would've fled from his caring and said, "Let's stay out of this. That man and his family are nothing to us now. We'll only get in the way." But Daniel did care, despite the complications. Zack loved him for that.

"Stay for dinner," said Elena. "There is plenty of food. We will have a feast. Maybe later we roast marshmallows on Daniel's fire?"

"Where's Papa?" asked Osh.

"He is meeting with an art dealer. Who has come all the way from Washington to see his work. I called him at school while we were out and he told us to go ahead and eat without him."

Mina didn't question her mother, but went along with the story. She seemed to have as much experience in accepting these stories as Elena had in making them up.

Elena started dinner: a stir-fry of lamb, vegetables, and rice for everyone except Osh, who ate only Tater Tots and hot dogs.

Zack turned on the TV news, as if hoping for something to explain Abbas's absence. But the local news was only the snowstorm, two fires, and a car wreck. The network news led off with a story on President Bush's upcoming State of the Union address, which was expected to include an official threat of war against Iraq. A lengthy report on the new fad in low-carb diets followed.

They sat down to dinner, and Zack couldn't help thinking, What if this becomes permanent? What if Abbas doesn't return? What if he and Daniel became responsible for this mother and her two children? Could they manage that?

"Save some for Papa," said Osh.

A phone rang, a landline in the kitchen. Elena jumped up to get it. "Hello?" she said and promptly began to speak French. Two sentences later she shifted to another language, a fierce crunch of consonants that Zack realized was Russian.

He exchanged a look with Daniel who lifted his eyebrows, then smiled blandly at the kids and continued to eat.

Only half of Elena was visible in the doorway. Zack saw her hair but not her face. She spoke for five minutes, then hung up.

"That was your uncle Hassan," she told the children. "Calling from Tehran to send his love."

"Hassan speaks Russian?" said Zack.

"Yes. Badly. But the little cabbages speak none at all."

Zack could wait until later to learn what had been said.

After dinner, Elena sent the children upstairs to take their baths. She put Mina in charge. "After you bathe, you can watch TV. Powerpuffs or Pokémon or whatever you both agree on. Just do not fight. Our guests are going to help me clean."

The adults crowded into the kitchen and actually began to wash the dishes. "Hassan was calling on his cell phone from Tehran," said Elena. "I called him earlier, and he only now called back. He says he is safely home. He was not arrested or stopped. He does not understand what the police want from his brother. He cannot believe they will arrest him. I hope the call was monitored, because he said again and again that Abbas knows nothing. Maybe we should not have spoken Russian? Who can guess what you Americans can and cannot understand? But Hassan advises us to sit tight and be patient. Last year he was questioned at Kennedy for twenty-four hours. Abbas has not yet been gone for nine. If we have not heard anything by tomorrow, he says he will start making inquiries through the French embassy."

She went upstairs to see how the kids were doing. It was almost eight but felt much later in a house full of children after a day of waiting. Daniel and Zack continued to wash the dishes. Daniel whispered, "How long do you think we should stay?"

"I don't know. We should probably go soon."

"It feels so unreal," said Daniel. "My emotions keep going in and out of focus. Sometimes I feel very anxious, but usually I feel nothing. I can't help wondering if we're just imagining things. Everything is fine and we're just being paranoid."

"Except we met the FBI agents, and they weren't imaginary. And Abbas isn't here. That's not imaginary either."

The front door softly jerked open. Zack assumed Elena had come back downstairs and was looking outside. He wondered what she'd heard. But when he stuck his head around the corner, he saw a strange man closing the door, a tall man in a heavy coat, a fur cap, and rectangular glasses.

The man resembled Abbas Rohani, only his face was paler, his eyes smaller. He looked less interesting than Abbas, less significant.

"Papa is home!" sang Osh upstairs.

He stood there, slowly removing his coat and unwinding a scarf, looking at the empty living room with the burning fire, then noticing Zack and Daniel staring at him from his kitchen.

Zack heard Daniel take a sharp, deep gulp of air.

"*Abbatushka!*" cried Elena at the top of the stairs. Her shoes came clattering down, and she looked like she was going to throw herself on her husband. She stopped and stood before him, staring.

"I am sorry," he said flatly. "I know it is late. I should have called. I lost track of time. I see you went ahead and ate dinner. Good. I am not hungry."

The children came down the stairs, both in their pajamas, Mina clinging to the rail and holding back, as wary as a cat.

Elena continued to stare at Abbas. She stole a quick look at the children, then at Zack, as if wondering whether he saw more than she could.

All Zack saw was a man stunned to find so many people in his house: not only his family but an ex-trick and the ex-trick's lover.

"I am fine. I am not hungry," he repeated. "Do not worry about me. Here. Let me sit by this fire. Such a nice fire. Come here, Osh. Come keep me company." He sat in a boxy cushioned chair by the fireplace and helped Osh climb into his lap.

The boy in his stretch pajamas, like a little blue union suit, was tickled to perch on the throne of his father's body. He turned sideways and curled against Abbas's chest.

"Where have you been?" Elena said drily. "You did not go to the Green Leafe to meet with these—art dealers."

"No. Richmond. They took me to Richmond. So we could do our business there." He wrapped his arms around Osh and rubbed his nose in the boy's wet black hair. Osh wiggled happily.

"You could not phone?"

"I wanted to. But they said we would soon finish. And more time kept passing. Until it was too late and I stopped asking."

He drew a loud snort through his nose, as if inhaling the aroma of his son's head. But no, he was sniffing back tears. He was crying in the boy's hair. He twisted his face in a rubbery grimace, trying to squeeze his tear ducts shut.

Elena clapped her hands. "Children! Time for bed. Chop chop. Your father is exhausted. Bedtime. Now. It has been a long day."

Osh wiggled down. Mina raced over and threw herself on her father's chest, trying not to look at his tearful face. "Happy dreams, Papa."

"Happy dreams," he murmured and petted her good night.

Elena herded the children up the stairs.

Daniel crept over to the fire to add a fresh log. He remained crouched between the blaze and Abbas. "You okay?" he whispered. "What did they do to you? Did they hurt you?"

"Nothing. They did nothing." Abbas wiped his nose on the back of his hand. "They talked at me. Forever and ever. It was like they would never stop talking at me."

"Did you want us to stay and we can discuss it?" said Zack. "Or would you rather be alone?"

"Stay. Go. I do not care." He heaved a heavy sigh. "There is nothing to discuss."

Elena returned. "Would you like a drink, darling? A glass of wine? I know I want one. Everybody? I will get the wine."

Zack went with her to the kitchen. He opened a bottle while she took down the glasses. They said nothing but acknowledged with an exchange of looks that this wasn't over, they weren't safe yet.

When they came back, Abbas was already telling his story to Daniel, in a low, steady grumble. Daniel sat on the floor with his back to the fire. Zack and Elena pulled up two chairs and leaned in close, so Abbas could keep his voice down and wouldn't be heard upstairs.

"They wanted to know about my brother's visit. That is all. Why he was here, who he was seeing, what branch of government he is with. That is how they started. No big deal. They suggested we go to their office, which is in Richmond, and they could finish with me for good. Fine, I said. I want to get this over. I have been questioned often before. By the police of many countries. But the French do this better. And the Germans, and the Israelis. These people are fools. They kept making threats, but they did it with smiles, pretending the threats were harmless remarks. They only *mentioned* deportation. And then prison. And then telling my children what kind of man their father is. 'What would they think of their daddy if they knew about his love life? Would they still love him?' "

Zack stole looks first at Elena, then at Daniel: both remained stone-faced.

"Which made me angry. Which was what they wanted. They said I should reconsider my position and tell the truth. When I said I was already telling the truth, they began to talk about how highly children are valued in America, how courts go out of their way to protect them, even the children of foreigners. A man who lives my kind of life might be judged a dangerous father. He might lose custody of his children."

"It's an empty threat!" said Zack. "An ugly threat!"

Abbas shrugged—it didn't matter if the threat were real or not. "So I told them: 'Threaten me like this and I will have no choice but to start lying. I will try to guess what you want and tell you that instead of the truth. Do you really want that? Because then you will never know what is fact and what is fiction.' They said no problem. They had a lie detector machine that would tell them what was real. 'So use it now,' I said. 'See if I am not already telling you everything.' And they gave me their test. Which I think is why they took me to Richmond in the first place. They knew I would want this test.

"They put me in a chair with a cord around my chest and a blood pressure thing on my arm, and my fingers on a metal strip. And they began their questions. Is your name Abbas Rohani? Are you the brother of Hassan Rohani? Did your brother come to this country to visit you? Was he here for other reasons? Do you love your children? Do you love your wife? Do you love America? Do you love Iran? On and on it went, serious questions and silly questions. I saw the little needles on their roll of paper, reading me like an earthquake. And when they finished, they did not tell me the results but looked very, very grave. They resumed the threats again: deportation, prison, my sex life, my children. But I was no longer angry. I was tired, I was numb.

"They left the room, both the man and the woman, leaving me to think of my future. But I was not panicked or frightened. I did not want to fight anymore. I knew I could do nothing. I found I could surrender to my fate. And it felt good to surrender. It was out of my hands. It was in the hands of fate or chance or God.

"Then they came back, grinning like hyenas. 'We believe you,' they said. 'You are telling the truth. We were only testing you. We are sorry to upset you. But we need the stress to tell for certain if people are lying or not.' And they drove me home, not both of them, only the blond man. Who was so friendly, asking me about Islam and Iran and being an artist, that I wondered if he were hitting on me. If he wanted to suck my dick. But I realized, no, he was only sorry. In that stupid, maudlin, American way. 'Sorry we beat you up. Sorry we humiliated you. But it was for a good cause, so do not take it personally. You must forgive us.' "

He shook his head and sighed, declaring his story over. His tone had remained low and steady throughout. He now sat very still.

"But it's over?" said Daniel. "You're free? They're not going to bother you anymore?"

Abbas shrugged, a contemptuous lift of one shoulder. "They say it's over. I don't know if I believe them. I don't know if *they* believe it. Because they are idiots. Total idiots. They do not know what they are looking for. They are little men pretending to be big men." He turned to Zack. "You think your country is different. That people are safe and secure here. But your country is as bad as the others. Maybe worse because your police do not know what they want." He shook his head again. "Iran does not look so terrible now."

Elena pinched her mouth shut in a tight little frown.

"But you're safe now," said Daniel. "They're finished with you."

"Maybe. Maybe not. I do not know. But I distrust this country. I do not feel safe here."

Elena jumped in. "So we finish the semester and go to Canada. As we planned."

Abbas frowned. "How do I know I will be safe in Canada? There is nothing for me in Canada."

"There is nothing for me in Iran!" cried Elena.

Abbas gave her a cool, steady look. He adjusted his glasses and sadly nodded. "Yes. I know. You would be miserable there. I cannot do that to you." He looked heartbroken, only it was hard to guess which thing pained him, his loyalty to his wife or his sudden homesickness for Iran. He wasn't as tough as he pretended.

"Look," said Zack. "You've been through a terrible experience today. Something that's left you feeling badly unraveled. You can't make any decisions about anything right now. You need to wait. Think about it a few days. You don't have to decide right away, do you? You can afford to wait and think and see where things stand."

"He is right," said Elena. "We should wait. We can talk about this tomorrow. Maybe we won't leave. But if we do, we do not have to go to Canada. We could go back to France. Anywhere but Iran."

"You don't understand," said Abbas. "Wherever we go we will not be safe. What is happening here can happen anywhere."

She was silent a moment. Then she said, "I do not want to fight. I want to be glad you are home. Glad you are safe and sound."

"Yes, I am home, aren't I?" His eyes roamed the room, seeing first his wife, then his American friends—only Zack feared Americans might not look friendly tonight—then he gazed at the ceiling, toward the rooms where his children were sleeping. He took a deep breath. "You are right. I cannot think clearly tonight. What day is today? I cannot even remember what day it is."

Zack suddenly couldn't remember either.

"Friday," said Daniel.

"Friday?" said Abbas. "Good. I do not have to face my students tomorrow. It is not their fault. Still—"

"You need time," said Zack. "Give yourself time. You've had a horrible experience. If there's anything we can do, you can call us." He slowly stood up, letting Daniel know they should go.

Daniel drew his legs together and got off the floor. "It's good to have you back, Abbas. We were worried."

Abbas only nodded. He refused to look at Daniel, as if he blamed Daniel—Zack was surprised to imagine such an emotion.

"Good night, Elena," said Zack as they pulled on their coats. "Again, if you need anything . . ."

She gave him a slight bow and looked back at Abbas, who remained sunk in his chair, staring at the fire.

The two men walked out to the Toyota. Zack still had the keys, so he got in on the driver's side. When Daniel sat next to him, Zack reached over, took hold of his hand, lifted it, and kissed the back of it.

"What's that for?"

"I don't know. Just to thank you for being you."

Daniel frowned. "For all the good it does anybody."

40

LIFE SHOULD HAVE GONE BACK to normal after that. Life should have felt good again. But it is hard to believe in safety after your imagination has lived with disaster for nine hours. Daniel's sleep that night was full of bad dreams. He could remember nothing about the dreams the next morning except a general sense of panic, but he lay in bed feeling like a hole had been punched in his world and all kinds of new catastrophes could pour in. He felt helpless, useless, stupid. He felt guilty, too, as if it were his fault he'd been able to do so little. He couldn't begin to guess what Abbas was feeling today.

Zack wanted to talk, of course, but Daniel preferred to be silent about yesterday. Real talk would only make him feel worse. So they said little to each other and the weekend passed slowly. Daniel suggested they give the Rohanis a breather for the next few days, and Zack agreed, but on Sunday, Daniel called the house to ask if Abbas and the kids wanted to go to the pool. It was Elena who answered. She thanked Daniel for the invitation but said Abbas was staying in bed today. He hadn't been sleeping well.

On Monday a special department meeting was called for one o'clock, everybody's lunch hour. Daniel arrived five minutes late, took a quick look around the conference room, and understood what the meeting was about. "Where's Abbas?" he asked.

"We decided," Jane began, "or no, *I* decided, that this would be easier if visiting faculty weren't present." She lowered her head, unable to look him in the eye. "Have a seat, Daniel. I was just telling everyone that things are fine now. The FBI learned what they needed to know, and we got a clean bill of health. So let's just forget last week ever happened."

The others at the table blandly faced Jane but were stealing peeks at Daniel—all except Samuel Clay Brooke, who only looked confused.

Oh shit, thought Daniel. The FBI had spoken not just to Zack and a few students but to his colleagues, too, asking questions and unleashing suspicions. Or rather, the questions must have confirmed suspicions, since there was already talk among the students, and students were the last to notice anything. Being the subject of gossip usually amused Daniel—he should be proud that people knew he was engaged in a sexy little soap opera. But today their interest felt different: cold, uneasy, judgmental. He could feel the eyes of his occasional friends—Warren Bates, Ginny McMullen, Bob Potts—dart around his face like flies.

"Excuse me, but am I misconstruing the topic?" Samuel blurted out. "Are you *implying* the FBI was here to look for *spies*?" He rolled his words in his mouth like marbles, randomly emphasizing this one or that.

"Nobody said anything about spies," Warren explained. "A member of a foreign government came here to visit his brother, who's on the faculty. The FBI just needed to find out exactly who the man and his brother are." They were carefully avoiding names.

"They didn't talk to you, Samuel?" said Jane.

"A man and woman came to my office. Never guessed they were *G-men*. Couldn't make head or tail of what they were saying. Something about Iran? Iraq? Something about two painters in *carnal* relations?" He scornfully twisted his mouth to one side. "People always talk rubbish like that about painters. Diddling each other when they aren't diddling each other's *wives*? Ridiculous. I told them nobody diddled anybody here. We're a good, clean *college* town."

As always with Samuel, it was hard to guess if this were sarcastic wisdom or total nonsense.

"Uh-huh," went Jane. "As I was saying? If the FBI is happy, I'm happy. End of story. Okay? That's all I needed to tell you today. Any other business can wait until our regular meeting on Wednesday. All right? See you on Wednesday."

People grunted and nodded, and chairs began to scoot back.

"Wait a minute," said Daniel. "Don't I get to say anything?"

Jane didn't turn to see who had spoken. "Not necessary, Daniel. There are privacy issues here. We don't need to open them."

"But you've already opened them. Everybody's going to walk out of here thinking God-knows-what about Abbas. And me and Abbas together. Can we quit being coy and say the rest of it?"

Ginny jumped in. "Your private life is none of our business. I don't want to hear about it." Leave it to Ginny, who taught art theory, pure theory, to end the discussion before it began.

"No, it isn't your business," Daniel said firmly. "But the FBI made it your business by telling you about us. I just want to say— There was nothing shameful or sinister about it. We were two good friends who had sex now and then. That's all. We had sex the same way other friends go bowling or fishing. The sex is over and we're still friends."

There were blank looks around the table. Then Bob snorted. "Remind me never to go fishing with you, Wexler."

"Go ahead. Laugh. I know how silly I sound." This was harder to discuss than he'd expected. "But don't laugh at Abbas. Because it's not funny what he's been through. He was hauled in by the FBI. For no good reason except that his Iranian brother came to town. And the FBI held him for most of the day. He didn't know what was going to happen. You met those people. They were idiots. Would you feel safe in their hands?"

"How we might feel is irrelevant," Warren solemnly declared. "National security is at risk. Our government has to protect us."

Daniel was startled that an art teacher could take the other side. Warren had hardened over the years, raising teenagers, writing about Thomas Hart Benton, but he had once been a long-haired painter.

"And how do you know there's no cause for suspicion?" Warren continued. "They must know something, stuff they can't tell us. His brother's a bigwig in the land of Islamic zombies. They think America is a cancer. Don't you remember the hostage crisis? Who knows what they're up to? Just because you had the man's dick down your throat doesn't mean you know everything about him."

A couple of teachers winced. "Guys!" said Jane.

Daniel stared straight at Warren, more stunned than angry, confused that Warren could think in such lame, xenophobic clichés.

He spoke slowly, carefully. "Yeah, I sucked his dick. And yeah, dicks lie. But I spent hours with the man. And we talked. After sex. Before sex. We talked about everything under the sun. Art. Life. Politics. Religion. Family. You name it. He doesn't give a damn about politics. He has very mixed feelings about Iran. Plus I met his brother. Zack and I had them over for dinner. I can't say I liked him. He was full of himself, like most politicians. And smug, like a Frenchman who'd found Jesus, even if his Jesus is Allah. But he's hardly a terrorist. Hardly a mastermind who came here to blow up Colonial Williamsburg. They're not the bad guys. Believe me."

Everybody was silent. Daniel felt pleased. It was a good speech, wasn't it?

"I believe you," said Jane. "We all believe you, yes?" She nodded at the others until they nodded with her. "The man is our guest for another semester. It's no good for us to wonder and worry about him. He's *not* one of the bad guys. He's a painter and a teacher. Thank you, Daniel. I'm glad we got that out in the open. Enough said." She stood up, signaling that the meeting was over.

The others, even Warren, stood and began to move out the door.

"Can somebody explain to me that *last* part?" asked Samuel. "Was the oral sex reference figurative or literal?"

It had ended much too quickly. Daniel understood that Jane just wanted to finish with it. He stayed behind to explain himself a little better.

She appeared nervous seeing him standing by the door as the others filed out, but she remained in the room.

"Sorry to put you through that," Daniel began. "But I couldn't let people think the shit they were thinking. Abbas isn't the enemy, despite what Warren says. But they all surprised me today, not just Warren. The way they looked at me, like I'd slept with Hitler. What's going on? Are people so afraid nowadays they'll trust their shitty government more than they trust people they work with?"

Jane nodded, moving her big butch head up and down, as if in full agreement. Then she said, "I don't know, Daniel. A man who can cheat on his wife, not just with another woman but another man, is not somebody *I* can fully trust."

Daniel was stunned all over again. This was Jane Morrison, whom he'd known since grad school, who was like a cousin.

"Come on, Jane. He's hardly the first married man I've had an affair with. Elena has known from the start. They have a very open marriage, you know."

Jane made a face. "No, I didn't know. You think I care about that? I don't care." She continued to make faces, scowling, smirking, frowning, searching for the right expression to capture what she felt. "I don't give a damn who sleeps with who around here. The messes you people get in are not my concern. Until the FBI comes to town, and suddenly I *have* to be concerned, I *have* to know?"

"You didn't suspect anything until they told you?"

"No. Which made me feel stupid. I like to know what's going on, even when I'd rather not. I thought you and I were good friends."

"We are, Jane. We're great friends."

She shook her head. "No, Daniel. Not this week. I'm very pissed at you. Aren't you old enough yet to keep your pecker in your pants? We're not in our twenties anymore. The seventies are over. I just hope the dean and president don't hear about this. *Or* the board of trustees and state legislature."

"You can't worry about *them*," said Daniel dismissively.

"Well, I do. All the time. I have to. It's my job." She stared at him in frustration. "Forget it, Daniel. You have a helluva lot on your plate already. I'm out of here. Goodbye."

Daniel watched Jane hurry off, feeling confused by her, annoyed. He did not want to feel guilty. He wanted to be pleased with himself for defending Abbas, for not backing down. He decided to go find Abbas. He suddenly needed to see his friend again face-to-face.

Abbas wasn't in his office. His classroom was open but deserted. The door to his work studio was closed. Daniel heard something being dragged across the floor inside. Abbas must be working again, which was a good sign.

Daniel knocked. The dragging stopped. "Who is it?"

"It's me. Daniel."

A long silence followed. Daniel wondered if he should knock again or go away. Then the door opened, and there stood Abbas in his bib overalls and thermal underwear shirt. He was frowning, his face smudged black with whiskers, not a five o'clock shadow but more like a five-day shadow. He hadn't shaved over the weekend. His chin and cheeks echoed the crew cut with its widow's peak. "Yes?"

"I just came from a department meeting. It was all about you. I thought you might want to know."

There was no change in Abbas's expression. He looked very tired. After a moment he stepped aside and let Daniel come in.

The room looked starker than before, more austere, and Daniel realized there was no music. Abbas was always playing something on his boom box, but not today. Then Daniel saw four or five raw wooden stretchers against the back wall, like the stripped bones of paintings, square skeletons of art. No wonder the room felt bare. A finished canvas from last semester lay flat on the floor: the big green one with Osh's red handprint.

"Do they know what happened on Friday?" asked Abbas.

"Most of it. The FBI talked to everyone last week. Which made them all suspicious. But have no fear. I defended you. I assured them you won't blow anything up."

It was meant as a joke, but nothing was funny anymore.

"They believed you?"

"Yes. Plus the FBI told Jane you were safe. They have amazing faith in their government."

Abbas nodded, then returned to the painting on the floor and lifted up one end. He'd been working on the back, using a screwdriver to pry the heavy staples holding the canvas to the wood.

"But they know I was arrested?" he said.

"You weren't arrested. You were held for questioning. That's all. For a very long time. But yeah, they know that."

Abbas gouged at one staple, then another, raising them a half inch or so. "But after the police touch a man, he is no longer clean. They know I am not one of them. I am a foreigner, a fanatic, a crazy towel-head."

Daniel wasn't sure how to respond. "No, they don't think that. They're probably more alarmed to learn you and I had been fuck buddies."

"Little potatoes," grumbled Abbas. "As if it matters to anyone."

Which couldn't help but sting, even as Daniel told himself the man was right.

Abbas continued to gouge and pry with the screwdriver. When he reached the corner, he put the screwdriver in his pocket and took out a pair of pliers. He pulled at the loosened staples like a dentist extracting teeth.

Daniel saw a stack of flayed canvases on the floor near the sofa, four or five squares of densely painted fabric with raw white borders. They looked like the hides of gaudy patchwork animals.

"Why're you taking your work off its stretchers?"

"I am cleaning house. Separating sheep from goats. Good paintings from bad paintings."

"Which are these?" Daniel pointed at the stack.

"The ones good enough to save."

Daniel went over to look. It was the recent work, the abstract studies of magnified letters from the Koran. On the top of the pile was the pale creamy orange canvas with a title like "Surrender to God." Daniel did not like these paintings half as much as he liked the older, looser, slightly cartoony work.

"Do you really want to do this *now*?" he asked. "Wouldn't you rather wait until things are calmer and you can be objective?"

"I need to do this soon so I won't leave any good work behind."

Daniel hesitated. "Where are you going?"

"I don't know. Nowhere, I hope."

He continued to pull slowly and steadily with the pliers. Twisted staples rang against the concrete floor.

"You still think you might be arrested?" said Daniel.

"Maybe. Or maybe I will flee. Either way, I must travel light. I cannot abandon my best work."

He sounded perfectly reasonable, utterly calm. The calm may have been only fatigue, but he did not seem paranoid, especially when one knew he had good cause to be fearful.

"But the FBI says you're fine."

"And you believe them?" Abbas continued to pull out teeth. "You are a Jew. You should know better than anyone what it is like to be hated. To be a foreigner wherever you go. They smile at us when they make their promises. But they are lying, always lying."

"Nobody hates you," Daniel claimed. "Nobody hates me either."

Abbas turned the painting around to its next side and continued to pull.

"Did you talk to your brother over the weekend?" Daniel hoped to find an explanation there.

"Yes. He wants me to come home. Elena thinks we should stay."

"She thinks the danger is over?"

"She says we have French passports. France will protect us. She wants to go to the French embassy and see what they can do."

"Sounds like a good idea."

Abbas shook his head. "She is talking in her hat. Because she hates my country. So much that she prefers to risk losing me rather than go over there."

Daniel paused again. "You can't believe that. Zack and I were with her all day Friday. She was very worried. Very upset. She cares about you very much."

"She says she cares, and maybe she does." He yanked out another staple. "Sometimes. But she is a Russian. They are a cynical people. She is always looking out for her own ass."

Daniel had told the department that he knew Abbas inside out, as if talking to a man when you're both naked gives you special insight. But Daniel didn't really know him, did he? He wished Zack were here. Maybe Zack could tell if this talk were crazy or not.

"Look, I got a class in fifteen minutes. Can we continue this later? We could meet for a drink this afternoon."

"No. Osh and I are going to the mosque this afternoon."

That took Daniel by surprise. "The mosque in Newport News?"

"Yes. It is a good place to think. I was first there with my brother, but I went back on Saturday. I find I can focus my thoughts there. I like the peace and order."

Now Daniel remembered the full title of the orange painting: "Surrender to God and you will be safe."

"I've never been to a mosque," said Daniel. "Can I join you?"

Abbas glanced up from his pliers. "Why? There is nothing to see. Only an ugly building, an old automobile showroom. Full of black Americans speaking bad Arabic. You will find it ridiculous. The calm is in this dome, not in that one." He pointed at his head. "Plus the place is watched by the police. They will see you with me and think the worst."

"I don't care what they think of me," said Daniel.

"I care what they think of *me*," said Abbas. "More important, it is a private place. A personal place. For me and my son. I do not want you there as a tourist."

"I'm not going as a tourist, I'm going as a friend."

Abbas frowned again. "Why are you so warm to me? Why do you want to look after me?"

The question threw Daniel. "Because you're my friend. Because I care about you."

Abbas shook his head. "Not for the sex? You are hoping we will have sex again?"

"No. I'm not."

"Because I am done with sex. With men *and* women. Sex makes one too vulnerable. It takes one out of the mind and into the body. The body makes life difficult."

Only now did Daniel realize that he felt no erotic tension today, none of the usual chemical density of memory and anticipation. The Iranian's presence was oddly weightless. Was it the five-day beard or the shadow of prison? Was it simply because Abbas felt no lust? Daniel was confused by the thinner air, but also relieved, pleased. If he wasn't here for sex, then his concern was purely disinterested, his friendship admirably selfless.

Abbas removed the last staples, and the canvas began to slide off the frame. Daniel hurried over to catch it. He held two corners while Abbas finished and then helped him carry it to the pile. A canvas off its stretcher is such a strange object, stiff and floppy, no longer solid but not quite disposable either. They laid the green canvas over the orange one.

"Are you going to ship these to Iran?"

"Iran would be a good home for them. I could roll them inside a carpet tube and send them to Hassan."

"And you and your family can follow?"

Abbas frowned. "I do not know. I cannot decide. Not yet anyway. But being ready to go will make me feel better."

Against the wall behind the sofa leaned a dozen or so older paintings, all face out: the less abstract work that Daniel preferred: Clemente-like animals, paisley Klee men, alphabet people.

"What about those?" said Daniel. "What will you do with them?"

Abbas shrugged. "They are trash. I can put them in the Dumpster. Or maybe pull off the canvas and let students work on the backs. It doesn't matter."

"But I like them. It's some of your best work."

Abbas could not have looked more disgusted if Daniel had farted. "No. These are bad paintings. They are garbage."

"You might think that now. But you can change your mind." Daniel was all too familiar with how artists thought about old work. "Let me take them. I can store them here or at the house in our basement. I'll take good care of them."

"No. They are no good."

"But I love them."

"That doesn't make them yours!"

The anger in his voice stunned Daniel. The contemptuous look in his eyes was even more damning, more hurtful.

Daniel stepped back. "Forget it. Do with them what you like. What do I know? I'm just a Jew in self-denial. But we all change our minds about what we love and what we hate."

⁓

That night Daniel told Zack a little about the department meeting, nothing about the quarrel with Jane, and a lot about his conversation with Abbas.

"I think he's having some kind of nervous breakdown."

Zack said it was possible but that it also sounded like the natural agitation of someone who'd been through a terrible ordeal. "His reality has been badly shaken. It makes perfect sense for him to turn to religion. He doesn't know what to do next, so he's going to be angry at his friends, including you. He can't trust anyone right now, including himself. We just need to give him time."

Daniel was surprised Zack wasn't more concerned, but he feared that it was his fault for not describing the encounter better.

41

THE PRESIDENT DELIVERED his State of the Union address on Tuesday, January 28, 2003. Zack watched it on TV, alone. Daniel couldn't bear to look at the man who represented everything he hated about rich people, the South, and evangelical religion. But Zack was cooler, more detached. He listened for the entire hour while the president smirked and frowned and lifted his eyebrows, like a bad actor practicing a speech in front of a mirror. The incompetence of his delivery only added to the unease produced by his words on weapons of mass destruction: nuclear warheads, sarin nerve gas, botulism toxin—things that already worried four or five patients. But war was no longer just rhetorical; it had become inevitable. There was no denying that Saddam Hussein was a vicious shit—Zack kept thinking of a line from a Marx Brothers movie: "Hey, you big bully. Quit picking on that little bully"—but the war against him felt faked, rushed, and unnecessary.

Zack spoke to Elena every day that week. She called him or he called her or sometimes they exchanged e-mails. She kept Zack posted on how they were doing, especially Abbas. He couldn't sleep at night. He was restless during the day, often quiet and withdrawn, then abruptly angry.

"He's like a different person since his FBI meeting?"

"Oh no. He is like always. But moodier. If only he were still painting, his moods might not swing so much. But he has stopped painting. He goes often to the mosque, with Osh, which worried me at first, but he always comes home calmer, more gentle."

They had met with Zack's lawyer, but Jeremy didn't put their minds at rest with his endless worst-case scenarios. On some days Elena wanted to stay put, other days she wanted to go straight to Canada. Abbas mentioned Iran again but withdrew the idea as soon as Elena vehemently resisted. "So we are paralyzed. We play a waiting game, only I do not know what we are waiting for. Sorry. I complain too much. But a Russian is like an onion. The more you peel us, the more you weep."

Zack asked if the FBI had been back, but no, the agents had made their trouble and disappeared.

"But they are out there, I know. Your secret police is more delicate than ours. More secret."

"And the neighbors? Has war talk turned them against you?"

"Oh no. Americans are always nice to foreigners. To their faces anyway. They might want to see us blown to bloody hell on television. But they try to be nice in person."

That weekend Elena called to ask for a special favor. They were driving to D.C. on Tuesday to visit the French embassy. Jeremy had set up a meeting to ensure their status as French citizens. While they were up there, Elena wanted to go to the Canadian embassy and check out the possibility of an early move to Toronto.

"I don't know how late we will be. Can Mina and Osh stay with you after school until we get back?"

"We'd be delighted."

On Tuesday, at two-thirty, the school bus dropped the kids off at Indian Springs Road. Daniel had come home early to look after them while Zack saw his patients, but Mina announced that she could take care of her brother, thank you very much. They went down to the basement to do their homework, watch cartoons, and hang out with Jocko.

"That boy is so spoiled," said Daniel with a laugh. "A regular little prince."

Zack saw three patients that afternoon, two college students and a middle-aged husband. He enjoyed working with students. Their problems weren't half as interesting as they thought, and they could be bottomless pits for advice and reassurance, but they were more flexible than adults, more open to change. Both of these students looked surprised when Zack asked if they were worried about the war. "What war?"

When he was done, he sat at his computer and typed up his notes. There was a timid knock on the door. It slowly opened: Mina.

"Oh, hi," said Zack. "How's it going? Find everything you need?" He automatically talked to her as a peer.

"Uh-huh." She stood at the door, her eyes climbing around the room. "You help people here? Don't you have a thing to lie down on?"

"A couch? No. I got rid of my couch years ago. Come on in. I'm done for the day. I'd give you a tour but I don't have much to show."

She strolled into the room, confident and composed, her slim, dark hands held away from her sides, her jet-black eyes taking in everything. There was a slight tremble to her hoop earrings. "Where do your patients sit?"

"There." He pointed at the leather straight-back chair. "Go ahead. Sit in it if you want to know what it feels like. I don't do anything weird or magical here. I just listen while people talk."

He thought she'd get giggly and nervous, but no, she went over to the chair, hopped into it, and sat up straight. "I came today to talk about my husband," she declared in a make-believe grown-up voice. "We argue all the time."

"I'm sorry to hear that, madam. What do you argue about?"

"Every little thing. What to eat. Where to go. When to sleep."

Zack didn't have a lot of experience working with kids, but he thought he could playact with Mina and learn something. "Have the fights been getting worse lately?"

"Oh yes. Because my husband wants to live on Mars. I want to stay on Earth. I can't live on Mars. The air would kill me. But my husband says the air on Earth is killing him. What should I do?"

Her eyes widened as she spoke, as if she were frightening herself with her game. It wrung Zack's heart.

"What about your children? You have children, right?"

"Yes, we have two beautiful sons."

"I thought you had a beautiful daughter?"

"We did. But we traded her for a son. Sons are more valuable."

He wanted to blame Abbas for her attitude, but this wasn't about blame. "I disagree. I prefer women. They're smarter and more sympathetic. They're more interesting."

"You would think that. You're a homo."

"True." Was this how he and Daniel were identified in that household: the homos? "Where do the children want to live?"

"It doesn't matter. They are like cats. They can always land on their feet."

Where had she heard that phrase? It was like eavesdropping at the Rohani dinner table. "But what do you think they would say if you *did* ask them?"

"The son can live anywhere. He's too young to care. But the daughter wants to stay here. Because she gets to wear dresses or jeans or anything she pleases. And everybody in her school looks different, not just her. She has friends here. People like her."

"I thought you said you had two sons and no daughter?"

Mina stiffened for a moment, like a small bird trying to make itself invisible, and Zack realized that he'd fumbled it.

"This is a stupid game," she declared. "I'm tired of playing." She jumped out of the chair and left the room in a brisk, proud, falsely nonchalant walk.

⁓ ⁓

Daniel cooked dinner that night: a hot dog for Osh, fried chicken for everyone else. Afterward he and the kids took Jocko for a walk while Zack washed the dishes. When they returned, Daniel built a fire in the rec room and they all watched Charlie Chaplin on DVD. The movies delighted Osh, especially when someone got kicked in the butt. Zack brought down ice cream for everybody.

Their parents still weren't back by nine. Daniel went upstairs for a minute, returned, and announced, "Your mom just phoned. She said they're running late but you should go to bed. They know you're here and they'll pick you up. Want to do a campout?" He brought out two old sleeping bags and opened them in front of the fire. Zack admired his way with kids. "Want to hear a

ghost story?" Daniel asked. Osh did but Mina didn't, so Daniel turned off the
lights. The kids lay snug and warm inside the two plump, pillowy bags in a
dark room lit by crumbling red coals.

"Like Hansel and Gretel," Daniel whispered. He and Zack crept up the
stairs. "I was lying about the phone call."

"I figured."

"You don't think anything happened, do you?"

"No. It's a three-hour drive. D.C. offices probably don't close until six.
Even if the FBI followed them, I can't imagine they'd be arrested. I mean,
they were going *into* the beast, not fleeing it."

"But you're worried too or you wouldn't have thought it out."

Zack paused. "Yes, I'm worried. A little."

A half hour later they heard a slam of car doors outside, and two people
arguing. Soon there was a sharp knock at the front door.

Zack opened the door. Elena stood on the porch, hissing in French at her
husband. *"Quelle merde! Tu es fou!"* She hurried past Zack without looking at
him.

Abbas closed the door, glowering at Zack. Daniel hadn't mentioned that
Abbas was growing a beard, a short, black, scruffy thing that climbed up to
his eyes. It was as though he'd decided that if people were going to treat him
as a Muslim terrorist, he would look like one. "Where are our children?"

"Downstairs, asleep. Why don't you come in and tell us what happened
first? Would you like some wine?"

"Didn't you know?" Elena called out from the living room. "He no longer
takes alcohol. He is preparing himself for paradise."

"Shut up," said Abbas. "Yes, I would like wine. One glass. But then we
must go. It has been a long and terrible day."

The Rohanis sat at opposite ends of the sofa and lit up two cigarettes.
Daniel opened a bottle and filled four glasses. Abbas took a deep swallow and
immediately began to speak. His tone was dry and hurried.

"The French say they cannot protect us. We are not French-born, we are
only aliens, naturalized aliens. Their government will not stick its neck out."
The Canadians, by contrast, wanted to help but advised them to wait until the
new job started in the fall, when Abbas would have his work visa. Once Abbas

was inside the country, there was a good likelihood he could stay permanently. In the meantime, however, they could not offer political asylum since he was not being persecuted. "Only if I am arrested do I count as persecuted. But if I am arrested I cannot leave, can I?"

"That is not what they said!" snapped Elena. "You are hearing only what you want to hear!"

"No! You are the one with selective ears."

"*No!* What the Canadians said was we can go ahead and come in. But they cannot promise anything until you begin your job."

"And those things include protection from arrest, protection from being returned to the U.S.! We will not be safe there either."

"They were talking only of permanent residency, immigration papers. You didn't want to hear because you want to go to Iran. You have already fixed your mind on taking us to Iran."

"And why not?" declared Abbas. "It is the best place for us. My brother offers us a good life there, a safe life. Here I may be arrested any day."

This was a new development for Zack, although clearly not for them. They sounded like they were repeating an earlier argument.

Elena softly groaned. "You think this is bad? This is nothing, Abbas. Iran is a police state. You do not know what it is like to live in a police state. I do. Where there is no private life, no family life. Where everybody is a busybody. Where children are taught to rat on their parents. It does not matter if the head cop is Brezhnev or Allah. Your life is no longer your own, and everyone is a spy. I refuse to put my family in such a place."

Abbas stared at her, unable to answer, which made him angrier.

Zack saw his chance and took it. "What about the war, Abbas? You'll put your family next door to a war. It isn't a good time. Don't you think you should wait?"

Abbas shook his head. "If there is war and we are here, we *will* be arrested. Like the Jews in Germany. Like the Japanese here."

Elena gave him a dirty look. She didn't know how to answer the charge; she must believe it herself. But then she said, "You see? You cannot reason with him. Because he has already made up his mind. He wants to go home to Iran. He wants to go home to his brother. He has wanted it all along, even before the

FBI threatened him. Ever since Hassan visited and promised him a new life. What's wrong with your old life? You have children who love you, a wife who loves you. Even men who love you." She avoided looking at Daniel. "What else do you need? A government that loves you? A God that loves you?"

Abbas scowled. "Leave God out of this. This is not about God. This is about being where I belong. Because I am nobody here. I am nothing. They could pick me up on the street and make me disappear, and nobody could help, nobody could save me."

Elena hesitated. "You are such a baby. You sit in police station a few hours and your world comes to an end. I see what you are doing. You are fixing the cards so we have only one choice. To go to Iran. All right then. Go. But you can go without us. Because our children and I are not going. You can go alone."

Abbas's face went blank. He must have heard everything else before, but this was new, this surprised him. He turned away for a moment, took a deep breath, then faced her. He spoke in French, a long, clear, careful paragraph. Zack's French wasn't good enough for him even to guess what he was saying.

Elena watched and listened, her eyes growing wider, her chin going up. "In English!" she cried. "Say it in English!" She bared her teeth, furious with what he'd said. "I want them to hear your craziness. I want them to know how nuts you are!"

"Very well." Abbas took another deep breath. "I said: You can stay here. You and Mina can stay here. I will go to Iran. With Osh. I will take my son home with me and give him the life he deserves. Everyone will be happy. We will all be satisfied."

Zack turned to Daniel, wondering what he made of this. Daniel was still staring at Abbas. "You're serious?" said Zack.

"Totally." Abbas did not turn to him but continued to face his wife. His tone remained cold and deliberate. "It is the best solution, don't you think? I do not want to give up my daughter. But I want to be fair to my wife. I cannot leave my wife with nothing. Even though she is willing to do such a thing to me. So yes. Let me have my son and she can have my daughter. We will go our separate ways."

Elena snapped her head to the left, then the right, as if looking for the proper angle to see her husband.

"What did I tell you?" she muttered. "He is crazy. He is nuts." She turned to Zack. "You're the psychiatrist. He is insane, yes? You can put him away. You can lock him up. For the good of his family. For his own protection. Yes?"

Zack stared at her. Was *she* serious?

"Before he hurts his children. It's not bad enough *he* wants to go straight to hell, he wants to take his son there with him. He is a danger to his children."

"No, you are the danger!" charged Abbas. "We are given a chance to escape and you want to stay, so I can be arrested? So I can disappear inside their system and you will get rid of me?"

Her mouth hung open in disbelief. She snapped it shut to speak. "You really are mad. You are talking nonsense. You are talking shit. You will not cut up our family like a pie. You will not take my son."

"He is *my* son, and you are a selfish woman. I will do with him what I please."

Elena turned back to Zack. "You hear that? He is threatening to kidnap Osh. He is a dangerous man. He is a crazy man. You must lock him up until he is sane again. A hospital is where he belongs."

"Elena. No. I can't do that." Strangers asked him to do this all the time, the families of patients. But friends never. The idea frightened Zack. "Once a person is hospitalized, it's out of your control. It's on their record forever. They'll never forgive you. It can lead to lawsuits and charges of malpractice. No. We do not want to go there."

"Listen to her," said Abbas with a sneer. "She thinks that if she calls *me* crazy, nobody will notice that *she* is crazy, that she is the one who needs to be put into a hospital."

Zack noticed Daniel watching him, as if wanting to know which of these two were insane.

"Please," said Zack. "You're both under enormous strain. It does nobody any good to call each other crazy. But if you want to continue this, why don't we go to your place? The three of us. We can leave the kids here. They can have a sleepover, and Daniel can look after them. The two of you can finish what you started. You don't want your kids hearing their parents call each other mentally ill."

Abbas and Elena were silent, unable to look at each other or anyone else.

"No. We are fine," Elena finally said. "I have said all I need to say. I want my children with me tonight. I cannot leave them."

Abbas nodded. "Yes, yes. We must take our children home. You have heard too much of our shit. You do not need to hear more."

"Uh, want me to go downstairs and wake the kids?" said Daniel.

"I will go with you," said Elena. "I want them to see we are back and they are safe." She followed Daniel out to the kitchen and down the stairs, leaving Zack alone with Abbas.

Suddenly Zack had nothing to say to the man. He was at a complete loss for words. Finally he said, "I'm sorry about what you're going through, Abbas. It's very unfair."

Abbas looked at him, expecting something more.

"I hear you're having trouble sleeping. Would you like me to give you something?"

Abbas angrily flared his nostrils. "I do not need your drugs. I do not need your pity. My life is none of your business."

"Maybe not. But my friendship with your wife and Daniel's friendship with you have made it my business. I only want to help."

Abbas looked colder than ever, stern and indifferent. But nobody could be as indifferent as he pretended.

Elena came upstairs carrying Osh, heavily asleep, sprawled in her arms like a big beanbag doll. Abbas tried to take him. She turned away. "*I* have him," she said. "You can help your daughter."

Daniel was leading Mina by the hand, a little sleepwalker stumbling along with her head down. She dreamily mumbled to herself when Abbas gently helped her on with her coat.

Zack followed Elena to the door. "If there's any trouble," he whispered, "call me." The boy's puffy, pouty face hung between him and her. "Don't hesitate to call me. Okay?"

She nodded, but in such a curt, dismissive manner that he felt he had failed her.

42

Daniel watched the Rohanis go out to their car in the cold, Elena lugging the sleeping boy, Abbas leading the half-awake girl by the hand. Not until they drove away did Zack shut the door.

Daniel remained shaken by the argument, the anger of the words, the bitter intimacy in the husband's and wife's attacks on each other. He and Zack never argued like that. Thank God. This went beyond a nasty marital spat into something that felt as fierce and physical and real as a tornado. Daniel almost envied the Rohanis their fine fury, even as he remembered that Abbas was crazy and getting crazier every day. And Elena kept adding fuel to the fire.

He and Zack returned to the living room, but only to pick up the wineglasses, as if afraid to stay in a room still radioactive with anger.

Zack said, "You would think an outside threat like this would bring them together. But it's made things even worse."

"It's like I said," Daniel replied. "Abbas has had some kind of nervous breakdown."

"It's possible." Zack had gone into shrink mode during the argument, and part of him remained there. Daniel often found his psychiatrist persona a challenge, both admirable and annoying.

They went into the kitchen and put the glasses in the sink, and Zack began to wash them.

Daniel came out with it: "I hate to say this, but I think Elena is right. I think Abbas should be hospitalized. For a week or two. Until he calms down."

"No. Absolutely not." Zack didn't even pause to consider the idea. "She shouldn't have mentioned it."

"But he's flying apart. He's having a meltdown."

Zack shook his head. "The man is not acting psychotic. He makes perfect sense. Unfortunately."

"But you heard him. He wants to take them to Iran. Which is like wanting to go to prison. It's totally irrational, completely self-destructive."

"It would be a terrible decision," Zack agreed. "But there's nothing pathological about it. He's under a lot of strain right now. Life has become very complicated for him. It's only natural he'd say and want strange things."

They remained at the sink, no longer washing glasses, just standing there, as if sitting down would signal a long, serious talk, which neither of them wanted.

"He threatened to kidnap Osh," said Daniel. "If Elena doesn't agree to go."

"He didn't call it kidnapping. Elena called it kidnapping."

"I think he could do it. He takes Osh down to the mosque in Newport News every other day. What's to stop him from going to the airport there, getting on a plane with Osh, and skipping the country? Do you want that to happen?"

Zack was losing his patience. "Look. If Abbas *were* committed, he'd be held for forty-eight hours. They'd examine him and either want to keep him there indefinitely, which would be disastrous. Or they'd release him immediately. If he were released, he'd be sure to skip the country. So no, it's not an option we even want to consider."

Which made so much sense that Daniel wanted to agree.

But then Zack said: "I respect your concern here, Daniel. But you're not an objective party."

"What does that mean?"

"You were in love with him. Remember?" Zack attempted a tiny smile. "You're still infatuated. A little." -

Daniel was hurt to be so misunderstood. "You think I want him locked up at Eastern State because I'm still in love and don't want him to leave?"

"That's not what I meant."

"No? What did you mean?"

"Only that—" He waved his hand, trying to erase his words. "You know him too well to be objective. That's all."

"I'm not infatuated," Daniel declared. "Not now. I'm not sure I ever was in love with the jerk. As soon as the sex stopped, I stopped feeling much of anything for him. My concern here is purely selfless. I want to save him *from* himself. I don't want to save him *for me.*"

Zack stared as if he'd just said something absurd. "Daniel. You *are* still in love with him. Especially now that you're not fucking."

Daniel was stunned. "Fuck off," he said. "No way." He couldn't understand why he was so angry. "What do you know about it? When was the last time you were in love? Sexually, I mean. You love everybody and nobody, and that doesn't count."

Zack's eyes grew wide, and Daniel realized he had jumped over the real subject into something else, a bigger, messier topic. Daniel quickly jumped back.

"I wish I *were* in love with him. Because that would make this sexy and dramatic. Instead it's just messy and ugly. I hate every minute of it. Because I can't do a damn thing to help him. You won't let me. Because he's your case now. Not mine."

Zack quietly said, "He's not a case. He's a friend. He's my friend as well as yours." He swallowed. "Just because I don't care about sex doesn't mean my love doesn't count. But why should that matter to you, since you're sure you're *not* in love with him?"

"You are so smart," said Daniel. "So on top of things. Is that why you won't commit him? You *want* him to skip the country, so you can get him out of town. But that would mean you're jealous, and you're never jealous. No, you're too selfless and perfect for that."

Zack winced. "I'm hardly selfless. A little selfishness is a good thing. I admire your selfishness. Sometimes. I even envy it. It gets you out of your head and into the world."

Daniel stared at him in disbelief. "That is so condescending. You don't envy me. You think I'm a silly, shallow, selfish sex junkie who can't help anybody, not even himself."

"Stop talking crap," said Zack. "That's absolute crap and you know it." He took a deep breath, keeping his temper, staying in control. "Why are we fighting about this? We both want to protect them. This isn't about us."

"No, it's never about us, is it? I'm not even sure there is an us."

"What the hell does that mean?"

Daniel had said it only because the words were handy. But they had a good, hard, brutal sound. "Nothing. It means I'm tired. I'm exhausted. I'm going to bed. It's your turn to walk the dog. Good night." He hurried down the hall to his bedroom before Zack could answer him.

He had said too much. He hadn't said enough. Why was he so angry with Zack? Why did he want to make Zack angry with him? He couldn't figure it out. Daniel suddenly felt he couldn't do anything right. He couldn't help people, he couldn't paint, he couldn't even tell if he were in love or not unless somebody else told him.

Daniel lay in bed in the dark, listening to Zack leave the house, then return, hoping he wouldn't come to his room and try to make peace tonight. He wanted them to stay unhappy with each other, for a while longer, as if pain would prove that an *us* did exist.

43

ZACK SLEPT BADLY THAT NIGHT and woke up much too early the next morning. His head was already full of Abbas and Elena. He knew he should also be worried about himself and Daniel and the terrible things they'd said to each other, but they could wait, they could fix themselves later. He sat in the kitchen in the dark, eating cold cereal and trying to come up with some kind of solution. Finally he went into his office and wrote an e-mail:

> Elena: I have thought long and hard about your proposal last night. I am sorry but I still believe I gave you the right advice. A man needs to be an imminent danger to himself or others before he can be committed, and by imminent I mean fatal. However, if Abbas tries anything with the children, call 911. The police will take your side. The children belong to you both. If worst comes to worst, we can get a restraining order issued. But we cannot hospitalize him. I hope you understand my position here. Call me later this morning.

He would've thought of the police last night if he and Daniel hadn't gotten lost in their own argument. After he wrote Elena, he stayed at his computer to make out bills and fill in insurance forms, good, mindless busywork. Eventually he heard Daniel in the kitchen, fixing breakfast, talking to Jocko. Daniel left for school without knocking on the door to say goodbye.

Zack promptly called Elena.

"Hello? Oh, Zack. Yes." She sounded remarkably calm, yet Zack couldn't tell if it were true calm or only exhaustion. She had already read his e-mail and thanked him for his advice. "Yes, you are right. I see that. And I already knew, if I put him away, he will never forgive me. But if he takes Osh, I will never forgive him."

"If he tries anything, Elena, call the police. Will you promise me that? And call here. I'll back you up, whatever you tell them. But if he runs off to Iran by himself, remember: You're not alone. You have friends here who want to help you and your children."

She was silent for a moment. "When I married a man I didn't love, I thought I would be spared all ugly complications. But such is not the case. We will talk tomorrow."

He got off the phone full of affection for Elena, her honesty and heart. He wanted to help her, and felt guilty he couldn't, yet Elena needed only so much help. So why did he imagine her and the children, without Abbas, being looked after by himself and Daniel?

Zack went on with his day, seeing patients and concentrating on *their* problems. He was pleased by his ability to compartmentalize. But he ended the afternoon with Carter Mosby, his sexual compulsive. Carter had gone to bed two weeks ago with a young, married, born-again Christian, a handsome cabinetmaker who'd recently begun work in Colonial Williamsburg. Carter had been showing him the ropes and invited the guy back to his place one night for a beer; one thing led to another. "He was *aching* for it. I could tell as soon as he came in the door," Carter said. He wanted to "do" the guy again, but the guy pretended nothing had happened, even as he avoided Carter at work. Carter wanted to punch his face in.

"So you see, Doctor, anonymous *is* better. Because men are liars. Married men are the worst. They hide in marriage. Marriage is nothing but one big lie. Love is a lie. Monogamy is a lie. I may be a shit, but at least I'm an honest shit."

Zack often disliked Carter, but today he actually hated him. He hated him so much that he couldn't speak for a long time. Finally he said, "You don't believe that, Carter. You'd like to believe it, but you don't. Let's quote Lacan again. 'There's no such thing as a sexual relationship.' Meaning sex is always about something else."

Carter sneered. "Only for losers. Only for wimps. For real men, sex stays in the dick and it doesn't go upstream."

———

The next day was Thursday, and Zack called Elena before he drove out to Eastern State. There was no answer, only the machine. He left a message telling her he would call again after work, but she could reach him on his cell phone if she needed to talk. Most of the morning was spent in the weekly staff meeting, where Roy got into a heated exchange with Aquino, the resident, about his overreliance on older drugs, like Thorazine. Zack was glad that he'd advised against hospitalizing Abbas. A quick stroll through the wards persuaded him an emergency stay would only turn Abbas permanently against them. He decided it was a good sign when Elena didn't call.

That afternoon Jocko had an appointment at the vet. It was nothing serious, only his annual checkup, but Zack and Daniel needed to go together— Jocko got suspicious if only one human got into the car with him. Zack drove and Daniel sat in the passenger seat, twisting around to chat with the anxious dog. Daniel was still brooding over the other night but was perfectly friendly with Jocko.

"How old are you, Jocko?" the vet asked the grinning dog, who stood on his examining table. "Ten years, huh? I'd never guess it. You must live a very happy, active life."

On the ride home Zack decided to risk the subject. "Did you talk to Abbas at school today?"

"No," Daniel said indifferently. "He wasn't in."

"Really? Does he often skip Thursdays?"

"Yeah. Sometimes. His big class is on Tuesday."

He sounded looser, calmer, and Zack saw a chance, an opening. "Look. Daniel. I apologize for the things I said the night before last."

"I don't want to talk about it."

"I had no business telling you—"

Daniel said sharply, "I told you, I don't want to talk about it."

Zack recognized Daniel must feel guilty for the things *he* had said, although Daniel probably believed he was only angry about Zack's words. They would need more time before they could fully apologize.

"Uh, can we swing by their house?" said Daniel. "We're not going to stop. Call me neurotic. I just want to see if they're home."

"Sure. I don't mind." Zack could've explored this with a few questions, but he decided to keep it simple. "Only it's not neurotic, it's just human worry. And superstitious. Like knocking on wood."

They came to Chandler Court, and Zack turned left, steering carefully between the brick posts at the entrance. It was already dark, and there were no streetlights back here. A few isolated windows shined in the tangle of bare dogwood and crepe myrtle.

"I had no business getting into a fight with you the other night," said Daniel. "I still don't know what that was about. Which is why I don't want to talk about it."

"Okay. We can wait. We can talk about it later."

Zack swung the car to the right, toward the Rohani house. The structure had disappeared in the black grove of cedar trees. The lights were off. The Saab was gone. The Toyota's headlights swung over a dark front porch and blank, black windows.

Zack stopped the car. He sat with the motor running, staring at the house. He switched to the high beams, and the house became fully visible, looking even emptier.

"Maybe they went out to dinner," Daniel said quickly.

Zack opened the car door and started toward the porch. Two tall shadows bounced in the twin cones of light projected over the house—he was moving more quickly than he intended. He ran up the steps and rang the bell. Nobody answered. He pulled open the storm door and knocked on solid wood. He tried the knob. It was locked.

Daniel came up behind him. "Maybe they went out shopping! Or they went to the movies!" He sounded as frightened as Zack felt.

The curtains were open, and the headlights shined straight into the living room, painting the walls white and casting a grid of lines from the window frames. It was like a blank canvas inside, only the room was hardly empty. There was furniture, but furniture came with the place. Then Zack understood what was missing: toys. Other items were absent, too, pictures on the walls, books in the bookcase, but what struck Zack first was the absence of children's toys.

"Hello?" cried Daniel. "Hello!" He tried the door, he rang the bell. "They're gone? They're really gone? Were they arrested?"

Zack's heart stumbled. "God, I hope not. I should call that FBI agent. She could tell us."

"No, Zack. Don't. What if they took off on their own? They won't want anyone knowing they're gone until they're safe."

"Of course. Yes. You're right."

"Right back," said Daniel. He ran down the front steps and toward the house next door.

Zack remained on the porch in the glare of headlights. The Toyota continued to seethe and steam in the cold. Zack returned to the window, put his hands on either side of his face, peered inside again and thought: *Where are you? Are you together? Are you safe? How did we let this happen?*

44

THE NEXT THING ZACK KNEW he was back at the car and watching Daniel in the distance, who stood outside the house next door, talking to a tiny old lady in a blue sweat suit. When Zack looked over at the Rohani house, he half expected to see himself still on the porch. Jocko paced around on their backseat, unsure what was going on.

Daniel returned. "She says they've been gone all day. When she got up this morning the car was gone. She didn't hear anyone come for them last night. But she's not friendly with the family, not since Elena chewed her out for scolding Osh when the boy got into her garage one afternoon. Did you want me to drive?"

"No. Why shouldn't I drive?"

"Baby. You look awful. Like you've seen a ghost."

Zack was surprised to hear that. He didn't feel anything. And he hadn't seen a ghost. He'd seen nothing at all.

He drove very carefully while his mind raced with questions: If they'd been arrested, would the FBI take the car? Would the FBI take the entire family? If they'd gone freely, wouldn't Elena call him? Could Abbas force her to go against her will? And where did they go? Canada? France? Iran?

"Hush, Jocko, almost there," said Daniel, and Zack saw they were still on

Jamestown Road, only halfway through a three-minute drive. Time had stopped while his brain rapidly worked through all the awful possibilities. It was adrenaline, he told himself, only adrenaline, yet he felt stoned, lobotomized, disconnected.

As soon as he parked the car in the carport, he ran inside and upstairs to the phone in the kitchen. There were no messages. He felt he should call someone, but Daniel was right, they couldn't call the FBI. He called Jeremy, their lawyer, but only got his machine. He left a message. "This is Zack Knowles. I was wondering if you've spoken to the Rohanis today."

Daniel already stood beside him. "You didn't want to tell him they're gone?"

"No. In case the FBI is listening." Not until now did it occur to him that their phone might be bugged. Adrenaline shook loose all kinds of new ideas. He tried Hassan—he still had the man's cell phone number in his wallet—but again he got a machine, only this one spoke French. "Hi, this is Zack Knowles in Virginia. I was wondering if you've spoken to your brother or sister-in-law today. Please call us."

"It's so unreal," said Daniel. "Like a bad dream. Nothing makes sense, so it feels like anything can happen. But people don't just disappear. Once we know what happened, then it'll feel real."

Zack sat at the kitchen table. He was exhausted. He hadn't guessed he was so tired. He waited for his mind to wear itself out and slow down, but it continued to run like a manic rat in a wheel.

"You want a drink?" said Daniel. "I could use a drink."

He turned away to get the ice and glasses. Zack noticed Jocko at his feet, nervously waiting, swatting the floor with his tail, as if sending a signal in Morse code.

Zack jumped up and hurried through the house to his office. He switched on the computer without turning on the light. The machine was still booting up when Daniel came in with two glasses of scotch.

"What're you doing?"

Zack didn't answer but took a swig of the scotch—he couldn't even taste it—and went online. The server took forever to connect.

He opened his mailbox. There was the usual queue of e-mails, from patients, pharmaceutical companies, and professional groups. Toward the top, however, was a post from "poetmother," sent this morning at 6:15. Zack opened it. The message was shockingly short.

> *Dear Zack: We are going to Iran. All of us. There is no other way. We leave for Toronto this morning. I know I am making a terrible mistake but see no alternative. I cannot explain. Maybe later. I cannot thank you for all you have done for us. Do not think badly of me. Elena*

"Thank God! Now we know." Daniel stood beside Zack, reading with him. Then he bent forward and read it again. "But Iran? They're going to Iran?"

Hearing the name of the country said out loud slapped Zack out of his trance. "Is she crazy? Is she nuts?" He shook his head in disbelief. "That stupid Russian bitch!" His temper took him by surprise. "She didn't have to do that! Why did she give in to him? We would've handled him! We could've protected her!"

Daniel stared at him, not in sympathy but disbelief, as if he'd never seen Zack so angry before.

"That idiot! That masochist! How could she give in to that bastard? What did he say or do or threaten to make her go?"

His rage lifted him like a wave, a surge of anger that poured down his arms into his fists. He opened his hands and tried to shake the anger out. "Damn her! Damn him! How could they fuck themselves over like this?"

Then the wave passed and set him down again, only he kept going down. The anger faded, and there was nothing to hold him up.

"Why did they do that? Why?"

He continued to sink, and a great weight fell over him, like grief. He couldn't remember experiencing such a heavy grief before, not even when his mother died. He took deep breaths. He clenched his teeth to hold himself together, bulging his cheeks out. He felt like he was making a fist with his face.

He must look like a gargoyle in the light of the computer monitor. Then his sorrow rushed out of his chest: a loud groan followed by raw gasps and burning sobs.

"Zack?" cried Daniel. He threw his arms around him.

But the embrace didn't stop the shake and shudder of his body. Hot water ran from his eyes into his cheeks and beard. He was crying, but why? Nobody had died. They were only going to Iran. But it was as if Elena and the kids had died. As if Abbas had killed them. Which was absurd—Iran wasn't death. It was only an impossible country on the other side of the world. But it felt as final as death.

And here was Daniel, with his arms around Zack, holding him up, standing so close that Zack couldn't see his face, couldn't guess what he was feeling.

Now we're going to make up, he thought. Finally. Was this the right way to make peace, a true way to resolve things? Surely not.

"Chill, Zack. Relax, baby. It's not the end of the world."

45

Daniel didn't know what to think. He wasn't even sure what he was feeling. His emotions kept changing from minute to minute. First he felt the loss of Abbas, harsh and sudden. Then he felt pity for Zack—he couldn't understand why Zack took this so hard. Then his anger with Zack returned, which surprised Daniel. When he released him, Zack had stopped sobbing, but his eyes wore dark, tragic, panda-bear slashes over his masculine mask of beard. He did not look like someone who deserved anger.

"Relax, baby. It's not the end of the world," Daniel repeated.

"I know. I know."

Daniel couldn't remember the last time he'd seen Zack cry like this. Zack often cried during movies, but softly, gently, nothing like this openmouthed orgasm of tears.

They went into the kitchen. They hadn't eaten yet. They both admitted that they weren't hungry, but it was early, not even eight, and they needed to do something, so they fixed dinner.

It still didn't seem real. If Daniel hadn't insisted they swing by the house tonight, they wouldn't know and could remain innocent. Daniel hoped the phone would ring and it'd be Elena saying they'd changed their minds in West Virginia and were coming back. Or that the e-mail was just a joke and they'd only gone to Richmond to buy clothes for the kids. But Zack's reaction made clear that this was real. Maybe that's why Daniel was angry with him.

"So what happens next?" Daniel asked. "What do we do now?" What he really wanted to know was: How do we make this real?

"We wait and hear from them when they get to Tehran. Or we hear from the FBI. Or maybe we don't hear a damn thing."

Daniel shook his head. "It's like a bad movie. People always say that, but we know stuff like this only from movies. The good movies leave out the boring parts, the parts that make no sense."

"It's like they died," said Zack. "I know they didn't, but that's how it feels."

Which was an extreme thing to say, but Daniel understood Zack well enough to guess where it came from. "But it's not your fault," he said. "You did everything you could. You can't blame yourself."

Zack looked surprised by the possibility. "It's not that. Well, it is that. Maybe. But something else, too."

Zack only picked at the dinner they put together—just soup and sandwiches—saying little, which was surprising. Usually Daniel was the one who preferred silence, while Zack insisted on articulating every damn thought. Not tonight. He looked so sad sitting at the kitchen table, so defeated.

When Daniel returned from walking the dog, he asked Zack if he wanted to share his bed tonight. "I think we both need company." Zack was pleased by the invitation, touched. They got into Daniel's double bed, Zack in his nightshirt, Daniel in his boxer shorts and T-shirt, and lightly embraced, hooking legs around legs, like the old days. Daniel couldn't remember the last time they'd slept together at home, although they often shared a bed on trips. There was nothing sexual about it, except for the sad reminder that they no longer felt sexual with each other. After a few minutes Daniel kissed Zack on the temple and scooted back, so they could have room to breathe. Zack rolled over on his back and sighed.

"I wonder if they've gotten to Toronto yet."

There was no way they couldn't talk about the Rohanis, was there? "I think it's like a twelve-hour drive," said Daniel. "Do you really believe Iran is such a terrible place?"

"It won't be an easy place for a gay man and a woman like Elena." Zack sighed again. "What did we do wrong? I keep asking myself that. What should we have done differently?"

"There was nothing else we *could* do," Daniel insisted. "It's like you said. If Abbas had been committed at Eastern State, he would've fled the country as soon as he got out." He paused to swallow. "And it's their choice. They're grown-ups. We can't feel responsible for the choices that other grown-ups make."

"Maybe," said Zack. "Maybe."

He let the repeated word hang there, open-ended, incomplete, unable to add anything to it.

He held his silence until he fell asleep. Daniel was surprised that Zack could doze off. Maybe he wasn't so upset after all. But Daniel was the one who usually had trouble sleeping in a shared bed.

Jocko jumped up on the mattress and made a nest in their valley of legs. Then Balthus came out of hiding and curled into a ball at the foot of the bed. Everyone could sleep except Daniel.

During their first ten years together, Daniel's body and Zack's had grown easy and familiar in bed. They were able to shift around in their sleep without crushing an arm or poking an eye. About the time they moved to Virginia, however, things began to change. They stopped having sex altogether, which was actually a relief. Sex had become infrequent, and their bodies fell out of sync; desire only caused aggravation. Now they could stop worrying about who wanted what and simply sleep together, which is a lovely act to share with another person. But as they got older, each began to experience insomnia, bouts of night fret, worry, sleeplessness, always suffered alone, although the awake party inevitably woke the other. So they took separate beds in separate rooms, and that worked well—they could talk to each other through their open doors—but they slowly forgot the language of each other's bodies.

Daniel lay in the dark, studying the silhouette of Zack's nose and beard, feeling the heat of his legs, listening to his breathing merge with the breathing of their animals. He was surprised at how calm he felt, worried but not panicked, sad but not devastated, nowhere near as upset as Zack had been. Which was odd, since Daniel was the one whose lover had run off. His ex-lover anyway. A piece of him was actually glad that Abbas was gone and their story was over. There was no way it could resume. It really was over.

⌒ ⌒

Early the next morning, while they drank their coffee, the phone rang. It was Justine Whitehurst, the FBI agent. "We're trying to reach Mr. and Mrs. Rohani. Can you help us?"

Daniel promptly passed the receiver to Zack.

Zack played dumb with the woman, pretending to know nothing. Then he said, "*Frankfurt?*" He lifted his eyebrows at Daniel. "Well, if you knew they flew from Toronto to Frankfurt, why are you asking *us* questions?" The voice buzzed again in his ear. "Are you serious? You make their lives miserable, you threaten to take the man's children away, and you ask *me* if I have any idea why they left the country? You people have no sense of human reality."

He hung up and told Daniel, "They're in Frankfurt. Where there's a six-hour layover before the next flight to Tehran. So they're going where they said they were going. And they're safe. At least at this end. The FBI can't arrest them."

Later they heard from Jeremy, who was not surprised by the news. "This is why I avoid immigration cases. More often than not, your client skips the country before you ever go to court."

They heard nothing from Hassan.

Friday passed, then Saturday. One can grow accustomed to almost anything, even a loss like death that isn't death. People leave town all the time, but this was different, stranger, final yet not final enough, as if there were ghosts who might return.

Telling friends helped, only there were few friends to tell. Zack phoned Ross at home and gave him the full story. "Crazy lady," said Ross. "I don't know what she sees in that man. He's hardly worth a trip back to the land of the garden of martyrs."

Daniel told Jane at school on Monday morning. "He's gone? Just like that? You're sure? You poor guy." Her sympathy surprised him. Then she said, "Oh shit. What am I gonna tell the dean?" She stopped worrying about

Daniel and worried about what to do with Abbas's class for the rest of the semester. Daniel volunteered to teach it.

The next day the department secretary came to Daniel with the keys to Abbas's studio. "We hear there's lots of artwork and art supplies in there. Could you look things over and see what can be kept or thrown out?"

Daniel had forgotten about Abbas's paintings.

He went to the studio that afternoon, fearing what he might find there. Slashed canvases? Trash cans stuffed with masterpieces? He nervously unlocked the door and opened it on a darkness full of the smell of oil paints, like beef stew gone bad. He flipped the switch; the lights fluttered on. The place was a wreck, but a familiar wreck, a friendly chaos. Daniel saw the old table heaped with dirty brushes and crushed paint tubes. Then he saw the green leather sofa, their old fuck sofa—he had forgotten it was green, Mohammed's favorite color. Behind the sofa stood a crowd of empty stretchers, a forest of squares and rectangles with the canvas stripped off. Daniel had been here for the stripping. Against the right-hand wall, however, stood frames with fabric still attached, their painted sides facing the wall, their marked-up backs facing out. Daniel tilted one away from the wall. The paint had not been scraped off or painted over but was perfectly pristine. This was the older work; the work Daniel liked best. The newer paintings were gone, shipped to Iran. But Abbas cared so little for the older work that he didn't destroy or cancel it, he simply left it behind, like so many shed skins.

Daniel was enormously relieved. Then he wondered how the pictures might look now, what they might mean to him.

He set the canvases out on the floor, a half dozen big, square carpets of color, giant playing cards, the oversize panels of a neo-Expressionist comic strip. Here was the orange gingerbread man tattooed with little bodies. Here was the family of ideograms on a beach fighting a giant fish—the fish resembled male genitals. How had he not seen that before? Here was a burnt sienna landscape full of sublimated body parts, a reddish brown desert decorated in icons like tongues, penises, and hearts.

The paintings were fun and playful, like sex. Sex with Abbas had been fun and playful. Yet somewhere, sometime, Abbas had stopped wanting to play.

He wanted to be serious, in painting, too, taking refuge in Arabic letters—the literal letter of the law. Why?

Daniel sat on the green couch and stared at the images. He missed Abbas's body. That was all he knew of him: his cock and tongue, his anus, his hands, his smile. Remembering sex did not help Daniel see the man. He didn't have a single photograph of him, not even a snapshot, only these strange pictures from inside the Iranian's head.

The terra-cotta gingerbread man, for example. Was that Abbas? It was covered in other bodies, full of other selves, a body of bodies. They marched through him like a broken alphabet. There were so many damn Abbases. There was the Abbas who gladly took Daniel in his arms. The Abbas who happily danced in this room with his children. The Abbas who could paint such beautiful paintings and then abandon them. The son of a bitch didn't even bother to write a note saying goodbye.

Daniel wanted to cry but didn't. He was cooler than Zack, tougher. But Zack was right: he *was* still in love with Abbas. It was easy to miss until after the fact. This love had never been hurt-me obsessive, like the infatuations of his twenties, or ego-driven, like the romantic sideshows of his thirties. No, this was gentler, subtler, more middle-aged. Daniel knew to expect nothing from this extra love, knew it wouldn't save him—he didn't think he needed to be saved. And yet he missed it badly. It had made him feel anxious, excited, physical, alive. Now that it was gone, he felt dead.

So who was Abbas? Daniel didn't have a clue. He wanted to forget him, which would mean destroying these paintings. But not yet. They were too beautiful. And Daniel couldn't help identifying with them. They were labors of love, yet Abbas had abandoned them when he fled into his new abstractions of God and country.

Daniel left the paintings on the floor, locked the studio, and went out to his car. It was an hour drive down to Newport News, but there was another piece of Abbas that he wanted to visit while his wounds were still fresh.

The mosque on Warwick Boulevard was a round, white building like a hatbox, a structure that made no sense until one recognized it was an old car dealership with the showroom windows painted over. Daniel sat in his car in the parking lot, unsure if he should go in or not. A marquee sign remained out front, no longer announcing what makes and models were on sale but displaying a verse from the Koran: "Those with God are not too arrogant to worship."

Daniel got out and drifted up the sidewalk to the glass doors to peek in. Other people were arriving, all men, a few with their sons. It was after five, and they were getting off work. Half of them were African American, the other half new Americans: Pakistanis, Turks, Palestinians, Saudis, and a solitary Asian man, maybe Indonesian.

The Asian stopped beside Daniel. "May I help you?"

"No, thanks. I was just curious. Just passing by."

The man's face lit up. "This is your first time? Please. Come inside. All are welcome in God's house."

Daniel followed the man into a front hall lined with shelves, a honeycomb of pigeonholes full of shoes.

"All we ask is that you show respect by removing your shoes," said the man. But he was studying Daniel hard, as if seeing him for the first time. The light was better here. He abruptly nodded and hurried off. Had he just realized that Daniel was Jewish? But in white-bread Virginia, a Jew looked as Other as any Muslim. Maybe he saw that Daniel was gay. Or thought he might be FBI.

Now that he was inside, however, Daniel wanted to stay, although he was reluctant to remove his shoes. He remained in the front hall, looking into the main room while men trooped by in their sock feet. He expected someone to ask him to leave, but nobody said a word. Nobody seemed to notice him. He was invisible here. He clasped his hands at his waist, bowed his head, and watched.

Two dozen men arranged themselves in three neat rows on the purple indoor-outdoor carpet inside, all on their knees, presumably facing Mecca. A man in a white fringe beard and a gray suit worn over a white turtleneck got up and began to chant. Some of the men chanted back, others didn't. Then the rows touched their foreheads against the carpet in unison.

Daniel had hoped to learn something about Abbas, but there was little to see here. The service was orderly yet loose and casual, like yoga. Men wandered in and out, joining or leaving, sometimes whispering to neighbors. This was not nearly as anal as the Catholic or Protestant services that Daniel knew from weddings. A few men wore skullcaps. It was all very calm and gentle. Zack might be able to read some deeper message here, but Daniel couldn't. Daniel had no feeling for religion. This was as meaningless to him as a basketball game. It was as masculine as basketball, too, with no women present, only men of all nations, in all kinds of clothes: business suits and workmen's overalls and baggy hip-hop jeans. They sat back on their heels and bowed forward again, their shirttails pulling free from their trousers.

Maybe Abbas no longer needed to have sex with men now that he could worship with them.

Was that what it had been about? Sex was a substitute for religion? Abbas had wanted Daniel for a while, until he grew bored with him and decided to want God instead. He had fled Daniel and sex and the FBI, and disappeared into God. Daniel couldn't follow him. He couldn't even begin to imagine what Abbas's new life was like.

It was late when Daniel got home. He hoped Zack had gone ahead and started dinner, but he opened the door off the carport and found him sitting in the rec room, grimly watching CNN. Daniel took a quick look at the screen: a pundit was pontificating.

"Is it war yet?"

"No. Just more experts saying how quick and easy war will be."

"Then don't watch. It's depressing."

Zack shrugged. "I'm depressed already. This makes my depression feel earned." He sat slouched in a corner of the couch, looking as shapeless and heavy as a laundry bag, his head resting in a hand that was propped on the armrest. He continued to face the TV. "Where have you been?"

"Nowhere." But Daniel had no reason to keep his trip a secret. "Actually, I drove down to that mosque in Newport News. Just to see what it looked like."

Now Zack looked at him. "Really? I wish you'd told me. I would like to have gone."

"Why? Abbas was my friend. Not yours." He didn't mean to be brusque, but Zack's interest annoyed him. "Nothing to see anyway. Just a lot of men on their knees bowing to God. I don't get it."

Zack gave Daniel a long, sad, puppy-dog look. "Well, I'd like to see a Muslim service. Just to attach a picture to what that man is doing to his family."

And Daniel's temper snapped. "Look, they're gone. Okay? Let's just wash our hands of them, okay? Can't we have some closure around here?"

Zack did not seem surprised by Daniel's anger, not nearly as surprised as Daniel felt. Then Zack shook his fist weirdly at the TV—he was holding the remote and repeatedly pressing it to mute the sound. "What did you see down there that upset you?"

"Not a damn thing. I'm in a shitty mood, okay?" Daniel walked behind the couch, headed for the stairs. He wanted to be alone with his self-pity tonight. He did not want to share it.

"You can't feel any shittier than I do," said Zack.

Daniel stopped. "Yeah? What do you feel shitty about? You miss your buddy Elena?"

Zack looked surprised, his expression like a wince. "I do, in fact. I miss the whole family, but especially her."

"Well, I miss Abbas. Because I was in love with him. You said so yourself. And I admit it. I was in love. It's not the same thing."

"Maybe. Maybe not." Zack turned away. "I'm beginning to think I was in love with Elena. In my oblivious, half-assed fashion."

Daniel cocked an ear at Zack, unsure he'd heard right.

"I always liked her," he explained. "I always enjoyed being with her. She's an amazing woman. Smart and open and brave. Not until she disappeared did I realize how deep my liking went."

Damn, thought Daniel. Of course. A laugh would be appropriate here, only he didn't laugh.

Zack continued to face the silent TV, where a female journalist stood outside a sunbaked village. Iran might look like that, yet this was probably Saudi Arabia. The crawl underneath read: "Weapons inspectors withdraw. The search for allies continues."

"That's what my grief was about the other night. That's why their leaving hit me so hard. I was in love with her. In my fashion." Zack turned to Daniel, a sheepish smile peeking through his beard. "I don't mean love in the way that you mean love. She's a woman. It's not sexual."

"Neither are we."

Zack looked startled, confused, worried. "True," he said. "True." He guiltily lowered his head. "All right. Categorize it how you like. It was like a crush, an office romance. But I *was* in love with her. And not just her. Her life, her kids, her situation. I'm still trying to understand it."

Daniel continued to walk around his thoughts, unable to get a fix on what he was thinking, what he was feeling. "So what did you want from her? Since you weren't going to fuck her."

Zack screwed up one side of his face.

"Did you want to save her and her family? Keep them here and take care of them?" Daniel heard himself sneering as he said it.

"Yes. Maybe. Something like that. But that part was fantasy." Zack was watching him, studying him. "Why are you so angry? They're gone. They're in another country. There's no reason for you to be angry. It was only platonic." His eyebrows came together as he understood something new. "Are you jealous? You're jealous of me and Elena?" His mouth opened in a mirthless grin. "That's crazy. She and I didn't do a damn thing except talk, and *you* get jealous. I've never been jealous of you."

"No. Because you don't love me as much as I love you."

Zack shook his head in confusion, like a cartoon character who'd been hit with a mallet.

Daniel's anger came out of pain, and his pain was like injured pride, but that was another name for jealousy. "All right. Maybe I *am* jealous. But I'm proud of being jealous. Which is more than you ever feel. You're such a cold, rational know-it-all. Leave it to you to fall in love with a woman. Who you're never going to fuck, so it's never going to get messy."

Daniel felt suddenly hot and uncomfortable, and he realized he was still wearing his coat. He hurriedly unzipped it and opened it, but he didn't take it off.

"Why are we fighting?" said Zack. "What is this fight really about? You want to finish what we started the other night? Is that what this is about?"

"What do you mean? What other night?"

"The night you said there isn't an *us* anymore. I said this crisis wasn't about us, and you said there isn't an us. I didn't pursue it because we still had *them* to worry about. Well, now they're gone, so we can pursue it. What the hell did you mean by that?"

What had he meant? Daniel couldn't remember.

His silence made Zack more persistent, even desperate. "Look, I know I'm not a romantic man. I'm not a passionate man. But I am a good friend to you, a very good friend. And you've been a good friend to me. What the fuck else do you want?"

The question took Daniel by surprise, so much that he wanted to answer truthfully. "I want meaning in my life. I want joy. I want to have something more to show for my time here than twenty-plus years of—*friendship*."

"Yeah. Because you're getting older. And you're a painter, only you don't paint anymore, so you got to fall in love." Zack remained sunk in his corner of the couch, his voice droning away, softly bitter, coldly angry. "And who do you fall for? Another painter, someone you admire. Someone you envy. Which is a recipe for misery. You don't want joy. You want to suffer."

The man's a psychiatrist, thought Daniel. He knows exactly where to put the fucking knife.

"What about you?" he replied. "A gay man who's given up on sex? Who falls in love with women in trouble but can't do anything to help them. You're no prize either."

"I never said I was." He lowered his head. "We shouldn't be talking about this now. When I feel so low and shitty that I can't control what I'm saying."

"But now I know what you *really* feel. What you've been hiding all these years."

"It's not what I've been feeling *all these years*," said Zack, gritting his teeth. "It's only what I feel this minute."

Daniel was hotter and more miserable than ever. He was still wearing his damn coat. "I got to hang up this coat," he said. "But I'm done. I've got nothing more to say. Let's stop while we're ahead."

Zack was watching him, looking very sad and desperate and confused. "Fine," he said. "Yes. Let's give it a rest."

Daniel hurried up the stairs, glad it was over, wanting to get away before they did further harm to each other.

In the kitchen, he heard a jingle like keys climbing the stairs. He turned around, hoping it was Zack coming to apologize. But no, it was only Jocko, his tags ringing as he crept up from the basement. He must have been napping in a corner. He guiltily cut his eyes at Daniel, as if sorry to overhear such a stupid, ugly quarrel.

The sound of the TV came back on. Apparently Zack preferred to feed his depression with bad news rather than come upstairs and finish this. But what was there to finish? They had talked themselves out of their life. They had revealed the lie of their years together. What else could they say to each other?

46

THE PHONE RANG, and it was Hassan, calling from Tehran.

"I have terrible news. There has been a traffic accident. They are dead. All of them. My brother, his wife, and their beautiful children."

Zack jolted forward, sharply sucking in air like an inhaled cry. He frantically looked for the phone—he must have dropped it—to ask Hassan for details. Who was driving? How fast? Had there been another car?

But there was no phone. He was sitting up in bed, in the dark, which meant he'd been asleep, which meant he'd been dreaming. The violent deaths were a dream, only a dream.

He lay back down again, not into peace and sleep but into grim, gray melancholy. The relief of knowing the traffic accident wasn't real lasted less than a minute before his depression returned. It's one of the worst feelings in the world, waking up depressed. Usually Zack didn't even have a bad dream to explain it. Luckily there was a little daylight in the window. He got up and went to the kitchen to start the coffee. He preferred starting his mornings early anyway, without Daniel. A week had passed since their argument. They were still angry with each other, but it was a buried anger, a neglected anger. Daniel didn't want to discuss anything serious, and Zack didn't press, for fear it would bring their anger back to life.

Zack needed to tell someone about his nightmare, but there was nobody to tell. Daniel hated hearing about other people's dreams, even in the best of times. He didn't deserve to hear this one. Zack went into his office, turned on his computer, and typed an e-mail.

> *Elena: I just had a terrible dream where you and your family died in*
> *a car wreck. Could you please write to me and let me know you're*
> *okay? Zack.*

There was still no word from the Rohanis. Elena's electronic mailbox remained open, but Zack didn't know if she had access to it. Writing notes to her was a neurotic compulsion, like writing to the dead, but he couldn't stop himself.

He showered and dressed and sat in the kitchen, drinking his coffee and eating his cornflakes, listening to the radio, which was turned down low so it wouldn't disturb Daniel. The fat crows croaking in the trees out back competed with the sinister whisper of news. Between NPR in the morning and CNN at night, the war came a little closer each day. No wonder Zack had dreamed about death. The radio mentioned again the major antiwar march scheduled for this Saturday in New York, where hundreds of thousands were expected despite the bitter cold. Zack knew he should try to get up there, but he couldn't bring himself to do much of anything nowadays outside of his usual, sad, well-established routines.

～ ～

"So it was three weeks ago they vanished, and I keep waiting to feel better, but I don't. I feel no joy, no energy. No, that's not true. I can be angry. I feel only anger or fatigue. Which leads me to believe I'm clinically depressed. Yes, I know, three weeks is nothing. Which is why I didn't want to prescribe anything to myself until I discussed this with you."

Zack sat with Roy Chadha in his office in Building 2, sharing a pot of English tea and talking. He had already filled Roy in on recent events: how Daniel and Abbas had stopped seeing each other, how Abbas's brother had come to town, followed by the FBI, and how the family had fled to Iran. It was strange hearing the emotional mess of the past months reduced to a relatively simple story line.

Roy kept nodding and smiling, a gently amused, philosophical cat smile. "How very interesting. And modern, too. When Anna Karenina committed adultery, she destroyed *her* family. Now when people do it, they extend their families, double them."

Zack frowned. "But we're not doubled. Half of us is in another country."

Roy shrugged. "Which is the case with my family, too. But just because they are in India doesn't mean they no longer matter." He poured more tea into his mug. "Your overextended family is trickier, true, but it sounds like you grew quite close to this couple. So you are grieving, and grief is work. How are you and Daniel getting on?"

"We're very angry with each other."

"Well, of course."

"But I'm not always sure what we're angry about."

Roy weighed the statement. "Maybe because neither of you could help and each blames the other for his helplessness?"

"Maybe," said Zack hesitantly. "But it feels darker, more selfish. We've been arguing like the Rohanis. As if we're copying them."

Roy nodded approvingly, until a new idea came to him. "Or maybe you're angry only because the excitement is over and now you are stuck with each other?"

The idea sounded even nastier coming from Roy than when Zack had thought it himself. "But this isn't about explanations," he argued, backing away from the idea. "It's not like I think I can find a magic key and everything will be fine again."

"I don't believe in eurekas either. But they give you something to talk about. Have you explored these explanations with Daniel?"

Zack made a face. "No. He doesn't want to hear. He's afraid of talking. He wants us to be silent for a while. I can't say I blame him."

"Yes, it's hard to live with a headshrinker," Roy agreed. "You get tired of talking, talking, always talking. You wonder if silence isn't better. I wonder myself now and then. But at a time like this, his silence must leave *you* feeling very lonely."

Zack was surprised to hear his emotion named. "Except I've always felt a little lonely. It *is* part of the profession." He disliked this topic even more than he disliked the topic of his sex drive. "I used to think a little loneliness would protect me from feeling *too* lonely, *too* hurt. And it usually does. I know not to expect too much from anyone. Even from Daniel. But I've never felt as desolately lonely as I do now."

Roy looked very sad, very concerned. "You should talk to him."

"I will. When the time is right."

"Would you like me to say something?"

Zack winced. "No. Not necessary. But thank you." He didn't ask what Roy might say.

Roy gently waved the thanks aside. "No problem. I know you can fight your own battles. But I am here if you need me." He took a big swallow of tea. "You might put yourself on Paxil. Until the warm weather arrives. This winter has drained the light from us all. And take a little exercise. Go to the gym and look at the pretty men. Maybe plan a trip to someplace warm and sunny. Alone." His philosophical cat smile was back. "Your depression does not sound medical, my friend. It sounds perfectly moral, perfectly human. Especially when we consider what else is going on in the world."

❦

A few days later Daniel brought Abbas's old paintings home from school and stored them in the basement, rolled up like carpets. Zack thought this was a big mistake, like preserving sorrow, but he couldn't tell Daniel that. They continued to avoid their serious issues. They ate dinner together, and watched movies on DVD, although they never seemed to like the same things anymore. But Zack was too tired to argue, his spirits too low. He kept postponing the day when he'd dig up the garden out back to plant their vegetables.

Spring came slowly to Virginia. Tiny white dogwood blossoms appeared in the gray woods behind the house, floating like suspended handfuls of confetti. Then dotted green buds showed on the tips of branches. And one night—March 19, 2003—the war arrived.

It opened with another speech by the president, followed by a long live TV shot of Baghdad on the other side of the world, where it was almost dawn.

The skyline, with a deserted elevated highway in the foreground, resembled Richmond, only with fewer tall buildings.

There was a missile attack that night on a nearby palace. Saddam was supposed to be there, but he wasn't home. The second night saw the launch of what the Pentagon called "shock and awe," with live footage of a government complex in Baghdad being blown to pieces. Fay Dawson's angel of death arrived in Iraq with the disturbingly familiar noise of car alarms. Then Donald Rumsfeld appeared, smiling and assuring the American public that modern technology was wonderful and civilian casualties would be minimal. In the nights that followed, there was no more video footage, only photographs and taped sound. Enormous trees of black smoke towered over a sea of flat roofs. Buildings on a river were silhouetted against a fiery sky.

The war existed only on television. It was like a new TV series that everyone was watching, with its own logo and theme music. Daniel often watched with Zack, but irritably, angrily, sometimes leaving halfway through a broadcast.

Zack worried that the administration might be right and Iraq actually possessed weapons of mass destruction. American soldiers would die by the thousands from nerve gas. Deadly germs and terrorist bombs would be unleashed in U.S. cities. The doctor wasn't entirely sure if his fears weren't also wishes. He was surprised by how angry he was with his own country.

He continued to send his truncated e-mails into cyberspace.

> *Elena: We assume you are hearing the same bad news we are hearing, but maybe more, since our government says nothing about civilian dead.*

> *Elena: The war distorts everything here, even the Oscars. As if to offset any antiwar speeches, there were news bulletins throughout the broadcast, although there was no news to report. These were like advertisements for war, commercials for war. Our media has sold its soul to liars.*

> *Elena: Are you safe there? Do your neighbors trust and accept you? Or are you tainted by your time over here?*

Still he heard nothing. He wondered if the war next door meant all communication between Iran and the outside world was shut down, or monitored so closely that Elena didn't dare write back.

~ ~

"This war is so sad. Yancy watches every night, but I can't even bear to look at a TV set. All those people in danger? I pray to God every day it'll end before more harm comes to anyone."

"A good thing to pray for," Zack agreed. "War *is* terrible."

Fay nodded and smoothed her skirt again. She was more distracted than usual, more nervous under her shell of composure. She spoke in crisp, hard, disconnected sentences. "But it makes a person think. War is good for that. It's made me realize that I need to be tougher. I've been giving myself one long pity party. But I'm not alone in this world. I can't just think about myself anymore. You got to wonder if God gave us this war because we were getting soft."

Zack shifted uncomfortably. "Soft, how?"

"Weak. Full of doubt. Doubt is not something we can afford."

"What kind of doubt?"

"Self-doubt. It's self-indulgent. Especially at a time like this. Our way of life is in danger. We can't afford to shilly-shally."

Zack was disappointed to hear Fay talk in White House buzzwords. "Are you referring to doubts about your own life, Fay? Or to doubts about whether we should be in Iraq or not?"

Fay stared at him as if the question were preposterous. "Well, about me, of course. I have no doubts about the war. But the war has made me realize that doubt is a bad thing."

"You don't think that doubt simply means stopping for a minute and asking ourselves if we're doing the right thing?"

"It can. But too often it's just an excuse to do nothing. And while we do nothing, they could be attacking and killing us."

"So we should hit first and ask questions later? Even if it means killing innocent people?" He spoke softly but was surprised to hear himself respond with such harsh words.

Fay stopped smoothing her skirt. "It's for God to decide if they're innocent or not. Only I can't believe they're so innocent. Not when they live under that dictator or believe that so-called religion."

Zack remained outwardly calm even as his temper rose. He knew he should wait and address this later, but he liked Fay Dawson and hated being angry with her. "I should tell you, Fay, that I feel very hurt right now hearing you talk like this. I have friends who are Muslims. They're not in Iraq, but I am concerned about them. I feel their lives are as valuable as yours or mine."

Fay grimaced and groaned, like a teenage girl who'd just put her foot in her mouth. But then she said, "I'm sorry about your friends. I truly am. But they are not my concern." She couldn't look at Zack. "I don't hate Muslims. But they hate us. I can't worry about their welfare. I have only so much worry to go around. No, my worry is for our men in uniform. And women. They're the ones I pray for." She continued to look away, unable to look him in the eye.

"I'm surprised at you, Fay. I'm disappointed." He kept his voice low, keeping anger out of his tone. "I have great respect for your Christianity. I always felt it was a force of love, a way of seeing the world whole. But you talk like someone who divides the world between good people and bad people, the damned and the saved. You speak with the hard-heartedness of the saved. I liked you better, Fay, when you were more uncertain."

Fay stared at him, her jaw thrust forward, her eyes shining. Her lips curled back. "What're you saying?" she snarled. "What business is it of yours if I'm saved or not?" Her eyes squeezed shut against a swelling of tears. "Malvern is going over there!" she cried. "Malvern has joined the army!"

"Malvern?" said Zack. "Your son? He's only a teenager."

"He turned eighteen on Friday! And he ran out and enlisted! And they're taking him, the day after he gets out of high school. He wants to be a man for his country, even if it means getting killed."

Zack was overwhelmed with confusion and sorrow. No wonder Fay was on edge today. No wonder she was talking so strangely. He reached for the Kleenex box and held it out to her.

"So don't tell me about your nice Muslim friends." She sneered. "And don't tell me doubt is good." She saw the tissue box and ignored it. "I believe our president when he says this war is necessary. I believe him when he says it'll be over soon, before Malvern finishes school, and he won't go over there. I need to believe these things! I don't need you filling up my head with things to be afraid of!"

"Fay. Listen to yourself. You're angry because I'm telling you things you already know. You don't trust our president either."

She glared at him. "Don't tell me what I think! People are always telling me what I think." She stood up, then sat down again.

"Fay. Wait. Just sit quietly for a minute."

"No, I won't sit quietly. I've been sitting quietly for months, and what do I have to show for it? A son who's joined the army. A husband who says I'm wasting money on a quack. A minister who thinks I'm spending too much time with an atheist homosexual. The damned and the saved, huh? The damned and the saved? Who are you to call me hard-hearted?" She was on her feet again and taking her coat off the rack.

"No, Fay. Sit down. Please. Let's talk about this."

"There's nothing more to talk about. I sacrifice my only son to defend my country, and all you can say is I hurt your feelings because you have Muslim friends? That I'm a hard-hearted bitch because I believe in Jesus Christ?"

Zack wanted to stand up and argue—he intended to argue—but he couldn't move. "That's not what I said. But that's what you want to hear? Fine. I'm not going to fight you. If you want to go, just go."

She opened the office door and stood there, like a child daring a parent to stop her. Then she went out to the front door. He heard her open and shut it and hurry down the sidewalk to her car—she was able to drive again. The car door slammed, and she drove off.

Zack fell forward in his chair, folding in on himself, feeling like a failure, a complete fuckup. Fay was his favorite patient, and he'd found a dark side in her, but he didn't blame her. No, she was upset about her son. He wished she'd told him sooner. So he wouldn't have lost his temper and righteously scolded her. He had been so damn full of himself, so superior and condescending.

He took two cushions from the chair, got down on the floor, and lay on his side, curled around his sorrow. It was the reverse of a panic attack, more like a numbness attack, a nothingness attack. He was amazed at how bad he felt. He breathed in and out, trying to breathe away the badness. He hoped to release his sorrow in tears, but he found no tears; he was bone-dry.

⁓ ⁓

He couldn't guess how long he had been lying on the floor when he heard the front door jerk open.

"Zack?" cried Daniel from the front hall. He ran into the office and dropped to his knees. "Honey? Honey!" He grabbed Zack's shoulder and pulled.

Zack rolled over and faced him. "I can't do anything right. I can't help you. I can't help myself. I can't even help my patients."

Daniel leaned back, blinking away his look of alarm. "Don't be an idiot. You help lots of people." He scrambled to his feet. "You scared the shit out of me. What happened?"

"I got into a fight with one of my patients. About the war."

"Not your born-again-Christian lady?" He sounded pleased.

"Yes. Her."

"Poor baby." He stood over him, shaking his head and smiling. "So what would you like for dinner? How about fettuccine Alfredo?"

"I can't think about dinner. I'm not hungry."

"What? You gonna fast? You wanna punish yourself more? Go ahead. I don't care. I'm hungry." Daniel irritably turned and left.

Zack felt he deserved to be left. He lay on the carpet, despising himself, hating his stupidity and smugness, wanting to disappear in a black hole of self-hatred, until Jocko trotted into the room, sloppily licked his ear, and trotted off again. Daniel must've let the dog out of the basement. Feeling chastised and corrected, Zack got up, went into the bathroom, and splashed cold water on his face.

He went out to the kitchen. "Time for the *NewsHour,*" he announced. "I'll be downstairs."

Daniel was at the stove. "What? You already feel like shit and you want to make yourself feel worse?"

"That's right. It's my way of working this out of my system."

Daniel frowned. "Look. I'm making dinner for us both. Whether you want it or not."

"Good. I think I'm hungry after all. Did you want to eat up here, or should I set up the TV trays downstairs?"

"Do I have a choice? Oh, sure. We can eat downstairs. I'd like to know who we bombed today."

Fifteen minutes later, Daniel came down to the rec room carrying two plates loaded with fettuccine and salad.

"Thank you," said Zack. "Smells good."

"Does it need more salt?"

"Oh no. It's perfect."

They sat side by side on the couch, eating pasta and watching war, first on PBS, then on al-Jazeera.

It was Ross who had told them that BBC America showed a full hour of the Arab news channel every night. What was censored on U.S. television was available here, while what one saw in American broadcasts was often missing on al-Jazeera. There were probably only a handful of people in town who regularly visited the enemy's favorite station, but watching Arab TV had become a private act of protest. And, as Daniel pointed out, al-Jazeera was the only place where one regularly saw handsome, well-spoken Muslim men.

Tonight was a typical broadcast: There was a tour of a shelled village but no corpses. The channel was notorious for showing dead bodies, Iraqi and American, but bodies were actually rare. An old Iraqi woman stood in front of her flattened house, screaming at the camera while an Englishwoman's voice coolly translated her words: "My children and grandchildren are dead. I call upon God to destroy the people who did this to us."

"This makes all other troubles look like nothing," said Daniel.

"Yes and no. It makes other troubles look small. But it doesn't mean we don't have to deal with them." Zack hesitated. Should they address their troubles tonight? No, not yet. "But it's something people like about war. It simplifies life. They don't have to ask themselves hard questions anymore. All they need to do is hate the enemy."

"Is that what you told your Christian lady?"

"No. But I don't think I could've."

A Saudi journalist politely questioned an American official who grew more and more irritated. The Arabic lettering along the bottom of the screen, an elaborate pattern of fishhooks and umlauts, reminded Zack of Abbas's paintings.

Daniel must've been thinking something similar because he suddenly said, "I wonder if they're watching this."

Zack didn't need to ask who. "Ross says al-Jazeera is banned in Iran but people still get it on satellite dishes."

"Do you think we'll ever hear from them again?"

"I don't know. But I hope so. One day."

Neither man looked at the other, only at the screen.

In a street in Kuwait, a half dozen women in black chadors stood in front of a camera and expressed their hatred of both Saddam Hussein and the United States. They looked as anonymous as penguins, yet Zack knew each woman had a distinct history and point of view hidden under her uniform garb.

"Why did she do it?" Zack suddenly said. "That's what I want to know. Why did she go? Did he bully her into going? Or did she do it just to keep their family together? Was it out of love for their son? Or love of him?"

Daniel was silent for a long time, as if embarrassed by the subject. Then he said, "I hope you never do anything so crazy for me. Because it *is* crazy. It's stupid. It's masochistic. All right. Maybe *you* would do it. But I couldn't. To be honest. I'd never sacrifice my freedom to be with you like that. Sorry. But that's how I am."

Zack continued to face the screen. "I'm not so sure I could do it for you. But I sure as hell don't want you to do anything like that for me. No. It's not the kind of love I want."

Right now there are readers saying to themselves: How self-indulgent. People are dying in Iraq and two men sit in front of the TV and try to talk about their "relationship." A different kind of reader is thinking: Forget Iraq. These men should turn away from the outside world, turn off the TV, and focus on their own messy lives, their own troubles, which they should confront head-on instead of discussing indirectly.

These are justified charges, and I don't know what to say in response except: So how do you live *your* life? Do you selflessly lose yourself in others, escaping the trap of self in good works or politics? Or do you cultivate your own private garden, an oasis of perfect love and honesty in a world you couldn't change even if you wanted to? You probably don't take either route. You live in both worlds, like we all do.

So how do *you* balance the two? Do you succeed in both? Do you succeed in either? Are you always honest with yourself and your spouse or partner or lover? Do you know what to say? Do you know when to stop talking? Are you really that much smarter than Zack and Daniel?

I'm not being sarcastic. I'm just asking.

Because I don't know how to do it myself. I don't have an answer here. I'm in the dark with Zack and Daniel.

47

WE QUARRELED FIERCELY, OPENLY, OFTEN. We fought every night for weeks until, finally, one night, I said, I am sick of fighting, I will go. And we packed our things before we could change our minds. We woke the children and went out to the car in the dark cold. We drove north toward Canada, into colder, whiter landscapes, while I thought: I am making a terrible mistake.

We flew first to Frankfurt and caught the night plane to Tehran. We arrived early in the morning, flying over a gray city—as ugly as the cement cities of my Iron Curtain childhood. There were miles and miles of squat, square buildings under a polluted, henna-colored sky. A new friend who once lived in California (we are not the only returnees) says Tehran is Los Angeles with twice the traffic and mosques instead of carwashes. She also says nobody ever smiles here, which isn't true, but people said the same of the Soviet Union. Our problem was our eyeglasses were crude, and so we always squinted. There is a squint here as well, but that's a different matter. Hassan was waiting at the airport with Roxanne and Samira, his two wives, welcoming us with open arms.

I am not sure how to tell my story, Zack. I have been working on this letter for two weeks now, and English does not provide the distance I hoped for.

I keep changing my mind and contradicting my words. All e-mail is examined, and anything in English is doubly suspect, so I assume this will be read by the police, both ours and yours. But I have nothing to hide.

We arrived three months ago. Your war has come and gone, only it refuses to end. People here are glad of that, since it means your country might leave ours in peace. We live in northern Tehran, in the hills above the city, in a new house in a walled estate next door to Hassan and his wives. We share a swimming pool and a beautiful garden. The trees and flowers smell delicious, a paradise for the nose and fingers. Five times a day, however, we hear calls to prayer from the mosques surrounding us. At first the sound worried me, like policemen with bullhorns ordering people out of their homes. Soon, though, the chants blended with the daily music of birdsong and children at play. Osh and Mina are very happy here, and why not? They have an uncle and two aunts who spoil them terribly. (Mina being Mina is sometimes guilty about her happiness.) I am friendly with Roxanne, the first wife, but not Samira, the second wife, who does not get along with anyone. They are both hypocrites, but amiably so, without righteousness. I am a great hypocrite myself.

Abbas is calm again, which makes him kinder, more thoughtful, almost apologetic. He broods only about his work now, hiding in his art. He is painting a huge mural in the lobby of the Ministry of Justice, an elegant abstraction that will be a nice change from the endless billboards of martyr boys and tulips. He doesn't know if anyone will see it, however. If the mullahs don't paint it out, he says, the bombs of the next war could destroy the whole building. Hassan was wrong. The reformers did not come to power, in part because you invaded Iraq. The old mullahs remain the big dogs.

I received your many messages, Zack, but did not write sooner because I did not want to think about why I came here. I still do not know. But I am here. And no matter where you go, there you are. Am I happy? No. Am I more miserable than I was in Paris or Virginia? No again, strange to say. I am a woman without a country. I will be a foreigner wherever I go. Why not here? They say that one writes prose at home and poetry in exile, and I am a poet, so maybe I will always be in exile.

But I do try to imagine another life. I could live without Abbas. He is so needy, unable to live alone, but I am stronger. I know how to be alone. Because being married to him is like being alone. Who am I kidding? I should delete those words. I have my children, who are like two extra husbands. I am not as alone as I pretend. I love Abbas more than he loves me, but I am used to that. It is the air I breathe, like the thin air of the mountains breathed by the goats who live in the clouds. And here is money, while in the U.S. I would be poor.

I am in the land of covered women, and it is not as bad as I feared. I can be myself indoors, reading illegal books and watching illegal DVDs. I despise the chador but have grown fond of silk scarfs, particularly on windy days. I learned early I cannot walk alone without strange men following me and going tsk tsk tsk. Luckily I have a son and daughter and two sisters-in-law and even a new friend to accompany me. I am surrounded by people, more than in Virginia. And yes, I often feel lonely, but I tell myself I should cherish my loneliness, since it is entirely mine, a free space inside me.

Do you remember Hassan's idiotic quote from Sartre, how the French were never so free as they were under the Nazi occupation? It is a stupid idea, a vile idea. As if a chained dog is freer than a stray, and prison the purest free-dom of all. Yet I understand the temptation. When we suffer our little private stories, we long to lose ourselves in a big public story. A public story is more important, more meaningful. But now I am trapped in a public story (war and religion), and I miss my private little narratives. Yet they are here, if I look for them. There will always be little stories. Many little stories in every life at any given time.

And how are you? What kind of story do you and Daniel live in now? Life must be wonderfully peaceful without us around. But you appear to miss me some, since you continue to write despite my silence. I did not think I missed you, Zack, until I started working on this letter. I like talking to you in my head as well as face-to-face. We were part of each other's stories, briefly, dur-ing our time in America: You and me. Abbas and Daniel. You were our friends in the Great Satan. But now we live in God. Which is a curious place to be.

You must come and visit us. One day. When you are ready. Before the next war. Please?

AUTHOR'S NOTE

Many friends helped with this novel, but I especially want to thank Dr. Richard Kassner, who patiently answered endless questions about the psychiatric profession. The painting described in Chapter 4 is based on a very real, wonderfully dangerous piece by Jamie Rauchman.

Christine Westberg has fed my mind for years with many things, including her stories about life in Iran before and after the revolution. It is a privilege knowing her.

And I am fortunate in my first readers. Ed Sikov, Paul Russell, Mary Gentile, Victor Bumbalo, Damien Jack, Patrick Merla, Mark Murtagh, Brenda Wineapple, and Draper Shreeve all provided advice, criticism, information, and support. My agent, Edward Hibbert, and his associate, Tom Eubanks, were invaluable, and my editor at Morrow, Jennifer Pooley, has been a pleasure to work with.